A Scandalous Life:
The Reputed Wife

a novel

Jo Ann Butler

Neverest Press

Copyright © by Jo Ann Butler 2013

Published by Neverest Press

Orders taken at: www.rebelpuritan.com

Email: joann@rebelpuritan.com

Printed in the United States of America by
Edwards Brothers Malloy Incorporated of Ann Arbor, Michigan

Publisher's Note: This is a work of fiction. Most of the characters and their actions are based on actual 17th century persons and events. However, presentation of these characters, their deeds, and their motivations arises from the author's imagination, and all persons and places are used fictitiously. Any resemblance to actual persons, living or dead, is entirely coincidental.

All rights reserved. No part of this publication may be reproduced, stored in a retrieval system, or transmitted in any form or by any means, electronic, mechanical, photocopying, recording, or otherwise, without prior written permission. Please contact joann@rebelpuritan.com for further information. Your support of the author's rights is appreciated.

Library of Congress Control Number: 2012921600

ISBN: 978-0-9829780-2-3

1 3 5 7 9 10 8 6 4 2

A worthy sequel to *Rebel Puritan*, but working equally as well as a stand alone volume, *The Reputed Wife* is the second installment in the saga of tough-as-nails Herodias Long. With straightforward, lyrical prose and vivid imagery, JoAnn Butler brings her spirited heroine to life in a beautifully wrought tale built on a solid historical foundation. At a time when one risked a death sentence by dissenting from popular opinion, this remarkable woman challenges convention. With her powerful act of defiance, Herodias shakes an entire community's perception of what they believe to be right.

Although the story takes place in the past, the women's issues brought to light in this illuminating work are as relevant now as at any time in history. And to anyone who thinks that the background of our own country is not as sensational as that of England or other popular European settings, this book—which I heartily recommend—will change your mind. Two thumbs way, way up for JoAnn Butler!
      Ginger Myrick, author of *The Welsh Healer*

This smoothly written sequel to *Rebel Puritan* gives us a compelling heroine with a spirit as courageous as her personal life is scandalous. As if her overabundance of children, common-law husband, and vengeful ex-spouse weren't enough to handle, Herodias Long takes on the repressive Puritan establishment and proves an outspoken defender of religious freedom. Her tale of family life, women's friendship, and heartrending bravery is taken straight from the historical record, and Jo Ann Butler has resurrected her strong-minded ancestress with creative skill and a wonderful eye for detail. Fans of colonial American settings will want to delve right in.
      Sarah Johnson *Historical Novels Review* book editor

For Richard Hale and Carrie Butler forever,
And for Carolyn, Christy, Christy, Esther, Ginger, Kay, and Marilyn,
My sisters from another mother

FOREWORD

HERODIAS LONG IS my 8th great-grandmother, and she was one determined woman. Since I published *Rebel Puritan*, distant cousins in many countries have told me that hard-headed women run in their family. There are worse traits to inherit, and we are all proud of Herodias.

Actual and fictional events are interwoven in *The Reputed Wife*. In the Author's Notes you can learn which incidents are fictional and find some of the records I used to write Herod's story.

Here's a note of thanks to the New England Historical and Genealogical Society, the LDS genealogical library in Salt Lake City, and the genealogical societies of Rhode Island, Massachusetts, and of Newport, Rhode Island. The historical societies of Rhode Island and Newport have proven very helpful. The Rhode Island and Massachusetts State Archives provided much-needed information. Lastly, public libraries around the country were invaluable as I wrote *The Reputed Wife* and kept in touch with *Rebel Puritan*. They all deserve our support.

I would especially like to thank Carrie Butler, Richard Hale, Marilyn Henetz, June Holden, Ginger Myrick, George Rogers, Carolyn Stone, and Kay Varney for their unwavering assistance and patient reading of my manuscript. Suzy Witten made invaluable suggestions, and Christy Robinson's Editornado editorial service cleaned up my anachronisms. Kristen and Ryann Seal are the lovely Herodias and Rebecca on my cover, Marilyn Henetz made the costume, and Rob Shepherd took the photograph. Numerous readers of *Rebel Puritan* have contacted me and they have been very patient, but insistent – I must keep telling Herodias Long's story! Now I have done so, and will continue to the end.

CHAPTER 1
June - July 1647

HERODIAS GARDNER KNEW a warning when she saw one. For the second time in three years she faced losing her home to flames, and she might not get another chance to ward off disaster. She would probably lose her ocean view, but it was ruined already.

During Herod's eight years in Rhode Island she dwelt on Newport's fringe, and loved it. The seclusion of the south bay reminded Herod of her childhood home, tucked away high in England's Devonshire hills.

For her, Newport's congested heart was far too noisy as boys and dogs herded sheep to the common, roosters crowed from back yards, and carts with ungreased wheels groaned along the narrow streets. Some of the houses were packed so tightly that people passing by could look right into your windows!

In contrast, when Herod opened her own door, the panorama brought a smile to her face. Whether she was tending her growing family, or her garden and orchard, Herod loved the parade of seasons and gaudy sunsets reflected in Narragansett Bay's chilly water.

For many years, only a gently sloping pasture lay between the Gardners' house and salt marsh stalked by graceful white egrets. However, Newport had blossomed from the scattering of huts that sixteen-year old Herod saw when she arrived with her first husband, John Hicks. Now the Gardners' home was surrounded. As new settlers cut reeds from the marsh and foraged for fish and clams, Herod was saddened to watch her favorite crook-necked birds flee to quieter waters.

The Lucar family now owned the lot next to the Gardners, where Herod had once lived. Though she preferred privacy, Herod didn't mind a few people living nearby. However, that morning Mark Lucar's hogs broke through their fence to root in Herod's garden.

When she heard the pigs' grunts, Herod shouted out the open door at them, but they ignored her. Herod's two young sons were playing in the second room, so she flipped a bench onto its side and dragged it in front of the kitchen hearth. 'I'll only be a moment,' she thought, praying that Benoni, an active lad who was not yet three, would stay in the storage room with his younger brother, Henry.

Grabbing a twig broom, Herod dashed outdoors, brandishing her improvised weapon and howling like a madwoman. The half-dozen hogs sped home, tails in the air and scattering peavines in their wake. Herod chased them to the fence. An eight-foot span of rails lay on the ground, and one of the posts tilted like a loose tooth.

"Lucar – your damned pigs are in my garden again!" Herod yelled, but there was no response. She straightened the post, stamped reinforcing dirt around its base, and put the rails back in place. Her repair job was flimsy, but she dared not work at it any longer. Benoni might already be in the kitchen, pulling the bench away from the fire.

"Stay away from here!" she shouted at the pigs, and then heaved a clod of earth at them. They snorted and ran off. "Eat your own garden," Herod muttered.

Steeped in ill will, she glared at the second irritant in her life – another new neighbor. Though no other houses lay between the Gardners and Newport's harbor, their property did not extend to the water's edge. The shoreline was reserved for businessmen.

There was now a boatyard blocking Herod's view, and that was only one of the yard's annoyances. Herod hated the assault on her ears while the men chipped ribs and keels into shape, and then pegged planks to them. She grumbled to George that they sounded like bewitched woodpeckers, but he merely chuckled.

The smoke was worse than the racket. Scrap fires burned from dawn to dusk as the builders steamed their planks into shape and roasted pine knots for tar. Westerly breezes sent fumes drifting over Herod's garden and rank smoke filled her house.

With Lucar's pigs routed, Herod trotted home anxiously, but her sons were safe in the second chamber. Henry had fallen asleep on his pallet, and Benoni barely glanced up at his mother from a fistful of wooden pegs whittled into crude human shape. Herod stood her broom by the door, and then paused to look down at the boatyard.

It had fallen unusually silent. As she watched, three shipwrights appeared with a yoked ox, dragging their newest creation into the water. The shallop – a sailboat which was small enough to row – did not have its single mast stepped yet, but apparently it floated to the shipwrights' satisfaction. Two of them began to row toward Newport. The third man led the ox up the road toward town.

With the crew gone, Herod beamed as she thought of the peaceful afternoon ahead. The boys could nap, and she needn't wonder what to serve for supper. There was plenty of pot liquor and scraps left from the stew they'd eaten at midday. She would thicken the pottage with oats to serve the same meal which many New Englanders ate in the evening.

Herod sat down with her sewing. Henry was toddling now, and Benoni's simple gown was too tight. It was time to put her oldest son in breeches and a shirt, and Henry would wear Benoni's gown. She coughed to clear her throat, threaded her needle, and set to work on the nearly-finished shirt.

A minute later Herod coughed again and rubbed her eyes. Then the hairs on her neck prickled. There was a gauzy veil of smoke in the kitchen. Her fire was down to embers, barely enough to keep her pottage warm, so where was it coming from? Fear made Herod's stomach contract – had her thatch caught fire?

She dropped the shirt, kicking it aside in her haste. When she got to the door, Herod emitted a wordless cry of horror. The breeze from the bay had freshened and smoke was streaming from the boatyard. A swirl of wind revealed flames – a glowing band thirty feet wide and knee-high – driving uphill toward Herod's home.

Last year the boatyard owner grew oats in the field between the yard and the lane. Six weeks ago seeds were sown among the old stubble. Jade-green oat stems now stood knee high, so the flames had plenty of fuel. A mere thirty yards lay between the fire line and the orchard in Herod's front yard.

Herod closed the second room's door, and then threw George's great chair against it. Benoni would have to shove it aside to get into the kitchen. Her frantic eyes spied an empty tow sack. A bucket of water always stood by the hearth for emergencies, and Herod upended it over the bag.

To keep her ankle-length skirt from catching fire, Herod reached back between her knees, pulled the hem forward, and tucked it into her waistband. The wooden clogs she wore on muddy days stood near the door, and she slipped her bare feet into them. Then she grabbed the twig broom and ran outside with the dripping tow sack in her other hand.

The smoke was thicker now, so Herod dropped the broom by the gate and guided herself to the fire by the crackle of the greedy flames. "Fire, help!" she shrieked, but the smoke choked her. She thought, 'Please God, spare my boys.' Then she smashed the wet sack into the flames at her feet again and again, advancing a pace each time.

Herod glanced over her shoulder. The flames to her right had weakened. If they reached the dirt road, sparks might set the Gardners' hayfield alight, but the wind would drive it away from her home. It was the flames ahead that were the enemy. If they crossed the road, the breeze would send them through the apple orchard straight toward Herod's home – and her sons.

She screamed for help again, but could barely hear her own cry. The smoldering sack would soon be alight, but her broom was at hand. Only fifteen feet to the road now, and Herod swung her now-flaming sack down onto the burning stubble as quickly as she could.

Ten feet to go, but a frantic glance assured Herod that sparks hadn't crossed the lane yet. 'I won't let you,' she thought furiously, 'Not this time! John Hicks, God rot his black heart, burned me out of my home, but I won't let it happen again.'

Then she saw movement – a shirtless man was slamming an iron-edged spade into the flames on the southern end of the line, and tossing dirt over the embers. Through a thin spot in the smoke Herod recognized Mark Lucar's stocky build. With a hasty prayer of thanks, she turned to work her way north again.

A jerk on Herod's arm sent her staggering. It was George, red-faced and panting. He snatched the sack away from her, crying, "You are on fire – get out of here!"

Herod ran toward the road, looking down at her skirt. No flames there, but charred holes pitted the sleeves of her white shift and her clogs were smoking. At once her feet felt uncomfortably warm. Herod retreated to the road and scuffed her clogs in the dust. She used her broom to beat out sparks crawling through the weedy strip under the orchard fence.

George had tossed aside the tow sack and was fighting the fire with a hay rake. Bob Stanton, who lived next to the Gardners, was battling the northern end of the fire. Attracted by the smoke, a couple of President Coggeshall's servants were trotting up the lane to join them.

Sparks skittered across the road on the wind, and Herod attacked them with savage glee. The fire was licked and her home was safe. When one of Coggeshall's lads took her broom to finish off the spot fires, she jogged up to the house to check on her sons. Now Herod felt a burst of gratitude that her neighbors lived so close at hand, and she would never curse Mark Lucar and his hogs again.

With the fire out, the Gardners shared a common thought – they would move away from that boatyard as soon as possible. After supper, Herod nursed Henry, and then laid the drowsy baby on the family's bed. Benoni played with George's hound pups, dragging the charred tow sack for them to chase. Herod sent him into the second room so Henry could sleep.

Grateful that the boys were settled at last, Herod let out a deep sigh. Standing behind her, George wrapped her in a hug and she turned to kiss him. Though she overtopped most women in Newport, she still had to look up into George's blue eyes. Her arms tightened around his waist. "I've an idea."

"Me, too." George pushed her cap back to finger her braided chestnut hair. "Something to pass our time when the boys are asleep."

Smiling, Herod said, "Later for that. We should build anew."

"A new what?"

"A new house. We've barely room for the four of us, and more on the way."

"Another?"

Herod laughed at George's dismayed tone, then assured him, "Not yet, but I'm barely twenty-four and doubt that God means to strike me barren. There will be more, and the boatyard is not our only problem. The garden is too damp and the wind is so harsh in winter."

"We could build further uphill, where 'tis drier." George stroked Herod's shoulders, and then his fingers slipped downward.

She squirmed away. "I thought to build elsewhere."

George's tender smile vanished. "Clear all that land for house and garden? You know not what you ask."

"Don't I? John Hicks and I cleared our Weymouth land. Remember the house that John burned the night he took our children? I had a hand in building it, and though I was big with child, I helped when you and John put this house up too."

George's grin returned. "So you did."

Encouraged, Herod went on, "We've been gardening here nigh ten years and the soil is playing out. Lucar's hogs rooted up my peas again, and even before the fire we were choking from that smoke. Let's build at the farm!" George had been granted several parcels of land. He and Herod lived on a four-acre lot, but raised most of their corn and kept a sheep on a much larger plot a half-mile southward. "What say you?" she asked.

George scratched at his closely trimmed beard. "Not a bad idea. There's timber there so I'll not have to haul wood, and I can keep a closer eye on the sheep. If I start cutting now, I should get the frame up before harvest."

"We could use these planks," Herod tapped the wall beside their bed. "They are sound, so no need to saw more. Keep the garden and orchard —"

"Or sell all to a newcomer. We could get a pretty price for a home and fruit trees already bearing." George reached for Herod's shoulder again. "What say you to picking a spot tomorrow?"

Though the Gardners found a site which suited them both, it would take months to build a new house. Their thatch had been leaking since spring thaw but George had ignored Herod's grumbles. When it rained she placed a bucket in the middle of the room to catch the drips, but day after day George had circled the container. When a new leak developed over the family's bed in July, he conceded that the roof had to be patched.

Herod took their sons outside while George crawled onto the roof to add new reeds. When he neared the ridgeline, one of the supporting poles sagged, and then cracked like a musket shot under his weight. George yelled as he fell through the thatch.

With a scream, Herod ran into the house. Planks pegged to the rafters formed a storage loft over half of the main room. Though George had landed near the edge, he was safe. His head and shoulders still protruded through the gaping thatch. He squatted and called down to her, "Look at that! The blasted pole split near in two."

"Are you hurt?"

"Not at all. Good thing I was at work here, not by the chimney." There, George would have dropped twelve feet to the cobblestone hearth. He reached into his loose-necked shirt and pulled out a handful of thatch.

Herod laughed, partly because more reeds were stuck haphazardly in his hair, but also in relief.

"Will the roof fall?" she asked, peering at the tattered thatch. A clump of moldering reeds the size of her head thudded to the floor.

"I'll pull down the loose stuff. With bracing, it will be safe." But when George was done, he told her, "Other poles are rotting too. 'Tis well we are moving or I'd have to replace the whole roof. After all the work I did on your house, John Hicks couldn't find time to help finish mine. I used poles I could handle myself, but never thought them hefty enough."

"John had no time for work not to his benefit," Herod scoffed. But then she thought about the shipwrights' fire earlier that year. Her mother had said that trouble comes in threes, but Herod could think of no other event that qualified. What was going to happen next?

CHAPTER 2
July 1647

HEROD DID NOT wonder what would go amiss for long. The next day she and George were ordered to present themselves at President Coggeshall's home. "What do you think he wants?" she asked George.

"It will be no social call. William Dyer is helping to draw up new laws, and told me that they are discussing adultery." George smoothed his braided hair, tugging the queue into place. "I told you we should have married."

"So you did, but Coggeshall did not send Constable Bull to jail us," Herod said. She felt calm, though the mood would be hard to maintain tomorrow. "Let's hear what he has to say before you put your head into the stocks."

Roger Williams, Rhode Island's famed peace-maker, had returned from England in 1644 bearing a royal charter for Rhode Island and Providence Plantations. His two-year negotiations gave legal standing to the colony at last. Larger Puritan colonies still coveted their neighbors' land and sheltered harbors, but could no longer seize them without risking the king's wrath.

Though the charter strengthened Rhode Island, it still took three years for Newport and Portsmouth to cooperate with Williams' Providence and the newer settlement of Warwick. In May 1647 Rhode Island finally formed a single government with equal rights for all towns. The first general election was held late in the month.

William Coddington, an ambitious merchant, had governed Newport and Portsmouth since Rhode Island was settled nearly ten years before. However, with votes from Providence and Warwick added to those of men who cared little for Coddington's patrician ways, the presidency was now John Coggeshall's. While Coddington still governed the island towns, he answered to Coggeshall on colony matters.

Coggeshall declared that Rhode Island should have laws equivalent to England's, and that those new laws would be enforced. Massachusetts, Plymouth, and Connecticut could no longer claim that Rhode Islanders – outcasts from those Puritan colonies – were lawless.

The Gardners were shown into the president's low-ceilinged parlor. Smoke-darkened beams made the space gloomy despite sunlight streaming through leaded glass windows. Coggeshall, stooped and gaunt, motioned them to a bench. He adjusted his full shirt sleeves as he sat back behind his desk, straightened wire-framed spectacles, and then riffled the corners of a parchment sheaf. "Do you know that Rhode Island has a new code of laws?"

"So I've heard," George answered, turning his broad-brimmed hat in his hands. Beside him, Herod gulped, but squared her shoulders and gazed at Coggeshall coolly.

"We've enacted a new marriage law that deeply affects you both –"

Herod said quickly, "It has naught to do with us. John Hicks abandoned me three years past and nearly killed me before he left. You know that Governor Coddington separated us, since you were his assistant. George and I are *not* adulterous."

"That is well, since adulterers may be put to death," Coggeshall said dryly. "I am more concerned with our law touching fornication." He took a parchment from the sheaf to read, "*For the preventing of many evils and mischiefs, no agreement between a man and woman to own each other as man and wife shall be owned as a lawful marriage, nor shall their children be legitimate unless they wed.*" Coggeshall squinted at them over his glasses.

"But Governor Coddington permitted us," George protested, his voice rising anxiously. "Mr. Dyer said the king himself allows common-law marriage."

Herod touched George's forearm as she said to Coggeshall, "I heard that you followed Mistress Anne Hutchinson's teachings in Boston. Remember when she said that marriage is an affair between a man, a woman, and their church? Magistrates have naught to do with it. George and I gave our vows before witnesses, just as she taught. That makes us wed, surely as if we spoke the words in John Clarke's church."

Coggeshall had set down his parchment, and now he slapped it. "That may be, but Mistress Hutchinson has gone to God, and Mr. Coddington is no longer governor. The new law stands, and you ignore it at your peril. You twain risk God's wrath not only for yourselves, but for all of Rhode Island!"

"Will you drag us before Pastor Clarke and force us to give our vows?" Herod cried. "I could not do it three years ago, and I will not do it now." She wanted to add that Coggeshall should mind his own business, but held her tongue.

"The law makes provisions for the likes of you," Coggeshall said. "All you need do is announce your intent at two town meetings, wed properly, and enter your marriage and sons' births in the records. All taint will be washed clean." Looking at George, Coggeshall asked, "What say you, Goodman?"

George had crumpled his felt hat. Now his callused hands smoothed it. "I wanted to marry then, and I still do."

Herod protested, "George, all of Rhode Island thinks us wed. If we go before the town now, they will point at our sons and say, 'There go George Gardner's bastards.'"

"They will be made legitimate if you wed properly," countered Coggeshall.

"I spoke your precious words to a minister with John Hicks, and see what came of it," Herod said bitterly. "Even without vows, George and I have led blameless lives, so leave us be."

George asked, "Can I go before the town myself?"

Herod glared at him. "Don't you dare!"

"Both parties must appear," Coggeshall answered.

"And if we don't?" George asked miserably.

"You and anyone who aids you will be fined five pounds and you will pay another five to her parents," the president tipped his head toward Herod.

Smiling, Herod told him, "Then he will pay me, for my parents are dead in England and I am their only heir. It was Governor Coddington who aided us. Will you fine him?"

"Do you find this humorous?"

"Not at all, but I will not paint my children as bastards to amuse the town gossips. George and I are bound as husband and wife by our vows."

"You are his *wife* by reputation only!" hissed Coggeshall. "God's law does not recognize your lying marriage. Neither does Rhode Island's."

Herod snapped, "So fine me all you like, for I've no money to give. Clap me in jail, and you'll have to nurse my son who is still suckling."

Coggeshall turned to George. "Goodman, do you refuse to obey?"

"Of course not, but I can't force her," George admitted. "Mr. Coddington couldn't make her wed, and you can't either. If you won't let me stand before the town by myself …."

"The law provides not for that."

"Then apply your laws to others if they grieve you, but leave us be," cried Herod. "Ten years ago you barely escaped banishment from Boston and fled here with the rest of us. Now you judge as harshly as the Puritans! Will you banish us now?"

Coggeshall stared at Herod for a long moment. His lips were pressed together so tightly that they were ringed with white. At last he replied slowly, "No, I will not."

"Leave things as they are. I swear to you that we will make no trouble."

"Don't think that I will soon forget this," Coggeshall warned them. "Goodman Gardner, take your … your *reputed* wife from my sight."

A few days later the Gardner family ate Sabbath dinner at the home of Herod's dearest friend, Mary Dyer. The Dyers' long table was crowded with the four Gardners, the Dyers, and their five children. Sam and Henry, Mary's eldest sons, ate standing at the sideboard with the family's servant girls; Peggy, and her little sister, Catherine.

The girls were new to the Dyer family, and Mary told Herod, "William got them from the captain of the *Princess* last week." Herod knew of the little ship which traveled the coast between Boston and New Haven; trading between the towns along the way. She also knew that was how bondservants often arrived in town. A ship's captain or a traveler to the colonies from England would pay the girls' passage. In turn, the girls would serve him for several years, or he would 'sell' them to a colonist on the same terms.

"Peggy is twelve now, and Catherine six. They will both be with us until they are eighteen," Mary told Herod.

"It's good that you kept the sisters together." Not only did the girls' plight remind Herod of her own losses, but she had nearly bonded herself out when she was only a year older than Peggy. Perhaps misfortune had played the same sad tricks on the Dyers' new bondservants as it had done to Herod.

Mary said, "The captain wanted to keep the little one for his sister in New Haven, but I couldn't bear to see them parted."

Her husband William added, "I paid him an extra pound for Catherine. It was worth it to see the smile on their faces – and Mary's."

Herod eyed the girls again. Dressed in a new skirt, Peggy seemed happy as she chatted easily with Sam, who was about her age. However, Catherine pressed against her older sister's leg and peered nervously at Herod past the edge of her cap. Little Catherine didn't know how lucky she was. Even if there was a sad tale in the child's past, she and her sister would have a good home with the Dyers.

After dinner, Peggy went to draw water from the well, and Catherine, the older Dyer children, and Benoni followed her into the yard. The Gardners seized the opportunity to describe their recent meeting to Mary and William. "We've heard no more of it from Coggeshall," finished Herod.

"*President* Coggeshall mentioned it to me," William told her. "He was plenty angry, but it should blow over if you trouble him no more."

"Trouble is the last thing I want," Herod assured him, but William's hazel eyes were narrowed. Though he'd helped to free her from John Hicks, sometimes Herod wondered if William thought that she'd brought John's wrath upon herself.

William took George out to the barn to show off twin calves. Peggy began noisily scrubbing a crusted roasting pan with sand and a rag, and Herod rinsed trenchers in a bucket of water warmed with a splash from the kettle. Mary wrapped uneaten bread in a cloth, asking, "What says George?"

Herod glanced at the servant but the girl was occupied with her chore, and probably couldn't hear. Quietly she answered, "Same as always. George fears that Coggeshall will sit him in the stocks." She picked up a shallow wooden trough large enough for two to share a hearty meal. Though it had been wiped clean with a piece of bread, Mary liked to rinse her tableware. Herod sloshed it in the bucket, and then set the dripping trencher on the table.

She realized with envy that Mary's home was always tidy despite five active children and her advancing pregnancy. Her clothes were near-spotless from the hem of her skirt to her bleached linen cap. Herod asked, "How do you do it?"

"What?" Mary, who was nearly a dozen years older than her friend, grinned at Herod.

"Keep everything so clean?"

"It will be easier with the new girls to help me," Mary chuckled. "But you can do what I do. When your boys are older, put them to work. 'Ben, sweep the floor. Henry, rinse those mugs.' It's a pity that John took your children. They'd be of an age to help you now."

"Betty and Hannah ... Betty is eight now, and Hannah will soon be ten," Herod mused bitterly.

"And Tom is five?"

Herod nodded. "When John took them to Long Island, all Coddington said was that by law they belonged to him. I'll not risk losing my sons again to a faithless husband."

Mary took a rinsed trencher from Herod and sat it on the hearth to dry. "You have nothing to fear. George adores you. It would take an army to wrest him from your side."

"I know, I know, but when I think of being bonded to any man, I feel ill. And if we go before the town now ...."

"Tongues would wag from here to Boston." Mary's freckle-faced smile was usually infectious, but Herod could only respond feebly. "Just remember that scandal is short-lived without fresh meat to feed on."

"That's not so. After John left, half the people in Newport no longer spoke to me. The rest of Newport shunned me when Benoni began to show. Anyone who could count to nine watched my belly grow, sniggering to each other, 'is it Hicks' or Gardner's?' I would have been chained up as a madwoman without you."

"And George," Mary added.

"You both saved me, Mary. George was stronger than any rock, but he paid dearly. Though he was an ensign in the militia before, George has held no office since he took me in. He says that he cares not."

"Do you think so?"

Mary's quiet question made Herod pause. She scratched a bit of dried gravy from a trencher and rinsed it again. "Yes. George doesn't like biting talk or jealousies. He is happiest when he's in his barn with his stock, or planting a furrow and watching the seed sprout. My George is a simple man, and it's easy to keep him content."

Herod gave the last wet trencher to Mary, and then dried her hands on her apron. She said, "As for you, I am not the first woman you have stood with. You walked out of the meeting house with Anne Hutchinson after she was banished from Boston, though that meant you had to leave Massachusetts too."

"Anne repaid the kindness many times over. Leaving Boston? It was no loss. William and I couldn't stomach the Puritans and their wicked acts. As for you; you would have stood with me then, and –"

"And I will do it now," Herod declared. "Whatever you need, Mary, call on me. If you need me to stand with you in Boston, I'll do it."

"You must help me here, for we'll never see Boston again," Mary laughed. "The Puritans can trouble us no more."

After admiring the newborn calves, George shooed the children out of the tiny barn. Dyer used it to store tools, and there was a pair of stalls for young or sick animals. When they were alone, George asked William, "Do you think Coggeshall will charge us with adultery? He said we could be hanged."

"He is not charging you," William replied. When George blew out a loud sigh, William held up a hand. Annoyed by the gesture, the shaggy cow brandished her horns at the two men, warning them away from her calves. They stepped back from the stall, and then William said, "Coggeshall had me place an entry in the town records, but you won't like it."

"What is it?"

"Remember John Hicks' letter?"

"How could I forget?" After Hicks had abandoned Herod three years ago, he sent Newport's governor a letter that dripped poison, declaring that he wanted nothing more to do with his wife. George reddened and asked again, "What did Coggeshall put in the record?"

"That Hicks was most willing to be parted since Herod had untied the knot of affection. Her whoredom with you freed him of any blame in the matter." William tossed a wisp of hay to the cow.

George cried, "Did Coggeshall write 'whoredom' for any man to read?"

"I pleaded for more considerate language, but he insisted on using Hicks' actual words because his intent is clear. So long as I am Rhode Island's clerk, no man will read that entry."

"But you won't keep the records forever. What then?"

William shook his head. "I never guessed John Coggeshall for a vengeful man. You must have pricked him."

George said sourly, "Not me – 'twas Herod."

William groaned. "Let me guess. 'I will not wed and you can't make me.'" He accompanied the falsetto whine with a stamp of his foot.

George laughed, but then admitted, "I've never been able to move her a finger's width on it. She was in such a state before Ben came that I didn't press her. After he was born, Herod still fretted about what people would say. I offered to take her to Providence or New Haven so nobody would know us, but she still refused."

"Is she ashamed now?"

George snorted, "Shame has naught to do with it! Herod cannot be forced to anything. If she gets a notion, I may as well give up and do as she wishes."

"I'm glad Mary's not so. She has her fancies, but I prefer a little give in a woman." William tossed another clump of hay to the cow, and then hung his fork where mice couldn't chew on the sweat-flavored handle.

"There's not much give in Herod," George admitted. "All I can do is keep her content so she will stay with me."

CHAPTER 3
October 1647

IN EARLY OCTOBER Herod was among several women who helped Mary deliver her sixth child. They crowded into her bedchamber to toast the infant with the last of the groaning beer, so-named because the brew eased the mother's pain during labor, as well as quenching her helpers' thirst. Dark-haired Betty Coggeshall asked, "What is the girl to be named?"

Mary's voice was slurred with weariness when she replied, "This one will be named for me." Her eyes dropped, and Herod's gaze followed to the swaddled child now suckling for the first time. Young Mary had delicate yellow fuzz on her head; a paler shade of her mother's hair. Herod mused that Mary's locks had faded over the ten years since they'd met. Her own hair had darkened, just as a penny does over the years.

The other women left, and William would soon return with their children, but Herod was staying overnight. She contemplated the fire. It wasn't safe to have a laboring woman get chilled, but with the birthing over, Herod wondered whether she should feed the flames again. Mary said, "Leave it be, and please take away my quilt. I'm stifling."

"It's plenty warm," Herod agreed. She set the coverlet aside and opened the shutters to admit cool October air. It was scented with smoke, probably from the Dyers' own chimney. She commented, "You birthed so quickly. It gets easier each time."

"Ah, that breeze is heavenly," Mary sighed. Wait 'til you are near thirty-five. You'll find that everything comes harder."

"If God has any pity in him, I'll be done with childbearing by then."

"The one you carry now won't be your last," predicted Mary. "But I know no other woman who was fourteen when she bore her first. Perhaps you will stop young too."

"George wants a big family," Herod said.

"It's all in God's hands," Mary replied, looking down at her newest daughter. "I am grateful that he has blessed me so."

The next morning Herod went home. Soon George came back from their new home site with Ben and Henry in tow. She told George about Mary's new daughter while they ate their midday meal, but he showed more enthusiasm for Herod's new pregnancy. "I hope it's another son. With luck I'll never build another house, but the boys can help each other." He took a big bite of stew, and then added, "Benoni's near ready to help in the sawpit now, aren't you, Ben?"

"Yes," said the three-year-old, but the lad was clearly confused.

"Papa's teasing, Ben," Herod told her son. Though the lad was as tall as Maher Dyer, who was a year older, he didn't have a quick wit to match his size. His father's jest forgotten, Benoni turned back to his food.

"Soon as the corn's in, I'll start hauling rocks for the chimney," George told Herod. "Lucky us – there are outcrops on the farm. I won't have far to haul the stone."

"You won't like them so well when we are picking them out of the garden."

"We'll plant here next year, so don't worry yet. Once the chimney's up and the ground freezes, I'll sledge our goods there. All I need is Jess and Shem." George couldn't be happier with his new team of oxen. The gelded steers were inexperienced, but willing and strong. "Why, it took less than a week to haul all the timber I needed for the house."

Herod sighed. She'd heard many times about the team's abilities, but it was hard to stop George once he got started. Then, hard rapping on the door ended her husband's flow of words, and continued as though the unseen guest thought the house's occupants were deaf. Herod rose, saying, "Do you expect someone?"

"Bob Stanton's hunting today. Maybe he needs help with a deer," George told her. Herod unlatched the door, but before she pulled it open, the visitor boldly pushed his way inside.

"What ...." Herod stumbled backward until she bumped into the table. The intruder was a short man in his early thirties, with broad shoulders and heavily-muscled thighs. "What's wrong, Herod?" the burly man asked. "Have you no kiss for your long-lost husband? Mayhap you can't see through my disguise."

George jumped up, knocking his bench aside. "How dare you come here, Hicks! What do you want?"

John Hicks bared his teeth in a phony grin. "I'm in town for a bit of business, and thought to see my wife again."

"She's no wife of yours," George grated. "You were separated by Governor Coddington three years back."

"Yes, Coddington," Herod cried. "I'll run for help!"

"Save your feet," John sneered. "Coddington is in mourning for his wife, so he'll have no time for you." In a kinder tone he added, "In truth, I mean no harm. I just came by for a chat." He closed the door gently behind him.

"We've naught to say to you," George told John.

Herod had planted herself between John and her sons. Benoni asked, "Who is that, Mama?" but Herod shushed him.

John craned his neck. "Two little ones already. Marriage to the likes of Gardner must agree with you. You *are* wed, or didn't Coddington give you leave to remarry?"

"None of your affair, John," Herod snapped.

"You are mighty bold in coming here after all you've done," George added.

"What could you mean?" said John, hanging his wide-brimmed hat on a peg by the door. "I don't say that I did a thing, mind you, but whatever happened, you deserved it."

"Who is that, Mama?" Benoni asked again.

George said to John, "Why, you took Herod's children and robbed her, burned her house, and tried to fire mine as well."

"I took *my* children and money," John said, his voice silky. "As for house-burning, I know nothing of it. The place looks as it ever did. A trifle snug for four, is it not?"

"If Mr. Coddington knew you were here, he would have you jailed," said George.

"President Coggeshall gave me leave to come here."

"I doubt that," was George's reply. "I'm of a mind to fetch him, and call Henry Bull to lock you up."

"That's not needed," Herod said. Her trembling voice was as sweet as she could manage. "Why don't you go out to the shed and get the last of the applejack?" George gaped at her, and she nodded reassuringly. "Please, for our guest."

She turned to John. "Have you eaten? We've stew and white bread, still warm. Remember you always wanted to grow wheat? We had a good crop this year. Let me take your cloak, and I'll fetch a bowl for you." She looked back at George and nodded toward the door. He went out reluctantly, leaving it open behind him.

Pushing her unfinished meal to one side, Herod held out a hand for John's cloak. He sat near the fire, saying, "Mighty kind of you."

"No reason we can't be polite," she replied, filling a trencher with venison stew. She broke off a big chunk of bread and placed the food before John. As he tasted the stew, she eyed him. Clean-shaven in the past; he now wore a beard, but not a fashionable chin tuft. Thick black growth hid his lower face. John's hat and jerkin were new, with a silk band and bone buttons, but his breeches were worn and one knee was patched.

Herod sat between her sons. "Eat, Ben," she said to the older boy, who still stared at the stranger across the table. She broke bread into small bits, sopped them in her cooling stew, and gave them to her younger son. "Here, Henry." The toddler crammed a piece into his mouth.

John was saying, "This is quite good. You've learned to cook at last," when George came back with a stoneware bottle in his hand. He thumped the jug onto the table by Herod, who said, "A mug?" This, too, was banged onto the table. Herod poured a couple ounces of the liquor into the wooden mug and passed it to John. George stood behind her and she leaned back against him, grateful for his solid warmth.

When John sipped his brandy, his eyebrows arched. "I didn't know you liked strong drink, George."

The tall farmer growled, "I don't."

"A keg of cider got so hard we put it in the shed to freeze," Herod explained, "and poured off the applejack for guests." His stew forgotten, John sipped the brandy and let out a satisfied "Ahhh."

"What's your business, Hicks?" George asked.

Herod said, "Don't be hasty. John, will you tell us where you have been?" Beneath the table, she wiped sweaty palms on her skirt. She knew John too well. A drink or two loosened his tongue, even made him jolly. More liquor released his anger, and she was grateful there wasn't much brandy in the bottle. Seeing John drink awakened bad memories.

"I live in Flushing, not far from Manhattan. A fine place: fertile land and plenty of it."

George seemed to be relaxing when he asked, "How is it living under the Dutch?"

When John grinned, big white teeth flashed through his beard. He sipped his brandy again and said, "I like them quite well, thank you. They're far more just than Coddington or the Puritans ever were. They welcome Englishmen, and we can worship how, or if, we choose. My name is on the Flushing patent, and this year I helped settle disputes between the Indians and villagers. Why, the Dutch treat me like a brother ever since I told them my family fled to Holland to escape English persecution ere we came to Massachusetts."

"There's a bold lie," Herod said, but her tone was teasing. "You and I came straight from England to Boston, and not a one of your family with us."

"They believe me, and that's good enough. They also think I graduated from Oxford."

Herod shook her finger reprovingly. "You told me you studied there but one year. You lie to your neighbors and sound proud of it." John raised his mug to her.

"Any wife yet?" George asked. "You always talked of getting a Dutch wife."

John's lips puckered and he turned his head to one side, as if he might spit on the floor. "Thank you, but no. I had as much wife as I want for a long, long while." He bared his teeth again in a smirk aimed at Herod.

She took a deep breath. "What of my children, John. How are they?"

"My children," he corrected, tearing off a bit of bread to pop into his mouth.

"Whatever you say. Tell me of them," Herod begged.

John sneered, "So that's why you were so nice – you just want the news. I knew Gardner couldn't have tamed you so readily."

"Hicks, you've had bread and drink in my house," George said. "Stop tormenting Herod and speak of her children."

John took a big bite of cooling stew and mumbled, "Very well." He swallowed and said more clearly, "Tom's five now, and a fine young man; bigger and faster than the other boys. He doesn't remember you at all." Herod sagged and George squeezed her shoulder. "He claims that he saw you brush your hair in the morning, but Bessie fills him with sentimental rubbish.

"Hannah fills your shoes nicely. Not even ten, but she's a proper little mother to the younger ones. Our neighbor is teaching her to bake, and already she's a better cook than you. Why, Hannah's only four years younger than you when we wed. She'll make a fine wife; far better than you ever were."

"Do you give her a chance to play, or is she your slave all the day?"

"Hannah is hardly a slave. She adores me, and never speaks of you at all." John shoveled in another big bite of stew.

"What of Betty?"

"*Bessie* is now 'Elizabeth, if you please.' She's the image of you. Red-haired and tall as Hannah, though she's two years younger. Got no more heft to her than a fishing spear. Acts just like you too; dreamy and idling about, telling Tom stories. 'Mama said this' or 'Mama did that.' Gets him all stirred up and asking why he doesn't have a mama. If I knew how difficult Bessie would be, I'd have left her with you."

Herod begged, "Keep the others if you must, keep my money, but if Betty's not happy, then bring her back to me."

"Are you mad?" John threw his spoon into his trencher, splattering stew on the table. "Why would I leave any of my children to your whorish ways? Who knows what you are up to when Gardner's back is turned; bringing men in here –"

"Mind your tongue in front of my sons," George growled.

John studied the boys; red-haired Henry munching his bread, and the wary Benoni, with silky blond locks curling to his shoulders. "Don't want the little bastards hearing the truth about their mama?" George started toward John, but Herod caught his arm.

"I heard that boy was born in December, and a fine, full-term babe he was," John crowed. "I abandoned this bitch only eight months before, and 'twas far longer than that since I last sullied myself lying with her. He's your son, and bred before I left town. Rhode Island has laws against adultery to put the two of you to death, and I'm still wed to her."

Herod shook her head. "Not at all. Coddington parted us."

"Did he? Well, we're still wed under Dutch law. I've not divorced you yet, though I've plenty of grounds."

"So what?" asked George. "You don't want her, and we live under English law."

John shrugged as his eyes went back to Benoni and Henry. "Two sons," he said.

Herod snapped, "And a third on the way. I should know when I'm carrying a boy."

"Hah!" John scoffed weakly. "How is it you've borne Gardner two sons, but only one for me?"

"Because he's twice the man you are, in *every* way," Herod snarled. "George doesn't need his fists to arm himself to bed me."

John's face went scarlet, and George said clearly, "Enough, Hicks. State your business, if you have any, and be gone."

Breathing hard, John reluctantly turned away from Herod. "Very well. I've been to see your new president."

George said, "You heard that Coddington lost the election, so you looked for revenge. What was your charge?"

John snickered. "I asked Coggeshall what Parliament might do if Rhode Island fails to enforce its own laws."

"And charged us with adultery," said Herod.

"Wrong! My main concern is the new law against exiling a man or seizing his property without trial."

Herod blinked, and George asked, "What of it?"

John grinned, his eyes cold and triumphant. "That is exactly what Coddington did. He took my lands and gave them to you. No trial, no chance to defend myself; just thievery. And he banished me in every sense of the word. Banned me from voting, and told me to leave or he'd make my life hell. Took my wife and gave her to you too, though I no longer wanted the treacherous bitch. Your new president righted some of those wrongs."

"How?" Herod asked.

"Remember my fifty acres at Newport Cliffs? Coddington gave them to your new man, but Gardner's done nothing with them. Coggeshall gave me leave to sell them."

Herod protested, "He can't take our land and give it to you."

John laughed. "He already has. Stuffy old duck – he said I must sell the land and never return, not that I want to see this charming place crawling with rogues again. He also told me to stay clear of you, but I couldn't resist."

George said, "Coddington still governs Newport, so let's see what he says. He still blames you for the fire at his farm, and you'll be lucky to escape jail for arson."

"Coddington knows all about the deal," John said. "He didn't approve, but couldn't help but submit to his president. Neither one told you because they didn't want to hear you whine. Go crawl to their feet! 'Twill do you no good."

"Have you any more news?" asked Herod.

John scratched his head. "Nothing more. I wish that Coggeshall would let me sell the rest of my land and jail you adulterers, but he won't."

"Then get out," George said, and took a step toward Hicks.

"Delighted," John said. With a courtier's flourish he bowed low to Herod. "A pleasure to see you again, my dear, and to meet your charming bastards. As for you, Gardner, pay heed. She'll betray you too, as soon as she finds another man to her liking."

Herod laughed, "Only you, John, and only after you started beating me. George is a true, loving husband and has nothing to fear."

"Remember my words, Gardner," John said, donning his cloak and hat. "Watch the bitch well – she's not to be trusted."

"Enjoy Hell when you get there, John," Herod said. He laughed, and slammed the door as he left.

"Can you believe that?" George said. He opened his arms and Herod fell into them. "I never thought to see him again."

"Nor I."

"Who was that?"

They both turned to Benoni, and Herod told her son, "A bad man. He was married to me before your Papa, but he ran away."

"He called me 'bastard.' What's that?"

George muttered something, but Herod asked, "Has anyone else called you that?" Looking at his trencher, Benoni slowly shook his head. "It's a very bad word, and I never want you to use it. That man was trying to make us all sad."

"Like when Buzzy Dyer called me a dung-head?"

"I don't want you to say that either. I thought Buzzy was your friend."

"He is," Benoni replied. However, when Herod was putting him to bed, he said, "That bad man said you had other children."

Herod sighed, "Yes, we did. We had two girls and a boy, and he took them far away."

"Will Papa take me away?"

23

"Nobody will ever take you from me," Herod said firmly, and hugged Benoni as her eyes flooded with tears.

The next day the Gardners confronted Coggeshall, who assured them that they need not fear John Hicks. "I forbade him to return to Rhode Island."

"Just as you forbade him from tormenting Herod, but he did," George cried. "Why should he not come back to demand more land or just to devil us?"

Coggeshall assured the couple that Hicks would be arrested if he ever returned, but it was a long time before Herod could answer the door without her heart pounding in dread.

CHAPTER 4
Late May 1648

"AT LAST!" HEROD looked around her new home with satisfaction. George had sledged in the last load of goods that morning. He was out in the shed with his oxen now, rubbing their sweaty coats dry. Spring was full-blown, with leaves emerging and fruit trees in flower, but ocean-chilled winds still blew cold on Newport.

Benoni and Henry had 'helped' their father move the last tools and feed from their old house. They were so worn out that they barely stayed awake for the midday meal. Their mother looked at the boys sleeping on their cornshuck tick and sighed happily. She stroked her swollen belly, but it seemed that even the baby had gone to sleep. 'Two months to go,' Herod thought.

Bob Stanton, George's long-time friend, had bought the Gardners' old lot. Now that the family was living at the farm, George would dismantle their former home. Planks and beams, already sawn and drilled, would make a fine loft and storage room for the new farmhouse.

Herod stepped outside to gaze around their yard. Their new home sat in a shallow bowl. A limestone outcrop to the south had provided slabs for the hearth and chimney which formed the entire western wall of the house. The Atlantic lay nearly a mile beyond, but she couldn't see it.

After the Gardners picked a new house site, they had planted apple, pear, and cherry cuttings right away. Most of them survived, but it would be a few years before the trees matured. Stanton would give the Gardners fruit from their former orchard for a few years.

The new trees waved jauntily at Herod from her left. To her right stretched a long swath of plowed dirt. It was planted in corn which was now beginning to sprout. To Herod's north was her kitchen garden. A hundred paces beyond the garden's fence lay a line of low hills. Those hummocks sheltered the Gardners' home from the wind, but they also blocked the family's view of the bay and Newport town.

Herod turned away from her imperfect view with a regretful sigh. It was time to wake her sons.

"You need not go," George said. "I'll tell you what Coddington says."

"I promised Mary that I'd mind her children. I'll not hear the meeting, but there's no reason that she should miss it as well." Herod held Benoni between her knees and pulled a long-sleeved shirt over his head, a miniature version of the one his father wore. She stuffed the hem into the top of Ben's breeches, though it wouldn't stay neatly tucked for long.

The Gardner family was on their way to Newport, for George was attending a special meeting. Only two weeks ago William Coddington had been elected president of Rhode Island's four towns. He'd stunned the colony by declining the office, and today he would explain his actions.

Benoni was dressed at last, but now he was daring Henry to chase him. 'To think I was worried that they'd be worn out from this morning,' Herod thought irritably. Ben eluded her awkward grab, and she warned him, "If you don't stop …." He laughed and darted away.

Henry was an easier catch, and Herod plopped him onto a bench. "Here are your shoes," she told him, but he kicked and squirmed. At last she said, "Go barefoot, but I'll not listen to complaints that your toes are cold."

"I don't want shoes either," said Benoni.

Herod rolled her eyes to heaven. "Very well, Ben, take them off." The tow-haired boy kicked the stiff leather shoes from his feet. One flew into the air and landed in the fireplace. Fortunately the flames were confined to the other side of the hearth, and the shoe landed safely. Herod growled warningly at her wayward son.

"Stay here," George urged. "Keep the boys and stay."

"I promised Mary."

"But it's so far to walk, and in your state …."

"I'm fit enough to walk to town on Sabbath, so why not today?" Herod said impatiently. "You sound like John." She swung a light cloak over her shoulders and gathered up the boys' wraps. They might want them later in the day.

George hugged Herod, saying contritely, "I am not commanding you. I only thought to save you a walk."

"I know, and thank you," Herod said, kissing his cheek. "Now, let's get these boys on the road lest they wear themselves out again."

At the Dyers' home, Mary thanked Herod for minding her children. "I suckled young Mary, so she may sleep until I return. It's a shame you can't hear Coddington explain himself."

"George will leave out half of it," Herod complained. "I hope you remember the details."

Looking out the window, Mary tapped her fingers on the sill. Then she said, "I have it. We'll all go to the meeting house and sit in the yard. I'll ask William to open the window so we can hear everything. Betty Coggeshall may sit with us, for she thinks that she is breeding. We'll all sit on the grass and nurse our babes and queasy bellies in peace."

When they reached the meeting house, Herod's sons ran off to romp with the younger Dyer children. She sat on the lawn and braced her back against the church's wall, sighing, "It's so pleasant here. You had a good idea, Mary."

Betty, who was a few years younger than Herod, plopped down beside her. Herod asked how she felt.

"False alarm – my courses came yesterday. John is disappointed, for we have been wed a year but no baby in sight." Betty was married to John Coggeshall Jr., and it was her father-in-law who had admonished the Gardners.

Herod told her, "Don't be hasty. At your age, I'd borne three children already."

Betty said, "Oh, that's right. You were wed to that other man."

"Old news," Herod said with a shrug. "I wager today Coddington will tell us about his old feuds." Her spine pressed into the planks behind her, so she stuffed her cloak between her back and the wall, wriggling to fit the padding into position.

"Will he speak honestly?" Mary asked. "Herod is right. It's bad blood that led to this, mostly with Samuell Gorton."

Betty said, "Gorton's not a Newport man, is he?"

Herod shook her head. "He and a few families live on the far shore of the bay, with Indians all around."

"So why should Coddington worry about him?" Betty sniffed.

Mary said, "Master Gorton troubles authorities wherever he goes. Samuell's been in New England eleven years. He's been chased out of Boston, Portsmouth," Mary ticked them off on her fingers, "seven towns by my count. Plymouth sent Gorton packing, Massachusetts banished him on pain of death, and Coddington ousted him from Aquidneck."

"I heard about that when John and I arrived," said Herod. She idly ran her fingers through the grass, looking for a four-leafed clover.

"After Plymouth cast out Gorton, he came to Portsmouth," Mary said. "Coddington governed us then." She moved her arm to cast more shade over the infant in her lap, and directed her next words to Betty, "He has every year except the last, when they elected your father-in-law, God rest his soul." President Coggeshall had died several months ago.

"You hens had best stop your cackling when Coddington gets here." The voice came from over Herod's head and she started.

Mary grinned up at her husband, who was leaning out through the open window. "Come now, we weren't even loud enough to wake your daughter."

"True, but you'll have to keep it down once the meeting begins."

"We're agog to hear Coddington, same as you. Seems like he's late," said Herod.

William nodded. "Perhaps he's reluctant to face Newport's freemen."

"Women too," his wife added tartly, and William shook his head before drawing back inside. Mary told her friends, "Did you know that last year, when President Coggeshall, John Clarke, and my husband drew up Newport's laws, they wrote all *men* may walk as God and their conscience guide them? It seems that they forgot about us women."

"Mayhap they think women have no conscience," Herod suggested.

Betty snickered, but Mary said flatly, "Some of them believe we have no souls as well."

Herod said, "Then I shall stop worrying that I might go to Hell."

Mary frowned as she replied, "*That* should worry all of us."

"'Twas but a jest," Herod said defensively. Mary eyed her until she added, "Pray tell us of Samuell, Mary."

After another moment Mary continued, "Not long after Mr. Gorton arrived in Portsmouth he and Coddington were at war. They got on just like a rat dog and tomcat well-matched in size. The terrier barks a brave tune, but won't risk those claws. The cat's back is up, but he won't give an inch. Neither will cry 'Enough!' for Coddington walks among us like a king, and Gorton loves a fight."

"Has Coddington ever yielded to anyone?" Betty asked.

"God, perhaps, but he fought the king." Herod smiled at Mary's jest. "My William says he refused a loan that Charles forced upon him years ago.

"As for Samuell, he found a kindred spirit in Anne." Mary's voice barely wavered, but Herod knew that her friend still grieved for Anne Hutchinson, dead several years ago at the hands of New Netherland's Indians. "Anne admitted to no governor but God, and Samuell agreed with her.

"Shortly after Samuell came to Portsmouth, Coddington went to Boston on business. As soon as he passed from sight, Gorton called for an election. Men whom Coddington had offended, and there were plenty, voted in a new governor: William Hutchinson. On the same day, my husband and those who cared little for Gorton's coup agreed to start anew in Newport."

"Tell Betty about the cow," Herod suggested.

Mary grinned. "Soon after, a cow strayed onto Samuell's land. When the owner came to fetch it, Gorton's maidservant attacked the poor old woman. The girl was ordered to court, but Gorton came in her stead."

"What a battle that was," said Herod.

Betty laughed, "Father said that Gorton mocked the court and called them Just-Asses."

"True!" chuckled Mary. Her daughter stirred in her lap, and then settled back to sleep. When Mary spoke again, it was more quietly. "Coddington called, 'All you that hold to the king carry Gorton to prison.' But Gorton replied, 'All you that hold to the king carry Coddington to prison!' Coddington had him whipped, but after it was done, Gorton chased after him with a chain dragging from one ankle, crying, 'You have but lent me this whipping, and you will surely be paid back.'

"Gorton tried Providence next, but didn't stay long. Roger Williams once spent a winter with the Narragansett Indians, but he couldn't stomach Gorton's whimsies. When Samuell tried Pawtuxet, they begged Massachusetts to annex the town and cast Gorton out."

"I met Mr. Gorton," said Betty. "He doesn't seem so troublesome."

"Samuell can be kind and generous, but he takes orders from no man. He never found peace until he went further south and bought Warwick from the Narragansetts."

Herod observed, "We Rhode Islanders are a touchy lot."

Mary nodded. "We will need God's help to stay bound under a single government. Our charter unites us, but while Coddington will consent to govern Gorton or Williams, a day will come when one of them is elected president."

"That will be Coddington's worst nightmare come to life," said Herod.

A stir of voices announced William Coddington's arrival. All three women peeked at him through the window. The portly 47-year old was immaculately dressed and freshly shaven, but there were dark rings under his eyes. He strode to the front of the meeting house.

"As you know, I was recently named president, but persecution forced me to decline the office." Coddington's voice was high-pitched from tension. "Now our worst fears have come to pass, and we have Gorton's puppet as president."

"You didn't attend elections, so you have no man to blame but yourself!" Herod could not recognize the unseen man's voice.

Coddington said testily, "No comments until I have done speaking. My enemies lay in wait with false charges, so I would not satisfy them by appearing. Mr. Jeremiah Clarke is a good Newport man, and stood in my place. I hoped that he would be chosen, but we have John Smith in his stead."

A different voice drawled, "We wanted Mr. Williams, but he declined."

"You prefer Williams?" Coddington sneered. "He professes liberty of conscience, yet persecutes men who do not agree. Do so much as build a shed in Providence without his approval, and there is no peace. What regard would he have for us in Newport?"

Herod jeered quietly, "So Williams must have command? Sounds like Coddington himself." Mary grinned her silent agreement.

"Remember how Williams returned with his precious charter?" Coddington asked the assemblage. "That charter which doesn't even name our Rhode Island, only his Providence Plantations? A flotilla of canoes led him home, puffed with pride like Alexander leading his troops into the desert, dreaming of empires."

"He's jealous," Betty giggled.

"Quietly," Mary gently shushed her.

Coddington continued, "What will happen when mainland rabble outnumber the gentlemen on our island? What sort of chaos will follow?"

A murmur floated through the meeting house. Nicholas Easton, who had often been Coddington's assistant, stood to say firmly, "We have chaos already. Because you declined your office, Portsmouth refuses to unite with Newport to govern our island."

"That is not my doing," Coddington blustered. "All men know that I wish for a joint government."

Mary twitched when she heard her husband say angrily, "We hear you are plotting to have our island swallowed up by Plymouth."

"I merely inquired about an alliance for our own protection," Coddington explained, but a pleading whine crept into his voice. "We are weak, so the Dutch encroach. The Indians have more guns every day. I spoke with Plymouth and Massachusetts about mutual defense and perpetual friendship, but never asked to be annexed."

William Dyer said, "We hear you have also approached the Dutch!"

"Only seeking arms for our protection. I've no more desire to live under Dutch law than any of you. As for Massachusetts and Plymouth, they will take our land if we fall to dissension. An alliance would end that hazard."

Another man sneered, "Or let them seize our island to 'protect' it. Did you not ask them to seize Providence and Warwick?"

Coddington hesitated. "That was long ago, and only for those towns' safety. Even now they are weak, and easily overrun by Indians or pirates. What if that land was held by enemies who could sail across the bay to attack us?"

"Consorting with the Dutch is treason!"

"A dangerous word," snapped the red-faced Coddington. "When President Coggeshall talked with the Dutch about trade and arms, you never accused him of treason. My only thought is for Rhode Island's safety and prosperity, and everything I do is to that end."

The accusations and Coddington's defensive answers went on until the governor finally stormed out. The meeting house only got noisier. Herod sat down, commenting, "I'll wait out here 'til George comes." Betty nodded her agreement.

Mary said, "Coddington has backed himself into a corner. He's not dishonest, but his hatred of Gorton colors everything he does. It's a pity. My husband once thought highly of him. I won't say that he's Coddington's enemy now, but …."

"My husband too," said Betty.

"George thinks the world of Coddington no matter what," said Herod. "But he wouldn't grant my divorce from John and left me forever tainted." She masked a scowl. Mary knew all about Herod's mock marriage, but would Betty notice?

Apparently not, for Betty commented, "Coddington makes his claims, but last week he asked my husband what he thought of joining with Plymouth."

"Mine too," said Mary. "Coddington told him, 'Rhode Island will topple if led by lesser men. We need strong leaders to hold off our foes!' He thinks he's God's gift to Rhode Island."

"He's made a botch of it. A woman might do better," Herod joked.

"A woman govern Rhode Island?" Betty laughed so hard that she fell over onto the grass. "That will never happen."

"Not while men write the laws and prevent women from voting," was Mary's cynical comment. "Half of Rhode Island is silenced, but I pray that men will come to their senses some day. Let us speak!"

Many of Mary's whimsies seemed improbable to Herod, but this time she said thoughtfully, "Amen."

CHAPTER 5
July 1648 - April 1651

GEORGE GARDNER JR. was born in July. When his father picked up the tightly swaddled infant, he gaped at the black hair crowning the baby's head. George joked, "Are you sure that's not John Hicks' get?" Chestnut-haired Herod assured her blond husband that the chubby infant looked just like her brother Jim, and at the next militia meeting the proud father bought a round of rum punch to toast his namesake's birth.

However, Herod fretted to Mary, "When do you think I'll birth another girl? I hope that John Hicks didn't steal the only daughters I'll ever bear."

"Herod, you are only twenty-six. You've plenty of time to have a little girl."

In August huge flocks of pigeons appeared. George, like every other New England farmer, feared that his corn and recently-reaped wheat would be devastated. However, a musket loaded with birdshot brought down dozens of doves with one blast and drove the rest of the flock away. For a few days, everyone dined well on fat pigeons of passage.

Their bellies were full and their crops flourished, but Rhode Islanders were still uneasy as William Coddington kept up his separation talk. He had a handful of supporters, but most men preferred to stay united with Providence and Warwick, not Plymouth.

Coddington had a new, sinister right-hand man. Captain Alexander Partridge had been ordered to leave Massachusetts because of his opposition to the Puritan leadership. However, it was said that he had fought with Cromwell's army against the king. William Dyer commented, "Strange man: it seems he was with the Puritans in England, but against them here."

Herod didn't trust Partridge at all. In Coddington's presence he was polite, but when his employer was absent, Partridge rarely bothered with courtesy. The man would fix his prominent blue eyes on a person and stare without blinking, so Herod snickered to Betty Coggeshall that he looked like a beached codfish. However, his caustic wit reminded Herod of her former husband, and her aversion was bolstered by gossip that he drank heavily.

In September, Captain Partridge accompanied Coddington to a United Colonies meeting. Once more they begged for Aquidneck Island to be allied with the Puritan colonies, claiming that they were supported by most of the freemen. Again they were denied, unless they were annexed by Plymouth.

Doing so would nullify the charter that united Rhode Island, and the isolated mainland towns risked being swallowed up by Massachusetts or Connecticut, just as a hungry gull devours a broken clam.

Even Coddington would not submit to Plymouth, but with his plots laid open to public scrutiny he became a very unpopular man. A fortnight later he confided to Roger Williams that he intended to visit England.

In the first days of 1649, William Coddington and his only child sailed from Boston, leaving Captain Partridge in charge of his affairs. He gave Newport's residents little explanation for his departure, and people speculated that he was seeking a rich husband for fifteen-year-old Mary. If Partridge knew what Coddington was up to, he kept the secret well. Newport heard little of him for over two years. In light of the ex-governor's schemes, nobody on Aquidneck missed him.

Whatever his plans, if Coddington had hoped for the king's help, he was out of luck. After battling Puritan armies for nearly nine years, King Charles lost the war. On January 30, 1649, only days after the former governor left Newport, the victorious Puritans beheaded their king. Coddington's pleas would not be aired for a long time.

"Let's go watch the sun set," Herod told her children, and they raced for the door. Though Herod was content in her new home, she sighed wistfully for the view from her former doorstep. However, on pleasant evenings a short stroll toward Newport gave her the scenery she craved. George could work in peace, the boys got one more chance to stretch their legs, and they fell asleep as soon as they slid under their quilts.

On this May evening, a seductively warm breeze blew from the southwest to riffle the bay. Benoni and sturdy, red-haired Henry wanted to wade along the shore but Herod told them, "Absolutely not – that water's cold enough to freeze your bones. Stay with me and I'll tell you about your grandpapa."

Benoni heaved a theatrical sigh, but Henry took his mother's hand. Herod settled young Georgie, now nearly a year old, on her hip, pointed inland, and said, "See over there?"

"Aye, Mama," said Henry, his eyes turning to the low green ridge that rose above Newport. Once it was crowned with huge pines and oaks, but the trees were thinning fast as they were chopped down for housing and firewood. The hillside was nearly covered with fenced orchards and kitchen gardens. The old one-room cabins were disappearing, replaced by larger houses as their owners prospered.

Herod pointed to the southern part of Newport's shoreline. "We used to live there, just by those trees."

"I know," Benoni said impatiently. He preferred activity to words, and the other Newport lads had learned not to taunt him with whispers that he was a bastard. Benoni was quick to defend his honor with his fists.

Herod ignored Benoni's pique, and said to Henry, "That hillside looks just like my home when I was little like you. But we didn't have the sea; just a big valley and a stream where I played. My papa raised sheep, just like your papa."

"He's not there now," said Benoni. The boy was getting caught up in Herod's story.

"No. He took sick and died when I was Sam Dyer's age." When she was twelve, Herod had helped with the futile care of her father and brother as bubonic plague slew them. Those memories still jolted her from sleep. She told her sons, "Mama sent me to London —"

"To live with Aunt Alice," smirked Benoni. 'Mean old Aunt Alice' was one of the boys' favorite stories, and Herod had fun with the legend. She hadn't adorned the merchant's wife with horns or a witch's broom yet, but Herod didn't need those embellishments.

"She worked me day and night, and I slept in a room so cold there was ice on the window and my covers froze."

"She didn't spank you," Henry prompted. The boy loved tales, and knew some of them better than his older brother.

"No, but she wanted to, so much that her fingers itched like ivy poison. I got married just to get away from her, and that's how I came here to New England."

Henry crowed, "You married the bad man!" The boys had heard about John Hicks too. George was shocked when Herod told them about her abusive first husband, but she replied, "I'm amazed Avis Stanton and the other gossips haven't already told them. At least they'll hear the truth from me."

Herod nodded at Henry. "Yes, he was mean to me, but your papa saved me." Soon she would tell them about their half-sisters and brother, living far away in New Amsterdam. But for now, little Georgie was asleep on her shoulder, the glorious sunset was fading, and the freshening breeze was no longer balmy. She told her sons, "Let's see if we can get home before it turns dark."

A few months later, workers began adding a second story and leaded glass windows to one of the better homes in Newport. Herod soon learned that the new owner was William Jefferay. Her heart leapt, because Jefferay had been her closest friend while she and John Hicks lived in Weymouth, Massachusetts.

Though old enough to be her father, Jefferay had not married until several years after Herod met him. To the amazement of all, he married a younger girl – thirty years younger. Mary Gould was only a few years older than Herod.

With their house rebuilt, it wasn't long before the Jefferay family sailed into Newport harbor with a boatload of possessions. Herod waited eagerly for Sabbath, when she would surely see her old friend.

As she waited for the welcoming crowd around the Jefferays to thin, she had a good look at them. William had been a wiry man, but now he'd grown a potbelly, his cheeks had filled out, and wrinkles had erupted around his eyes and across his forehead. He wore his hair long, but his crown was nearly bald now. Mary stood at his side, clutching his arm possessively. Herod regarded her with distaste.

Before her marriage, Mary had also lived in Weymouth. One might think that girls so close in age would be friends. However, she would barely speak to Herod, who overheard Mary sneering to others, "I heard she got in trouble. Why else would she wed so young?" It wasn't true, but the stinging rumor persisted.

Mistress Mary Jefferay was dressed in lush indigo satin, and a strand of seed pearls was woven through dark hair which fell in to her shoulders in carefully formed ringlets. The once-slender girl was even plumper than her husband. The tops of her breasts bulged above her tightly laced bodice, pressing her lace-trimmed neckband upward. 'Her servants must do all the work while she sits on a pillow and eats sweetmeats,' thought Herod. 'I may work hard, but I don't look like an old brood sow.'

When Mary stepped away to talk with the Coggeshalls, Herod came up behind her husband and said in his ear, "It's a pleasure to see you, William. Welcome to Newport."

Jefferay turned, grinning widely. "The day is blessed by your presence, young Herodias."

She told him, "Few here know my full name, and it isn't a thing I share willingly. Not even George knows it."

"No?" Jefferay shook a finger at her. "A secret from the world, but why have you not told your husband?"

Herod shrugged. "It never arose. What might he say if I told him now?"

Jefferay said teasingly, "Fear not. It is safe with me, but 'tis a perilous thing to keep secrets from your husband."

Mary came toward them, wearing a bright smile, but her narrowed eyes were pinned on Herod. Her husband said, "Surely you remember my wife. Dear, Goodwife Gardner has kindly welcomed us to Newport."

"Oh my, I thought your name was Hicks," Mary said as her grin broadened.

"When charged for beating me, John Hicks fled to New Amsterdam like the cowardly pup he is," Herod said coolly. "Now I'm wed to a fine man, George Gardner, and have three hearty sons. And you?"

"Perhaps Hicks did what he thought right," Mary sniffed.

William squeezed his wife's arm and whispered in her ear, while Herod took a deep breath, reminding herself to be civil. Then he told Herod, "We've a lovely daughter, and another child waiting offstage."

"How lucky for you –"

Mary interrupted Herod. "Look dear, the Eastons are here. We must greet them before they go." To Herod she said, "I'm sure we'll see you soon, and be the dearest of friends." William was barely able to call, "Goodbye," before Mary towed him away.

Herod watched them disappear, thinking sadly, 'There goes a good friend. I'll not see much of him with that snippy little witch standing between us.'

In the year which passed after the Jefferays moved to Newport, Herod's sad prediction came true. She saw little of her old friend, and his wife's sly insults made each meeting tense. Herod mourned, for she missed William's wry wit and keen advice.

'At least I still have Mary Dyer,' she told herself. 'What would I do without her?'

Shortly after that consoling thought, Herod awoke one hot August dawn with sweat slicked across her face and throat. The wind rose steadily, flipping leaves over to show their pale underbellies. Heavy rain pelted the house, and after it stopped bronze clouds raced across the sun, sending shadows fleeting over the land. The boys were cranky and restless, and Herod felt a prickly unease.

She climbed the low hill behind her house, but there was so much mist in the air that the ocean was invisible. However, when Herod turned toward town, she saw long waves rolling across Narragansett Bay and splashing over Newport's wharves. Boats tied to the docks rocked in the surf, their masts clocking back and forth like crazed pendulums. There were no sails on the frothing water – no sane mariner would venture out under such ominous skies. George and Herod marveled at the weird weather over their noontime meal.

Mary Dyer knocked at the door while Herod was still cleaning up. Her three younger children were in tow and her youngest, six-month-old Charles, named after the beheaded king, rode in one arm. "Hurricane weather, don't you think?" she asked Herod.

"George and I thought the same. Remember the storm ten years ago in Boston?"

"Twelve. 'Twas in 1638," said George.

Herod said, "I pray we don't get another like that. It blew our cornfield flat, and John and I crawled in the mud for days propping the stalks up."

"All in God's hands," was Mary's answer. "Before he decides, we must see the blowhole. If it's not spouting today, I don't know when it ever will."

George declined to go, saying he'd get things under cover before the storm arrived. "Take the boys," he suggested. "A walk should settle them."

The women set out for the southern shore, with their children tumbling along in a cheerful, raucous mob. "I see but four of yours," Herod said.

"Sam and Willy are too old to see the sights with their mama," Mary laughed. "They'll go with other lads, if they remember." The wind blew the women's skirts flat against their legs, and Herod shook her waist-length hair out of its braid and let the wind toss it into a wild reddish mass. "You'll never get the tangles out," Mary commented.

"I love to feel it blow."

"If I loose mine, poor Charlie will be smothered," her friend said. Ahead they saw a white puff rise above the rocky shore. "Look at that!" Mary cried. She called out a warning to the children running ahead, and they reluctantly waited for their mothers.

"I've never seen it blow," said Herod.

"Nor I. I hear it takes just the right tide and wind, so it's a rare sight. The Indians say it foretells disaster. If the hurricane hits, they may be right." When they crested the last knoll above the beach, Mary suggested, "Let's watch from here, where it's safe."

"I'm not going any closer," Herod said cautiously. "I've never seen surf like that." Dark, foam-streaked waves rose to twice a man's height before hurling themselves onto gray rock ledges armoring the island's rim. Each breaker produced a burst of spray, and the children danced in the wind-driven shower.

"They'll be soaked," Mary warned.

"For certain, but the air's so warm, it feels good."

A hulking wave crashed against the rocks, and from an insignificant-looking crevice in the granite, a gush of water and spray blasted into the air, accompanied by a loud, "Whoof!" The next wave was even larger, and so was the towering column of mist. The vapor showered the watchers. "Breath of God," Mary sighed.

"Nay – 'twas his sneeze," giggled Herod. "When we sailed, the crew told me of sea monsters that spouted so."

"A true leviathan. That blast must have been three-score feet."

"Tall as St. Paul's in London."

The two friends sat side by side to watch as tall waves marched from the south in disorderly rows to destroy themselves on the Aquidneck shore. Mary said, "I wonder where those waves come from, and what they've seen."

"John said that hurricanes come from the Indies, where they never have winter. I wish I could go there."

"I'd rather go back to London," Mary said wistfully.

"Whatever for?" Herod scoffed. "Nothing there but muddy streets full of dung and smoke, and people jostling you all the time. I like it here."

"So do I, but I ache to go back to England and see my family and friends who stayed behind. I dream of them, and they haunt my waking thoughts. Don't you miss them?"

"Anyone I wish to see is long dead."

"That grieves me," said Mary. "You weren't close to your mother, but if you saw her after all these years, she'd look just like an angel."

"Standing by Aunt Alice and singing sweetly to me," Herod laughed. "I won't see them 'til Judgment day."

"Oh, but I can see them, standing by St. Martin's altar with the choirboys. Outside, London's streets are bustling." Mary's eyes were sparkling and long strands of golden hair streamed behind her on the wind. "Just think of the preachers. You can hear any sort you want, even the Adamites, who preach naked."

"All I saw were Puritans," Herod snickered. "You needn't go to London, for there are a-plenty of them in Boston."

"Puritans – Hah! They just talk at you, quoting the Bible in Greek and Latin to flaunt their learning. No other man, and never a woman, may speak a single word. I mean the Seekers, the Ranters; that sort. If you're moved to speak, you may."

Herod nodded. Her friend had seemed restless these last few years – was this the source of her discontent? Mary was saying, "John Clarke is a fine teacher, but he never touches me as Anne Hutchinson did. What think you of him?"

"I know not," stammered Herod, unsure how a trip to the beach had turned into talk of theology. "Mr. Clarke is better than the Puritans."

"Puritans know nothing! Remember how Anne said we should listen in our hearts for God to speak to us? He does, you know – God spoke to her, and I hear him in my heart too."

Herod nearly asked, "What does God sound like?" but knew that her joke would fall flat. Mary's faith ran far deeper than her own, and her friend's cheeks were flushed by excitement which Herod did not share. Though Herod had been instructed by a dozen Anglican and Puritan ministers, God had never spoken to her. In fact, Puritans said that God no longer spoke to men at all. What was Mary hearing? Herod had been told that Satan would whisper sweet deception into men's ears like poisoned honey — what of that?

She was for silent long enough that Mary sighed, "Forgive me; I know that you have no taste for such talk. I simply ache to see my mother and friends in England again, and soon I'll be too old to make such a trip. Look, the wind is starting to veer." Mary pointed southeast. Sure enough, the blowhole's spray, which had been drifting straight into their faces, was headed toward the western shore of Narragansett Bay. "Maybe the hurricane will stay out to sea."

"Well, I'm soaked to the skin," said Herod. Her hair, darkened by spray to the color of black walnut, was now plastered to her back. "My boys look like they've been swimming. I think I'll take them back and tell George about the blowhole. He can see it before the storm breaks over our heads." Herod was glad to have an excuse to leave. If she had asked Mary whether she was actually hearing Satan's voice, another type of storm would surely have broken over Herod's unwilling head.

Mary's peculiar agitation increased as winter arrived, and Herod was more worried about her friend. She told George that Mary spent long hours on her knees. "William says she is praying for guidance."

"In what?"

Herod said dully, "She wants to visit England, but 'twould mean leaving her family behind."

"They could all go."

"Remember your own crossing? The storms and sickness? Just imagine such a trip with our little ones. Also, William refuses."

"Of course he won't go! This year William is attorney general, and he'll not walk away from his office like Coddington did. Mary's unease will vanish when spring arrives."

Herod relaxed, saying, "We'll both have spring fever until we can start working our gardens." But several times in late February Herod saw her friend head to head with other Newport women; conversations which broke into nervous laughter, or subjects which changed when Herod came within hearing. When she heard rumors that Mary truly was going to England, she confronted her.

Mary's welcoming smile faded. "Herod, it is true. Sometimes when I am at prayer, I hear my mother calling. She was ill when last I had a letter from her, and that was months ago. What if she needs me? I fought my desires all winter but they grow stronger each day."

"What of your father or brothers?"

"They died before I crossed the ocean, so Mama needs me."

"Your children need you far more! Charlie is but one, and Henry barely three. How could you leave them?" At the same time, Herod felt a hint of jealousy. Mary would be freed from husband and children both. 'I can barely remember what that is like,' Herod thought as she pictured herself running over England's hillsides as a girl.

"They'll not be fending for themselves," Mary was saying. "Our servants will help William, and Christian Easton promised to keep an eye to all."

A lump was swelling in Herod's throat. Her voice quavered when she asked, "When do you leave, and how long will you be gone?"

Mary gave a nervous laugh. "The first ship. I'd best go quick before William changes his mind. And it won't be forever, just a year or two."

"You're out of your mind! Your little ones won't even remember they had a mother when you return."

"Don't you think I know that?" Mary said, blinking back tears. "I thought you would understand! Being wed to John Hicks taught you what it is to live every day aching for change, but naught you do will bring it about.

"Herod, my soul is withering here, and it is tearing me apart. Not one preacher in New England touches me, not even Pastor Clarke. Nobody since Anne. You will always be my dear friend, but Anne's soul twined with mine. Have you ever found a clearing in the woods, full of sun? Anne's faith shone just like that. Now I wander deep in the forest, searching for light, but I cannot find it." Tears crept unheeded down Mary's cheeks. "Have you heard of the Seekers, with such ideas as we colonists never hear? Perhaps I can persuade such a man to bring the light to us."

Herod said skeptically, "If you bring a naked Adamite, Boston will send an army to arrest both him and you."

"So long as he reaches my heart, I care naught what a preacher wears, or wears not."

Herod laughed at Mary's jest, but her heart felt like lead as she watched winter's snow melt and the ice vanish from Newport's shores. In the beginning of April, the first ship of the year left for England with Mary waving enthusiastically from its deck.

With tears streaming down her cheeks, Herod waved back. She thought of the blowhole she had seen with Mary last summer. Perhaps it had been an omen of disaster after all.

CHAPTER 6
July - October 1651

ON A SULTRY day near July's end, Herod arrived at Newport's waterfront with George and their sons, along with anyone else in Newport fit to walk. A ship had anchored less than an hour ago. The passengers would soon debark, and though Herod was far along in her pregnancy, she was trying to meet every newly-arrived ship. Perhaps Mary would be among the passengers.

If George had figured out why Herod was haunting Newport's docks, he remained tactfully silent. He had come today for a different reason, and many in Newport shared his interest. William Coddington was on that vessel after a thirty-month absence.

Rumors of Coddington's return had been flying since the first ship from London had arrived a few months earlier. Alexander Partridge, who managed the ex-governor's affairs in his absence, had begun enlarging Coddington's already spacious Newport home. However, Partridge proved close-lipped when asked if the building's owner was coming home soon.

"I hear that ship is loaded to the deck with Coddington's fancy stuff," George said.

"I heard he has a new wife," commented Herod.

"I don't know about that. I'm more interested in what mischief he has wrought on us," said William Dyer, who had paused to greet Herod and George.

The same ships which brought rumors of Coddington's return also carried news that Parliament had made him permanent governor of Newport and Portsmouth. Few island residents favored that move. Dyer declared that he'd rather hang than be ruled for life by Coddington.

A shallop rounded the bow of the anchored ship. Its sail was flapping uselessly in the languid breeze, and three sets of oars rose and dipped like a giant water bug's legs. To the anxious watchers, the boat seemed to take hours to cross the harbor. At last the red-faced crew lowered the sail, shipped their long oars, and tossed lines to waiting hands at the dock.

Though it was no easy feat to appear regal while clutching a mast for balance, William Coddington arose. The first thing that Herod noticed was the strange device he wore on his head. Coddington's hair was thinning long before he went to England. Now it was thick and curling again, though a darker brown than before. Herod soon heard that it was something new worn in France – a wig.

The second thing she saw was his stylish great boots. Nearly knee-length, the tops flared so widely that Herod thought she could pour a couple pints of cider in each and not spill a drop. Those boots looked marvelously well after having spent two months crossing the ocean, and so did Coddington's freshly pressed clothing.

Beside him sat a well-dressed woman clutching a blanket-wrapped bundle to her breast, and a teenage girl. 'A baby already?' Herod thought. She stood on tiptoe, but could see little of Mrs. Coddington or her infant.

"Welcome back to Newport, Governor. Every man rejoices that you are safe." Behind her, Herod heard William Dyer snort.

It was Alexander Partridge who had spoken, and the hard-eyed man helped the beefy Coddington step to the dock. Though he tried to make it look like he was shaking Coddington's hand instead of hauling him up from the shallop, Herod noticed the effort. She turned her head to hide a derisive grin.

Nicholas Easton, Rhode Island's president, stood near Partridge. His face was scarlet, and he clenched and re-clenched his hands behind his back. "Poor Nick," George said. "He'd rather toil in the stink of his tanyard than see Coddington return."

Dyer laughed sourly, "No doubt he wonders if he is truly greeting our new governor-for-life, and whether Coddington will have an office for him."

"Or whether he will take it," Herod added, and Dyer chuckled.

The teenage girl climbed to the deck behind Coddington, and then Partridge stepped down into the shallop to take the blanketed armload from the other woman. He gingerly passed it to the girl waiting on the dock. Herod had never seen her before, and judged by her simple garb that the newlyweds had hired a servant in England.

The maid's bundle was wailing now, affirming that it was a tightly swaddled baby. Coddington said proudly, "My son William, nigh seven months old. This is my wife, Mistress Anne Coddington."

Partridge reached to help the woman to her feet, but she nimbly stepped up to the dock, her fingertips barely touching the agent's outstretched hand. Then she doffed her cloak and laid it over the surprised Partridge's arm. A murmur went through the crowd when they got a good look at her. Coddington was near fifty, but his new wife's age was far less. "Why, she's younger than me," gasped Herod.

"By a good five years," agreed William Dyer, and Herod's gaze slewed irritably to him.

William Coddington was wearing a plain traveling suit, but his wife had dressed to impress Newport. She wore a low-necked green silk dress with dramatically puffed sleeves which ended at her elbows, and were slashed to show pale blue undersleeves. She paused to adjust her sun bonnet and pat her curled brown hair back into place. Then the group headed uphill toward Coddington's home.

As they passed, Coddington gave the slightest nod to Dyer, who inclined his own head an inch or two. The governor's eyes met George's for a moment, and then flickered to Herod. She tucked her chin, but kept her gaze on Coddington out of the corner of her eye. Perhaps it was unwilling, but the governor smiled.

He paused to tell Dyer, "I came here via the Indies islands, to see the horses we bred in Rhode Island now toiling in the Barbados sugar mills. The growers are delighted with our stock, and will take all the beasts and salt mutton we can send. Captain Partridge tells me I've had a good increase in horseflesh during my absence. They will go south as soon as possible. In return, I'm getting a shipment of molasses and sugar."

"That should please you," Dyer commented.

"Indeed." Coddington recommenced the walk toward his home.

As she watched the little parade stroll up Marlborough Street, Herod smiled mirthlessly. His wife didn't have to tote her baby uphill – she had a maid to carry it for her. Then Anne Coddington, with one gloved hand tucked in her husband's elbow, glanced dispassionately at Herod: a fashionable young beauty assessing a big-bellied colonist's wife clad in fading homespun. Herod's smirk vanished.

When Coddington was out of earshot, George sniffed, "He said naught of that new governor affair."

"Did you expect him to spill his news at the dock?" asked William Dyer. "We'll know quick enough, but I doubt we'll like what we hear."

Coddington was not seen on Newport's streets the next day. On the following morning President Easton, William Dyer, and other prominent townsmen demanded to meet with the merchant. George wandered into town in the afternoon, hoping to hear some news. He soon returned and told Herod, "I asked William Dyer to sup with us. Mr. Porter is coming too, seeing as he's staying the night with William and they have nobody to cook for them."

"Porter of Portsmouth, Porter of Portsmouth," Benoni chanted, and Henry joined him.

Herod reddened when she heard that the distinguished Mr. Porter was coming to dine. She told the boys, "Hush now. Take yourselves out and fetch some wood." Turning to George, she asked, "How soon are they coming?"

"Not long. Why?"

"You might have given me time to get ready," she snapped. "There's much to do, and you can start by killing a chicken for the pot." She looked around the room. "What luck – I baked this morning, so we've fresh bread. For heaven's sake, George, go get that chicken, and take the red one that eats eggs."

Despite her pregnancy, Herod cleaned house like she hadn't done since spring, spurring George to scrub the table and sweep the floor. She sent Benoni to the garden for a basket of beans, while Henry kept Georgie from wandering. Herod scoured their trenchers and spoons. She might not be able to serve Mr. Porter from pewter, but his wooden tableware would be spotless.

When their guests arrived, the five Gardners, from senior George down to young Georgie, wore clean linen. Every face and pair of hands in the house was pink from scrubbing. George scoffed at Herod's cleaning frenzy, but he had washed his hair and it was still dripping water down his back. After all, it wasn't often that the Gardners entertained one of Rhode Island's wealthiest men.

John Porter lived on the northern end of Aquidneck Island. Consequently, Herod didn't see him apart from court days. However, she admired Porter and thought him handsome, even if he was old enough to be her father.

She was also grateful for his help after John Hicks abandoned her. Governor Coddington had been ready to throw Herod in jail unless she married the father of her unborn child. However, Porter, who was Coddington's assistant, suggested that the couple declare themselves married until Herod trusted Gardner enough to formally wed him.

When Dyer and Porter entered the Gardners' home, John bowed over Herod's hand. He murmured in a baritone as smooth and warm as fresh cream, "It's ever a pleasure to see you, Goodwife Gardner. How good of you to welcome me with little warning, and in your condition. If I'd known, I wouldn't have intruded."

"Think naught of it, Mr. Porter," Herod replied. She smiled demurely, but her arms broke into gooseflesh. "I had help in getting ready. Even Georgie took part by picking beans."

John had unusually dark eyes, like jet beads. His black gaze took in the three-year old hiding behind his mother's skirt and he grinned. "'Twould be simple for the lad. He wouldn't have to stoop for them."

"Herod drove us like slaves, a-scrubbing this thing and that," laughed George. "You might think the king was coming to call – if we still had a king."

"Governor-for-life Coddington is near enough," growled William.

"It looks like Goody Gardner has a fine meal ready, so let's sup," suggested John. "We can speak of Coddington later."

Herod ladled stewed chicken and vegetables into trenchers, filled a pitcher with new beer, and placed a round loaf of rye bread on the table. She shared a trencher with Henry and Georgie, and the boys' father ate with Benoni, so John and William might each have their own bowl of stew.

Sopping her bread crust in gravy, Herod asked John, "What of Mrs. Porter? Did she not come with you today?"

"Mrs. Porter dislikes sailing, for we had a stormy passage from England. She swore she'd never cross water again." John took a bite of stewed chicken and said to Herod, "Tasty cooking, Goodwife." William agreed, and Herod blushed.

"I thought your wife was ill," said William to Porter.

"So she said, and mayhap it was true." Herod raised inquiring eyes, and John added, "Margaret has a weak heart, or so she saith."

"What makes you doubt her?" George asked.

Georgie was starting to squirm, so Herod offered him another piece of bread with gravy. He pushed it away, so she told the older boys, "If you are done, go and play in the second room, but be quiet about it."

John was saying, "Many a time Margaret has dismissed me, saying she is too ill to get out of bed or even to eat a bite if I fetch it. But let me return after she thinks I have gone away, and I oft find her eating bread and cheese by the parlor fire. At such times I suspect she is not so ill as she claims." John hunched his shoulders irritably. "Margaret's maids will keep her comfortable tonight, so enough about her complaints. William has a letter from his wife, brought by Coddington's own hand from England."

Herod sucked in a breath of delight, and George said, "I'm surprised that he would help you, William. You are at each other's throats with lawsuits."

"We were friends until his overreaching began, but he could not say no to Mary. He is truly fond of her."

"As we all are," added John. "What do you hear from her?"

William pulled a folded paper from inside his jerkin. "Let Mary tell you with her own words." His gaze skipped halfway down the sheet to read,

> *Mother lives comfortably here in London. I urge her to come over to Newport but she is sickly and I fear she would not survive the voyage. I told her of your work as keeper of Rhode Island's records, and now as the colony's attorney, and she is full of praise. I also tell her of her grandchildren. Sadly, she will never see them.*
>
> *London has grown, swelled with refugees from the late wars. Puritans also fill the city, crowing with victory and their murder of our poor King. Their dowdy clothing and cropped hair are everywhere, and I so miss the silks and finery. The only hats they wear are common felt, like black beehives to house the mindless insects that fill their head in place of brains.*
>
> *Not every church has turned Puritan. Every Sabbath I hear a different preacher: Seekers and Ranters, but I have not seen naked Adamites preaching on the street corners yet. Anglican services can still be found, but not easily.*

Herod laughed, "And she so wanted to see Adamites, too."

"Surely she only wanted to hear them," joked William. He cleared his throat, and then continued,

> *I bore your greetings to Sir Vane, who sends his warmest greetings. Sadly, he has little time for me of late, but will write to you soon. He did tell me of Mr. Coddington's grant from the Council of State: no doubt a far different accounting than you will hear.*
>
> *Mr. Coddington told the Council that he himself discovered Conanicut and Aquidneck Islands, and purchased them from the Indians, and they are mere knobs of rock washed by the waves. The few who dwell there are devoted to him, or so he claimed. Coddington wisht to have those islands granted to him to govern by English law, and it was done, so that Coddington may now rule as he sees fit, or so Mr. Vane warns us.*
>
> *Finally, bring my greetings to my dear friends, and assure them that they fill my thoughts and prayers. I miss you all, and we shall meet again soon.*

William took a sip of beer before saying, "It seems that Coddington got his commission with a bold pack of lies. Today we refused to leave until he showed us the grant, and it is as Mary wrote. Our island is now his personal realm for life. Coddington alone decides who may vote, and since he holds the deeds, he can send men he doesn't like a-packing."

John said, "I never thought to see Nick Easton refuse a battle, but he will surrender his office until this is settled." His dark eyes turned to the Gardners. "Note you that our charter is now negated. Nothing can stop the Puritans from taking our lands by force and banishing us as heretics."

"Parliament is too busy to notice," said William.

"Or to care," added Herod. John nodded his agreement, and her cheeks grew warm. She rose to refill the beer pitcher, and then topped off his tankard. He thanked her with a smile.

"Who can stop Coddington?" George asked while Herod refilled his mug.

"What the Council of State has done, it can undo," replied John. "Especially since it based the grant on Coddington's lies."

William said, "We will petition the Council to that end, and over a hundred freemen in Rhode Island will sign. A mere handful support Coddington. Henry Vane has Cromwell's ear and will surely help. With able men bearing that petition …."

"Roger Williams, for one," John suggested. "He got the charter in '44."

"Will you sign the petition?" asked George.

John nodded, and William said grimly, "Of course."

Their eyes turned to George, but he said uneasily, "Suppose you can't undo Coddington's grant? He may persecute those who signed."

"We'll overturn it," growled William.

"I don't understand why Coddington has done this," said Herod. "Why should he weaken us?"

"Breaking the charter frees him from Roger Williams," Dyer told her. "When Williams brought the charter, Rhode Island greeted him like Moses bearing the Ten Commandments. It must have galled Coddington to crawl ashore with his commission under one arm, and all of Newport scowling at him."

"Revenge," laughed John. "He'll be free of Samuell Gorton as well. No man calls Justice Coddington a 'Just-Ass' without risking vengeance."

"He freed Herod from John Hicks," George insisted. "Should I not repay him with loyalty?"

"Some help Coddington was," Herod scoffed. "I begged him for a real divorce. We live in this mock marriage because he claimed to fear God's wrath. If —"

"The sham was your doing, Goodwife," John chuckled. "After the governor separated you from Hicks, you refused the wedding with Goodman Gardner." Herod wanted to sting him with a witty retort, but John disarmed her anger by saying, "Wedding or no, 'twas your husband's fortune that Hicks cast a jewel into the dust."

George eyed Porter as though he was calculating whether John had insulted or complimented his wife. Herod coughed and said, "I know why Coddington hates Mr. Williams. He is loved. Everyone calls him peacemaker for his Indian treaties and the charter. Nobody likes Coddington, so he's bilious with envy." William and John laughed, and after a moment, so did George.

"Whatever the reason, we needn't fear Coddington for long," William said. "Parliament will annul his grant when they learn that our island is more than a mere rock in the bay."

George asked William to examine a sore on his ox's neck, but Porter said that he knew little of cattle, and remained inside with Herod. The restless boys reappeared from the second room to follow their father.

When they were gone, John said to Herod, "You were wise when you said that Coddington was envious. Most men don't see past his ambition, but his very soul aches from jealousy. It blinds him to many things, including the wisdom in you."

"If I am so wise, then why did I marry John Hicks?" Herod scoffed.

"You were too young to see his wrath. Coddington never understood why you would not marry Gardner. He thought you defiant, but you simply wanted to keep your freedom."

"Freedom," mused Herod. "I wed John to be freed from my aunt, and I wouldn't accept a forced marriage with George, but still I am trapped."

"How so?"

"We can't wed without scandal, and if we part I lose my sons."

Herod piled the dirty trenchers one by one, and then pushed her bench out to rise. Her belly bumped the table, and John said, "Rest, and let your boys do it later." Herod eased back to her seat. "You are better off in one way," John told her. "Since you aren't wed, George can't take your money."

"Hah! I have none, for John took the only inheritance I'll ever see." Herod added boldly, "For all your wealth, you are still tied to Mrs. Porter."

With a chuckle John said, "Not so. Should I choose to leave, Margaret can't stop me. Oh, I'd toss her a settlement, but I can leave whenever I wish. So can you. All you need do is withstand the chatter."

Herod threw back her head to laugh. "I've seen far more than my share of gossip. I'm not going anywhere."

"You never know what the future holds, Herodias."

The laughter died in Herod's throat. "How do you know my full name?"

"William Jefferay told me. You have many admirers."

"No, they admire Mistress Dyer. I am merely bait for gossip."

John shook his head. "Perhaps, but you deserve a better life. George wants to see you happy, and Jefferay and I would both like to see you succeed. I won't speak for Coddington."

After Porter and Dyer had gone and George was asleep, Herod lay awake, reliving the evening. When she thought how the esteemed Mr. Porter had called her wise, she glowed with pleasure.

Though Porter's compliments eased the sting of not receiving personal greetings from Mary, Herod thought sadly, 'She is too busy with Mr. Vane and the Seekers to write to me. What sort of trouble will she find with them? Maybe George is right when he says that women have no place speaking in church. That's what the preachers tell him, but he agrees.

'George values wisdom more in a hunting dog than in his wife,' Herod thought sourly. 'Come to think of it, what does he ask me about, apart from our children? He's just like John Hicks, who tried to limit me to the children, chickens, and corn patch. At least Mr. Porter thinks I have a mind.'

CHAPTER 7
Autumn 1651

ANNE CODDINGTON MAY have been the only person in Rhode Island who wasn't displeased with her husband. It was reported that, though the young woman found Newport backward compared with London, she was pleased with her surroundings.

Coddington's next acts pleased almost nobody. He appointed a council, but most Newport men refused to serve. His few supporters filled those posts, and Partridge set about cowing the rest.

If the new governor hoped that Newport and Portsmouth would submit quietly, he was disappointed. William Dyer had been swapping lawsuits with him for years, and was foremost in writing Newport's petition to the Council of State. He informed the Gardners, "Every man in town, save Coddington's puppets, will gladly sign." However, Herod noticed that George turned silent while his friend talked about the petition.

Not long after the Gardners spoke with Dyer, they cleaned the barn together. George had brought the emptied sledge in for the last load – a pile of chicken droppings which Herod had scraped from under their night roost. He began tossing the mess onto the sledge, and she asked the question that had been on her mind since they had talked to Dyer. Would George sign that petition?

George examined the toe of one boot, reminding Herod of their youngest boy caught in wrongdoing. "I dare not."

"Why?"

"Coddington holds our deeds and the council is larded with his men. They could throw every signer off his land, including me."

"This isn't Boston, where John wouldn't let me bid a good morning to Anne Hutchinson, lest he be marked," Herod scoffed. "You have nothing to fear."

George grounded his shovel. "Was Hicks wrong? Those who defied the Puritans were exiled! They excommunicated Mrs. Hutchinson, and your friend Mary was lucky to escape jail after she paraded out of church with her."

"But William Dyer says that Coddington will be overthrown. If every man signs –"

"And marks himself as Coddington's enemy," snapped George.

"Coddington has done little for you," Herod said hotly. "He didn't separate me from Hicks just for your benefit."

"He asked me to serve in his government," George said, so low that Herod could barely hear him. He scraped up the last of the litter and tossed it onto the sledge.

"Truly?" Herod gasped. What did this mean? No respectable man would work for Coddington. Most of his supporters were men from society's margins. Was George tainted by rescuing her, or was it their unconventional relationship? Was she also stigmatized? Herod said, "I hope you didn't agree."

"I told him no," George replied, tossing dirt over a damp patch on the packed earth floor.

"Good," Herod sighed. "When Coddington's rule gets overturned, you don't want to be part of his government."

George's anguished gaze turned to Herod. "I don't want to be in *any* government!" He set his shovel in a corner. "It was John Hicks who ached to hold office, not me. I just want that!" George waved a hand at the open door, out toward their fields. "I just want to live with you in peace. They can leave me out of their schemes, because the whole affair makes me ill."

It took two months to finish Newport's petition, and the writers used the time to prepare for their voyage to England. At first Roger Williams refused to go. He'd spent nearly three years prodding Parliament to create the colony's first charter, and it might take another year or two to get Coddington's commission undone; enough time for Roger's youngest sons to forget what their father looked like. After much persuasion Roger – perhaps convinced that only he could get the job done – sold an Indian trading post on the far side of Narragansett Bay to finance his journey to England.

William Dyer was eager to go. With luck, negotiations with Parliament would go quickly so he could bring Mary home in the spring. Samuel would turn seventeen soon, and could handle nearly anything which came up. The bondservants had settled into the family's life long ago and Peggy, a few months younger than Sam, was a capable housewife. Nick and Christian Eaton would oversee the rest.

Herod offered to take one of the younger boys, but William said, "I am grateful, but you have that new baby, and I would not burden you further." Willy Gardner had been born only a few weeks after Coddington's return with that Puritan commission. Herod named him for her brother who had died fighting for King Charles.

Dyer also signed away most of his assets – a piece of land here, a team of oxen there. All would be returned when he came back from England. He brought a cow in milk to the grateful Gardners, explaining, "If I leave so much as a pair of threadbare breeches where Coddington can find them, he'll seize them as soon as my ship leaves the dock. I don't want to find myself a pauper when I return."

John Clarke, Newport's doctor and pastor of the Baptist church, would lead the party to England. The pastor had spent much of his summer in Boston's jail after holding a Baptist service in Massachusetts, and his absence had delayed Newport's petition. Clarke was lucky to escape with a fine and imprisonment. One of the other Baptists would not pay the fine, and was whipped so severely that he crawled on hands and knees for weeks.

Clarke had no children to worry about, and his wife would go with him, because there was no telling how long he would be gone. Clarke also had little fear of having his goods seized by Coddington, since he didn't share bad blood with the governor. From the pulpit Clarke told Newport, "Though I am sad to leave the fairest land anywhere, I am content. I am serving my beloved Rhode Island."

In mid-October the petition was ready to sign. Three days were picked for Newport's freemen to come to Dyer's home and sign or mark the document. On the first day, Herod was surprised to see George preparing his shot bag and musket for hunting. "Shall we starve while I scratch my name on that paper?" he said defensively. "I'll be back with plenty of time."

Instead, he returned as the light was fading, a stiff-legged doe splayed awkwardly over his shoulders. When Herod helped to hang the carcass, the young animal's body was little warmer than the evening air, as though George had waited a long time before coming home.

The second meeting was seven days later. George rose before dawn and went out, Herod supposed, to visit the privy. Then she found that his coat, axe, and water jug were gone. Again he returned at dark, telling Herod gruffly, "There's another chance to sign next week."

"Your last chance," she observed. "William and the others sail the next day."

"I know, I know," grumbled George.

Just before the final signing day, Herod answered well-spaced thumps on the door. She thought it might be William, come to persuade George to sign, but it was Alexander Partridge. His pale eyes stared boldly at her. "Goodwife – ah – Gardner. Is your *husband* at home?"

Annoyed by the man's insinuation, Herod fought to keep from slamming the door in Partridge's face. It seemed that Coddington had shared gossip with his agent. "Just a moment," she said. Without inviting the governor's most hated henchman inside, she called to Henry, "Go fetch your father." Still blocking the doorway, Herod asked, "What brings you so far from town?"

Partridge had been peering into what he could see of the house's interior past Herod's shoulder. He turned back to her and with the barest hint of a smile, said, "Nothing to concern you. I'm here on the colony's business with your husband."

"The governor has no doings here. Perhaps I can help you."

"I'm sure you can't," Partridge smirked. "It's nothing you could understand." Herod's fingers tensed on the door's planks.

Just then, George came around the house's corner, trailed by Henry. The farmer's tanned jaw tightened as he recognized Partridge. He told his son, "Go back to the barn and help Ben." When the boy was gone George asked Partridge, "What do you want?" His words were clipped and his voice was higher than usual.

"Let us speak in private," Partridge replied, as his eyes roved over Herod again. It was not the admiring stare that she sometimes got from men, but a cold appraisal, as though she was a pup that Partridge thought wasn't properly housebroken.

"We'll speak with my wife here," George said. When he placed a callused hand on Herod's shoulder she smiled, gleeful that George was taking her part.

"Very well," said Partridge coldly. "It's come to our notice that you have not signed that treasonous document."

"I've been busy."

"Even so, Governor Coddington welcomes support in such rebellious times." Partridge's gaze shifted once more to Herod. "Are you sure we cannot speak one man to another?"

"Herod stands for me in my absence, just as any good wife would," George said. "Let her hear what you have to say."

Partridge snorted. "Very well. As I said, the governor looks kindly on men who stand with him. He might place you on his council. Smooth the path to formalizing this marriage of yours. Legitimize your sons. Give you a higher footing in Newport, which *you* would help govern."

Herod laughed aloud and Partridge reddened. "Eight years ago Coddington overlooked our union," she scoffed. "Why the haste now?"

George squeezed her shoulder. "If Herod prefers not to wed, I'll not force her. The governor offered me a position and I turned him down, so you have nothing that I want."

"Ah, but Mr. Coddington has the weight of Parliament behind him. Those who rebel may wish to find more friendly places."

"Do you say that I'll be turned off my land if I sign that petition?" demanded George, staring straight into Partridge's eyes until that icy gaze slewed away.

"Of course not!" Partridge backed a few steps toward the lane. "No man will be banished, but Mr. Coddington will remember who supports him." He retreated even further when George followed him between rows of apple-laden trees until they reached the gate.

Partridge flinched when George reached toward him. Grinning at the agent's reaction, Gardner opened the gate so Coddington's man could edge by. "Let me tell you what I've told others who ask: I want no part in this."

"So you will not sign?"

George growled, "I am not Coddington's man, nor William Dyer's either. Leave me out of your schemes." He closed the gate and made sure that it latched.

"Governor Coddington has ignored your sinful life – *all* of it – but his patience does have limits." Partridge's narrowed eyes were fixed on George, and Herod saw the farmer blanch. "I hear that governor helped you substantially years ago, and he has kept secret your youthful errors. Were you to turn your back on him now ...."

The blood rushed back into George's face. "Errors which were properly paid for!" he shouted. Herod looked uncomprehendingly between George, with his hands clenched so hard on the gate's top rail that a knuckle cracked, and Partridge with his malicious grin.

"But so embarrassing if they were aired." Partridge winked at Herod. "Stand by Governor Coddington and he will stand by you, but he will not forget disloyalty."

"And I'll not forget threats," answered George. He jerked a thumb toward Partridge's tethered horse. "Leave me alone." The agent untied the horse's reins from the Gardners' fence, swung into the saddle, and hauled the animal's head northward. When he dug his spurs into the horse's sides it grunted, and then leapt down the lane toward Newport.

George followed Herod back to the house and closed the door behind them. He collapsed onto a bench with his head down and hands trembling. "George, what was he talking about?"

He didn't answer for a minute, and then he looked sidelong at her. "Herod, I was born to a big family. Three older brothers, a fistful of young ones, and sisters. A lot of mouths to feed. Land and stock to feed us, but never enough. We were always hungry.

"When I was fifteen, I stole bread from a market stall. Stuck it under my jerkin when the baker wasn't looking. I hid in our barn to eat it. Though I was terrified that I'd be caught, bread has never tasted so good!

"All children steal apples and such, and so did we. Nobody cared, because the neighbors' kids stole from our orchard too. But in '32, sickness went through our chickens. It killed the cockerel and left us with naught but the old cock. No new chicks hatched, so our mother said we needed a young rooster.

"Mother could have got one from the neighbor, but she was sickly from breeding and didn't do it right away." George swallowed. "I found one of our neighbor's cockerels loose on the common. I stuffed it under my arm to keep it quiet, ran home, and tossed it into our pen. Figured I'd leave it there a day or two – let it jump all the hens so they'd lay fertile eggs and we could raise cockerels of our own. Of course I would turn the bird loose again, close enough to home that the Beamans would find it, and who would know?

"But that afternoon Goody Beaman brought a posset to my mother and recognized her rooster. Then others complained of things gone missing. Though I'd taken none of them, the sheriff didn't believe me. I faced a whipping and an afternoon in the stocks." George's voice cracked, and he cleared his throat.

"William Coddington was in court on a matter of his own, and he said he would take me as a bondservant to pay for my crime. I crossed the sea with him a year later, and served as a farm hand on his land in Mt. Wollaston."

"I remember," Herod said. She sat on the bench beside George and put her arm around him. He looked up from his hands. "The day John and I landed in Boston, you and I met. You told me that you worked on his farm."

George smiled feebly. "So I did. I turned twenty-one not long after that, but kept working for Mr. Coddington until we went to Portsmouth and I got land of my own. The following year I came to Newport and met you."

"So Partridge threatens to reveal this?" Herod thought for a few moments, and then said, "Let him. Who cares about a chicken stolen twenty years ago? Let Partridge make all the threats he likes!"

George wiped his forehead on his sleeve. "William Dyer and John Clarke make no threats – not so much as harsh word. Why should I let that toady make me crawl?" He pulled Herod close and stroked her hair. "I'll sign that damned document, and let Partridge say what he likes. But if any man tries to put me off my land, I'll shoot him in his treacherous face."

CHAPTER 8
Winter - Spring 1652

ROGER WILLIAMS, JOHN Clarke, and William Dyer sailed for England on the last ship to leave Newport in 1651. Rhode Island's vigil began, and Coddington's hand-picked government lurched along, with its every act resisted.

The governor sued Dyer in absentia, appointing Partridge as judge since no other man would try the case. Coddington won a judgment against Dyer for 'stealing' cattle awarded to him in a previous trial. Since Dyer had signed his property away, there was little for Coddington to confiscate. However, his victory soured Newport's mood even further.

In midwinter George returned home from an errand, ruddy-faced and out of breath. "Herod," he panted, "there was a riot."

"In town? Was it Indians?"

"No, 'twas at Coddington's own home. Officers from New Amsterdam were there –"

"Are we not at war with the Dutch?" Herod asked.

"Nearly so, but Coddington met with them anyway. Word got out and men came running until his fancy house was encircled. Most of 'em were armed with muskets or clubs. Mr. Easton broke in, along with Captain Morris."

Morris' name was not familiar to Herod. "Who?"

"Portsmouth man and captain of our militia," George explained. "He's no friend of Coddington's, that's for sure. You could hear them shouting from the street. Easton called Coddington a treasonous bastard for making secret deals, and Coddington said he need not justify his doings to rabble. 'Defy me, and you defy Parliament, who set me in my place,' he said.

"Easton shouts at him, 'So long as you plot to bring us down, so God will bring you to ruin, and anyone who shares your betrayal!'

"Well, that broke up Mr. Coddington's court. The Dutchmen fled for their ship with a goodly mob at their heels. Easton and Morris went to Nick's home, while Coddington stuck his head out the door to shout for them to take their 'tumultuous crew' as well. I've never seen him look so a-frighted."

Herod said wistfully, "I wish I'd been there instead of stuck here with Willy. A riot's more fun than a colicked baby."

"You would have enjoyed it," George agreed. "There was one odd thing. Know you a man named Tom Painter – big man with sandy hair?" Herod shook her head. "He picked me out in the crowd and asked if I was George Gardner. Later Henry Bull asked if Painter had found me, for he'd asked Bull to point me out. A friendly fellow: we chatted about how we all came from Massachusetts. Then Painter asked if I'm still living with that red-haired woman."

Herod had been half-listening for sounds from Willy, who had finally gone to sleep, but George's last sentence brought her fully alert. "I told him my wife has red hair. 'So you are still dwelling with her,' he says, like he knew somehow that we aren't wed. Just then the Dutchmen come out and dash for their boat. Painter runs off too, so I couldn't ask just what he meant. I bumped into Bull and we went straight to the docks. The Dutchies were half the way to their ship, with Painter pulling at an oar like one of their crew."

"I've never heard of the man," Herod told George. "Aren't the Dutch from where John lives now? Maybe Painter knows him."

"Hicks is in Flushing, but the Dutch came from Manhattan. Maybe 'twas just a happenstance." George could shrug off the encounter, but Herod remained uneasy about Thomas Painter, whoever he was. If John Hicks was truly involved, the meeting was no coincidence.

The first ship of 1652 arrived from England in March. William and Mary Dyer were not aboard, but there was news which cheered Rhode Island. Parliament had pledged to review Coddington's commission and until they made their decision, Easton and other officers elected in 1651 were reinstated. Herod thought this was surely the end of Coddington's governor-for-life status, but she was wrong.

Coddington refused to relinquish his office. "I have heard nothing from Parliament that my commission is revoked. Until then, I dare not step aside, lest I be punished for abandoning my office."

Nearly three weeks passed: uneasy days when Newport's folk gathered on corners and in taverns to talk about what might come. In mid-March young Will Dyer pounded on the Gardners' door. "They are blowing up Captain Partridge!" the boy panted. "He's hiding in a house with his men, and they are fetching cannon to knock it down if Partridge won't come out. I'm going to tell Mr. Brenton!" the lad concluded, and jogged off toward Brenton's Point.

George was stitching a new strap on an ox harness, and sighed as Will spoke. When Herod asked if he was going to watch, he said, "It's naught but rumor, and nothing will happen."

"I could go if you would mind the baby. I just suckled him, and he's content," said Herod hopefully.

"You might come to harm."

"No harm in watching," Herod scoffed. "It won't come to cannon fire, but I'll keep to the common lest I be trampled by excited fools."

"Maybe you should take Benoni with you."

Herod laughed again. "The boy's only eight, and what if I lose him in the crowd?"

George frowned again, but said, "Please yourself. Keep a distance, and swear to me that you'll leave if there's danger."

"I will," Herod promised. She set off for town with a smile on her face, thinking how reasonable George was. 'If I were still wed to John, I'd have had to sneak off to see this.'

She had no trouble finding the excitement. Shouts and curses led her to a flimsy little house, with Coddington himself standing before the door. The crowd shifted, revealing the militia's tiny brass cannon pointed at the building and a torch-bearing gunner ready to set light to the fuse. Hatless and scarlet-faced, Coddington was arguing with the mob. He punctuated his words with broad gestures, but Herod couldn't hear him over the noise.

Then she spied her old friend, William Jefferay, at the edge of the common. Herod sidled over to ask, "What's afoot?"

"My dear Goodwife Gardner, it's so pleasant to see you at such an exciting moment," Jefferay said, doffing his knitted cap to her. "My wife wouldn't dare expose herself to such a dangerous event, but I might have expected to see you here.

"Captain Partridge is the villain today, in trying to evict his tenant. Nat Dickens has nowhere to go, so his friends took up arms to aid him. Finding himself in very unfriendly waters, Partridge is now holed up inside, but one of his party fired on Nat's friends. One was kilt and the other looked likely to bleed to death whilst they were carrying him away. Now Coddington pleads for calm, but there's no chance that Partridge will fly free." At that moment the door opened and Partridge himself appeared.

"Murderer! Butcher!" shouted the mob. Partridge's face whitened under his untrimmed whiskers.

Coddington raised both hands in the air. "Can we not have peace?" he cried. "Here stands Captain Partridge, and I will see to his trial myself. Let the man post bail and we'll pick an impartial jury and judge."

"Too late!" called a man. "That's my brother's blood at your feet, and it cries out for justice."

Jefferay said to Herod, "Henry Bull told me they fetched his chains, so Partridge won't get off with a mere scolding." The crowd closed in around Partridge and the other men who had crept out of hiding. Cheers rose, along with cries of, "Justice at last!"

The throng surged toward Herod and Jefferay on their way toward Henry Bull's jail. Partridge stumbled by, with cuffs and chains clanking on his wrists and ankles. He tripped and would have fallen if a score of hands hadn't borne him along to chants of "Murderer, murderer."

"There goes the most hated man in Rhode Island," marveled Jefferay. "I wonder if Bull can prevent that mob lynching him without trial."

"I thought Coddington the least-loved man in town."

"In his way, he believes he's doing best for us. He's providing good, stable government for as long as he lives, instead of letting that rabble vote for incompetent leaders," Jefferay told her. "As for Partridge, he's a malicious little man who has bullied or back-stabbed nearly every man on the island. He did it for Coddington's silver and to watch men squirm under his threats. He may not live to see the sun set."

Herod asked, "What will the governor do?"

"If I wore his boots, I'd be packing my valuables and hoisting sail for Boston, fast as I could."

"He can't go very fast with that great belly of his, nor toting all his gold."

"His servants will do the toting," chuckled Jefferay. "Coddington will be listing reasons that all this," he nodded at men who had lingered to argue with the governor, "was not his fault. He already complains of evildoers who were allowed to settle here in his absence. Too bad Dyer's in England, or Coddington could say 'twas his fault. Mayhap he'll point at Gorton."

"I don't see the man anywhere," laughed Herod.

"Nay, but he'll claim that Gortonist agitators roused the rabble."

Nick Easton was one of the men still arguing with Coddington. He broke away and stomped toward them, his face as scarlet and sweaty as the governor's despite the cool spring air. "What tidings, Nicholas?" asked Jefferay.

"Good news, if we are finally rid of Coddington's assassin," said Easton with a feral grin. "Coddington can't sweep this one away or let Partridge slip off in the dark. If Coddington's so-called council won't try Partridge and the other shooters, we'll do it ourselves and see justice done at last. Good day to you both." Easton hurried away toward the jail.

When Jefferay turned back to Herod, his eyes were weary. "It's sad that we've come to this. If Coddington had stepped down, his henchman would have skulked off and none of this would have happened. Now, if I don't get home soon, my wife will cause another riot."

"My sons too," said Herod. "'Twas a joy to see you, William. Let's not wait for another battle to say hello." William chuckled as he bowed over Herod's hand and bid her farewell.

The first trial to decide Partridge's fate ended in another near-riot. Coddington and Easton both claimed authority to call a town meeting. When one was arranged, Coddington pleaded for peace but was shouted out of the meeting house. He wrote frantic letters to the governors of Massachusetts, Plymouth, and Connecticut, pleading for help, but they stayed out of the dispute.

Partridge didn't wait long to learn his fate. Another unruly meeting was held, with men from Coddington's council and some of the governor's staunchest enemies as a jury. Neither of the Gardners attended. George said it was none of his business, and Herod didn't like hangings.

In London, at the urging of a fellow servant girl, she had watched a thief go to the gallows. The criminal died slowly because the drop hadn't broken his neck. Though his hands and legs were bound, the man wriggled like an eel on a fishing spear, dragging in croaking gasps until Herod ran away in horror.

Bob Stanton did go, and that evening told the Gardners that Coddington's defense of his henchman could barely be heard. "No man could prove who fired the fatal shot, Coddington says. Even if 'twas Partridge, he was merely defending himself and his men. Weren't they faced with a violent mob with a cannon? Fine Partridge or banish him, but don't take his life on a charge that can't be proved."

"There was peace before Partridge evicted the man," Herod commented. "Let him pay the cost."

"The riot wasn't his doing," George countered.

"A dozen men swore that Partridge fired first," Stanton said. "Partridge said there wasn't shot in his gun, just powder, and he fired in warning. Then the mob shouts that they couldn't know he wasn't fully loaded, so they must defend themselves. Coddington says again that Partridge also had the right to defend himself, but they cussed him down. There was another shouting match saying how Partridge caused the trouble in the first place by evicting Dickens."

"Just as I said," Herod observed.

Stanton continued, "Aye, but Partridge says if he'd let Dickens stay when he wasn't paying rent, then Dickens was robbing him surely as if he'd picked his purse.

"Then Easton says, 'If we let murder stand as a means of eviction, you'll see plenty more. Coddington holds our deeds so we can prove naught. He'll turn us all out.' Coddington cries out that eviction wasn't the issue, but he's shouted down again.

"It went quicker 'n thatch in a fire after this. One man after another cries out that Partridge was the shooter. 'It sounded like his gun,' calls one man. 'The barrel looked like his gun,' cries another, and at last one lad shouts, 'I saw him pull the trigger.'

"That was the end of reason. They shout, 'He done it.' Someone calls, 'Is he guilty?' and a hundred men call, 'Aye!'

"They get Partridge's hands tied behind him, drag him out to the nearest oak, and sling a noose over his head. 'Any last words?' some man asks.

"'Go to hell,' is what Partridge said, and they call, 'No, that's where *you* are going!' They haul him off the ground, kicking and squirming. A drop from the gallows would have broke his neck quick, but he choked his life away slow-like." Herod winced.

"Easton told me Coddington had tears in his eyes, but some said he wept 'cause his own life was in peril. 'Won't you please let him live?' Coddington begs. 'Banish or jail him, and I'll pay any fine you ask. Think of his family.'

"The mob screams that Partridge didn't think of Dickens' evicted family, nor the man he slew.

"'There's life in the man yet,' Coddington says. 'Spare him.' Dickens was watching Partridge flop like a gaffed salmon. He hands his musket off, grabs Partridge's feet and jerks down, shouting, "That's for my brother!" You could hear Partridge's neck snap, and Dickens laughs, 'Ain't no life in him now, and you're next.'

"Coddington shrieks like a girl, and then tells Easton, "This is your fault!' He points at Partridge still twitching on the end of his rope, and I could see his hand was shaking. 'That man's blood is on your hands, and God will judge you all for this.'

"Easton's face goes red and he shouts back, 'You left Partridge to lord it over us while you got your lying commission. You broke the peace and Partridge broke God's laws. He's paid full price. Will you?'

"The mob starts shouting, 'They chopped off King Charles' head for a tyrant, and we can do the same to you!' Coddington goes white and runs for home, and he hasn't come out yet. The mob was a-cheering and toasting with rum when I left, but Easton didn't stay. He and Morris had their heads together, somber as a bunch of preachers. Looks like Coddington is through," concluded Stanton.

Later that afternoon, Governor Coddington and his family were seen on a northbound ship. Within the week his servants had packed his goods and locked up his new house. As William Jefferay had recommended, Coddington fled to Boston. However, he took Rhode Island's record books and deeds with him, either to hamper the colony's government in his absence, or to give himself a bargaining tool if he ever wished to return.

"Good riddance," said George, "Maybe there will be peace at last." While Herod was relieved that the strife was over, she thought it amusing that Coddington had taken refuge in the same Puritan town which had ejected him fourteen years ago.

Still, she felt a little sorry for Anne Coddington. Though the governor's young wife looked down her nose at everyone in Newport, she had been forced from her home by the mob. Perhaps Partridge and Coddington had been punished appropriately, but Herod wasn't so sure that Anne deserved her fate.

CHAPTER 9
Autumn 1652 - Winter 1653

WILLIAM CODDINGTON WAS right about one thing – there was a different sort of settler in town these days. When he was in charge of Rhode Island, the governor rarely let a stranger stay for long unless he had money or a good name elsewhere. Now there were many new faces on Newport's paths. Some had slipped out of Massachusetts or Plymouth to dodge punishment for breaking Puritan laws. A few had drifted in from France or other American colonies.

Lately, Rhode Island had seen an influx from New Netherland. For years England tried to break the Dutch stranglehold on shipping, and they finally came to blows in 1652. The result was a handful of naval battles overseas, and increased tension between America's English and Dutch colonies. Englishmen living in New Netherland, including John Hicks, had to decide whether to stay under Dutch rule. John was content in Flushing, but those who felt more comfortable under English law left their Manhattan and Long Island homes.

It didn't matter to Herod who was in charge, as long as they weren't Puritan. With four young boys to raise she was too busy to worry about strangers. She and George had recently calculated that at the age of twenty-eight, Herod had been changing whittles without letup for nearly fourteen years. "Half of your life with babes in your arms," he marveled.

"Even longer, with caring for my sister's little ones," she moaned as George chuckled at her plight. However, while she felt like she had little control over her life, Herod was not unhappy.

Disruption finally came to Goodwife Gardner's life in late October, shortly after word arrived from England that the Council of State had removed Coddington from power. Herod thought hopefully, 'William Dyer and the others succeeded. Soon they will return, and Mary will come with them.'

However, the Dyers did not reappear that fall. Instead, Thomas Painter and his family took up residence in Newport. It wasn't long before the newcomer sidled up to Herod on a breezy Sabbath morning. She and year-old Willy both jumped when an unfamiliar voice behind her said in a throaty, intimate tone, "You must be Goody Gardner."

The fuzz on Herod's nape prickled as she faced the stranger. The burly man had sandy hair as curly as a ram's. He squinted at her as though he had trouble seeing well, but held out a broad-palmed hand and said jovially, "Thomas Painter, at your service."

Herod shifted Willy to her other hip, ignoring Painter's outstretched hand. He smiled anyway, saying, "I've heard much about you. Now that we meet, you are twice as pretty as I've been told."

Herod's neck prickled again, but she replied casually, "Who would say such a foolish thing?"

"Oh, people here and there, there and here," Painter replied airily. "I'm no idle flatterer." He moved closer and Herod stepped back. "I seek new friends, for I have just come to Newport." He chuckled, "*New* friends in *New*port, you see? I'm sure we shall be friends, for we have much in common."

"And that is?" Herod asked, stepping back another pace.

"We both have had our troubles with Puritans." Painter tugged down his brown wool jerkin, stretching it over a protruding belly.

Herod thought for a moment before replying. "I have no quarrel with them. You mistake me for someone else."

"Your friends were jailed and banished, were they not?" Intrigued despite her suspicion, Herod nodded. Painter fiddled with his cuff, fingering a carved antler button. "You see, I am lately of Massachusetts, and can I tell you of Puritan cruelty! I refused to have my son baptized into their unchristian church. They instructed, and compelled, and at the last they flogged me, but they couldn't break me. I hear that they could not break you either."

Herod eyed the big man. "Someone is misleading you."

At that moment, a skinny little lad about the same age as Benoni ran up to Painter. "Papa, Mama told me to find you."

"And so you have." To Herod, Painter said, "This is my son Shubael, whom the Puritans would have forcibly baptized. I did well to deny them, for God bore me up in my time of trial as a sign of his favor." Painter's words tumbled out, as though it was important for Herod to hear his tale. "Now, Shubael, run and tell Mama you found me, and I will be along soon."

"I want to stay," said the boy.

Painter hissed in Shubael's ear, "I said I will be there soon." He turned his son around, and with a shove sent the boy staggering toward the meeting house. "Go on now," he added. Shubael turned, and his eyes were reproachful behind the fine, dark hair which had tumbled over his eyes. Then he fled.

Painter turned back to see Herod also watching him warily. "The boy must learn to do as he's told, even as we must obey God," he said defensively.

"I suppose he must." Herod unconsciously squeezed Willy until the squirming boy tugged at her cloak. Relieved for an excuse to get away, she said, "My son has had a long morning, and we must be going. Good day." She dodged Painter's hand, stretched out again for an unwelcome shake.

His brown eyes narrowed so closely that they looked like dark slits, but Painter called after her cheerfully, "Until later, Herodias!"

Herod didn't break stride, but her heart pounded as her grip tightened on Willy again. When she found George, she told him she felt too ill to stay for the afternoon service.

"Your face is scarlet," George told her, touching her sweaty forehead. "Do you want to rest first?"

"No, let's just go."

On the path home, Benoni roamed widely, climbing fences to teeter along the rails, and shouting at sheep just to watch them startle. Young George, half his brother's age, aped Benoni's every move.

Henry, as he often did, disdained the company of his older and younger brother. Instead, he listened to his parents talk. Herod thought to chase him out of hearing, but then remembered sitting on the stairs in her childhood home, listening to her mother and father. She'd pretended that they were including her, and felt older and wiser than her years. Herod smiled to herself and let the boy stay.

Willy was far too tired to toddle home, so Herod toted him, shifting the little boy from one hip to the other. George said, "Let me carry him."

"He's soaked through."

"You can't ride my shoulders then, can you lad?" George laughed. He settled the child on his own hip.

Shaking a cramped arm in relief, Herod said, "George, there was the oddest man at meeting. I've never seen him before, but he spoke like he knew me."

"How so?"

"He called me Herodias."

George's jaw fell open as he turned to Herod. "Is your name really Herodias?"

"I thought you knew." Herod laughed nervously. Someone had warned her against keeping secrets from her husband – was it William Jefferay? No matter. This was no secret, just a name she didn't like.

"No. I can't believe …."

"I haven't used that name since I was twelve," Herod said. "Our Puritan minister told me that I was going to hell, just like Herodias in the Bible. After my father died, my mother sent me to my aunt and uncle. They were Puritan too, so Mama shortened my name before I went to London."

"Herodias," George said, drawing the syllables through his lips as though tasting the word.

"Herodias?" asked Henry. He began to skip, chanting, "Herodias, Herodias."

"That's Mama to you, young man," Herod said crisply. She motioned the red-haired boy closer. "'Tis a private name, Henry. Only special people know it, and they must never tell."

"Does Ben know?" Henry whispered back.

"Not even Ben, because he can't keep a secret like you. Can you keep it quiet?" Henry nodded earnestly, and Herod thought, 'And he will, too.' Just as Betty was her most beloved Hicks child, Henry was her favorite Gardner boy. He preferred helping her to working with his father and older brother, and Herod shared little treats with him in private. As far as she knew, Henry had never bragged to Ben about getting an extra piece of cake, so he probably wouldn't spill 'Herodias' to the world either.

She told Henry, "Good. Now, go tell your brothers not to climb Goodman Lucar's fence, because the rails are rotten." Henry ran ahead, shouting to Benoni. Ben jumped down, but Herod saw him give Henry a shove for passing along his mother's order.

George's reaction to horseplay was, "Boys are like that," so Herod shrugged at Benoni's roughness. She turned back to George. "Who else knows about your name?" he asked, bouncing Willy to keep him amused.

"Mr. Jefferay, for he read a letter that my brother sent to me. Mr. Porter, too, but they promised to hold it secret. Nobody else, not even Coddington."

George pulled his blond hair from Willy's impatient fingers as the couple followed Henry and the other boys. "John Hicks knew, did he not?"

"Because I told the minister when we wed. But John's in New Netherland. Painter's from Massachusetts, or so he said."

"Painter?"

"Thomas Painter. Tall as you, brown curly hair."

"Now there's a name I've heard before." George shifted Willy to his other arm, frowning at the damp patch the boy's wet whittle had left on his jacket. He finally shook his head. "I just can't place him."

"Well, I'm staying far from the man unless you are with me. Let's see how bold he is to your face."

Winter snows returned, but Mary and William Dyer did not. Herod mourned, for with the onset of stormy weather, she would not see her friends until the ocean could be crossed safely next spring.

Thomas Painter haunted her thoughts like a hulking ghost, and she stayed by George's side whenever he might be seen. The stranger came close enough a time or two to murmur a greeting to "fair Herodias," but before George could challenge him, the big man slipped away. After a couple of innocent encounters, George declared that Painter didn't seem much of a menace, and his vigilance relaxed. A week later, Painter approached Herod again.

"At last we meet." The jovial voice startled Herod and she whirled to see Painter behind her, so close that his lips nearly brushed her ear. "Have you dismissed your *husband*? Is he off to toast the Christmas season and left you all alone?"

"My *husband*," Herod emphasized the word even more forcefully, "has charge of our sons and I must help him. Good day."

Painter wrapped a big hand around Herod's bicep. "Don't rush off, Herodias. Your haste seems unfriendly. I just want to talk."

Herod tugged away from Painter's grasp. "I've naught to say to you."

"But we have so much in common. The Puritans whipped me, and they cast out you and your first husband, did they not?"

"Who are you?" Herod cried. "How do you know John, and where do you come from?"

"I told you," Painter beamed. "Massachusetts, where I was sorely abused in Hingham. As for Hicks – all in good time."

"If you don't leave me in peace, I'll report you."

"What for, asking friendly questions? And who shall get this report? Rhode Island has no governor and Gardner is busy playing at nursemaid. I merely wish to discuss matters which you might not want aired."

"I've naught to hide," snapped Herod. She turned and walked away.

Painter called after her, "Are you certain, Goody Hicks?"

George was just as frightened and angry as Herod. "This Painter has no cause to harass you so. I'll speak to Mr. Easton."

"Let me talk to Mr. Jefferay first. He's an old friend, and might know what to do," she suggested. George wanted to accompany Herod, but she persuaded him to stay home with the boys. "We can't drag them all into Mr. Jefferay's parlor. I'll ask his advice, then you and I will decide what comes next."

She went to her friend's home on a fair January day, when the air was warm enough to set icicles dripping and soften the hard-packed snow. However, fat clouds racing across the sky foretold that a cold reckoning for Newport's balmy weather was on the way.

Herod banged confidently on Jefferay's door. The man had certainly built a fine home, with costly leaded glass windows and massive stone chimneys on both ends. As she waited for an answer, Herod feared only one thing. What if Mary Jefferay came to the door?

The latch lifted, the heavy panel swung inward, and Herod's worst fear appeared. It was Mary who stood in the doorway, plumper than ever after the birth of her fourth child. She wore a thick green jacket over her unlaced bodice, and loosening ringlets hung lankly over her shoulders. Mary glared at Herod as though she had come to the door to beg. "What do you want?"

"I've a question for your husband. Nothing to concern you, Mrs. Jefferay," Herod said soothingly.

"You've wasted your time, for Mr. Jefferay is not home. Even if he were, I'll not have the likes of you troubling him."

Herod said humbly, "Mary, I'm just seeking advice about that new man, Tom Painter."

Mary came out onto the stoop, closing the door behind her. "I care not if you came asking about Jesus himself. You tempted Britton in Weymouth, and half of Newport's men while you were wed to Hicks. Look at the trouble you caused that poor man; cuckolding him and getting him turned out of town. What harm you are wreaking on that dumb farmer you have now? I'll not have you tempting Mr. Jefferay, so clear off!"

"Why do you hate me so?" Herod pleaded.

"Hate?" Mary's voice cracked. "I disdain you. Married and breeding at thirteen like a cheap London doxy –"

"I was wed a year before Hannah came," Herod said indignantly. "I would show you the license if John hadn't burned it."

Mary gave a dismissive snort. "Cheap talk. You flaunted yourself at my husband, big belly and all. There are plenty here who think Goodman Hicks was right to tighten your reins. If you've got men bothering you now, then Hicks didn't correct you enough."

"Mr. Jefferay and I are just friends," Herod said. "As for John –"

"I care not," Mary rasped. "My husband has no need for your sort of friendship. You are naught but trouble, and I'm not the only one who thinks so. Now you need advice. What are you up to with – what's his name – Painter?"

Herod almost left Mary standing outside her door without an answer, Then she took a quick breath before saying, "Mary, I'm sorry for disturbing you. Please, just tell me if you've talked to Painter about John Hicks and me."

Mary glared silently, and then spat, "I've never spoken to the man."

A small, relieved sigh escaped Herod's lips. "Mrs. Jefferay, I'll never trouble either of you again. But I beg you as a wife and a mother, promise that you'll not tell Painter about this. I don't know what he wants, but he already knows too much about me. Please don't arm him further. Perhaps even God thinks I deserve punishment, but George is innocent."

Mary's stony expression softened. "Very well. Not that I'd speak to the likes of him, of course, but your secrets are safe so long as I never see you near Mr. Jefferay again."

"Thank you, Mistress Jefferay." Herod was walking away when Mary called after her, "Come around here again, and I'll see you arrested for trespass!"

Though it seemed that Mary wasn't spreading tales about her, Herod didn't feel any better. When she got home, her pent-up questions tumbled out to George. What would she do about Painter now? She couldn't avoid him forever. How much did he really know about her, and what trouble would he cause?

"Come here," George said, opening his arms. Herod nestled her face against his chest, burrowing into his comforting warmth. "I don't see how he can hurt us," he told her.

Herod said, "The way Painter speaks, he must know that we aren't wed. If he tells President Easton, we could be whipped."

George had been stroking Herod's head, but his hand froze. "Just remember that I want to get married," he said somberly. "I have begged you time after time. If we get whipped, you are the one who called it upon us."

Herod broke away from him. Angry words were on her lips, but when she saw that George's hands were shaking, she held her tongue.

CHAPTER 10
February - May 1653

THE LAST THING anyone in Newport expected to see in early February was a ship entering the harbor. The captain must be insane to risk the frigid winter crossing. However, this ship bore welcome news, and even more welcome passengers. William Dyer and Reverend John Clarke stood at the rail, bearing a writ from Parliament which permanently revoked William Coddington's commission as governor.

Word that Newport's envoys had returned spread through the town like sunshine after a blizzard. When she heard it, Herod raced hopefully to Dyer's new townhome, passing celebratory bonfires already lighting Newport's streets.

William was there, but his children and servants were away somewhere when Herod knocked on the door. "Welcome home," she said. "I'm glad to see you back with us."

"It's good to be home," William exclaimed, ushering her into the dark parlor. "Somehow I knew that you would come calling today. And to answer your question; no, Mary has not returned."

William drew back the thick curtains behind his desk. His face was chapped and wind-burned. In the fifteen months since Herod had last seen him, his hair, once the color of newly-split oak, was turning gray.

"Is Mary waiting for fair weather?"

"Her mother is gravely ill," William told Herod. "Mary will return after she passes, but for now she gave me a letter to read to her friends. I can tell you the heart of it. She is besotted by a preacher in northern England, George Fox. Not by the man himself, for she has not even met him, but by his words. His followers preach in London and call themselves Seekers."

"I remember how she spoke of Seekers. What are they like?"

William gave a derisive snort. "I heard them at Mary's insistence. Akin to Mrs. Hutchinson, I suppose. 'Let the Inner Light guide you, not preachers' babble.' To me it was near-nonsense, but Mary has taken it to heart. She sends her love, but cannot come home until she meets 'The King of the Seekers' and hears Fox speak with her own ears."

"How foolish," scoffed Herod. "You and her children are here, and Newport has preachers. Why can she not be content with them?"

"How I wish you would go plant your common sense into my wife. I could not, though I wore myself hoarse with arguing. She wept most plaintively and promised that she will return soon, but for her mother's sake she must stay. However, I fear that she will delay to hear Fox."

Another matter loomed in Herod's mind, but should she let Dyer rest before raising it? William must have sensed her conflict, for he asked, "Is there something else?"

"Since you left, a man named Painter settled here. Somehow he learned that I was not properly divorced from John Hicks." Dyer's smile vanished. "Just last week he demanded money to remain quiet, or he will expose George for adultery."

When William scowled, Herod wished she had remained silent. "Goodwife Gardner, I have not shaken the salt from my cloak nor got my trunk from the ship, and you bring me your woes. I helped rid you of your first husband. Can't George handle this man?"

"I don't understand George," Herod burst out. "He dreads scandal, but won't consult President Easton or write to Hingham, whence Painter came. Ignoring the man hasn't made him vanish, but that's all George will do. Mr. Jefferay is no help, for his snippy wife threatens me with trespass if I speak to him. I know not what else to do."

"Poor Herod: your life is in disarray again, with nobody to pull you from the fire this time." Dyer's voice was heavy with sarcasm, and Herod eyed him uneasily. Then he sighed. "Herod, our marriages are both in disarray, and I hope you will excuse my rudeness. You have naught to fear."

"Naught but jail or whipping!" Herod cried.

Dyer sat on a corner of his desk. "Your separation from Hicks is in Newport's record, if you can pry it from Coddington's hands. Perhaps I can do that, but cannot help you further, for I shall be occupied for some time.

"Parliament made peace with Holland, but Dutch ships may not carry English goods, nor enter our harbors. I am commanded to pursue this matter in Rhode Island, and seize Dutch ships if necessary."

Herod's eyes widened. "Will Parliament send a navy?"

"No," William replied. "I am authorized to raise a crew and arms, but —"

"What arms can you raise here?" Herod scoffed. "Newport's only cannon is that brass peashooter the militia totes around. You might take a fishing sloop, but nothing larger."

She had misjudged William's exhaustion, or overestimated their friendship, for Dyer exploded into anger that Herod had never seen before. "I'll not have you mock Parliament's commands, nor me either. Solve your own problems, Goodwife."

Herod stared at William, wishing she could take back her words. Then they heard calls in the lane, drawing closer, "Papa, Papa!"

"I apologize, William. I spoke hastily."

William blew out a long breath. "Regrettably, so did I, but I still can't help you with Painter. I'll be busy for months to come, perhaps years." Herod heard footsteps running up to the house, and William looked out through the window and smiled. "And now I must greet my children. Give my regards to Goodman Gardner."

Herod sniffled back tears as she walked home, mourning Mary's absence, the seeming loss of William's friendship, and even George's frustrating inaction. Once more she wished that her father hadn't died when she was twelve. Most women her age still had their fathers to ask for advice. Why had God taken hers? Herod thought, 'Nothing has gone well for me since he died.' She felt more alone than ever.

Newport and Portsmouth were quick to embrace Parliament's writ. They reorganized under the original charter and held elections in May. However, Providence and Warwick suspiciously refused to unite.

A familiar face was seen in the crowd at Election Day. Admitting that he had no more right to Aquidneck Island than any other man, William Coddington had cautiously returned from Boston. He wasn't chased away, but wasn't elected to office either.

William Dyer was elected the colony's Attorney General. Rhode Island followed Parliament's recommendation to name Dyer as Commander in Chief upon the Sea, with authority to seize Dutch ships and confiscate their cargo.

George nudged Herod when that news was announced. "Just think — our William is a commander. How about that?"

"Too bad Mary's not here to see."

Betty Coggeshall was standing with the Gardners, while her two young children cavorted with Herod's sons. She smirked. "So he can take Dutch cargo. Seems to me that he's no more than a pirate."

George explained, "Pirates keep their loot. William must account to President Sanford for what he captures and give Rhode Island a share." He and Betty went on talking about Dyer, but Herod's attention drifted. She was still hurt by William's refusal to help, and wondered if he and Mary had quarreled, and was that why she stayed away. The dry-witted William Dyer who liked fiddle music was certainly more somber, and Herod didn't think that his new office was enough to account for the change.

Her eyes went past the new officers standing on their platform, and over the surrounding crowd. Now that Rhode Island's government was reinstated, several new freemen were admitted to the colony. One of them was William Haviland, a raw-boned young man who had been Newport's church warden several years ago. He had drifted away, but recently returned with a new wife – or so Herod had heard. Nobody had seen the woman.

Another new resident, Benedict Arnold, was also given the right to vote. The son of a pro-Puritan gadfly from across Narragansett Bay, Benedict was well-spoken and literate. Everyone said that the confident young man would surely rise in Rhode Island's government.

Standing near Arnold was the Portsmouth delegation. Betty Coggeshall's father, William Baulstone, was foremost, clad in a knee-length French coat and sporting a waxed goatee. Betty's husband, John Coggeshall, stood at his side. "Look, Betty, there's John," Herod said.

"So there he is," Betty sniffed. "Colony treasurer this year, so there'll be no living with him." She often spoke sharply about her husband, so Herod paid little mind. Betty was like a kitten – sweet tempered when things were going well, but sharp-clawed without warning. While the girl was a lively companion, Herod had seen enough sulky behavior from John Hicks. She was glad that she didn't have to live with Betty.

Beyond Baulstone stood John Porter. He wore the lightweight woolen jerkin and breeches commonly seen on Newport's streets, but unlike many New England men, he shaved his beard.

Herod said to herself, "Now there's a handsome man." She thought back a few years ago, when Dyer brought him to the Gardners' home for dinner. 'Mr. Porter called me wise when I said that Coddington was jealous of Roger Williams. If I'm so wise, why can I not think of what to do about Painter?' Then excitement seized Herod.

She elbowed George. "Do you see Mr. Porter?" The farmer nodded. "Go ask him what we should do about Tom Painter."

"Porter? Why should he know?"

"Because he has stood for Portsmouth in so many matters that he should be president." George hesitated and Herod prodded him again. "Go ask!"

He wove through the crowd to Porter's side. Herod watched hopefully as they spoke, and then George pointed to her and Porter waved. George came back to report, "He will see us tonight after court is over."

Sure enough, before dusk the Gardners heard hoofbeats on the path to their house. Herod and the boys dashed out to see Porter riding up to their gate. He was mounted on a tall chestnut horse with a bold white blaze on its face. It tossed its head nervously when Benoni and Henry ran to open the gate. Porter called, "Slowly, lads."

He spoke to the horse quietly as the animal sidled this way and that. At last the horse calmed, Porter dismounted, and led it through the gate. "Forgive Thor, he's young and not used to children," he said. "Goodman Gardner, he might be happier in the barn while you tell me of your difficulties."

The two men returned to the house shortly. Herod had already sent the boys to the second room with a promise of ginger cookies if they were quiet. The Gardners outlined their encounters with Tom Painter, and George concluded with, "He will charge us with adultery if we don't give him one hundred pounds."

"He said he would tell the Puritans, and they would capture and hang us," added Herod.

John grinned derisively. "There's a pretty fantasy. Massachusetts scorns us for our tolerant laws but they have more urgent matters than pursuing adulterers across Rhode Island."

"But we still could be whipped or fined," said George.

"Sanford won't whip you, and a fine would cost far less than one hundred pounds paid to a blackmailer. You have naught to fear from either," John said. His voice was so reassuring that relieved tears stung Herod's eyes. "I was there when Goody Gardner was separated from Hicks, and Dyer tells me it's in the records. Even Mr. Coddington will testify on your behalf, but that won't be necessary."

"But if he —" Herod began. John held up his hand.

"If there was anything to Painter's threat, he'd have done it already. I think he's harmless, but let's smoke this weasel from his burrow. I'll write to a friend in Hingham where Painter said he was whipped. It will throw some light on his past, and there could be other matters he'd rather not see aired here."

"Would it be better to face him now?" asked George. Herod hid a smile, for this was the first time that Gardner had ever suggested confronting their adversary.

"Do you hunt?" asked Porter, his dark eyes glittering mischievously in the firelight. "Shoot before your turkey is in range, and you lose your dinner. Do you know what Painter really wants?"

"Money," said George.

"Could be there's even more to it, so let's draw him out. We need bait, of course."

"He's already nibbling at it," said Herod. John chuckled, but George looked confused. "I'm the bait," Herod told him.

"Absolutely not!" George said.

"She doesn't have to grapple with the man," Porter told him. "Ask him questions; see what he tells you. What think you, Herod?"

"I'll do it," she declared. "I won't let him find me alone, and he dares not touch me with others near."

"He knows that Herod could clip his ears," Porter added. "Are we agreed?" Herod nodded with gusto, but George fretted before reluctantly giving his assent.

At last the Gardners followed John to the barn to fetch his horse. George stifled a curse when he saw one of his oxen grazing in a field behind the barn. "I always leave Jess inside at night to keep him safe from bears," he said. The ox's rope was hanging loose in its stall and George shook his head. "I know I tied him."

Porter laughed. "I should have stabled Thor further away. He's clever with knots." The gelding stood close by where Jess had been tied, watching them innocently. His own rope was securely knotted. "No harm, George. At least there's still enough light to catch your ox."

George grumbled as he set out to bring in Jess. The ox saw him coming, and headed toward the top of the pasture. "He doesn't want to come in," Herod laughed.

John reached for his saddle, and Herod asked him, "Can I give your horse something?" She'd picked out a wizened apple from the last of their stored fruit. "My sister's husband had a horse and I remember it liked apples."

"He'll be your friend forever," Porter said. Herod laid the fruit in her palm and held it out to Thor. The gelding picked it up daintily, and then nuzzled her arm as it munched. She stroked the animal's velvety nose, saying, "I really liked Blackie. Sometimes Edward let me ride him, and 'twas so much fun." She patted the chestnut's neck, wishing she had another apple to spare. "What does his name mean?"

"Thor, the Viking god of thunder and war. Funny, Thor's skittish of thunder, and I doubt he would care for cannon fire either. Some war horse."

"He's too pretty for war," Herod said.

"Just the color of your hair."

"George said that long ago in Boston." She had playfully feigned offense with George then. John's comment now didn't sound insulting to her either.

"You'd be good on a horse," Porter said. He set the saddle on Thor's back, reached under the animal's belly for the girth strap and buckled it snugly. He held Thor's bridle, but wasn't in a hurry to put it on the animal. "You've got light hands."

"I've got …?"

"Easy on a horse's mouth." John took the reins in one hand, saying, "Not like this." He jerked them as though he were sawing the bit against a horse's jaw. Thor's ears went back and he pulled away. "See, he doesn't even like me doing it in jest.

"You are right – riding is fun. I've done it all my life; riding to hounds, a steeplechase here and there. You'd love a brisk canter, or even better, jumping."

"Over a fence?" Herod laughed. "I couldn't."

"Perhaps," John conceded. "You wouldn't jump on a saddle like this. Ever seen a lady on a sidesaddle?" Herod shook her head. "You'd be good with a mare, but they can be touchy creatures. I had a stallion in England, a big gray who would have loved your hands."

"Why?" Herod asked, looking at her callused fingers. Burns reddened two fingertips, and she closed her hand to hide them.

"Firm, yet sensitive, just as you are with your children."

"Or husband."

"Like all men," John chuckled. "You must tell them how to behave and don't accept any nonsense. But if you don't handle them softly, they will panic. That gray, now, when he was listening …." Porter laughed again. "You must think me senile, babbling on like this."

"Not at all. You make me want to ride," Herod said wistfully.

"Next time you come to Portsmouth, you shall. I have a pony to suit you and a sidesaddle that Mrs. Porter has never used. Stop by, and I will take you for a stroll by the sea."

"Done!" said Herod. Then George came through the barn door with Jess in tow. John bade them farewell as he bridled Thor, and then rode off to his lodgings in town. Herod watched them go, picturing herself at John's side, riding his gray stallion off to some adventure on a sidesaddle – whatever that was. She couldn't wait until her next journey to Portsmouth.

CHAPTER 11
Summer - Autumn 1653

RHODE ISLAND'S FOLK turned thrill-hungry eyes to Commander-in-Chief Dyer and his tiny naval force as they began harassing Dutch ships. Their flotilla consisted of locally made vessels which were, as Herod had noted, incapable of capturing a Dutch man-of-war. But even a lowly canoe could sidle up to an anchored merchant vessel in the dark, letting its paddlers surprise sleepy guards or disable the rudder.

Dyer confiscated any English goods the Dutch ships were carrying, and triumphantly displayed the wares on Newport's docks before he and Nicholas Easton sold them as prizes of war.

Herod's private battle with Thomas Painter didn't go nearly as well. One day when she was seeking a couple of lobsters at Newport's fish market, she saw Painter. She boldly walked up behind him and said, "Greetings, Goodman."

The big man jerked and his felt hat fell askew. When Painter leaned closer to peer at her, the hat dropped to the ground. He bent to pick it up and Herod started giggling, but she stopped when she saw his face. Painter's squint sharpened his vision, but it also made him look furious. Then he recognized her and laughed. "Dear Herodias, you gave me a fright."

"'Twas not my intent. I merely thought to say hello. We've not spoken for a while."

"Gardner clings to you tighter than any tick, but I don't see him today. Has your bodyguard abandoned you?"

"He's busy elsewhere. George doesn't care for Puritan talk, but since he's not here, you can tell me of your trials. The Puritans never ill-treated me, but my friends were banished. What of you?"

Painter grinned happily. "Well, I told you that they whipped me for refusing to have my son baptized by their unchristian church."

"Where was that?"

"At Hingham, not far from your home in Weymouth."

Hingham was indeed a few miles from Weymouth, but Herod had never told Painter that she once lived there. She asked, "Do you mean Boston?"

"Nay, Weymouth." Herod decided not to ask how Painter knew. The man would probably lie anyway. Instead, she asked, "Where else did you suffer?"

"Suffer?" Painter laughed. "Every moment was agony when I lived with Puritans, stood in their courts, snored through their sermons …."

"I marvel that you dwelt with them for so long. Your whipping was near ten years past, was it not?"

Painter looked closely at Herod again and his smile vanished. "You are curious about me all of a sudden. Why the change of heart?" He took a couple of paces closer, and Herod retreated.

A woman excused herself as she brushed past Herod, giving her a moment to think. "Because you know much about me," she admitted. "You know where I lived and my full name, which I save for my dearest friends. If that makes us dear friends, then I should know more about you. How have you fared since your whipping?"

Painter said evasively, "My life is dull, Herodias, and I lived quietly after the Puritans abused me, hoping they would take no more notice. I would know more about you –"

"But I also live quietly," she protested.

"What of your first husband, or should I say your only true-wedded husband?" Painter asked slyly.

"Good riddance to John Hicks, and to you too," Herod cried loud enough that others turned to look. "You pretend friendship only to plague me. Come near me again and I will –"

"What?" Painter scoffed. "Carve me up with a knife?"

Herod stared in dismay at the smirking man. There was no doubt that Painter had spoken to John Hicks. She had indeed used a knife to defend herself against one of John's attacks. Few knew that, and of them only Hicks would have told Painter. A scathing retort eluded Herod so she simply walked away from her tormentor.

When Herod rushed to tell George what Painter had said, she found him pruning apple trees in their young orchard. "I am sure he talked to John," Herod said excitedly. "He knows my name, about Weymouth and the knife, and even called me a red-haired girl. It's gone brown now, but 'twas red when John knew me. Nobody but John would have told Painter these things."

George dug at a mosquito bite near his ear. "Red hair – where have I heard that? Damme if I recall it." He wandered away to cut a couple of leggy sprouts. Then Herod saw him stiffen and he dropped his knife. Grinning triumphantly, George told her, "Recall that riot when the Dutchmen met with Coddington? Easton and his crowd were ready to hang the bunch."

"What has that to do with Painter?"

"A stranger asked if I was still living with that 'red-haired girl.' Henry Bull and I trailed him to the docks and saw him rowing the Dutchies out to their boat. 'Twas Painter."

Herod wanted George to confront Painter immediately, but he said, "I'd rather take the constable or Bob Stanton with me, but I can't ask them this late. Painter's not going anywhere, so we'll do it tomorrow."

It was after noon the next day before George got going, and he came back sooner than Herod thought. "Bob and I couldn't find Bull, so we went to Painter's place ourselves. He's gone."

"Gone?" cried Herod. "Where did he go?"

"Westward on the Pequot Path. His wife said he hired a boy to sail him across the bay this morning." Herod pictured Painter's wife, with wide, round eyes like a rabbit's. The poor woman was thin to the point of illness, but so were Painter's children. Was Tom Painter the only one who got enough to eat in that house?

George was saying, "She thinks he is bound for New Haven. They lived there once, so perhaps he went to visit friends."

"But from New Haven he can easily get to Flushing, where John Hicks lives," Herod cautioned. George nodded unhappily.

At Herod's urging, George walked nearly ten miles the next day to tell John Porter about Painter. Again she was surprised at how quickly he returned.

She heard Porter's horse approaching the gate. Trailing the tall chestnut was a rotund gray pony, and astride that panting beast was George, red-faced and clinging to the animal's mane. Herod turned her head so George couldn't see her grin. Though the pony was nearly horse height, George's legs hung well below its belly. She wondered if he'd had to raise his feet when they waded through streams.

George's sons surrounded their father, chattering loudly as he slid off the pony. He groaned when his feet hit the ground. Herod timidly held Thor's reins as Porter dismounted, and then she patted the horse's nose. "Lovely day for a ride, Herod," John said.

She laughed, "George looks like he'd rather be doing anything else. I've never seen him on a horse."

"You'll never see it again," moaned George. "Next time I'll walk home."

Herod was eager to talk of Painter but her sons clustered around John, begging for a ride. He told Herod, "Rides first, or they'll never let us speak in peace." He boosted Benoni into the chubby pony's saddle and placed Willy in front of him. "Benoni, you must keep your brother safe. He's too little to hold onto Shorty by himself." John led the pony up the lane at a sedate walk, and then back at a bouncy trot that left both boys squealing. They clamored for more, but John told them, "It's your brothers' turn. If you behave, you shall all have another ride before I leave."

After taking Henry and young George on a similar ride, John asked Herod, "Would you like a turn, goodwife?"

"She can't – she's expecting," George said before Herod could reply.

"That won't bother me," Herod said.

John added, "A gentle walk would be good for her. After all, Amazon women gave birth on horseback, or so I'm told."

"And I don't want Herod doing the same," grumbled George.

"Let's talk first and ride later," suggested Herod.

"I don't have anything new," Porter said. "Now that you told me about New Amsterdam, I shall send to Stuyvesant's clerk. Good thing Baxter's English, so I needn't write in Dutch."

"Do you think Painter's there now?" asked George.

"It wouldn't surprise me. Perhaps he needs to consult with Hicks. I doubt we are rid of him for good."

After John gave the boys the second ride he had promised, he said to George, "Herod will be safe on Shorty. My daughter learned to ride on him and survived to make me a grandfather. That beast is too old for nonsense now."

"Just up the lane and back," Herod added. She gave George such a pleading look that he nodded reluctantly.

Porter fussed with the stirrups, shortening them to fit Herod. "I could have brought my sidesaddle, but George wouldn't use it. You'll be safer astride, and I'll not peek at your legs," he concluded with a wink. "George, I'll hold Shorty, and you can help her mount."

He led Herod up the lane toward Newport. Her legs were bared nearly to her knees, and she said, "Good thing nobody lives near. I wouldn't want to shock them."

"A little shock is good for the soul. A reminder of what we are missing," scoffed Porter. "Are you comfortable?"

"Very. Next time can I ride Thor?"

"After you try a sidesaddle on Shorty first. Thor's a bit spooky, you see, and sidesaddle's tricky. I wouldn't want you to slide off. George is watching us like a panther, and I don't want him to slay me if you get hurt." Herod beamed happily – apparently John would let her ride again, even if she had to wait until after her child was born.

With John leading the pony, they walked farther than he had taken her sons. When they crested a gentle hill, Narragansett Bay sparkled before them, with Newport town clinging to its eastern shore. A few fishing boats with sun-bleached sails skimmed over the whitecaps, escorted by gulls hoping for scraps. "How beautiful," John marveled. "Why didn't you build here?"

"Stand here during a winter gale and you'll know. We stay warmer in our little valley, and 'tis not far to walk for the view." The breeze tickled Herod's legs and she tipped her head back to giggle. Then she looked down to ask if they could go further.

John's dark gaze was fixed on her, his eyes wide and lips parted. A hint of longing was gone so quickly that Herod decided that she'd imagined it. Still, she looked away, fiddling with her skirt and tucking it under her knees more securely. "If I could ride every day, I'd come up here to see the bay."

"Let me …." Porter's words seemed to stick. He cleared his throat and said more clearly, "Let me give Shorty to you. He'll be dead before my grandchildren are big enough to ride, but your boys are just the age."

"Won't Thor be lonely?"

"He'll never notice that Shorty is gone. If he pines, I'll get a companion for him. There's a sweet little mare I'm eyeing, and Thor adores her. She'd make a fine mount for a lady – just the size for you to try."

Herod's pulse quickened when she pictured John teaching her to ride that mare. In fact, she would enjoy just about anything she did with him. He didn't talk of planting, hunting, and oxen the way George did. John dealt with governors and royal representatives, and traded in far-off places. And he had called her wise: a concept which George had never voiced.

'It's a pity that John is married.' Herod turned that fleeting thought around in her mind long enough for her palms to grow damp. But then she thought of the life she now had, content with her children and the man she loved. She'd yielded to such impulse once before – to make a decision and leap, trusting to land on her feet. Just look where it led her. Making her wedding vows to John Hicks, only to beg for a divorce from him.

'If he'd been like George, we'd never have separated. John Hicks was smart and a hard worker, but he was a cruel little man too. George is nothing like that.' Images ran through Herod's mind – George's tender smile as he closed in for a kiss, gazing in wonder at their first son, and the night she fell into his arms after holding John off with a knife. 'George is my husband, just as sure as if we married,' Herod told herself. 'Enough of these foolish notions.'

Patting her belly, she told Porter, "Maybe I can ride again after this little one comes."

He might have blushed, but Herod couldn't tell for sure since his face was deeply tanned. "Next spring, then," he said, turning Shorty to take Herod home. John walked briskly enough that the pony jogged a few steps, jouncing Herod and making her laugh. She didn't notice that his eyes were fixed on her face again.

"No, Ben, you and Henry can't sleep in the barn," Herod admonished her sons. They were so enraptured by Shorty that they could barely keep their hands off the animal. Porter had warned them that the pony was very old so they could only ride it once each day. The boys were already arguing over who would be first to ride tomorrow.

Surrounded by her sons' excited chatter, it took a while before Herod noticed that George hadn't said a word since Porter left. She shooed the boys out of the barn. "George, what ails you? Are you tired from your ride?"

"Are you?" he asked curtly.

"No, 'twas just a walk to the hilltop." He didn't reply, so Herod asked, "What's wrong?"

George forked wisps of hay to his oxen and Shorty. He finally replied, "You could have been hurt or harmed the baby."

"Nonsense. John was holding Shorty the whole time."

"You call him John now?"

"Why not?" Herod asked. "You do too." George could turn mulish when annoyed, but Herod's irritation was rising too. "What ails you?"

"That," he said, glaring at Shorty. The weary little animal was nodding over the remnants of its hay. "Why is he gifting us?"

"John said the beast probably won't last the winter. Our sons might as well have fun with it," said Herod.

"Why should he take such interest in our family at all?" George complained.

"There's no harm in it, and never forget; you asked him to help us with Tom Painter."

"But 'twas your idea," George said.

Painter returned a couple of months later, and the Gardners never knew for certain whether he had gone to see John Hicks. George clung more tightly than ever to Herod, so Painter never did more than leer at her. When her pregnancy began to show, Painter's unwelcome attention ceased.

In the fall, John Porter rode down from Portsmouth to tell the Gardners that he had received a letter from Massachusetts. He complimented George on his care of Shorty and gave the older boys tips on riding.

At last he told George and Herod, "It seems that our friend made himself unwelcome throughout Massachusetts. He tried Hingham, and Rowley, and Charlestown too, but never stayed long in any place. He left Hingham soon after his flogging in '44, but nobody there knew where he went.

"Roger Williams informed me that Painter was given a home lot in Providence, but he never lived there. They gave the land to another man years ago. Just as well, for the Massachusetts clerk said the town had to feed and house his family wherever he lived."

George said, "He supports himself here, and he's no longer bothering Herod. I think we can forget about him."

"Let's wait until I hear from New Amsterdam about this rogue," suggested Porter. "I don't believe for a moment that we've heard the last from him."

CHAPTER 12
Spring 1654

DESPITE HER UNCERTAINTIES over Thomas Painter, Herod was feeling remarkably content. Her sons were delighted with their new pony, and it had thrived over the winter. While she watched her happy children Herod smiled nostalgically, recalling her own childhood. When her fifth son was born in February, Herod named the boy Nicholas in honor of her father.

While Herod's family life was going well, there was one source of discontentment. She acutely missed Mary Dyer and hadn't found a friend to fill that void. Betty Coggeshall was once a good companion, but her behavior was increasingly erratic.

Betty had married John Coggeshall when she was near twenty, but he was ten years older. The marriage united two of Rhode Island's leading families but the couple seemed a poor match. Betty loved nothing more than lively conversation, and even before the wedding she joked cuttingly about her somber groom.

It didn't take long for Betty's comments to turn caustic, and she began to aim them at her husband in public. Though she doted on her children, her mood could quickly turn morose. Herod was worried enough that she brought Nicholas with her and stayed with the young woman for a few weeks after Betty's son was born in the spring.

"Look at that babe," said Betty. William was just stirring from sleep and Herod gave him to his mother to nurse. Instead, Betty laid the swaddled baby on her lap and eyed him. "Think you he looks like John?"

"I think he favors you."

"What about that hair?" Betty sneered. "John's is black as a coal pit and mine is dark, but that boy is as yellow-haired as your husband."

"You can't tell this early. Perhaps it will darken." The baby was whimpering and Herod commented, "He wants nursing." Betty still didn't move, so Herod loosened the girl's bodice and put William to her breast.

When the girl sat passively, Herod wrapped her arm around the child and pressed it into place, as though Betty was a scarecrow.

The younger woman's eyelids fluttered as though she was blinking back tears. "Your Georgie has black hair. Was there talk when he was born?"

Herod laughed uneasily. "He favors my mother and brother, and that's what I told anyone who stuck their nose in far enough to ask. Is that what's ailing you?"

Betty shrugged, dislodging William from her breast. She moved him back into position, and then stared vacantly at the suckling child. There had been rumors last summer that she dallied with a Long Island stonemason who worked on the Coggeshalls' new home. Some even speculated that he had fathered Betty's new baby.

Weymouth had buzzed when Herod chatted with James Britton. It was just an innocent friendship, but people had noticed. How ironic that she would now be counseling Betty on how to behave.

"Come, Betty, they can't hurt you with talk. You just have the blues. We'll go for a stroll when Willy's done there, and you'll feel better."

"There's only one thing to make me feel better," whispered Betty. "I want to go home."

"You are home," Herod said, feeling even more uncertain. She pulled back the curtains and opened the door a few inches to let in some fresh air.

Tears dripped down onto William's head. "I hate it here and I want my mother."

"What of John?"

"'Twas a mistake when we wed, but our fathers would have it so. I begged them —"

"But it's a fine match," Herod protested. "John treats you well and he'll be governor one day."

"He's treasurer these last two years, and all he cares about is his precious office. If he's president I'll never see him, not that I care to. John is as cold as that bay out there. Where is he now? At town. Was he at my side for Willy's birthing?"

"No," Herod admitted.

"George stayed with you for Nicholas, but John hates me," Betty cried. "You got rid of a husband. How did you do it?"

"I was a foolish little girl when I wed John Hicks," Herod said sternly. "Your husband is high-born, so if you separate they will give him what he wants. You know what will happen if he casts you off?"

"I don't care," Betty wailed. William began slipping from her arms. Herod took the crying infant to comfort him, but Betty didn't notice. "I just want to be free!"

"Do you want to be free of your children? I have three on Long Island that I've not seen in years. Divorce John and you might never see them again."

Betty's narrowed eyes held more defiance than woe. "He won't want them – he's too busy. That little one especially …."

"Think well, Betty," Herod pleaded. "If you part, all you keep is your dowry. I was left with nothing. Will your parents take you back? Will they accept your children – supposing that John doesn't keep them to spite you?"

Red-faced and trembling, Betty leapt to her feet. Her bodice fell open, exposing one plump breast, but she ignored it. "I knew you would take his side," she shouted. "You are just like him, telling me what to do. Well, I care not what you think, nor anyone else in Newport. Lord, I just want to go home."

"Perhaps you shall," Herod said coolly. "Look, William has spit up on my shoulder. Let us both clean up and take that walk."

"Clean yourself up and go home, and take your babe with you. Take that one too, if you like," Betty said curtly. She jerked her bodice over her breast, and then strode to the door and went out into the spring chill.

Herod closed the door which Betty had left hanging open, and then picked up her own whimpering son. She sat in Betty's rocking chair with both babies in her lap. Sooner or later, Betty would have to return.

No other women lived near Herod, and now Betty would barely speak to her. One more rejection left her feeling more isolated than ever. She wished she could see John Porter at elections in May, but they were held across the bay in Warwick so she did not go. Nicholas Easton was chosen as president, giving him more power to assist William Dyer.

Commander Dyer's harassment of Dutch ships resumed that spring, despite complaints from Providence and Warwick. Massachusetts and Connecticut also protested that these actions might provoke bloodshed.

Easton helped Dyer appraise and sell the captured goods, including a ship seized from a Dutch inhabitant of Connecticut. That last step may have been too bold, for lawsuits were filed and complaints sent to Sir Henry Vane in England that Dyer was enriching himself through 'unrighteous plunderings.' Privately, Herod thought that accusation might be true, since Dyer's new home was more lavishly furnished than it ever had been while Mary dwelt there.

George returned from elections full of admiration for Dyer's naval exploits, but Herod scoffed, "So William is getting rich from piracy. He must be so proud. What will Mary think of that? She doesn't know, for she is still touring with Henry Vane."

Roger Williams and Mary Dyer were both visiting Henry Vane at his country home, Belleau. They had sent letters home in March, and Williams planned to return to Rhode Island by summer. Mary would stay a little longer, for after the death of her mother Henry Vane had introduced Mary to Lord Thomas and Margaret Fell.

That couple owned a manor on England's wild western shore, and their Swarthmore Hall was now the headquarters of a religious group called the Seekers. Their leader, George Fox, had taught at the manor and Mary wrote that she would soon go there to study. The group also referred to themselves as the Society of Friends, but their enemies called them Quakers.

"I don't know why you are so angry with William," George told Herod. "It's not his fault Mary won't come home. Besides, I've other tidings. Our friend Painter is up to tricks again."

"He's no friend of mine," Herod snapped. "What's he about now?"

"Bob Stanton and Mark Lucar both told me that he asked just when you and I were wedded, and did we ever meet behind Hicks' back before he was gone."

"Mark came after John left, so he couldn't tell Painter anything."

"Mayhap Painter didn't know that. He asked Bob whether you had ever dallied with him or other men."

Herod laughed, "Why, Bob's over fifty. What interest would I have in him?"

"None, I hope," George exclaimed. "Bob said that Painter claimed to be curious, seeing how he lived close by us. I've seen Painter talking with other men, that Haviland boy for one."

"Up to no good." Then Herod mused, "Haviland has been in town for a year but I have never seen his wife. Was she at court?"

George shook his head. "I've never laid eyes on her either. But here is something you will like. Mr. Porter wasn't at election, but sent word that he has news for us. He'll come down to Newport soon."

When Herod heard a knock a few days later, she thought it was Porter with his new information. Her welcoming smile disappeared when she saw Tom Painter on her step. An ingratiating grin was on his lips, but his eyes narrowed to ominous slits as he squinted to identify who had opened the door.

"What do you want?" Herod demanded.

"No courteous greeting?" he asked. She tried to close the door in his face, but he pushed it open and boldly walked inside. Georgie had been helping Herod scrub the hearth, so she grabbed the boy's hand and tugged him to the open door. She pointed as she told the four-year old, "See where your Papa is planting corn?" The boy nodded. "You run and tell him to come fast, because Tom Painter is here. What's his name?"

"Tom Painter," Georgie repeated.

"Good. Now hurry." He ran toward the cornfield, and Herod turned back to the smirking Painter. "You have no business here. Will you leave now or wait for my husband to force you?"

"I'll wait." With her arms folded on her breast, Herod stood between him and Nicholas' cradle. Painter stretched his neck to look past her. "A new babe? I hadn't seen you for some time, and prayed that you weren't ill." She refused to answer. "Cat got your tongue? Take care he doesn't bite it off."

Then George burst through the doorway. His eyes roved wildly from Painter to Herod, and then back to the bulky man. Painter stuck out a hand to shake, but George brushed by it. "Are you alright, Herod?"

She nodded. Painter told him, "No harm done. I just dropped by for a chat."

Herod snorted, but George said, "Let's be frank. We know that you've met with John Hicks more than once. What do you want?"

Painter's squint went back and forth between the couple. At length he said, "Very well – I have met Hicks. After the Puritans misused me I went to dwell near Flushing. I liked both the town and the man well."

"If you liked it so, why did you leave?" asked George.

"The Dutch war. If England and Holland came to blows, I didn't want to be caught on the wrong side. I think I'll stay in Newport, for there's much that I like here." He leered at Herod.

"What of John?" she asked. "Is he coming back too?"

"That fine man is happy where he is. You both wronged him. Hicks stands for the town with Governor Stuyvesant and the Indians, and both English and Dutch look up to him."

"He's a drunkard and wife-beater," growled George.

"Must be the company he kept," Painter chuckled. "I never saw him touch a drop, and he hasn't a wife – yet. He's courting a widow, so maybe that has changed.

"The poor man has sad tales of his short stay here. He had a fine farm and a young, beauteous wife. Then that fickle bitch gave her affections to a man who claimed to be a friend. When Hicks tried to correct her, she spun a tale of abuse. A fair governor would command her paramour to keep his distance. Instead, Hicks' treacherous wife and his land were wrested away and given to her lover, and he was banished. They even tried to seize his children, but he rescued them."

"That liar took *my* children after agreeing to leave them with me," Herod cried.

Painter grinned. "There are two sides to all tales. By the by, I came to know your children well. Amazing that such charming little things could spring from a debauched she-wolf. Your little Bessie is particularly toothsome."

Herod's knees felt weak. This disgusting creature had spoken to her children? Touched them? All this time she thought he wanted easy money or to run his fingers over her unwilling flesh. But had he laid them on her daughter? A pulsating buzz filled Herod's ears, pounding with each beat of her heart. She looked around for some weapon she could use to stop the flow of words from his loathsome mouth.

George was growling at Painter, "Why do you torment her?"

"I merely thought she might like to know of them," Painter replied sweetly. "How much is word of your little ones worth, Goodwife?"

George spoke again, but Herod couldn't hear his words. Breathing hard, she stared hot-eyed at Painter. He sneered, "Fifty pounds for news of your son? One hundred for a few words about Bessie? John says she's your pet. Could be one of them is ailing. Don't you want to know?" The Gardners searched for words. Painter squinted at Herod and said, "There's another way you might loosen my ...." His tongue slid out and he flickered the tip of it at Herod.

A cry broke from the frantic woman's throat, and she rushed to Nicholas' cradle to scoop the baby into her arms. George grabbed Painter's jerkin and threw him against the wall by the door. Painter raised a meaty hand, but George grabbed the fist. He clenched his other hand around the struggling man's throat and pinned him against the wall.

The panting men locked eye-to-eye. Painter thrashed, but couldn't break George's grip. "You need to chop a few more cords of wood, my boy," he mocked. Painter tried to answer but George tightened his grasp.

"Hear me well, Painter." George's voice was laden with quiet menace. "I can feel your heart in your throat, squirming in my hand like a trapped mouse. I will set it free if you harm one of mine or come on my land again." George's muscles bulged as he lifted the other man a few inches into the air. Then he opened his hand and Painter's feet thumped back to the floorboards.

George nodded at the open door. Painter coughed, and then rasped, "You've not heard the last of this. As for you," he glared at Herod, "Favor me or not, Goodwife. I've heard plenty of talk about you. What if I tell the world that we met for a tumble in the hay and you screamed your pleasure to the skies? Plenty will believe that you bartered a fuck for news of your darlings."

"You wouldn't dare," George grated.

"We'll see," sneered Painter.

Another week passed before John Porter rode up to the Gardners' house on Thor. If illness had kept him from May elections, it didn't show. John's cheeks were flushed from his ride and he was whistling a cheery tune when he dismounted at the gate. The boys ran down to greet him, demanding that he come and see how Shorty was doing.

"He's fatter than ever," said Benoni.

"He's an old fellow and needs plenty to eat," John said. "You aren't riding him too often or too fast, are you?"

"Just like you said," Benoni replied. "Once a day and no more than a trot."

"Less'n he wants to go faster," Henry suggested. "Once he galloped back to the barn and Georgie fell off." Georgie nudged his older brother irritably.

"Right in a puddle," Benoni jeered, and Georgie gave him a harder shove. Herod started to reprove them, but Porter crouched down to Georgie's level.

"Did you cry, or did you get back on?"

Georgie growled, "Got back on."

"That's the spirit," said Porter. "Back in the saddle with no tears, and no man can ever call you a baby. Now, you let us talk in peace and you'll all have a canter on Thor before I leave." The boys ran off, whooping to each other about their upcoming ride.

Herod was waiting for Porter at the door. A broad smile spread over her face as John took her hand and bowed. "A fine day to you, Herod."

"And to you." George followed Porter inside, and also bowed over Herod's hand, flourishing an imaginary hat. She giggled and rubbed the back of her hand lightly against George's lips. Then she told John, "George says you have tidings."

"A letter from New Amsterdam." They went into the low-ceilinged main room and George pulled out the tall wainscot chair at the head of the table for Porter. He sat on a bench, and Herod gave them mugs of new beer. John took a long sip and smiled. "Good ale, Herod."

"I got new barm from Betty Bull, and it brewed well."

George said, "Guess who came here a few days back?" He related what Painter had said, and John nodded.

"I got a letter from George Baxter in New Holland confirming all that you said. It seems that Painter lived there 'til recently. He caused no problems and neither has our old friend Hicks. In fact, Hicks is well-respected.

"He has asked for a divorce from the Dutch governor so he can marry again. Baxter says he's collecting affidavits from men who know him, attesting to his good character."

"I'll send an affidavit," growled George. "Skin Painter and use his hide for parchment."

Porter said, "If Painter brings testimony from Rhode Island that Herod caused their divorce or still misbehaves, maybe Stuyvesant will favor Hicks."

"I think he seeks money or me, whichever he can get," said Herod.

"No matter what he says, we won't pay," added George.

John asked, "What if he accuses you in court?"

"On what charge?" said George.

"'Twould be adultery if she were still Hicks' wife. Does Painter know that you twain aren't wed?"

Herod said, "Few in Newport know, and John left before we …."

"Kept house together?" Porter added. "Some must wonder why you never wed in Newport's church, and they might share their suspicions with Painter. Hicks hasn't divorced under Dutch law yet, so Painter might think he can claim adultery."

"They can hang adulterers," George said, picking at a scab on his knuckle.

John laughed. "President Easton won't hang you, even if that is the law. There's a half-dozen men who can swear to your separation, myself included."

George said, "But until Hicks gets that divorce –"

"Dutch divorce, English law," Porter said calmly. "If Painter charges you under English law, you were separated ten years ago. That Dutch divorce means nothing here. Ignore Painter and let him sue. Easton may flog him for blackmail, and the Devil will take him for a lying rogue."

Herod couldn't walk through Newport without wondering who might have told what lies to Painter. When she saw Mary Jefferay after Sabbath, Herod couldn't stop herself. "Mistress Jefferay, I'll not bother you again, but please tell me if Thomas Painter has talked with you."

At first Mary would not even look at her. She faced the waterfront, saying to the empty air, "Why should I dirty myself by speaking to such a scoundrel? Or to you, for that matter?"

The insult barely stung Herod in comparison to her anxiety. She said, "I kept my word and have not spoken to Mr. Jefferay. Painter is up to something, and I wonder if he's come to you."

Mary turned to face her. "Whatever our differences, you honored your pledge so I shall keep my word. That man did ask what lay between you and Goodman Gardner while your first husband still dwelt here. I told the swine that I've heard nothing. Good day." With her nose in the air, Mary Jefferay strolled away.

Herod felt like she was treading on air. So Mary had spurned Painter. If Mistress Jefferay treated her well, the rest of Newport should, too!

CHAPTER 13
Autumn 1654 - Summer 1655

AS HEROD HAD predicted, Betty Coggeshall was notified in September that her husband wanted to end their marriage because, though he had tenderly tried to win her affections, Betty had refused to perform her wifely duties. Now persuaded that she had never truly loved him, he was sending Betty away from his house.

In return, Betty testified that everything Coggeshall said was true and that she also wanted to dissolve their marriage. She had hoped that he would be ordered to support her and their three children. Instead, he cast them off with their mother.

A year ago, Betty had told Herod that she wanted to go home to Portsmouth. Now she did, taking her rejected children with her. Before going, she came to see Herod. She offered Betty a seat, but the other woman shook her head. "I'm not staying."

"I'm so sorry about this," Herod told her.

"Don't be," Betty replied with a skeptical sniff. "Did you regret when Hicks left you?"

"Only that he took my children," Herod said. "There was no love left between us."

"John doesn't love me, and I'm glad to quit of him, but John proved what a good papa he is by tossing all three of our babies out the door with me. I knew he didn't want Willie, but I thought he would fight for the others." Betty looked out the window, perhaps to hide the tears in her eyes. "I told him that they are all his, but he believed me not. We're off to Portsmouth to live with their grandpa."

"Is your father angry?"

Betty shrugged. "All last year, I told Father that it would come to this. He's taking us in anyway. I'm his only child now, bringing his only grandchildren. My mother dotes on babies, so she'll love Willie – far more than she did me." Betty's voice was flat and indifferent.

"What will you do now?"

Another shrug. "Find a new husband, I suppose."

"With three children as baggage?"

"Is that a jest?" Betty gave a single, hard laugh. "I bear the Baulstone dowry like a golden halo. Suitors are already sniffing the air for money." Betty smoothed her skirt over her thighs. "I married a 'good match' that my father bought. My next husband will be a man that I like. Tom Gould, perhaps. You know, Mistress Jefferay's brother. He's biddable and likes me well, and I'm fond of him." Betty forced a smile at Herod. "I'm sailing with the tide, so …."

"I'm glad you came to say goodbye," said Herod. "I'll come see you when I visit Portsmouth."

Betty's wry grin returned. "Remember when I asked how you got rid of your husband?" Herod nodded. "It's easy, and you can do it again if you like. Confess your sins, a little public shame, and then you are free."

"Mary Dyer said there are laws for kings and laws for common folk," Herod countered. "A Baulstone or Coggeshall might not stand in the stocks or be flogged for their sins, but what of a Gardner? Besides, I'm not going to rid myself of George."

"Would you think different if George beat your children or you caught him with another woman?" Betty asked earnestly. "What if you loved another man and he loved you, and George neglected you and your little ones? What then?"

"What if you could pick rubies from a cherry tree?" laughed Herod. "Go on with your silly questions. You'll miss your boat."

After George's confrontation with Tom Painter, the blackmailer muttered threats to the Gardners, but never dared come to their home again. He was gone for several weeks during the fall, and Herod wondered if he had abandoned his family. However, their antagonist returned before winter with no explanation for his absence.

He approached Herod at Sabbath meeting. With Nicholas riding one hip, she was waiting for Willy to come out of the privy. Painter sidled up to her and boldly said, "Did you miss me, Herodias?"

She had seen Painter earlier so she was not surprised. "Just as I missed the smallpox once I was well," she said without looking at him.

"Last chance, Goodwife." Now Herod did turn. There was a malicious grin on Painter's ruddy face. "I've been patient, but this is your last chance."

"For what?"

"The day of reckoning is near." Herod looked around for George, but Painter laughed, "You'll not get help. He's hauling firewood for Pastor Clarke."

"See here, Painter, you've done your worst to disturb my peace but it's come to nothing. There's been no adultery. If any man dares speak for you, God will strike him down for lying. Why don't you give up?" The privy door opened and out came Willy, still buttoning his breeches. Herod called to the three-year old, "Go play with Charlie Dyer for a moment."

"I don't need witnesses," Painter replied. "There's work afoot, my ignorant little slut, and you know nothing about it. Two hundred pounds buys my silence."

"I thought you wanted one," Herod observed.

"I raised my price. Two hundred, or face the hangman."

"Be it two or two hundred, you get nothing from us."

"So be it. See you in court."

Herod believed that Painter intended to act, and soon. George scoffed at her fears despite the finality of Painter's ultimatum. "He is just seeking money."

"But he said something's coming."

"The man's all bluff," George replied. "You'll see." Perhaps George was right, for Painter left the Gardners alone over the winter.

George went to Providence in May 1655 to vote for president. He favored Newport's representative, Benedict Arnold, but Roger Williams was again voted to lead the colony. George's report of the elections was dull listening, but he had a surprise for Herod.

The Coggeshalls' divorce was finalized, and John as an 'innocent, suffering person' was given leave to remarry. Perhaps as a consequence of the Coggeshalls' parting, a new divorce law was drawn. Formerly, divorces had been granted only for adultery, but now the court might let couples divorce for other causes. However, if they parted without the court's approval, they would be whipped and fined.

Herod was skeptical about the new law. A divorce for adultery would have embarrassed Betty's powerful father. The court had enacted that law to let the couple claim incompatibility, but now that path was open. Which dissatisfied Rhode Islanders would be next to try it?

The final chord in the Coggeshall divorce came when Betty was also given permission to remarry. She didn't wait long to wed Thomas Gould.

The colony's Court of Trials met at the end of June to hear lawsuits for debt, assault, and other such cases. To the Gardners' amazement, George was ordered to attend. "I don't know why," he said, shaking his head. "I've done nothing wrong."

"Nor I," Herod assured him.

"Of course not, or they would have called you too," George said irritably. They took their children to Avis Stanton's home and walked to Portsmouth for court.

Outside of town they stopped at John Porter's home to ask if he knew what was afoot. It was a small building with plastered walls revealing a heavy timber frame and roofed with a thick layer of thatch. A stranger might not have known that an affluent couple lived there.

However, when the Porters' maid opened the door, Herod caught a glimpse of their parlor. Massive imported furniture and gleaming silver in the cupboard belied the home's modest exterior. A spotty-faced maid in a white cap informed them that Mr. Porter had already gone to court and that Mrs. Porter was not receiving visitors.

The first face that Herod recognized inside Portsmouth's meeting house was Thomas Painter's. When close enough for his squinting eyes to identify the Gardners, he walked boldly up to drawl, "I told you a reckoning was at hand."

"Half a year back," Herod snapped. "What mischief are you up to?"

"Your *husband* will find out, soon enough," he sneered. "You'll wish that you had paid me when you are salving the welts on his back."

George pulled Herod away. They sat on one of the wooden benches to wait his call, with George clutching Herod's hand in his sweaty palm. "I told you we should have wed," he whispered to her.

Herod silently searched the meeting house for John Porter. She saw him near the front of the building with President Williams and his assistants. When he noticed that she was watching, he nodded to her.

All too soon the summons came for George Gardner and Thomas Painter to approach. Herod also stood, but the court's clerk shook his head at her.

Roger Williams had come from Providence to judge the session. It was the first time Herod had seen Rhode Island's peacemaker, but she was so nervous that all she saw was a broad-shouldered man clad in a black suit and white linen neckbands as severe as any Puritan minister's. Williams asked the clerk to read the charge.

"I, Thomas Painter, present George Gardner for keeping John Hicks' wife as his own, contrary to law."

The charge was adultery after all, not the fornication of two unwed people. Herod covered her mouth with her hand. Though George's back was turned, she saw his shoulders twitch as though he was equally surprised.

When asked for evidence, Painter produced folded papers from inside his jerkin. "This is a true copy sent me by Mr. John Hicks of Flushing, in New Netherland. On the first of June the Dutch governor ordered him divorced from Herod Long. Until that day she was still Hicks' wife, even though she has dwelt with George Gardner in an illegal and adulterous way.

"Perhaps Gardner thought he married her honestly, but she has been Mr. Hicks' wife all these years. Gardner is an adulterer and his children are bastards," Painter concluded. He grinned triumphantly.

Williams asked, "Goodman Gardner, can you prove that this charge is untrue?"

"Governor Coddington separated my wife from Hicks over ten years ago because of his abusive ways," George declared firmly. "Mr. Coddington, Mr. Dyer, and Mr. Porter can all attest to that. Hicks abandoned her, and Mr. Coddington gave her leave to remarry."

"Very well," Williams said. "A grand jury will investigate the matter, to be judged at October's court of trials. This case is suspended until then. Painter, you may leave those with me." Williams held out a callused hand for Painter's papers.

He protested, "Are you not trying them now?"

President Williams aimed a keen look at Painter. "There are prominent men who may well prove your charge false. We need time to interview them and to allow Goodman Gardner to gather evidence for his defense. For now, you may take yourself away. Next case."

When Painter did not move, Williams added, "Shall I have the sergeant remove you?" Painter stormed angrily up the aisle, his face brick-red. He glared at Herod as he passed her.

George turned more slowly. Unlike Painter, his cheeks were pale. His shoulders slumped as he took Herod's hand to lead her from the building. They saw Painter far down the street, walking swiftly toward the waterfront. Then, behind them came a call, "Herod, George, wait!"

It was John Porter who had followed them from the courthouse. The older man chuckled when he caught up to the couple. "Painter reveals his plot at last," he said as he doffed his hat to Herod, and then smoothed back his hair. "The fool aimed for the wrong target. I'm surprised the charge wasn't bigamy. Either way, a half-dozen men and the colony's records will prove him wrong." Herod's gloom lifted, but George said nothing. "Why the long face?" Porter asked.

"Even if they prove Painter wrong, what if it is revealed that we never wed? We may yet get flogged for living in sin," George said unhappily.

"Didn't you heed Williams' voice? He despises falsehood and Painter reeks of it. I'll testify, of course, and if you don't wish to ask Coddington and Dyer to do the same, I'll be pleased to. I've not seen the governor for some time, and I'll have fun needling Dyer about his pirate's life."

Herod told him, "Mr. Dyer will speak for us."

"Coddington, too," added John. "He still holds tight to the record book but he'll produce it if needed. Remember a few years back, when Coggeshall entered Hicks' letter in it, calling Herod …." He hesitated, and then said, "Well, it left no doubt that she'd been abandoned.

"Methinks that Hicks and Painter have concocted quite the plot. He supplies Painter with evidence that Herod is still wed to him, at least by Dutch law. You pay Painter to shut him up, and they split it. He was probably conferring with Hicks whilst he was gone from Newport."

Herod said, "Mayhap Painter found someone to testify that George and I lay together while I was wed to John. The charge would still be adultery." Porter glanced at her, and she wondered if there was speculation in his eyes. "I didn't, of course!"

"He'll be disappointed," George said, but his voice rose like he was asking a question.

"Just so," said John, sounding more confident. "Go home and forget about Painter."

"What of October?" Herod asked.

"What of it? George will be cleared. Should anything else arise, Painter will have tossed away his credibility with a false charge."

As they walked home, George fretted, "We *did* lie together that one time. I wasn't keeping you as my wife then, but it was adultery."

"If he had proof, he'd have charged us so," Herod told him. "Stop worrying."

One more thing bothered George. He said to Herod, "Porter has done so much for us. Writing to Massachusetts and New Netherland, and testifying for us. He even gave our sons a pony. Why is he helping us so?"

"Mayhap he is lonely," Herod suggested. "Mr. Porter has but one daughter and she lives with her own husband. Maybe he likes our sons."

"That could be," George admitted, and Herod wondered why he sounded so relieved.

The Gardners struggled to put Painter's accusation aside until October, but fallout spread. A few weeks later Benoni and young George came home bloodied, but triumphant. Ten-year old Ben had a black eye and swollen nose, but Georgie, three years younger, had come off worse. When Herod examined his mouth, she found two teeth were missing. "You are lucky they were baby teeth, young man. Now, what happened?"

"Nobody will call us bastards," the boy said scornfully.

"Not without paying," added Ben. He told his parents that the older Bassett boys, sons of Coddington's former henchman, had taunted them. "We showed 'em. Three of them and two of us, but we taught 'em, didn't we, Georgie?"

"We sure did!"

"Good for you," was their father's response, and pride filled Herod's heart. She'd endured much over the last two decades to keep from being cowed, and she was delighted to see that her sons felt the same way.

CHAPTER 14
Autumn 1655

OCTOBER'S COURT OF Trials came too quickly for the Gardners. George urged Herod to stay home because her latest pregnancy was advancing, but she ridiculed the notion. "I feel well and the trial is here in town. How does that differ from going to Sabbath?"

"I don't know why you are so merry about this. Your back won't get the stripes."

"Of course it will," Herod laughed. "If you are found guilty, they'll lash me too." George glared, but she told him, "Remember what Mr. Porter said? They will all testify for us, and you will be cleared."

"I'm not ready to celebrate," George said sullenly. "Someone else may want to bring us down." Herod sobered. Though Mary Jefferay would keep quiet, perhaps they did have other enemies in town.

The Gardners took their seats in the meeting house and the bailiff called for order. Then John Porter rushed in, trailed by a curly-haired young man and a cloaked woman. Herod recognized William Haviland, Newport's one-time church warden.

The cloaked figure joined other women standing in the rear. Haviland ducked into a seat near the door, but Porter headed for the front. He paused to mutter to the Gardners, "I daren't delay court, but let me assure you that whatever Painter says, you will be acquitted." The sergeant-at-arms coughed and Porter waved at him before telling the anxious couple, "We will meet later."

Once more George stood before President Williams and the court of trials. This time, a twelve-man jury sat before him. Herod was elated to see that William Jefferay was one of the members. Now she knew that George would get a fair hearing.

Tom Painter repeated his claim that Goodwife Gardner was wed until her husband obtained a divorce in New Netherland. "Mr. Hicks never got a divorce in Rhode Island. George Gardner is guilty of adultery and so is his wife," Painter concluded.

The first to testify on George's behalf was Mr. William Coddington. The ex-governor may have lost his post, but if the cut of his blue satin coat and the glint of silver on his buttons and shoe buckles were evidence, his wealth hadn't suffered. Though Rhode Islanders sniggered at the French affectation, Coddington wore his wig at all times.

"Have you evidence touching this case?" Roger Williams asked.

Coddington said genially, "I governed during the years that John and Herod Hicks dwelt together in Newport, so I have long familiarity with the twain. The man beat his wife with increasing frequency and severity. I, with Pastor Clarke and my assistants, counseled Hicks many a time to soften his wrath, but though we bound him to the peace, our labors came to naught.

"Goodwife Hicks, now Gardner, repeatedly begged us to divorce them, saying she preferred to flee or to take her own life than to dwell with him. In December of 1643 the goodwife came to us grievously injured. We were certain that Hicks' next attack would cause her death."

"Why did you risk her life? You might have separated the couple sooner," said Williams.

Coddington shifted in his seat. "We had no divorce law then, and I was loath to break that sacred bond. Might such an action bring God's wrath upon them, our colony, and myself? But when the girl came to me with broken bones and bruises from Hicks' fingers printed on her throat, I was convinced that God himself had parted the pair. They agreed to separate and I witnessed their pact. Hicks fled Newport the next day."

"Did anyone else view this agreement?"

"The elder Mr. Coggeshall, Mr. Easton, and Mr. Porter were my assistants at the time. Mr. Dyer was Rhode Island's secretary, and therefore present as well."

"Have you anything further?" asked the president.

"I judged that Hicks had abandoned his wife. When we found whereto he fled, I directed Mr. Coggeshall to write and discover his intent. Hicks' response was more than clear – he wanted no more to do with the goodwife. Being abandoned, she was given leave to remarry."

Herod held her breath; what would Coddington reveal next? His eyes roved over the crowd and met Herod's. He inclined his head to her before turning back to Williams. "I have no more to add in the matter."

William Dyer spoke briefly, affirming what Coddington had said. His coat was nearly as elegant as Coddington's, and Herod thought, 'He must have done well in the piracy business.' Complaints that he and Easton hadn't given the colony its fair share of seized goods were mounting.

The last to testify was John Porter. As Herod watched him speak, her mind wandered back to his visit a few days ago. John had told the Gardners, "Painter still presents a danger. He may yet uncover your real crime."

"We aren't married," George said.

"Exactly. I doubt President Williams knows that, for Providence had little to do with Newport in those years, but he will not look favorably on such a revelation. Here is how you defuse the problem. When you are acquitted, Painter must pay the court's costs. You nobly offer to pay them."

"I'll be damned if I will!"

"George, you'll be damned if you don't," John laughed. "An angry Tom Painter keeps digging, and some disagreeable soul reveals that you aren't wed. But if you pay the costs, a grateful Tom Painter leaves you alone."

Herod smiled, but George said, "The cost —"

"Is less painful than the penalty. If you are convicted for living in sin, you will pay a ten-pound fine and they will flog both of you in Newport and Portsmouth. Pay the six shillings and mark yourself as a generous, forgiving man." George began to smile as Porter's advice sank in.

The jury conferred after Porter's testimony, and quickly gave their verdict – Thomas Painter had not proven his accusation. Williams asked the packed meeting house, "Can anyone contribute further to this case?"

Painter turned to face the crowd, smirking broadly. However, there wasn't a sound. He squinted harder, and Herod followed his gaze to the men's side. The only movement came from William Haviland. Shaking his head, he looked down at his hands. Then a cloaked and hooded figure hastened outside from the rear of the women's side.

Painter's face turned crimson and he croaked, "Hav …."

"Have you nothing further to say?" Williams asked. Painter's mouth opened and closed a few times. He finally replied, "No."

"Then Goodman Gardner is acquitted," Williams declared. The sergeant notified Painter that the costs of hearing his case ran to six shillings. Then George called out in a strained voice, "President Williams, I will pay the fee." A murmur went through the crowd.

As soon as court adjourned, John Porter rushed to meet the Gardners in the aisle. "You were right," George exulted. "I can't thank you enough."

John shook his hand, saying, "No doubt that will be the last we hear from Mr. Painter. I have seen a busy morning on your behalf. I met with Painter early, urging him to drop the charge. 'Why bother a couple who have done you no harm?' I asked him.

"He said, 'They are hardly innocent. I have other witnesses.' Who – or to what – he wouldn't say, but I've a man with a tale to tell." He looked over George's shoulder and called, "Goodman Haviland!"

The long-limbed young man was now standing in the aisle behind them, his eyes flickering between Porter, the Gardners, and the open door. John said, "Tell them."

Haviland stammered, "I didn't tell Painter this, but I was not going to testify. We already changed our minds, both me and Hannah."

"Hannah?" asked Herod.

"My wife. She's waiting outside. Mr. Porter didn't want to shock you, not in your condition." Herod smiled at Haviland's concern, for she was only four months pregnant and wouldn't lose this baby to mere upset.

"What's going on?" George demanded.

John said, "Let's go outside, and Goodman Haviland can tell us on the way." They worked through the thinning crowd as Haviland reluctantly spoke.

"You know, I used to live in Newport in 1646 when I was church warden." Herod remembered a lad just released from servitude, working for a few pence and a place to sleep. He'd left Newport shortly afterward. "I went to the Long Island."

"Did you know John Hicks?" Herod scowled when Haviland nodded in agreement. "Was that what you meant to tell the court?" she asked.

"Both me and Hannah were supposed to, but we decided against it long before today."

Porter blocked the door to tell them, "As I said, I talked to Painter today, even offered money to retract, but he refused. When he said there were other witnesses, I remembered seeing him jaw to jaw with Haviland.

"So, I went to have a chat with young William. That's why I was late. He and his wife live in Newport, but in the north, nearly to the Portsmouth line." John said to Herod. "Have you ever seen Hannah Haviland?"

Surprised, she said, "No."

George said, "I heard that she's ill."

"Or breeding," Herod added.

"Or disinclined to meet people who might recognize her." John said gently, "Herod, your daughter is his wife."

"My Hannah?" Herod gasped, and then she rushed to the door. Outside, still cloaked and hooded, stood the mysterious woman. Slowly she pulled the hood back to her shoulders.

Though it had been eleven years since John Hicks took her from Newport, and Hannah was only seven then, Herod recognized her daughter in an astounded heartbeat. She rushed toward Hannah, but the girl didn't move. Hannah gazed at her mother with John Hicks' brown, tear-filled eyes. She had his broad cheeks, but her pointed, trembling chin was shaped just like Herod's.

"Mama?"

Herod opened her arms and Hannah fell into them. "It is you!" she exulted, stroking her daughter's dark hair. "I've dreamed of this day. When did you come here?"

"With my husband, over two years ago."

"Why didn't you come to me?" Herod asked, swallowing to clear a great lump closing her throat. "Why did you hide yourself?"

"I had to!" wailed Hannah, burying her face deeper into her mother's shoulder. Curious court-goers were staring, but when John told them gruffly, "Please excuse us," they drifted away.

In fits and starts, Hannah's story emerged. After the Hicks family fled to Flushing, they became acquainted with John and Florence Carman, neighbors in Hempstead. Carman soon died, and Hicks and Florence began courting. Two years ago he sought a divorce so they could marry.

Hannah's brother Tom, now thirteen, got along well with Goody Carman, but their sister, who was two years older, barely spoke to the widow. Herod held her tongue when Hannah referred to her sister Elizabeth as 'Bessie.' It was John who had bestowed that nickname on the baby to irritate Herod, who preferred to call her second daughter Betty.

"Widow Carman walks through the door like she owns the place, and says that the house is dirty." Hannah protested, "I kept house for Papa all these years and he never complained. She and those brats of hers were there all the time but never moved a finger to help me and Bessie, though half of them are older than us. So when she came to call, I ran off. Father got mad, but I left anyway. Sometimes I'd go see Will."

Herod almost laughed aloud. How many times had she been scolded by her own mother for running off like that? She would have to tell Hannah about that some time.

Will put his arm around Hannah as she said, "We were friends ever since he came from Newport, and we'd talk about what we remembered. It wasn't long before we fell in love."

"When did you wed?" asked Herod.

"Two years ago," Hannah said sheepishly. "Just before I came here with Will."

"Oh, Hannah, you were only fifteen," Herod sighed.

"You were only thirteen – Papa said so!" Hannah replied defiantly. Then her chin quivered. "He was furious, 'cause we *had* to get married."

George chuckled, squeezing Herod's shoulder gently. "Does that mean you're a grandmama?"

"Aye," Will admitted. "Our boy Joseph is two now. He's with friends today, but do you want to see him?"

Herod said, "Of course," but George reminded her, "It's been a long day for the Stantons minding our boys. You have five brothers," he said to Hannah. The girl began to address Herod, but stopped before the words left her mouth.

"It's been a long day for all of us," Herod agreed reluctantly. The Havilands made plans to come to the Gardner's home the next day, and then said farewell.

George and Herod walked toward the waterfront with John Porter, who was staying at an inn there. "I can't thank you enough for your help," George said to him. "You pulled our irons out of the fire again."

"And found my Hannah," added Herod. "I can't believe that she's been in Newport this long and we've never met."

Porter chuckled, "So, you're a grandmother now."

"I'm only thirty-one!" Herod exclaimed. "How can that be?"

"You were but fourteen when Hannah was born," said George. "You were really a grandmama two years ago, when you were but twenty-nine." He laughed, "I was near that old when you and I wed!"

Heat bubbled up in Herod, and she was turning on George when John chuckled, "You were waiting for Herod to be free, Goodman. A prize like her is worth the wait. As for you, Goodwife, you are the fairest grandmama in all of Rhode Island."

CHAPTER 15
October 1655 - February 1656

THE NEXT DAY the Havilands came calling. Joseph, Herod's new-found grandson, was a charming little boy with curly chestnut hair and wide brown eyes. He was too shy to sit on Herod's lap, but curious about Nicholas, who was nearly his age. Before long the two had their heads together, drawing on the floor boards with charcoaled sticks.

Hannah frowned as she watched them. "They are making a terrible mess."

"I don't care," laughed Herod. "They are quiet and happy, and I will scrub the floor later. For now, we can get acquainted." Mother and daughter sat in the two good chairs, pulled close to the fire for warmth. Will sat on a stool near Hannah, and George hauled a bench from the table and placed it next to Herod. He slouched on it and began whittling a scrap of wood. Chips and shavings soon littered the hearth. Hannah's eyes went to them often enough that Herod wondered if she thought it messy too.

"Let's start at the beginning," Herod suggested. "How did you meet?"

"Will came to Flushing a few years after Papa brought us there," said Hannah. "When he said that he'd come from Newport, Papa wanted to know everything about you and Goodman Gardner."

"I didn't have much to tell," Will said. "I came to Newport in '46. Mr. Hicks was two years gone and you were wed." He blushed when he said to Herod, "I thought you were pretty, you see, and you were kind to me, so I remember you.

"Like Hannah said, Mr. Hicks asked me all about you — were you troublesome and what did people say about you, especially the men. I told him, 'Nothing,' but he kept asking. Hannah was just ten, but she did a good job of minding her little brother. I felt sorry for her having to be his mama, and not having a mama of her own. Whenever I saw them, I said hello to Hannah."

"That was when I fell in love with Will, even though he was near twenty," Hannah laughed.

Will said to Herod, "Bessie kept asking about you; what you looked like, where you lived. She cried when I told her that your home had burned, and she wanted to know what this house looked like. Bessie was such a mopish little girl I felt sorry for her, too."

"Why was Betty so sad?" Herod asked Hannah.

Hannah jutted her lower lip out derisively, just like she did when she was little. "Oh, she cried to me that she missed you, but she only said that to Papa once. He told her to go find you and locked her out of the house overnight. The next morning we couldn't find her for the longest time until I saw her in the chicken house. Bessie never spoke of you to Papa again, but I was too busy to dwell on it the way she did."

Herod bit back rage as she pictured her red-haired little girl hiding among the hens. She told Hannah as calmly as she was able, "I'm sorry that you had to work so hard. I begged your father to leave you all with me."

"Really?" Hannah asked, leaning toward her mother a trifle. "He said that you didn't want us. You told him to take us far away."

"No doubt Hicks told you all sorts of lies," muttered George. "That was only his first. So, what did he want you to do here?"

Hannah reddened and looked away. Will said, "It began after Mr. Hicks started courting widow Carman near three years ago."

"No," Hannah interrupted. "It started before that, with that nasty Painter fellow. He already dwelt in Flushing when we got there, but when the war with Holland began, he was scared to stay under Dutch rule. I remember Papa telling him about Rhode Island, 'They aren't Puritan and won't ask questions.' Painter left not long after."

Will picked at a spot on his sleeve as he added, "Before we came hence, Mr. Hicks said he'd told Painter about you two. They had a plan." He cleared his throat. "This is hard to say, now that I know you better.

"Mr. Hicks said that you two were – er – cuckolding him. You left him for Goodman Gardner and abandoned Hannah and the others. He told me, 'When you get there, look hard at their oldest boy. He's Gardner's son, all right: got on her well before I rescued my children and left her.' Benoni is the image of his pa, so I believed the rest."

"Did he send you to help Painter make trouble?" Herod asked.

"We came because of Joe," Hannah said with a nod at her son, "but I wanted to get away from *that* woman. I don't know what Papa likes about her; maybe it's her money and land. Whiny old thing and five of her brats set to move in with us. The littlest boy is blind, and guess who got to look after him when they came to call?

"So I left when they visited. Will lived nearby, and one thing led to another." She glanced at Will and blushed. "When Joe started to show, everybody said we should wed."

Will said, "Of course we wanted to."

"Papa was mad," Hannah told them. "He said, 'You're just like your mother.' Widow Carman said we should leave Flushing and take our scandal with us, so Papa sent us to Newport."

"Let me guess," Herod said wryly. "Not Puritan, no questions asked." Hannah smiled back at her mother.

"But before we go, he tells us about Tom Painter," Will said.

Hannah added, "Painter was so nasty that I stayed clear of him. Will did the talking."

Will told them, "Mr. Hicks said that Painter was going to make as much trouble for the Gardners as he could. They might pay him to shut him up. Then he said to me, 'Help Painter all you can, but hide Hannah. If they see her they will guess something is afoot.'

"It took Mr. Hicks longer than he thought to get affidavits from his neighbors. He also had to get what Painter learned about you and Goodman Gardner, and send it all to Governor Stuyvesant."

"So we had to stay hidden for two years!" Hannah told Herod. "It was awful hard. We pretended I was sick. Mostly I stayed to home, and we went to Portsmouth when I needed to see people."

Will continued, "I asked people about you two and told Painter. Wasn't much except ...." He stared doubtfully at Hannah.

She said grimly, "Tell them."

"If Painter's adultery charge failed, Mr. Hicks told Hannah to testify that she saw you two ... well ... lying together before Goody Gardner ran off from him."

"When I heard that you might hang for that, I said that I wouldn't," Hannah said. "But then they changed the law so you would just be flogged ...." She looked down at George's shavings and sniffled. "I was still so angry that I said I would."

"Angry at what?" Herod asked. She wasn't surprised. John must have filled his children's ears with endless poison.

"You cheated Papa! I saw you with Gardner all the time, giggling and whispering to each other." Hannah's words came faster now, and she looked straight at her mother. "One time you locked yourself in his house for hours. You left me outside with Bessie and Tom while you frolicked with Gardner."

Herod swept tears away with her sleeve. "Hannah, I remember, but it wasn't like that. I learned that my brother was killed fighting for the king. He was my dearest brother, and his name was Will, too. But when the letter came, your father just laughed at me. I was so sad that I needed to talk to a friend."

"Oh." The single word fell like a stone from Hannah's lips. After a long moment, she said, "That's what Papa told me, but I remember all those fights. Papa said he was trying to keep you from him," she jerked her head at Gardner. "I suppose that was a lie, too."

"Do you remember how he got drunk night after night?" Herod asked.

Hannah wouldn't look her mother in the eye. Will said, "I never saw him touch a drop."

"Then he had the strength to quit after he left Newport, because he was a sot here," George said.

"Not all the time," Herod amended, "but oft enough. When he was drunk, he was angry."

"At you?" asked Will.

Herod sighed. "Sometimes, but when he felt slighted, whether the Puritans wouldn't make him a freeman or the governor didn't give him enough land, John beat me." Awkward silence stilled the room except for Nick and Joe's chatter.

Will finally said, "After me and Hannah got to Newport, we never heard a harsh word about either of you. There was a little talk that Benoni came mighty soon after Mr. Hicks left, but everyone said he was awful hard on you. Mr. Hicks was so kind that I didn't know what to believe. But so is Goodman Gardner, and so are you," he said to Herod. "Even before Mr. Hicks got his divorce and Painter accused you in June, me and Hannah agreed that she wouldn't testify."

"We just didn't tell Painter." There was a wan smile on Hannah's face again. "We were scared of what he might do, so we figured that we wouldn't go to court at all. We weren't there in June, and wouldn't have been there yesterday if Mr. Porter hadn't fetched us."

"Mr. Porter is a smart man," said Will, who was grinning again. "Told me that we should both attend, so Painter wouldn't suspect. Let him say his piece, but when it was our turn to speak, we say nothing. Let him look like a fool and a liar."

"I walked out," Hannah snickered. "I thought Painter would faint."

"But why didn't you come to see me after you decided not to testify?" asked Herod.

"Suppose he saw us together?" Hannah said earnestly. "We didn't know who to trust, so we kept to ourselves."

Herod nodded, but wondered irritably why they didn't confess to the plot between Hicks and Painter earlier. The charge could easily have been dismissed in June. Why had they waited? Was it to punish Herod a little longer for 'abandoning' Hannah and preferring George Gardner?

In the end, Herod put her anger aside. Hannah had made the same errors that she had, and for much the same reasons. They both had married far too young, trusting their men to solve their problems. Herod had finally escaped John Hicks and his violence, but only after a long and painful struggle and the loss of her children.

Hannah had undergone her own trials, hiding from her mother for two years. It was all too easy for Herod to picture John's anger at his daughter's premature pregnancy, and his glee over the plot against the Gardners. Now Hannah was clearly regretful at her role. She had suffered enough, Herod decided. They all had.

It seemed that the rest of Rhode Island could live in peace, as well. In March William Coddington finally surrendered his claim to the colony's leadership, along with Newport's record book, bartering deeds and probates, births and deaths for acceptance by his neighbors.

That proud man stood before the court of trials to state "I, William Coddington, do freely submit to the authority of his Highness in the colony as it is now united, and that with all my heart." In return, page after page of citations critical of Coddington were cut from Newport's interim record and given to him. All lawsuits against him and his supporters were dropped.

The contentment which spread through Rhode Island didn't reach Herod. She ached to sail to Flushing so she could see Betty and Tom. "Not to talk to them," she told George. "I just want to look at them from afar."

George earnestly discouraged the notion. "Winter is coming on and you are breeding. If you do meet them, Tom won't even remember you. You can't steal them back –"

"Of course not!"

"– and Hicks will never let them go. If Betty recognizes you, she will be miserable all over." At last Herod reluctantly agreed.

She was saddened because she rarely saw Hannah, and finally asked Will Haviland what was wrong. "It's those terrible things that Mr. Hicks said about you," Will replied. "Hannah knows they aren't true, at least she says she does, but she can't forget."

Then Will looked her in the eye and added, "She can't abide Goodman Gardner because he should have stayed clear of you. He's what caused the trouble between you and Mr. Hicks. I don't think Hannah will ever forgive that."

Though Painter's adultery suit was dismissed, the Gardners still endured a long autumn under Newport's watchful eyes. The post-trial gossip didn't bother George. He shrugged it off like raindrops rolling from a lily pad, just as he had after Herod moved in with him.

However, sometimes Herod wanted to lock her garden gate and never come out. With Mary Dyer's loving support she had endured being abandoned, but now her friend was an ocean away.

Betty Coggeshall had met her tormentors with a defiance that Herod admired. "I don't see how you can stand the talk," she told Betty after the girl's pending divorce became known.

"They are just a lot of frogs in the mud," Betty said. "It all goes silent when I walk by. Then, 'Peep! Peep! Peep!' the chirping starts again. Just let 'em croak all they like."

Herod tried to imitate Mary's cheery acceptance, and if that didn't work, she turned away with Betty's feigned deafness. Harvest, with its multitude of tasks for everyone, finally put an end to the whispers and smirks.

Herod's ninth pregnancy went well until winter's cold deepened. Several weeks before the baby was due in March, her head began to throb and her face and hands bloated. She complained to Newport's midwife, "My legs too – they look like rising dough."

"That is normal, but not this," Sarah Grand pressed a knobby thumb into the back of Herod's hand. A dimple appeared in the puffy flesh and remained for several long moments. "Take to your bed and stay there 'til the babe arrives."

Herod's voice was shrill with dismay when she pleaded, "How am I to do that? I've five boys to tend."

"Get a girl to help you. You aren't so bad now, but you risk losing the babe, or worse." Herod reluctantly took to her bed. Hannah was sympathetic and visited more often, but wouldn't come to stay. Instead, Bob Stanton sent his daughter Mary to live with the Gardners. When Herod's birthing time came, Hannah would take the younger boys to her own home.

At ten, Mary Stanton was two years younger than Benoni, but the quick-handed girl was willing, and gifted with her father's dry wit. Herod appreciated the assistance, and it was a joy to have the girl in the house. As she listened to Mary giggle and argue with the boys, Herod's longing for her daughter Betty eased just a little.

In February Herod delivered her infant. The tiny girl was born nearly a month early, but Herod finally had a Gardner daughter. After the birthing George kissed his wife tenderly, commenting, "A girl at last. I know that you've longed for one."

Herod's health improved immediately after the baby was born. She and George marveled at her quick recovery, so swift that a few days later they took the infant to be baptized by William Jefferay. Because he had been educated at Cambridge and still favored the Church of England, Jefferay often performed such services. Pastor John Clarke and his Baptists would not have baptized an infant, even if he had been in Rhode Island instead of England.

Jefferay complimented Herod on her quick recovery, and George told him, "It's like Herod was raised from the dead."

"You look amazingly fit. We should rename you Dorcas," William told her.

"Why would you do that?"

"Because Dorcas was raised from the dead by Peter, Christ's disciple," Jefferay said. Herod giggled, and he added, "Now, what is the child's name to be?"

"Mary," said George.

"Dorcas!" Herod cried impulsively.

George gaped at her. "You said that you wanted to name the babe for Goodwife Dyer."

Herod grinned back. "Dorcas has a pretty sound."

"An auspicious start for your life, Dorcas Gardner," William said, and gently dripped a bit of warmed water on the baby's head.

Herod felt blessed that she recovered so quickly, but she did little in those first few weeks apart from nursing and comforting the sickly Dorcas. The fragile mite barely seemed to sleep, and protested her early entry into life with hiccupy wails.

George was delighted by his first daughter. When he came in from the fields, he gently lifted the swaddled little Dorcas from her hearthside cradle. He sat by the fire to croon *Come Live With Me and be My Love* in his sweet tenor voice while he stroked the sparse golden fuzz which crowned Dorcas' head.

He warned the boys, from Ben down to the toddler Nick, "You must take care with your sister. Hold her so …." and he demonstrated how he cradled the infant in his arms. "Never jostle her." When he offered to let the older boys hold her, Ben said scornfully, "That's for girls," and Georgie echoed him. Willy, a chunky four-year old, just shook his head.

Henry let their father place Dorcas in his arms. However, when she spit up some milk, he complained, "Take the baby back. She's got white stuff in her mouth." Henry hastily surrendered Dorcas to her laughing mother, shaking his hands as though they were contaminated.

During her pregnancy, the thought of raising yet another infant had filled Herod with dismay. She was not just physically exhausted – her emotions were as taut as a fiddle's strings. She nervously told George, "I'll be thirty-two, come June. I could bear another three or four babies before I'm done."

"God sends 'em, we'll raise 'em." Herod threw a wet whittle at him, and George chuckled. "I'm glad that came from the washpot, not from Dorcas."

Herod cried, "What if I get sick again? George, another birthing might kill me! Sarah told me that I'd best hope that God strikes me barren. Most women who swell like that are far worse with the next babe."

"Maybe it won't. Why fret before there's need?"

Herod tried to heed George's advice, but Sarah's warning haunted her. A phrase she'd heard in church when she was a girl came back to her; something like, "Mary kept these things and pondered them in her heart."

When she asked her father what it meant, he told her, "Mary thought things over." It was a strange way to say it, but Herod thought of the phrase when she had things on her mind. It was comforting to realize that, in this small way, she was just like Jesus' mother.

Now Herod remembered that verse. She had been pondering things in her own heart for many years. Events which she could not control, like her father's death and her mother sending her away from home, her own mistakes, and John Hicks' unreasoning fury. Now, with her fears of another pregnancy and George's seemingly careless attitude, Herod had more pondering to do.

CHAPTER 16
July - August 1657

"THE QUAKERS ARE coming!" For a decade New England's Puritans had been reading tales of a new sect in their mother country. What they learned was appalling. The Society of Friends – called Quakers by the scornful – disrupted Sabbath services, refused to pay taxes, and encouraged women to preach. Worst of all, those heretics claimed that God spoke directly to them. That alone proved to Puritans that the Quakers were under Satan's influence.

English Puritans had overthrown King Charles in their pursuit of corruption and heresy. The once-dominant Anglican Church had gone underground, but the Quakers had no interest in establishing a new church. They were determined to purify the Puritans, and then spread their restored faith to the rest of the world. George Fox had begun preaching his new beliefs in 1646. Eleven years later the Society of Friends numbered in the tens of thousands, and their eyes were turning to New England.

In July, Herod was preparing to dye some fine wool for embroidery. She had saved onion skins and picked laurel leaves to color her yarn yellow. Black walnut hulls from last fall would make her lambs' wool a deep brown. Sassafras roots yield a reddish-orange, and steeping her wool in red maple bark would turn it black. She and her sons scoured the hayfields for wild indigo blossoms, and had enough for an ample pot of blue. Treating some of her blue-dyed wool with hickory bark would turn it a lovely green.

Madder root made the deepest, purest red, but Herod had none. However, she did have a hoard of pennies and wampum from selling butter, and took it to the market on Thames Street. If she had any money left after buying the dye, Herod hoped that the vendor would also have some silk thread for her needlework's finer details.

After her dyed yarn was spun, Herod planned to make a set of curtains for the bed she shared with her family. She would embroider entwined flowers and leaves on the side that faced the room. However, if she could find the time, Herod wanted to expand her decorative efforts.

Mary Dyer had shown Herod a stunning silk dress she'd worn at her wedding. The glossy fabric slipped through Herod's fingers as smoothly as an icicle during a January thaw, but what really caught her imagination was the embroidery that Mary had scattered over the silk. The bodice bore an intricate white-on-white design, while multi-colored flowers, birds, and butterflies of wool, silk, and silver adorned the apron. That is what Herod wanted for her bed-curtains. She couldn't afford silver thread or the thick silk which Mary used for her dress, but if Herod's colors were strong and her embroidery skillful enough, she would be content.

As she examined silk thread at the merchant's table, Herod considered designs again. The tree of life was popular, but she wanted something different. She had seen a tapestry hanging in a London store window which featured Adam and Eve. They stood in Eden, surrounded by fearsome creatures, with the serpent twining up a tree between them. Some might find that image too daring, but Herod was tempted to try it.

"Goody Gardner!" Herod always relished market days because she never knew whom she was going to meet. The man who called her name was one of the first friends she had made in New England.

"Mr. Jefferay!" But then Herod hesitated. At the elderly man's side stood Mary, clutching her husband's arm and assessing Herod with cool eyes.

After the Thomas Painter affair, Herod had kept the promise she made to Mary in return for the woman's silence. Though Herod would not ignore William if he spoke to her, she had not sought his company since he baptized Dorcas. However it was William who had called to her today, so Herod felt free to respond.

"My dear goodwife, it seems years since we have spoken."

"Our lives are busy," Herod replied. "You have four children now?"

"Five," said Mary. "I bore Susannah last year."

"And you have a daughter at last. How is the babe?" William asked.

"Quite well." Herod turned to Mary. "Dorcas keeps me close to home but she was napping, so I slipped away to buy some madder." Mary smiled politely in response.

William said, "When I spied you, I thought perhaps you had come to see Mr. Dyer before he goes to Boston."

"Boston?" Herod asked. "Why is he going there?"

"To fetch his wife."

The madder root slipped from Herod's fingers. "Mary is back?" she asked faintly.

It was Mary Jefferay who reached out to steady Herod. "Mr. Jefferay, you shouldn't shock her so!"

William began to apologize, but Herod said, "Tell me of Mary."

"I know little, except that Mr. Dyer received word from her yesterday. He told me that she's been lying in Boston jail these last ten weeks, imprisoned as a Quaker. Just now your friend got hold of pen and paper and slipped a letter through a crack in the shutters. You might think that Governor Endecott would notify her husband, but he never saw fit," William sniffed. "Dyer goes tomorrow to fetch her and to swap harsh words with Endecott."

Herod's heart was racing in a mix of fear and joy. "Is she well?"

"Who can say, for she has rotted in an unheated cell for months," Jefferay replied.

His wife added, "I am surprised that the Puritans didn't turn her away at the docks."

William told them, "The Puritans didn't have laws barring Quakers last year. Now whipping, fines, and a long stay in jail await them. That will probably inspire the Quakers, but a £100 fine makes ship captains think twice. Mistress Dyer probably came in from Barbados where there are many Quakers and also some very bold captains."

"Will Massachusetts really whip Quakers?" asked Herod.

"They've been doing that in England for years," William told her.

"Those Quakers know what they will get in Boston, and so did your friend," Mary Jefferay sniffed. "It's her own fault she's lodging in Boston's jail now."

Herod stared at her in disbelief. "I thought Mistress Dyer was your friend too."

"Lawbreakers –" began Mary, but William stopped her by clearing his throat.

"Anne Hutchinson was Boston's treasured friend," he reminded Herod. "Yet she was banished and condemned to hell. They have hanged people merely for adultery."

"Rhode Island also had that law when I came here," mused Herod.

"But no longer. Our governors look the other way – on many things," William said. His eyes sparkled mischievously, and Herod wondered what he knew about her and George. But if William had heard that the Gardners weren't married, he merely smiled blandly as he continued, "As for our Puritan friends, they will do whatever it takes to keep their colonies pure. To that end, all other faiths, be they Baptist, Jew, or Catholic, are unwelcome. And they will not stop at whippings."

"But surely Parliament will protest," said Herod.

"Parliament is Puritan," replied William. "They won't punish their own."

Herod raced home with her dye and silk thread, but her purchases were nearly forgotten. One thought pounded in her mind – Mary is back, but she could be ill. Her friend might need help.

She found George in the kitchen, escaping July's heat with a mug of beer. He'd been hoeing the cornfield and sweat was still dripping from his chin. He raised a weary hand to Herod but before he could speak, she told him, "Mary Dyer is back."

George blinked in surprise. "Here?"

"No, in Boston. Mr. Jefferay said she's been in jail for months."

"The poor woman. Will she be freed soon?"

"William is going up there to scold the governor and bring her home."

"Good." George took another swallow. "Corn looks like it might come early this year."

"Did you not hear me?"

He stared at her over the rim of his pewter mug. "Mary is in Boston. What of it?"

"I should go there with William."

"To show him the way? He doesn't need you, Herod."

"George, remember what happened to those Quakers in Boston?" The first missionaries, a brave pair of women, had arrived a year ago. Their names were marked with a *Q* on the passenger list. With a glance, the Puritan magistrates knew exactly what they were – a threat to be stamped out. The rest of New England soon heard how the women fared. "Those poor women were stripped naked and searched for witches' marks!" Herod told George indignantly.

He started to snicker, but stopped when Herod glared hotly at him. "We've heard that English Quaker women strip themselves bare to show that Puritans are spiritually naked," he said. "They beg to be jailed —"

"Think of that mole on your shoulder, George. If one of those Quakers had such a mark she would hang as a witch! Do you think that they stripped Mary?"

George's voice went up nearly an octave when he cried, "If so, she brought it on herself!"

"I still want to go to Boston. What if she is sick?"

"Have you lost your mind? William can care for his wife, but what of Dorcas? I cannot suckle her, and taking the babe through the wilderness will surely kill her. When you reach Boston, *if* you do, you will join the Quakers in prison. Don't be stupid."

"Don't call me stupid," Herod spat.

"Then don't talk so," George retorted, and slammed the door as he stomped outside.

William brought his wife home, and Herod thought, 'What a strange reunion it will be.' Mary had been gone six years, and her oldest children were nearly grown. Charlie was only a year old when his mother left. He didn't remember her at all.

Herod waited a week before she walked up to the Dyers' new townhouse. Charlie and young Mary were weeding the kitchen garden. They waved, but did not come to the fence to talk. The older boys and William were nowhere to be seen.

With her stomach fluttering nervously, Herod tapped on the door. "Come in," called the voice that she had ached to hear. The massive door swung open and there, rising from a rocking chair by the parlor hearth, was Mary. She opened her arms and Herod rushed into them. Burrowing her face into Mary's shoulder, Herod heard her murmur, "I knew thou would come." Herod could feel Mary's ribs and knobby spine through her plain gray dress.

"I knew thou would return," Herod answered, the intimate word coming easily to her lips. She drew back so she could see Mary. The older woman's face and hands, pale from long imprisonment, glowed like Chinese porcelain. Mary's braided hair, once thick and blond, had thinned and was streaked with white. Herod blurted, "You look like Mrs. Hutchinson."

A smile lit Mary's face. "What joy, to be likened to a saint! And thou do not look a day older than when I left."

"I wish 'twere true," Herod said. "So many things have happened. My Hannah is back in Newport; wed, and a mother already. George was tried for adultery, but they found him not guilty. I bore three babes —"

"A daughter?" Mary asked, beaming hopefully.

"Aye, and two sons. We feared for Dorcas since she came early, but she thrives now. Your children must be happy to see their mama."

When Mary's face turned woebegone Herod wished that she could take back her words. "More surprise than pleasure," her friend sighed. "They know not what to say to me. The little ones take care to not call Christian Eaton 'Mama' in my hearing."

"What can you expect?" Herod said, keeping her voice gentle despite a surprising surge of anger. "She has been their mama for six years."

"Sometimes God requires sacrifice," Mary said firmly. "Let us speak of that anon."

Herod gave a relieved nod. "William said you were in Boston jail."

"Aye," Mary said with more energy. "I arrived from Barbados two months past. Sister Burden came with me to settle her husband's estate, for they once lived in Boston. Instead of greeting old friends, Governor Endecott rushed us into jail and destroyed our possessions. We lay ten weeks in the dark and might have starved, had Brother Upsall not bribed the jailer to feed us. I slipped a letter to him and he sent it hither. If not for him, Sister Burden and I would still be in prison."

"I didn't know you had kin in Boston."

"When Brother Upsall and Sister Burden declared themselves Friends, they became my brethren, just as I hope thou and I shall become sisters." Mary's smile returned, brighter than ever. "My dear William scolded Endecott for an ungracious host and brought me home."

"But why did you go to Boston? Why not come home first?"

"Most ships land in Boston," Mary said patiently. "Besides, we have much to do there. My Friends and I bear God's word for everyone in New England."

Herod asked, "Is his word not already here?" but the older woman shook her head. "But Mary, every preacher claims that he speaks God's word. They all say that women are not fit vessels for such work."

"They are wrong," Mary said. "I am not the same woman who left here, for I have been transformed. God speaks to me and through me. He speaks to thee, though thou need to listen for his voice. I will help thee, if that be thy wish."

Mary's eyes shone like the embers in her fireplace and some color had risen to her cheeks. Though Herod felt a touch of her friend's enthusiasm, she thought of Anne again. The last time she saw Mrs. Hutchinson the older woman had also burned with a zealot's fervor and said that she spoke to God.

Doubt grew within Herod as Mary continued, "I have learned that we all bear Christ's Seed within us. All thou need do is to nurture that Seed. Ministers can't help – they but stand between thee and God." Mary's breathless words stopped and she cocked her head as she examined her silent friend. "I must sound mad to thee."

Herod didn't know how to answer. Instead, she asked, "Why thee?"

"I knew thou would ask." A man and wife might use that intimate form of address, or mothers speak to their children so, but it was rare in common usage and certainly no way to address one's superior. Mary explained, "We are all equal in God's sight. Not even a king stands higher than the lowliest clam-digger. I honor God by calling him 'You.' Thou art my equal, as is my husband, and even our governor, whoever he is."

"Roger Williams."

"When I speak with Mr. Williams, I will call him 'thee,' just as I do thee, Herod."

"I see," said Herod. In truth, using 'thee' in everyday speech seemed awkward, and she could not imagine saying it to the dignified Roger Williams. However, she was so delighted to have Mary home that she would do anything to make her friend happy.

A few days later, Herod returned to the Dyer house to see her friend again. Instead, Mary's grim-faced husband met her at the door. "She is gone," William said.

"But she just came home," protested Herod.

"Word came that another boatload of Quaking fools landed in Providence, so away she went. A sensible person would cling to her family after six years gone, but Mary has lost all reason." William had been aloof after refusing to help the Gardners with Tom Painter's accusation. Now, to Herod's surprise, he waved her into the parlor. He pulled out one of the high-backed chairs for her and sat on the other side of the table. "Tell me, Herod, what think you of this business?"

"I wonder if Mary left her mind in Boston jail," Herod said. "She says that she is transformed, but to what?"

"Not a good wife or mother," William scoffed. "What sort of mother would leave her children as she does? I plead with Endecott to release her. She thanks me by dashing off again.

"We fought the entire time she was here. I should say that I argued, and she told me sweetly, 'Thou wilt understand when the Light comes to thee.' She even rebuked me for acting against the Dutch. I followed Parliament's command and no man was killed, yet she scolds me for making war."

Diamonds of light from the leaded glass window behind the table cast Dyer's face in harsh relief. There were deep circles under the man's eyes, as though he hadn't slept well since Mary's return. He finished angrily, "If George Fox stood before me now, I would horsewhip him for wife-stealing. That man and his notions have taken Mary from us all."

"Perhaps she is over-wrought. Let her have her say, and Mary will be herself again."

William laughed bitterly. "I don't know what 'herself' is like any more. I married a girl with golden hair and a laugh like silver bells. Now she is faded and somber. Mary can read and write, and once she turned her studies to family and God. Now it's these ghastly reforms. If she remains as she is now …." William looked at Herod with anguished eyes. "I fear this will end badly. Must my children lose their mother to please God? Must I?"

"I pray thou art wrong," Herod said.

William scowled at her, and she responded with an impish grin. Slowly, a smile came to William's face and he said, "Herod, I pray thou art right."

CHAPTER 17
August 1657

MARY'S ABSENCE WAS brief. In mid-August she surprised everyone by returning from Providence aboard the *Woodhouse*. That little ship, chartered by eleven Quakers, had recently come from England via New Amsterdam. The *Woodhouse* left five Quakers in the unreceptive Dutch colony and brought the rest to Providence.

There they found a warmer welcome at the home of Richard Scott and his wife Catherine, the sister of Anne Hutchinson. The Scotts were congenial hosts, and were soon convinced Quakers. Their guests rested after their voyage and planned their conversion of New England. Then two of the men walked off to Plymouth to begin their ministry.

The *Woodhouse* brought Mary and two Friends south to Newport. William could not conceal his dismay when Mary informed him that the Quakers would be staying at their home.

Living on Newport's southern edge meant that Herod didn't learn of events right away. She hadn't heard about the arrival of the *Woodhouse*, so she thought that Mary was still in Providence. But there at Sabbath meeting was her friend and the two Quakers, surrounded by curious Newporters. Carrying Dorcas on her hip, Herod joined the throng.

Her sons wouldn't have waited quietly, but Dorcas preferred to be carried in crowds. She sucked her thumb and twirled a strand of blond hair as Herod watched the Quakers talk. One was a recently-shaven young man, tanned from weeks at sea.

The other was a middle-aged woman clad in dark brown, with a plain white cape covering her shoulders. Her eyes went straight to the little girl in Herod's arms and she smiled. Dorcas shrank, hiding her face against Herod's shoulder. Then she peeked to see if the Quaker was watching.

The woman moved a little closer and winked. Dorcas hid again, but now it was a game. The motion attracted Mary's eye, and she saw Herod.

"My Friends, let me introduce you to Goodwife Herod Gardner, the sister of my heart. These are my brethren …." Herod didn't catch the woman's name, but Humphrey Norton was so unusual that it stuck in her mind.

The minister's arrival sent them all to their seats. George and their sons already occupied benches in the center of the meeting house. Herod took a seat near the door, for Dorcas was not one who would sit quietly for two hours. Escape with a fretful child was but a few steps away.

Though Mary ranked a seat in front, she and the female Quaker sat next to Herod. The man sat across the aisle from them. As the service began, Herod thought of the tales she'd heard of Quaker disruptions. What was going to happen here?

She was a little disappointed when Mary's friends sat quietly, listening to the sermon. However, Dorcas was anything but quiet. She stood on Herod's thigh, peering past Mary to the woman sitting by the aisle. Dorcas turned fussy when her mother made her sit, and the tantrum grew as Herod tried to hush her. It was time to take the child outside before she disrupted the service far more than these Quakers had done.

With the thrashing child in her arms, Herod tried to slip quietly past Mary and her new friend. Just as she reached the aisle, Dorcas wailed and then set a cascade of vomit down the flustered Herod's apron. Herod groaned, and Humphrey Norton rose. "Let me help thee," he said quietly.

"My cap," Herod said through gritted teeth. Dorcas had pulled it off and still had a grip on her hair. Norton loosened Dorcas' fingers, and then followed Herod to the door.

Once outside, Herod glared at her soiled apron. Dorcas' white gown was almost untouched, so when Norton held out his hands for the child, Herod handed her over. 'That girl will pitch another fit,' she thought.

Amazingly, Dorcas settled down in Humphrey's arms. Herod untied her soiled apron and slipped it carefully over her head. "What a mess," Humphrey said sympathetically.

"It's not the first time," Herod told him. She shook the garment, and then rolled it up, saying, "Dorcas has a weak belly."

"Dorcas – what a charming name. Know thou that it is Greek for gazelle?" Humphrey had the brightest blue eyes that Herod had ever seen, like Narragansett Bay in the sun.

Herod realized that she was staring at Humphrey like a teen in love. "What is a gazelle?"

"A creature like a deer. But Dorcas is also a woman in the Bible."

"Mr. Jefferay said that Peter raised Dorcas from the dead," Herod told him. "I hope he will raise my Dorcas. She's so sickly that I worry about her."

"She looks well enough to me," Norton commented. Herod told him that she was taking Dorcas home. "I will walk with thee to help with the child."

"Thank you, but it's not far," Herod said. Humphrey bid her farewell and returned to the meeting. Herod started on her two-mile trek. Despite what she told Humphrey, it was a long walk. However, she didn't want to take it with a stranger, no matter how charming.

A couple of days later, Herod got Dorcas to sleep under Mary Stanton's care, and then walked up to the Dyers' home. She hoped to catch her friend alone but Mary was sitting with one of the Friends in the orchard. Herod recognized Humphrey Norton. As she walked up to the pair, she watched them converse.

The man was young enough to be Mary's son, but Herod mused, 'They look almost like lovers, sitting there with their heads together.' Mary said something that made Humphrey laugh. When his head dropped back, he saw Herod coming up the path. "Goodwife Gardner," he called, waving a welcome.

"What a pleasure to see thee!" Mary exclaimed. "Join us, if thou will. Do thou remember my brother, Humphrey Norton?"

Herod tensed. It wasn't idle chat that she sought. She urgently needed advice, for she was pregnant again. How could she ask Mary about the illness that had accompanied Dorcas' birth in front of a man she barely knew?

"Welcome, sister," Humphrey said, reaching up to help Herod to a grassy seat. "How does thy little girl today?"

The Quaker seemed genuinely concerned and Herod's apprehension eased. "Dorcas has but a squeamish stomach. I hope she will grow out of it."

"The child is like that twig," Humphrey said, pointing to an apple sapling. "Its leaves are few and blighted as it struggles to grow. In time, with water and sun, it will prosper." He waved at the mature tree shading Herod, laden with hard apples beginning to blush. "God watches over thy Dorcas, just as he sends sun and rain for this orchard." Then the Quaker intrigued Herod by adding, "Last night I saw her as a woman grown, with babes at her feet."

"Brother Humphrey is noted for prophesy," Mary informed Herod. "He foretold that God would hide the *Woodhouse* from their enemies as if a great mist surrounded them, and so it happened. He also said the exact day they would land in New Amsterdam."

"Really?" Herod breathed. If Humphrey could foresee such things, then maybe he was right about Dorcas too. Perhaps her delicate little girl was destined to thrive.

"A lucky guess," said Humphrey. "It was God who led our vessel, as a man leads a horse by the head. When we met the fatal currents at New Amsterdam's Hell Gate, the Lord sent a shoal of fish to steer our ship.

"God sends what all of his creatures need. Thy darling daughter has a loving mother. These trees take in God's sun and water, and they nourish us." Humphrey looked up into the tree over their head. "That's a nice crop coming, Sister Mary. Thy husband cares well for his orchard."

The three of them formed a lopsided triangle, and Mary leaned into it. "Brother Norton knows his apple trees. Did I tell thee he worked in the orchards at Swarthmore Hall?"

Norton grinned. "At Swarthmore Brother Fox often taught us in the gardens. We Friends prayed and sang together; such glorious song like you never hear in a Puritan church. Brother Fox teaches that we all are planted at birth with Seed from which Christ grows, just as these apples bear tiny seeds in their cores. Sister Dyer and I bring this truth across the ocean, not only to the Puritans, but also to share with our friends in Christ's haven."

Mary helpfully supplied, "He means Rhode Island, Herod. Thou art lucky to live in such a friendly place. We sheltered here when Puritans cast us out. Now, just as Christ found rest in the Garden of Gethsemane, we Friends have a safe haven for the jailed to recuperate." Mary was still thin after her ordeal, and had a lingering cough. "When Brother Fox was in jail, Humphrey begged Lord Protector Cromwell to free our brother and take him instead."

Herod shifted irritably. She was losing interest. Worse, she was running out of time. Dorcas would wake soon, ready to nurse, but Herod still needed to talk with Mary about her pregnancy. But Norton looked far too comfortable to leave.

"This is where we will prepare to spread God's truth," he said. "Soon I may follow my brothers to Plymouth, and Sister Clark set off for Boston this morning."

"Who is she?" Herod asked.

"You met her yesterday at the meeting house," Mary said. Now Herod remembered the broad-shouldered woman who had winked at Dorcas. "God called her to Boston." Mary pointed northward and Herod's eyes followed, but the Quaker was long gone. "She will seek friendly ears and beg the magistrates to soften their hearts."

"She went alone? Don't you fear that she will be jailed?" asked Herod.

"Sister Clark and the rest of our English brethren walk many roads alone, and they have been persecuted for years," Mary told her. "We cannot change those evil laws unless we go there and speak with them."

"So that is what we shall do," Humphrey said. "We shall talk, and question, and beset them until they listen."

"Like a plague of mosquitoes sent by God?" Herod asked ironically. Humphrey and Mary laughed, but Herod added, "The more you bother the Puritans, the worse their laws get."

"What if Christ stayed silent in fear of the Romans, who needed his teachings the most?" asked Humphrey. "Brother Fox brought the truth to all of us. If we spread his word among the Puritans, they too may come to the Light."

"Christ said. *you shall know them by their fruits*," Mary concluded.

It wasn't the 'Seed' that was growing in Herod – it was irritation. She'd come for advice and the intimacy that she and Mary had once shared, but neither were to be found today. The Quakers were a kindred pair and Herod was the outsider. She scrambled to her feet and announced, "I told George that I wouldn't be gone long. I bid you good day."

Sensing her friend's distress, Mary said, "Wait –" but Herod was already striding back along the orchard path.

As she walked the dusty road toward home, Herod felt like crying. Her emotions were on a hair trigger these days – one of the things which let her know that she was breeding. Instead of suppressing them, she let her tears flow.

'What ails Mary? She will never be the same friend as long as she is with them.' Herod kept picturing the Quakers side-by-side under the tree. To her it seemed more intimate than two friends talking of the faith that absorbed them.

'I don't know why William doesn't throw that Norton fellow out of his barn,' she thought. 'Maybe he will take himself to Boston to preach and the Puritans will shove him onto a boat back to England.'

Wrapped in bitter musings, she didn't hear a horse approaching from behind. "Is that you, Herod? What brings you to this end of Newport?" The rider's voice made her jump, but then she recognized John Porter astride his chestnut gelding, dressed in a loose white shirt, comfortable breeches, and tall boots.

Herod hastily dried her eyes with her sleeve and called, "Hello, John. I came to see Mary, but she is busy with *Brother* Norton."

"Plotting their conquest of Massachusetts?" John reined Thor to a halt, but the horse sidestepped. "Whoa, there," he said soothingly to the animal, and then dismounted. To Herod he said, "Not polite to talk to you from on high." Noticing her reddened eyes, John added, "Something wrong?"

"No, I'm just …."

"Disappointed?" John suggested.

Herod nodded. "I was so glad when Mary came home, but since then I scarcely see her."

Thor nudged John hard enough to make him stagger. He tugged the horse's bridle in reproof, telling Herod, "He hates to stand. Are you going home?" She nodded. "Then Thor and I shall escort you since my meeting with Mr. Easton is done. Would you ride?"

Herod beamed at the suggestion, but thought better of it. She didn't know what caused her illness while she carried Dorcas, and dared not risk anything new during this pregnancy. "Mayhap I shouldn't," she regretfully told John.

"I'll give you a leg up." Herod shook her head and John urged, "It's a warm day for walking, and I heard that you'd been sick."

At John's mention of her illness, Herod blinked back tears again. He said, "Something's wrong, isn't it? You can tell me."

Herod looked away from John's dark, probing gaze. "I – I am breeding again, and I'm so afraid," she whispered. "I was so sick before Dorcas came. They made me lie abed for weeks, and my head felt like someone was splitting it with an axe, and I swelled …."

The words caught in Herod's throat when she repeated, "I'm so afraid. I lay wake every night because they tell me it could happen again. The midwife said the babe and I might die. I can't ask Dr. Clarke because he's still in London, so I meant to ask Mary."

"But she is busy," John finished her thought. "Too bad Mrs. Hutchinson is gone. She was a fine midwife, and brought my own daughter. What thinks Goodman Gardner?"

"George just says, 'Maybe it won't happen.' Perhaps he's right. I feel well now, except I can't stop crying." Herod started walking, with John keeping pace at her side.

"That's natural – you are breeding," Porter said in the same soothing tone that he had used on his horse. He held Thor's reins in a casual grip, letting the animal grab a mouthful of grass. Thor ambled contentedly, swishing his tail at a fly on his flank.

"I know little of your ailment, but more about your fear," John said. "You know that Margaret and I married late." Herod's eyebrows rose, for John rarely spoke of his wife. "She had another husband before me, but he died as a young man. They had but one daughter who survived. She is Philip Sherman's wife."

Herod barely knew the Shermans, for the couple lived at the northern end of Rhode Island. Like many other island residents, they had come from Massachusetts to escape the Puritans.

"Margaret was near forty when we wed; several years older than me. She bore our daughter not long after. Lord, was she ill. She lost another two before they were born and was sick with them too. Margaret was as fearful as you are, so we dared not risk any more births."

"How?" Herod asked eagerly. Herbs might end a pregnancy, but she knew of no way to prevent one.

"One part luck, three parts reluctance," John said ruefully. "You may be as glad to see the change of life as we were."

Herod was feeling better – simply telling John of her dread had eased her mind. She sighed deeply, just as Porter said, "Would you like to hear a secret to sweep your blues away?"

She smiled wanly. "A secret? What's afoot?"

"I'm negotiating with the Narragansett chiefs to buy land on the west side of the bay. The deal's not done, so don't tell. I don't want anyone bulling in on it."

"You and Mrs. Porter?"

"Friends of mine. John Hull – he's a goldsmith in Boston. Sam Wilbore, who is married to my daughter, and two other Portsmouth men."

Another wave of desolation swept over Herod – would John be leaving her life, too? Porter might not be the close confidant that Mary had been, but he was a resourceful friend. Herod swallowed before asking, "Are you going there soon?"

"Not at all," he said. "For now I'm happier in town. It's wild land and more of an investment now, but it is so beautiful. The Narragansetts call it Pettaquamscutt. It's set back from the sea and sheltered from storms. There are fields already cleared by the Indians for their corn, so it's ready for farming or livestock."

Herod's pulse quickened. She and George often talked about buying more land, but Newport land was expensive. George owned enough to support their family, but what would they do when it came time to pass it to their sons? If they split the land equally, none of their boys would get enough to make a living. Should they give most of it to Benoni, with a pittance for the other four? What of a dowry for Dorcas? She asked John, "Is your land cheaper than it is here?"

"By far," he laughed. "We may get as much as Newport town rests on for twenty pounds. I make no promises, but if the Narragansetts sell good land at such prices, perhaps you and George should consider it."

Herod raised her eyebrows in mock horror. "What – live with the Indians?"

"You prefer the Quakers?"

"There aren't many of them."

"There will be," John chuckled. "Mrs. Dyer is making her converts and young Norton has girls swooning at his feet. Every heartsick maid will soon be a Quaker."

"Mary seems besotted," Herod said sourly. "I don't know whether by Humphrey Norton or those strange notions."

"I can't speak for Norton, but Quaker beliefs aren't so outlandish. They are much like Mrs. Hutchinson's, and you regarded her well."

"I never saw Anne sit under a tree, waiting for God to put words into her mouth."

"But like her, the Quakers want their revelations straight from God, not from a preacher. Methinks I know what Mrs. Dyer likes best about the Friends." Herod looked questioningly at John. "She can preach. Even here in Rhode Island, where we value our soul liberty, you have never heard a woman preach. Your friend has power like she's never seen in her life."

Herod smiled. "Mary may preach, but one of her Friends sees the future." John snorted in disbelief. "She said that Brother Norton foretold the day they would land."

"A fortunate guess?"

"That's what Humphrey said," laughed Herod. "He also said God sent a shoal of fish to guide them through Hell Gate."

"Fish ride the currents through there every day," John scoffed. "Might have been shad or herring. If they glitter in the sun, any competent captain can follow them to the fastest water."

"Follow the fishes," Herod chuckled. She pictured Humphrey peering over the side, pointing the way to safe passage. Then a more sobering image came: Mary pointing northward. Would she soon lead the way herself? Herod said, "At least Mary did not go to Boston and Plymouth like her brethren. There are three of them in jail now and who knows when they will be freed?"

"Mistress Dyer already spent months in Boston's jail," John reminded Herod. "That won't daunt her. For now, she's content to win friends in Rhode Island. What will she do when one of her converts faces the lash?"

"She may go to Massachusetts," Herod said uneasily.

"Governor Endecott might remember her fondly from the years that her family dwelt there, but he's not a forgiving man. If she does go to Boston, I tremble for her."

CHAPTER 18
September - December 1657

AS HEROD'S PREGNANCY advanced, she remained healthy. Everyone said that her fate lay in God's hands, so telling herself that dread would change nothing, Herod put her fears aside.

At the end of summer Herod also put aside housework and gardening. The risk of illness rid her of chores for the first time since she was a very young girl. Mary Stanton did most of the cooking under Herod's supervision. George and the boys tended the garden and harvested crops. Herod didn't even have to fetch water. She was free.

September was a golden month in New England, and Herod took to exploring the island's southern paths. Not so many years ago Benoni and Henry would have shared the walk with her, and she'd carry Georgie on her hip. But the older boys were haying with George, and the midwife had warned Herod, "Don't go toting that little girl everywhere." Dorcas stayed home with the Stanton girl.

Herod liked taking six-year old Willy or the younger Nick when they didn't have chores, but Georgie was a puzzle. He adored Ben and tried to best Henry feat for feat, but couldn't seem to leave his little brothers in peace. Splashing Willy at the beach or scaring him by leaping out of the dark was Georgie's delight, so Herod often kept them apart. Now Georgie was raking hay with their father. If his pranks bothered his brothers, they would keep him in line.

'I wish that Willy stood up for himself,' Herod thought. Willy had George's slate-blue eyes, and also his father's preference for avoiding trouble. He quietly did as told, and then slipped away for solitary pursuits. Even when he was walking with his mother, Willy didn't have much to say. He couldn't walk by a flat rock without tipping it up to see ants and grubs underneath, and then showing them to his mother. She had liked the same solitary rambles as a girl, so if Willy would rather amuse himself than walk with her, Herod didn't mind.

Chubby little Nick was the cheeriest of Herod's boys, and people said he looked the most like her. Nick roved widely and darted after butterflies as fast as his three-year old legs could go, but he wore out quickly. If Herod wanted to go far, Nick stayed at home too.

September's balmy days blended into October's crisp afternoons, which lingered into November. Winter's cold seemed loath to invade Herod's enchanted world. She took advantage of the fair weather to stroll lanes fenced with rails or stone walls, converse with lads tending flocks of sheep, and make friends with their dogs.

If Herod tired, she picked a knoll to enjoy whichever view she chose. In the north lay Newport and its lovely, sheltered harbor. Westward lay Conanicut Island, and behind it the blue-green hills where John Porter was buying land. To the south, the ocean beckoned with foaming sapphire waves. The sea turned as gray as Rhode Island's headlands in foul weather, so Herod saved beach ventures for fair days during that magical autumn.

'If only this season could last forever,' she dreamed. 'If only my babe would come now, not in winter.'

Those dark days lay ahead, and Herod dreaded them. Never feeling warm enough, the windows shuttered and doors closed tight to keep out the frost. There were no more fresh vegetables dripping dew from the garden; just turnips and carrots slowly moldering in the root cellar, dried beans, and withered pumpkin rings.

The hens would soon quit laying and the calves were weaned, so there would be no more eggs or fresh milk. Herod had made plenty of cheese and butter during the summer, and there would be fresh venison if George was lucky at hunting. Otherwise, the family faced tiresome meals of salt pork and smoked hams or bacon.

Herod sighed when she thought of winter's constant crowding, with eight Gardners and one Stanton shut in two rooms. Five boys made a lot of noise, and though Dorcas looked like a wide-eyed fairy child with silky blond hair, she was perfecting a toddler's tantrums. She ruled her father like a charming tyrant, but George claimed he was happy to take the child off her exasperated mother's hands.

'Thank God for Mary Stanton,' Herod thought. The girl was only twelve, just Herod's age when her father had died, but she could cook a stew and was learning to bake. Remembering how much she had relished free time at that age, Herod released the girl for a while each day. In return,

Mary brought back bouquets of asters and goldenrod. That morning she'd returned with hawthorn fruit, like tiny apples cupped in her apron.

George was a busy man at this time of the year, with turnips and corn to harvest, wheat to sow, and firewood to cut. He could barely stay awake through supper before tumbling into bed to snore the night away. To Herod, the best part of winter was seeing more of her husband.

Ben, broad-shouldered and proud of his growing strength, could split wood as easily as his father. Each brother lightened George's burden in his own way. Even little Nick tossed cracked corn to the chickens and picked up kindling. The boy also sat with Herod to pick bits of hull from dried beans while they told stories to each other.

Red-haired Henry, now eleven, was another fine storyteller, and Herod wished that he could walk with her more often. The cleverest of her boys, Henry was most likely to volunteer when his mother asked for a helper. He might get stuck scrubbing the hearth with Mary Stanton, but Herod relished listening to the pair as they teased each other like brother and sister. When the chore was done they all enjoyed a slab of warm bread and fresh butter before Henry went off to the fields.

Whether she was walking or daydreaming, Herod thought most about the baby growing in her belly. Plenty of people had told her what she risked. Even old Jane Hawkins, Rhode Island's most experienced midwife, had repeated Sarah Grand's warning – Herod would be wise to end this pregnancy. "Take the herbs now," the wizened woman said flatly. "The drink alone'll make you wish you were dead. Wait 'til you are sick, and it will kill you."

Herod listened to the callous advice calmly, and then refused Jane's drink. Many years ago she'd been desperate enough to take her own life, but did not because she was carrying Benoni. If Herod protected this tiny life now, as she had spared Benoni, surely it would not harm her. Or so she hoped. The knowledge that Herod was carrying her last baby brought peace and gloom to her in equal measure.

In October, Humphrey Norton went to Plymouth to protest the abuse dealt to English Friends that summer. The rest of the English Quakers went on similar missions to Boston, Sandwich, and New Amsterdam. During one of her visits, Mary Dyer worried to Herod, "No doubt they are all in jail. I pray to God they aren't being abused."

With Humphrey gone, Herod thought that surely she would see more of Mary. At times she could lure her friend into telling her Newport gossip, but Mary was far more concerned by what was going on in the Puritan colonies. "Massachusetts has just passed more laws barring Friends," she told Herod. "They lashed two of my brothers thirty strokes each, but whipping is no longer punishment enough. A man who speaks his mind will be flogged. If he returns, they will cut off his ear as well. Let him return a third time, and the governor will order his tongue bored through with a red-hot awl."

"It's good that George and I aren't going hence," Herod joked uneasily.

Mary said earnestly, "Only God knows what may come. Thou may visit Boston again."

"Not willingly," was Herod's reply. "I pray that you won't go there."

"Not until God calls me."

December's arrival finally banished Indian summer with six inches of snow. It grew cold enough to freeze water indoors unless the shutters and doors were closed tight, and Herod's mood tumbled with the temperature. As she began her pre-birth confinement, every twinge brought dread that her illness was flaring.

The Gardners' home seemed increasingly smaller. The shed was too cold for sleeping, so the older boys nested together in the loft. The youngsters filled George and Herod's bed like a litter of leggy hound pups. Herod's embroidered bed curtains helped keep them warm at night, but the confined air was near-stifling.

In mid-month Mary came to visit, bringing a familiar pair of Friends. Herod remembered seeing the broad-shouldered woman at Sabbath meeting that summer. The Quaker had winked at Dorcas just before the little girl puked on Herod's apron.

The other visitor was Humphrey Norton. "Sister Gardner, thou look well," he exclaimed. "I told thee that God was watching." Norton, however, was thin. The brown curls that once fell to his shoulders were hacked so short that his scalp showed.

Then Georgie chased Willy in from the second room. Herod shouted over their din, "Willy, back in there with you. Georgie, have you fetched water yet?"

"No, Ma," he said warily. Herod looked sternly toward a yoke and buckets that the lad had dropped by the door an hour ago. Georgie shouldered the yoke and went outside.

Mary frowned. "What a racket when thou might take ill! I will tell thy Hannah that she must take these boys home with her."

"She will after Christmas," Herod assured her friend.

"I hope that is soon enough," Mary said. Then she turned to Herod's other guests. "Brother Norton has just been released from jail in Plymouth."

"I went there to spread Christ's word," Humphrey reminded Herod. "The priests were hostile, but many were curious. We could find Friends there if they aren't too fearful."

"Will you go back?" Herod asked.

"The magistrates arrested me, but then I waited in jail as they decided what to do," Humphrey said. "I demanded a trial, which at length they granted. I was the lucky one, for I was never abused. Now I am banished."

"I hope you won't return," Herod commented.

"God is calling me to the Long Island. Puritans in Southold need the Light as sorely as Massachusetts does. Sister Clark came from Boston." Norton looked to Herod's other visitor.

Herod thought that Sister Clark would have looked more at home on a milking stool, with a bucket between her knees and calming a nervous cow. Though she was a large-framed woman, Sister Clark was gaunt, and looked like she shared Humphrey's exhaustion.

Mary said, "Sister Clark has just been set free. She and Brother Norton will pass the winter with us."

George was sitting by Herod's bed, his chair protectively placed between her and the Quakers. He broke his silence to ask, "What thinks William of that?"

Mary confessed, "He is not pleased."

"He is still a courteous host," Humphrey added. "If God softens his heart, we may yet convince him." George snorted skeptically.

Sister Clark said from her hearthside seat, "When God called me to spread the truth, he never spoke to my husband." She was watching Dorcas and Nick play with longing eyes. "I've not seen my children in years."

"Amen," murmured Mary.

"What will God demand next?" Sister Clark asked hoarsely. That forlorn gaze went to Mary. "It is not God's will to separate thee and thy husband. We will shelter elsewhere if our presence drives you apart."

"That will not happen," Mary said confidently.

Herod asked the group, "How can you endure this? Your families are torn apart, you are tortured —"

Norton said, "Plymouth did me no harm past cutting my hair to suit them." He fingered his ragged stubble. "But Sister Clark had a more harrowing time."

The woman from London was spreading her hands before the fire. She rubbed them as though to press the flames' warmth into chilled flesh. "Aye," she said at last. "Three months in their jail. No light, no fire, fed scraps that I'd have tossed to the dogs."

"I remember it well," said Mary, "though they kept me but two months."

"But they didn't do *this* to thee," said Sister Clark. She loosened her jacket and tugged her blouse from one shoulder. Turning her back, she displayed several scars. Fading welts draped themselves across pale flesh like the cords that had created them. Herod gasped.

"Twenty stripes, laid on with fury," Sister Clark exclaimed. "Locked in the dark like a mad dog."

"I know," Mary said soothingly.

"But thou had Sister Burden to huddle with for warmth, and to whisper with at night after the jailers mocked thee. The miserable girls who shared my quarters for scolding or theft feared to speak, lest they be deemed Quakers as well. If I return, the punishment will be far worse."

"Thou and Brother Norton need not return," said Mary. "Thou must rest. Stay on Rhode Island and teach our converts. I shall visit the willing in Boston."

Herod and Humphrey cried, "No!" at the same time. He added, "Remember what the magistrates did to our brethren? Two of them were given thirty lashes. That would kill thee, Sister Dyer."

"Even if they don't take the lash to thee, a winter in that jail will kill thee," Sister Clark added. "We made our plan with Brother Fox and will keep to it. We, with the other *Woodhouse* brethren, will seek those we can convince."

"I can do that as well as thou," Mary declared.

"But who better speaks to Christ's Seed in Rhode Island? Thou art one of them, Sister Dyer. Thou have already convinced the Scotts ...." Humphrey glanced at the Gardners, but Herod silently shook her head. George would not meet his eyes. Humphrey barely hesitated before finishing, "Teach here, Sister, and we will reach the Puritans."

"I'm not afraid to test their laws."

"No?" Sister Clark looked levelly at Mary. "Thou should be."

CHAPTER 19
January 1658

A LONG WALK IN JANUARY'S first week brought Mary Dyer to the Gardners' yard. The lanes were well-trampled, but snow between the road and the Gardners' door was broken only by a single set of tracks. It came nearly to Mary's knees, and she was puffing when she knocked on the door.

There was plenty of noise inside, but nobody opened the door. She pounded harder, calling "Herod, 'tis Mary." This time she heard an answering call, so she let herself in.

Mary found Herod lying in bed with a damp cloth draped over her face. George was nowhere in sight, but Herod's younger boys were wrestling noisily by the fireplace. Georgie had Willy pinned to the floor, and he looked up at Mary guiltily.

Nick had apparently caught an elbow to the nose, for he sat to one side crying and dabbing at the reddened appendage. Dorcas stood by Herod's bed, wailing, "Mama, Mama, Mama," bouncing on her toes and tugging at Herod's quilt.

With a single glance at the chaotic scene, Mary snapped at Georgie, "Young man, what are thou thinking? Let thy brother up, both of you into the second room, and I don't want to hear another sound from thee.

"Nick, show me thy nose." The sniffling boy trotted over and leaned close to Mary. A firelit exam showed that his nose was not bleeding, so Mary kissed it. "That will fix thee. Now, go keep an eye to thy brothers. If they make trouble, come and tell me."

Herod pulled the rag from her face when she heard Mary's voice. With her bloodshot eyes and blotched and puffy face, she looked as miserable as Nick. She reached for Dorcas, but Mary got there first. "Dorcas, thy skirt is soaked. Herod, has she another?"

"In that chest," Herod said. A tear oozed from the corner of one eye, but she was smiling gratefully.

Mary deftly changed the little girl's skirt, asking Herod, "Where are thy husband and the Stanton girl?"

"Avis had need of Mary today, and George went to fetch the midwife. They should be here soon."

As if on cue, the door opened. However, it was Henry, with an empty chamber pot in one hand and a wooden bowl filled with snow in the other. He grinned when he saw Mary. "Mrs. Dyer, am I glad to see you. Mama's sick."

"And he's the finest nurse," Herod added. The lad made an exaggerated grimace. "Ben is bringing more firewood," he said, "and here's some fresh snow." He wrapped a handful of snow in Herod's face cloth, and then shook it out and gave the rag back to her.

Herod gasped when the chill hit her forehead, and then sighed. "Thank you, Henry; that feels good. I wish we had snow when I nursed my father." To Mary she said, "The sickness is back."

"So it seems, Herod. Thy head?"

"I want to split it with an axe to let the pain out. When I stand –"

"Don't stand," Mary advised. "Thy belly?"

"It hurts and I'm puking. Poor Henry just took a pot to the privy." Mary took one of Herod's hands. Bones and veins were hidden under mounded skin. There was no doubt – Herod's hands had swollen and her cheeks remained puffy, even though her crying had stopped.

The door flew open again. This time it was Benoni, barely able to see around a towering armful of firewood. He called, "Mama, I saw Papa in the lane with the midwife." Then the thirteen-year old saw Mary. He let the wood clatter to the hearth with a relieved "Whew! I am glad you're here, Mrs. Dyer."

"And I'm grateful thy mother has such fine help," Mary replied.

Jane Hawkins was too feeble to travel from Portsmouth in winter, but Sarah Grand was well-known for her able help at birthing. She checked the younger woman thoroughly; poking Herod's thickened ankles and prodding her abdomen hard enough to make her wince. "Your babe's fine so far," Sarah announced. "It's kicking like a mule. As for you …." Sarah shook her head, and Herod winced again. "We figured that you're due in six weeks?"

"Aye."

"You remember what I said – this babe might well kill you."

George blanched, and Herod groaned, "How could I forget?"

"And you still won't take the herbs and end this now?"

Mary expected tears from Herod, but instead her jaw muscles stood out in knots before she said resolutely, "Not if God himself ordered me."

"Then your life and that babe's await his pleasure," Sarah said heavily. "You stay in that bed until it comes. Piss in the pot, and don't stir unless the house catches fire."

Sarah couldn't stay long, but as George fetched her cloak, she told him loudly enough for Herod and Mary to hear, "That wife of yours used to be such a beauty, but look at her now. She looks as old as me! She is breeding herself to an early grave, so not one more babe if you want to keep her. Do you understand me?"

George nodded reluctantly as he reached for his own coat. "Nay, Goodman, I'm going no further than Coggeshall's place. You stay with your wife and think on whether you want to keep her." Sarah shut the door behind her with an angry thud.

Herod's tension had eased when Sarah said the baby was still healthy. But when the midwife spoke of her premature death, she'd pulled the damp rag from her ashen forehead. She asked Mary quietly, "Do you think I might die?"

"We all shall die," Mary replied. "But I do not believe that God means to call thee yet."

George was glum-faced. "Maybe she's right. You should take the herbs."

"Not you too," Herod growled.

"What if this child kills you? Better to take this one life than to lose you both."

Herod struggled to sit upright, and then cried out and gripped her head with both hands. Mary dampened Herod's rag to wipe her friend's face. "Lie back, dear. Thou must stay calm."

She said to George, "Herod has made her decision, so speak no more of that. Let's bring some peace into this house. Herod, I thought Hannah meant to keep thy babes."

"She will when my time is closer," Herod groaned, pressing the cold rag to her closed eyes.

"The time has come. I will send one of my sons to tell her to fetch the little ones without delay. Benoni can stay here and help us."

"And Henry," cried Herod.

The boy rolled his eyes at Mary, but told his mother, "Me too."

"Hannah will take good care of the others, but I shall stay with thee."

"But it's near two months before this babe comes, Mary. I can't keep you from home for that long."

"I won't be here all the time, Herod, but thou art in need. William has Kate for help." Now sixteen, the bondservant Kate was skilled at housewifery, and had learned to read and write. Her older sister, Peggy, was freed from servitude when she turned eighteen, and had married a Portsmouth man.

"William will miss you, and so will your children," Herod warned.

"They will understand," Mary assured her.

"I doubt that," was George's reply, and he was right. After the next time he spoke with Dyer, George confided to Herod, "William said they are husband and wife in name only. She is angry over his naval ventures, and because he won't become a Quaker. Well, he is angry because she *is* one, and says their rift may never mend."

"How sad," Herod said, for she shared William's sense of loss.

Apparently, word got out that 'Sister Gardner' needed comfort. Humphrey Norton was her first visitor. "I came to bid thee farewell," he explained. "I'm off to the Long Island."

"To preach to the Dutch?" Herod waved a dismissive hand. "Don't bother yourself with John Hicks."

"Nay, it's the souls at Southold I mean to reach." Connecticut's Puritans had established that outpost on eastern Long Island nearly eighteen years before. "I hope to find friendly ears there, and it may be some time before I can return." He startled Herod by asking, "Would thou mind if I bless thy child?"

"Blessings might do us both some good," Herod answered. Tears came to her eyes when Norton bowed his close-cropped head, placed his palms on her swollen abdomen, and prayed silently.

When finished he asked, "Remember when I told thee that God would protect thy little Dorcas?" Herod nodded. "And now she is doing well." Herod nodded again. "I pray thou will bear another fine girl."

Herod could barely breathe. "And do you see her children, as you saw Dorcas with babes at her feet?" She hoped for a mystical revelation, but Humphrey merely shook his head. She thanked him, adding, "I want so much for this one to live. Whether it's a girl or not, she's all I can think about now."

"Don't be afraid. God will preserve you both."

"I *am* afraid, but still hopeful," answered Herod. "This babe feels stronger than Dorcas was. Perhaps it's a boy, and he is well. Thank you for your blessing." The jealousy Herod once felt toward Humphrey was long gone, and she felt a chill when she concluded self-consciously, "I pray thee meet no harm on Long Island."

Humphrey beamed at her. "Whatever happens, God will give me the strength to endure, just as He will bear thee up when this babe comes."

Herod's next visitor was Sister Clark. Now that her cheeks were filling out, Sister Clark, whose given name was Mary, looked more youthful. At first she seemed ill at ease, chatting about Herod's health and her children. When Herod told her that Dorcas and the other little ones were at her daughter's home, Mary said ruefully, "I hoped that they would be here."

Herod shook her head, and then said, "Mrs. Dyer says you have children in England."

Mary Clark looked into the fire, and then suddenly clapped her palm over her mouth and sniffled. "When I heard Brother Fox preach in London, my heart melted. I had no choice but to follow him, for my soul was dying before I heard his words." Herod murmured encouragingly. "Losing my children was a terrible blow, but I had to do it.

"Thy daughter is so like mine when I left her." Then the words came tumbling out. "When I saw thy little girl, I thought she was a ghost. My Priscilla and her brothers live with their papa and grandmama, so they are well cared for. I will return to them when my mission is over."

"When will that be?"

Sister Clark gave Herod a wan smile. "When my heart tells me I've done enough for the Lord."

"Isn't being whipped enough?"

"I know not," Mary Clark admitted. "It is not in me to return to Boston. Some of those Puritans have souls as black as night and cannot be changed. They nearly killed Brother Holder when they flogged him, but he's returning. His heart is braver than mine. After lying in their jail for three months, I've seen enough of cold cells. In the spring, I will go where God calls, but pray it is some warmer place."

"I'm with you," Herod chuckled.

Mary Clark smiled, but continued earnestly, "I see that thou are not drawn to the Friends. God has gifted Sister Dyer to awaken the Seed in us. She hopes to persuade thee, but thou belong here with thy family. Follow thy heart."

Feeling a rush of kinship with the Quaker, Herod said, "Thank you. I would tell you to do the same, but fear that you would follow it back to Boston. Let the Puritans save themselves, and come to see me when this babe is born."

"I will, and hope to see that lovely Dorcas too," Mary said. "I pray that thy birthing goes easily. My life has been hell at times, but I am here at God's wish. He will surely heed my prayers and look kindly upon thee."

Long winter nights were hard for Herod to bear. When the fire burned down to embers and the room cooled, she awoke. With George or Mary's support, she'd squat awkwardly over a chamber pot, ashamed at piddling in front of everyone like a toddler. If the weather permitted, George went to the outhouse. If it was stormy, he peed in a pot in the second room. When he returned, he fed the fire and tumbled back into bed.

The main room, used for sleeping, kitchen, and parlor, was kept so well-heated that Benoni and Henry slept in the loft overhead. Mary Stanton had shared the Gardners' bed before Mary Dyer came to stay, but now she slept at home if she could travel.

The room soon warmed with fresh wood on the fire, but the adults still huddled under their quilts. Herod slept nearest to the fire for warmth. On some nights Mary slept beside her, but often George lay by Herod, surreptitiously cupping her breast with a comforting hand as he relaxed into sleep. Soon he began to snore.

Herod often lay sleepless for hours, and sometimes the sun's first light outlined the shutters before she finally dozed off. It was during these bleak wakeful periods that she feared death the most, or worried that the babe would emerge from her womb blue and lifeless. She relived tales of the monster that Mary had birthed. Her heart and head throbbed in a jagged tempo while Herod wondered if the little one she carried would be marked by her illness. What if the baby was simple or sickly? And what if she herself remained bedridden for the rest of her shortened life?

Mary became more precious to Herod than ever during these fear-ridden nights. Sometimes while George fed the fire, she moved next to Herod. Then, whether she couldn't sleep herself or sensed Herod's distress, she silently rubbed her friend's back or draped an arm over Herod's waist and massaged her aching belly. It was during these times of wordless comfort that Herod knew that she would do anything for Mary Dyer.

An impressive thaw came in the last days of January. For three days a southerly breeze set the eaves dripping. Mary threw open the shutters and door. Herod wanted to see outside, so George and the boys moved Herod's bed. Henry brought in an armload of willow switches. When set in a bucket of water, they soon sprouted fuzzy gray pussy-toes.

Mary pounded a handful of corn and tossed it over the trampled, dirty snow. Soon Herod watched bold blue jays, cautious doves clad in modest tan, and chickadees with perky black caps dart in to peck at their feast.

When a horse and rider came into view, Herod cheered even further. Who else would come here on horseback but John Porter? A little closer, and she could see that the horse wasn't the chestnut gelding that John usually rode. It was a chunky gray, like the elderly pony that John had given to the Gardner boys, but taller.

Herod didn't recognize that horse, but it was John after all. Ben and Henry ran out to hold the animal while he dismounted. John untied a sack from his saddle and gave it to Ben. Henry took the horse to the barn. With John at his heels, Ben cradled the bundle in his arms and brought it to his mother.

"What's that, Ben?" Herod asked, trembling with excitement.

"Mr. Porter says they're eggs."

"At this time of year?" asked George.

"Why not?" John said. He untied his cloak, but waved off Mary Stanton. "Don't bother yourself, young lady. I can hang it."

He opened the sack and showed Herod straw-wrapped bundles the size of his fist. "I coated them in lard for a mid-winter treat. Crack 'em in a bowl before you use them, for sometimes they spoil. I borrowed that mare to bring them to you. Thor would buck like a colt in this balmy weather. You'd have scrambled eggs."

"Why, thank thee, Brother Porter. They will be a treat," said Mary Dyer. "How would thou have them, Herod? Fried? Pudding?"

"Boiled," suggested George.

"Cake!" shouted Ben, echoed by Henry and Mary Stanton.

John said, "There are a dozen so you may try them all ways, if they are still good."

"Let's soak some pumpkin for pudding, and tomorrow I will help thee with a cake," suggested Mary Dyer to the girl.

"And boil a couple," said Herod. "I'm tired of venison, but can't abide salt pork at all," she told John.

He pulled a chair closer to sit by Herod's bed. "Now, tell me how you fare."

"Not too bad, so long as I lie here and do nothing," she replied. She waved at the open door. "Just seeing the sun makes me feel better. Too bad it can't last."

"Not much longer," George agreed.

"I'm afraid so," said John. "Clouds in the northwest are getting thicker. Change is in the air. I got my trip across the bay done just in time."

"You crossed at this time of year?" asked George. "Tip over, and you would be dead in a minute. What could be so important?"

"Couldn't resist that fair sailing weather, so I hired Sam Dyer and his ketch. Remember that Indian land I spoke of?" Herod nodded. "I just signed the deed with the Narragansett chiefs. Ever see that big rock above the bay's west shore? Can't see it from here, for Conanicut Island is in the way. You have to be out in the bay."

Herod shook her head, but Henry crowed, "I have – Ben and I have been a-sailing with Sam too!"

"Well, my partners and I own that rock now, with the land all around it, clear down to the Pettaquamscutt River. Nice land, George."

"Full of Indians," was George's placid comment.

"We'll let the Narragansetts hunt there, but they promised to leave when settlers begin to come. I set my earmark on the strip along the river, but there's enough good land for all your sons to have their own farms." John spoke casually, but Herod saw that his dark eyes were fixed keenly on George.

The farmer frowned and sat up straighter on his bench. "I hear those Indians have guns from the Dutch, and Mr. Coddington brought a load from England that he never accounted for. Could be those Indians have enough arms to make trouble."

"You are thinking of the Pequots," John said. "Their war was twenty years ago, and they are broken up now. The Narragansetts willingly sold us the land. They don't want trouble – in fact, they want to sell more land to us."

"George, we must look at it," Herod implored.

Mary added, "Might be the chance of a lifetime."

"Perhaps in the spring," George conceded. "I'm not crossing the bay in winter."

"The land won't be divided for some time," Porter admitted. "We will hold onto it until the bounds are settled with Connecticut."

Mary nodded her approval, and Herod gripped her friend's hand in excitement. However, George's gaze flicked from Porter to Herod and back again, and he was frowning. "I'm not sure that I want to go there at all," he grumbled. "I prefer to buy more Newport land. I've more sheep than ever, wool's fetching a good price, and Mr. Coddington is shipping salt mutton to Barbados for me. Soon I can buy more land here, and not battle wolves and Indians."

"My William is shipping mutton south as well," Mary said.

"What thinks he of John's land?" George asked.

"He's been too busy to look at it, but in the spring …."

George slouched lower on his bench, biting his lip and bouncing first one leg, and then the other. Herod knew these signs well. George would not change his mind any time soon. She wanted to throw her mending at him for his stubbornness, but instead suggested, "George, you could go with William."

"The spring it is," John said smoothly. "Look, I don't want to excite Herod. We can speak of it when she's past her illness. Perhaps I should go now."

"No!" Herod protested. "You just got here. I swear that I'll be more upset if you leave without telling me what's new."

So John lingered, telling them of his meeting the Narragansett chiefs at Richard Smith's trading post. Then he said that he must get back to Portsmouth before dark, and rode away.

As soon as he was gone, George began checking his shot bag and powder horn. "You can't go hunting now," Herod said.

"Weather's changing. If you want fresh venison, I should go while I can," he replied, biting his words short. He avoided meeting her eyes when he kissed her forehead, and then out the door he went.

"Why must George go now?" Herod asked Mary fretfully. "It will be dark soon."

"Brother George may not have to go far. He told me that he tossed some corn near the woods for bait," Mary explained. "If he doesn't go now it will be wasted."

"I suppose he must," Herod agreed. "Any way, there's no way to stop him once he decides to do something – or not. I don't know if he will ever go see John's land."

"Give him time to think."

"He can be hard to move as a chestnut tree," Herod insisted. "Some things I can bear, like when he won't fix a frayed latch string before it breaks, but why does he dig in his heels on buying land for his sons?"

"Thou know Brother George better than I, but might he be jealous of Brother Porter?"

"Why? John helped us so much with Tom Painter. And I never see John without George there, so he can't be jealous in *that* way."

"Art thou sure? Thou call him 'John,' where I call few men by their first names."

"Because Mr. Porter insists that we both call him John. We are but friends."

"Of course, but I wonder how my William would feel?" Mary mused. "Also, Brother Porter has enough wealth to make many a man envious, and he represents Portsmouth in everything. Remember how badly thy first husband ached to hold office?"

"George cares nothing for offices, but since he was tried for adultery, he hasn't even been asked to sit on a jury," Herod admitted. "He says he is delighted."

"So he says. Mayhap in his heart he is wounded. Thy sons adore Brother Porter."

"Because he gave them a pony."

"He may be jealous because Brother Porter was wealthy enough to give them a pony."

"That pony was old, and didn't last two winters," Herod said stubbornly, but yes, it seemed that George might have cause for jealousy.

The daylight faded, but George had to wait for a deer to come to his bait for longer than he thought. After sunset Herod told Ben to go look for his father. The boy came back after a few minutes and said, "Papa's in the smokehouse, hanging up a deer. I'm going back to help."

George came in sticky with deer's blood, but Herod kissed him anyway. During the night while she lay awake once more, she resolved that she would quit prodding George. So far her urgings only made him more pigheaded. Surely, when spring arrived, George would get over his stubbornness and decide to buy John's land.

CHAPTER 20
February 1658

"SPEAK TO ME of George Fox, Mary. Tell me of him." Herod lay abed, swollen and lethargic from poisonous humors seething through her body. Too restless to sleep and seeking diversion from the nausea that plagued her that afternoon, Herod turned to Mary Dyer, who was knitting stockings by the fire.

Mary raised her head to smile. "I'm glad thou asked, Herod. What interests thee?"

"Why do people risk prison to follow him?"

"Think first of Mistress Hutchinson. To me she is Sister Anne, for she would be a Friend. Remember when she said that a man needs no schooling to teach God's word?" Herod nodded.

"George Fox did not sit in any school, but he is blessed by God. When first thou see Brother Fox, thou think him a simple, kindly man. I think he is near thirty-four – about thy age. Though he wears his hair long enough to annoy Puritans, he shaves his face clean, and has eyes that pierce straight into thy soul. He was born to a weaver and apprenticed to a cobbler. He still dresses in cobbler's clothes – leather breeches and a plain shirt, just like your George.

"His mission has taken him north to Scotland and south to Cornwall. He walks wherever he goes and sleeps in haystacks or hedgerows. Brother Fox wears such a hat," Mary waved her knitting at her own broad-brimmed hat which hung on a peg by the door, its brown felt beginning to fade. Herod had noticed that the other Friends wore similar hats. "It keeps the sun and rain from him, and he's become famous for it."

"How can a man be famed for a hat?" Herod scoffed.

"Half of England knows that Brother Fox won't remove it for any man. God alone deserves such homage. He has been jailed for refusing to doff it to magistrates, and so have other Friends."

"I feel honored that you aren't wearing yours," said Herod, and Mary grinned back at her. "What says his wife when he wears it to bed?"

"No wife, no children," replied Mary. "His mission keeps him busy."

"Mission?"

"Brother Fox says that every woman, every man, and even each child has a mission in life. We must discover it, and then follow as God bids. I began my mission eight years ago, when I left everyone dear to me and returned to England. I thought 'twas a mere visit to my mother. Now I know that I was destined to meet Brother Fox, and my mission lies in helping my Friends spread his word."

"So where will God lead you next?" Herod asked.

Mary gazed into the fire. "I know not."

"What do you suppose I am meant to do?" Mary turned to look at Herod, who had raised herself on one elbow.

"How am I to know? Ask God."

"You say that he speaks to you, but he hasn't told me." Herod spoke lightly at first, but then frustration welled forth. "I'm stuck here in bed like a sack of meal, and all I've done in my life is bear one baby after another. What sort of mission is that?"

"Perhaps thou are meant to be a good mother, just as Mary was tasked with birthing the son of God."

"Which of my children will … no, better not to know," laughed Herod. Mary might take that joke too earnestly, and Herod's head ached too much to pry into her own beliefs that day. She circled back. "So, Brother Fox won't doff his hat. What else does he teach?"

"He loves the outdoors because that is where he most often finds God. To be jailed is worse than a whipping because he is shut away from God's sunlight. Brother Fox often speaks of the sun because God's Seed dwells in each of us. Plant a seed in your garden, and with sunlight, water, and tender care it will become a carrot or pea –"

"Or a preacher," Herod finished.

"Just so. As a seed seeks the sun, Brother Fox teaches us to seek Christ's Light." Mary paused a moment to count stitches as she turned the heel on the stocking she was knitting.

"Thou will like this part, Herod. Remember in Boston, when Reverend Wilson claimed that a woman has no immortal soul? That little notion infuriated us. Anne won that argument when they excommunicated her. By doing so, they admitted that she had a soul that could be condemned to Hell.

"Brother Fox says that his mother had a quicker mind than many men, yet she was chastened into silent obedience. God also speaks to women. We all have a voice, and Brother Fox encourages us to speak our minds."

"But you worship in silence, don't you?"

"At times we wait for God to reveal his will. We also share our thoughts and prayers, just as Christ and his apostles worshipped together. Like them, we need no church. A field or clearing brings us closer to God's creation – and to God himself."

Herod propped herself on her elbow again. "Mary, my father told me that the Puritans sought to be like Christ and his apostles. I remember when they took away the stained glass and painted over the saints in Burlescombe's church. The Puritan preacher said 'twas to be simpler and more Christ-like. Now you want to be even simpler than them."

Mary smiled. "Not just for simplicity's sake, Herod. Puritans put too much faith in what they learn in college. Remember their sermons, showing off how much Greek and Latin they could spew? I wager only a dozen men in Boston knew what they meant, and I watched them put thee to sleep."

"You know, there is advantage to illness," Herod commented.

"What could that be?"

"I need not sit in that cold meeting house for hours. Very well, Sister Mary, I will try one of thy meetings after my baby is birthed."

"I can bring my brethren to pray with thee, but –"

"I can't even bear the noise of my own children," Herod groaned.

"I spoke in jest."

Herod sat up, and Mary helped adjust a pillow behind her back. "I know, Mary. But a single word from you, and there would be a dozen crowded around my hearth. People all over Rhode Island look to you. Mr. Porter says you have power like never before."

Mary shook her head. "That's not power."

"Of course it is," Herod scoffed. "Apart from Anne, what other woman dares speak her mind to so many? None. If that's not power –"

"It is freedom," Mary finished. "I have a mind as good as any man's, and I am free to speak what God puts there. Thou art free to listen if thee wish, with thine own good mind." Again Mary fell silent as she finished rounding the heel of her knitted stocking. "My freedom has limits, Herod. I am not free to visit friends in Boston or to take a ship for England because Puritans deem me a dangerous heretic."

"You – dangerous?"

Mary said seriously, "There is much danger wherever souls are jailed for liberty of conscience. It is my mission to warn the Puritans to mend their intolerant ways. God wants me to do this, Herod. I am certain, and thou art my witness."

The cold, short days of early February found Herod four weeks into her enforced bed rest. "Lying like a turtle on my back, too bloated to even roll over," she complained, "aching from head to foot."

Sarah Grand shook her head over the ailing woman. "You should have taken the herbs whilst you still could. Now they would kill you. But there's one other thing you might try."

Herod stared at the midwife with miserable eyes, but George eagerly asked, "What?"

"You take to that bed too, Goodman, and lie with your wife just as hard as you can."

George's mouth opened and closed before he finally uttered, "But why?"

"Birthing that child is the only cure now. A good prod might start her laboring."

Herod struggled to sit upright despite the remorseless throb in her head. An angry gleam was in her eyes when she protested, "Sarah, that babe has a month to go."

"Dorcas was near that early, and she's fine," said George. He sat beside Herod and took her hand. "Maybe we should."

"And Dorcas nearly died," Herod told him through clenched teeth.

"This is a big, strong baby," was Sarah's reply.

Herod didn't seem to have heard. She said to George, "Don't you remember how tiny Dorcas was? Squeezing milk from my breast to drip into her mouth when she was too weak to suckle? I'll not risk this one's life."

"Then you are choosing its life over your own," George cried bitterly. He dropped Herod's swollen hand and left her side to pace the room. "You are more precious to me than that child. We have six already."

"I have nine!" Herod shouted. "I lost two to John Hicks, and he stole Hannah's childhood from me too. If I save my own life by sacrificing this last one," she splayed a protective hand over her belly, "I couldn't bear it." Her sobs turned to retches and she coughed up a mouthful of vomit.

Mary was quick to hold a chamber pot so Herod could spit into it. After a second spasm, Herod waved her away. "We shall speak no more of it," Mary said soothingly, fixing George and Sarah with a firm stare. "Please, don't upset her further."

Her admonition was too late. Herod cried out, "Oh God," and clapped one hand to her head.

Mary looked into Herod's eyes and blanched. "What's amiss?"

Herod couldn't focus on her face. Mary seemed to be leaping from side to side. The room began to darken, but she could still see her own puffy fingers wrapped around Mary's arm. Her fingertips were twitching, though she tried to still them, and her hands began to tremble. Someone said, "Sarah, something's wrong." Then the room went black.

A soft, golden glow opened before Herod, like parting the shutters on a warm spring day. A shadowy figure appeared and, as it moved closer, became clearer. Herod saw a woman, clad in a dark skirt and jacket, with a snowy linen collar spread over her shoulders. She did not wear a cap, and her hair flowed down her back like a sable cape. It couldn't be Mary, whose hair was a pale mixture of ash-blond and gray. When the woman spoke, Herod knew her.

Anne stood before Herod, younger than when they had met in Boston twenty years before. There wasn't a trace of gray in Anne's hair, and her broad cheeks were unlined. When Anne smiled at Herod, her brown eyes sparkled like a happy child's. "Mistress Hutchinson?"

The woman nodded. "Please, dear girl, call me Anne."

"Anne, am I dead?"

"Not at all. Now is the time for life to begin."

"My child?"

"Just so. God is not ready for you yet."

"Does my child live? Did my sickness harm it?" Herod held her breath for Anne's reply.

"The child is strong, Herod, and so are you."

"Why have I suffered so to bear it?"

"Suffering is the lot of all women – our sacrifice to God."

Herod said emphatically, "Everyone wants me to sacrifice this child to save myself. It is more precious to me because I have suffered to give it life."

Anne nodded in approval. "Eve bore her sons in pain because of her sin."

"Have I sinned?" Herod asked.

"Who has not?"

But when Herod pressed Anne to name her sin, she merely smiled. "We are all Eve's daughters and pay for her sin, but that is not the only cause of our suffering. I was tried by the Puritans and cast from Boston. Had Mary not fled, she would have suffered my fate. Even now Quakers lie in Puritan jails awaiting trial."

"John Hicks beat me, but the Puritans forced me to remain with him."

"Men write the laws, women suffer them," Anne said testily. "If women were let to speak, they might convince men to change those harsh laws."

"Mary and her Quakers are trying to change them," said Herod. Anne's smile returned. "Would God spare my child and me if I pledge myself to speak against laws that whip women for their faith, cast them from their homes, and force them to stay wed to cruel men?"

The glow brightened around Anne. "God pays heed to all prayers," she replied. "If you take up his cause, he will bless you."

"Will you bless me and my babe?" asked Herod.

Anne placed her hands on Herod's taut abdomen and her lips moved silently. Then her eyes caught Herod's once more. "But you must help us, Herod. It's time for you to help us."

The aura around Anne flared until Herod had to close her eyes. Heat seared her face. At the same time, Anne's hands tightened, wrapping around Herod's belly in a cruel grip. She writhed and cried out. Then the pain eased and she opened her eyes.

Herod was sitting upright on her own bed, leaning back against another person; a woman whose wiry hands were wrapped around Herod's belly, rubbing and squeezing her womb. Herod's shift was shoved up around her waist and her legs were spread wide. Between them worked Sarah, with a hand plunged into Herod's crotch. Her fingers were deep inside, massaging Herod's cervix. The midwife muttered, "This babe will come now, even if I must reach in there and pull it out by its feet."

The pain began again, a massive tightening that Herod now recognized as a birthing pain. Her head rolled back against the unseen woman supporting her. One of her hands came up to clasp that woman's arm.

"Herod!" cried Mary. "George, Sarah – it's Herod."

Sarah's head came up and she eyed Herod. "Good. Now you can help us."

"What?" Herod groaned, still gripped by the labor pain.

"Herod, thou had a fit and it started thy labor," Mary explained. "With God's help, the babe will come fast."

Her head rolled to the right. George was kneeling by her bed, his face puckered with fear. "Is our baby well?" she asked him.

"I feel its pulse now," Sarah told her. "Its head is coming into the passage." She reached up to take Herod's hands, her fingers wet from birthing fluids. "Squeeze my hands." When Herod complied, Sarah smiled. "You don't feel weak, so perhaps the fit did no harm. This babe will be here soon, and then you will get better."

CHAPTER 21
February 1658

SARAH WAS RIGHT. The baby – a tiny, red-skinned girl – came quickly. She began breathing after a single slap on her wrinkled haunches, and suckled with little assistance.

The midwife stayed at the Gardner home that night, but Herod needed little help. Her bleeding stopped to Sarah's satisfaction, and Rebecca was big and strong for a girl born a month early. "Mayhap we had the date wrong," Sarah suggested. "Even so, you and that girl-child are lucky to be so well."

With the swaddled Rebecca held close to her breast, profound sleep claimed Herod. When the baby finally stirred her into wakefulness, Herod felt almost like she was floating. The newborn girl's head wobbled as she sought her mother's breast, but Rebecca was strong for such a puny infant, and so very determined. Herod wept grateful tears even as she smiled. Both she and her babe had survived!

She ruffled the infant's downy hair. Though the fire painted everything with a rosy glow, Herod was certain that Rebecca's hair was going to be red. It was hard to say whether she would share Henry's wiry brick-red curls or wear the lighter copper color of Herod's youth, but Rebecca faced years of being called 'Carrot-Top.'

By morning, Herod was using the chamber pot copiously. "Good – you'll piss away all that bloat," commented Sarah. "Get back on your feet soon as you feel up to it, but remember that you've lain abed a month. Don't be over-quick and collapse halfway to town."

"I know," groaned Herod. "I don't think I could walk as far as the outhouse. But my headache is fading." Sarah nodded her approval.

Mary went home for the day to see her family and to tell Hannah about her new sister. By midday Herod was feeling so well that she told Sarah, "I think you could go home too. I've plenty of help from George, and Ben and Henry are close at hand."

Sarah checked her once more and said, "You are doing fine. But before I go, I've something to say." She gave George a stern look. "Sit down, Goodman." George sat beside Herod, as meek as one of their sons.

"We spoke of this before, but I tell you now, this must be her last child. I am certain before God that another will kill her. Goodman Gardner, you can't lie with her for a two-month anyway. You twain must decide whether to risk getting her with child again."

George's face went scarlet. "I have already resolved to do – or should I say *not* to do –what I must. Precious as that babe is, Herod means more to me."

"Good," said Sarah. Her eyes turned to Herod. "Now, there are things which might keep you from catching. He can wear a length of lamb gut, you can stuff sheep's wool up yourself, and I can give you herbs to cast out a babe before it quickens." Herod shook her head. "The only sure way is to quit lying together until you go through the change."

"Is there no safe time?" George stammered.

"Perhaps she won't catch during the dark of the moon, but you are playing with fire. The only safe way is for you to keep *that* inside your breeches," Sarah said, with an emphatic nod at George's crotch.

When Mary returned her mood was somber. Herod wondered what was wrong. Her friend reported that Hannah was delighted by the news, and that Herod's children sent their greetings. Then she added, "If thou are still improving tomorrow, I shall take myself home. The Stanton girl will be back, and Hannah will bring thy little ones and stay with thee a while."

"Of course," Herod said. "I have kept you here too long." Mary hadn't been at her side for the entire six weeks, but she was at the Gardners' home more often than not.

"I may go to Providence for a few days," Mary admitted. "Humphrey Norton has been jailed on Long Island for at least a month. They will take him to New Haven for trial soon."

"He said the Puritans there are not as harsh as at Boston," Herod commented.

"I pray not," said Mary. She made a bundle of her belongings and refused George's help in carrying it home. "It's a light burden, George. Thou must stay with Herod."

Ben and Henry had gone to help Hannah bring the Gardner children home, so when Mary closed the door behind her, it was the first time in six weeks that Herod and George had been entirely alone. Herod thought, 'I feel as nervous as a new bride.'

George apparently felt the same, for he fussed over the fire, shoving in a chunk of fast-burning pine for light and then selecting the proper split maple for long-lasting warmth. At last he turned to ask, "Are you warm enough? Can I get you something?"

"I'm fine, George. Come and sit." His eyes went to the swaddled Rebecca at her mother's side. Herod told him, "She's fed and asleep, so we have a quiet moment."

The straw tick crunched when George sat by Herod. Their feather mattress was still rolled up in the second room, but would soon return now that Herod's birthing and the attendant mess was done. Herod curled to lay her head in George's lap and stroked his hard-muscled leg. She asked, "Have you thought on what Sarah said?"

George's leg tensed under his thick woolen breeches. "I've thought of little else, and I meant what I said. I won't lie with you if it risks your life."

"There are ways we can please each other," Herod said, sliding her hand up George's thigh until he squirmed.

"We've done it before when you were breeding," he said. "We'll do naught else, for I don't want to lose you. When you had that fit, I thought you were dying."

"It wasn't so bad."

"You didn't see it," George replied plaintively. "You shook and frothed, and your eyes glared like you were dead. Then you went limp and we couldn't rouse you. I thought you would never wake. I'd rather sleep in the barn than chance you dying for another child. We may yet lose this one. She's so small."

"No smaller than Dorcas," Herod said. "Rebecca's going to live."

"You're so sure. No doubt you are already thinking of her first shoes and counting pennies for her dowry." George smiled as he spoke, but there was a gruff edge to his voice.

"So what if I am?" Herod said, sliding a hand up his leg again. "Never too soon to plan."

George brushed his wife's hand away, and then slid out from under her head. "You complain that I can't provide for our family. Have any of our children gone hungry? I pay the Stantons for their girl's help – have you suffered?"

Herod sat upright and reached for George, but he pulled away. "George, I never said that you don't provide."

"What of all your talk of land, and sheep, and dowries?"

"Don't you wonder what future our sons face?" Herod asked. "Will they be able to stay in Newport, or must they go elsewhere because we haven't enough land for all, and I'll never see them again like Betty and Tom?"

"Now we have two girls to dower – you needn't say it," George added bitterly.

Herod bit her lip, and then began quietly, "When I was twelve my mother gave me to her sister as a slave because when my father died, he left *nothing*. My brother got a flock of sheep on leased land, an old stone house with leaky thatch, and no money to pay the rent.

"I won't do that to my children – send them off as servants or hire them out. I hated it, and I'd hate myself for doing that to them." By then Herod was shouting and she was in tears.

George stared in dismay, and then sat back down and put an arm around Herod. "I didn't mean to upset you. Calm yourself before you get sick again.

"Our sheep increase every year and money is coming in from selling mutton, so we'll buy more land. I need the boys too much to hire them out, and you will need the girls' help, so they can stay home too. Now, would you stop fretting about Rebecca's dowry? That's years away."

A new sound came from outside – excited children's voices on the path. Herod hastily wiped her face and asked George to hand her a wet rag. By the time the door flew open and Georgie and Willy raced inside, Herod had washed her face and was smiling with pure pleasure. Trailed by Nick, they surrounded their mother's bed.

"One at a time," she laughed. 'My arms aren't big enough to hold you all."

Will Haviland appeared in the doorway with his son Joe. Imperiously straddling Will's shoulders was Dorcas, with a dainty foot protruding on either side of his bead. "Have to take you down, little one," he said. "You don't want to hit your head." When her feet touched the floor, she ran to hug George's legs before greeting her mother. Then her blue eyes went to the whimpering infant lying beside Herod.

"What is that?" Dorcas demanded.

"Your baby sister, Rebecca."

Dorcas tried to push Rebecca aside to climb onto Herod's bed. Hannah rushed to restrain the toddler. "Careful, you might hurt her." Hannah gingerly picked up her half-sister. "Look how tiny she is! I've seen newborn puppies bigger. Mama, I'll swaddle her for you."

"She doesn't like it," Herod said. Hannah sniffed skeptically. Laying Rebecca on a clean cloth, she wrapped the baby into a tidy little package. Only the infant's face protruded from her bindings. That face scrunched into a little red knot, and then Rebecca let out an outraged howl.

Herod loosened her shift to suckle Rebecca, but the baby refused to nurse. "I told you she doesn't like it," she chuckled. Freed from confinement, Rebecca sprawled contentedly over her mother's breast, and Dorcas made room for herself under Herod's other arm.

"Mama, her legs will go crooked if she's not swaddled," Hannah scolded.

"Yours didn't."

Hannah sniffed again. Then, eyeing Herod's face, she said, "I thought Mistress Dyer said you were well again."

"I am better," Herod replied. "I walked to the outhouse this morning. Perhaps this afternoon I'll get as far as the gate."

"Your eyes are red. Why were you crying?" Hannah looked suspiciously from Herod to George.

"Tears of joy," said George before Herod could speak. "Your mama is happy to see her children again."

Usually George wasn't so fast with a glib answer, so when Hannah's eyes went back to Herod again, her mother was openly amused. "He's right, Hannah. I'm glad to see *all* of my children again."

Hannah planned to spend a week or two with the Gardners, helping Herod get back on her feet and getting the youngest children acquainted with their new sister. However, even before her husband and son went home that afternoon, Hannah was tossing distrustful glances at George. Herod sighed, wondering how soon the blowup would come. A week? Three days?

Less than eight hours, as it turned out. Before sundown, the whole gang of children went out to the barn to see a new litter of kittens, with

Dorcas insisting that Henry carry her so her feet wouldn't get wet. Herod walked unsteadily around the room, warming water to wash Rebecca's whittles. "Let me do that, Mama," Hannah said. "You'll make yourself sick again."

"The only sickness I have is sick of lying abed."

"If Mama's so fit, then why was she crying when we arrived?" Hannah's demand was directed at George, who sat on a bench by the fire, drawing on his boots to fetch firewood for the night. He clumped one booted foot to the floor, looking uneasily from Hannah to Herod. "What did he say to you?" Hannah asked her mother.

Herod said coolly, "We were talking of my illness, and that I can't bear any more children."

"That's good, isn't it? Seeing how sick you were?" Hannah said uncertainly.

"Not that I can't, but I mustn't." Herod clarified. "Do you know the only sure way to not start another?"

Hannah's gaze flicked to George and they both reddened. The girl looked quickly away with her teeth bared in distaste. "With seven children, he needs no more," she muttered. "That shouldn't be so hard."

"Hard for him, or for me?" Herod asked.

Hannah's mouth compressed, then angry words burst to her lips. "That's always been the problem, hasn't it? He could not keep his hands off you, and you would not stay away from him!"

Herod cried, "Hannah – what a horrid thing to say!"

"I have heard enough." George jerked on his second boot, then stamped to seat his foot properly.

Herod said grimly, "Wait a moment, George. Explain yourself, Hannah!"

"You and him," Hannah said, her breath catching as though she was fighting sobs. "If it hadn't been for him you wouldn't have left Papa."

"That's not true and you know it. When your husband breaks your bones, it has a way of driving you apart. All *he* did," Herod nodded at George, "was give me a safe place to run when your father tried to kill me."

"But you liked him better," Hannah insisted. "I remember how you giggled behind Papa's back. He had to stop you somehow." To George she added, "If you hadn't been there –"

George said something, but Herod's voice was louder. "I'd be dead, and your father hanged for murder."

"Peace, you two," George said. "Your mother's going to get sick again. Hannah, this happened so long ago. Can't you leave it be?"

"No," Herod snapped. "Let's finish this. Hannah, you were fifteen when you wed. I was thirteen. What do girls so young know of men? Wedding your father was my first chance to flee my aunt, but I made a horrible mistake. Some people are simply not meant for each other, and your father was a poor choice for me."

"And he picked poorly when he took you," Hannah said.

Herod gasped, and then found her voice. "Perhaps, but your father wanted his freedom too. If you don't believe me, ask Mrs. Dyer. It was Governor Coddington who forced us to remain wed."

"You can't stable a lion and a goat together," added George.

Hannah laughed bitterly. "Is she just the lioness for you? What of my poor father, with his land taken? I remember getting into that boat when it was still dark, Bessie and Tom were crying –"

"And I was still bleeding from your father's last attack." Herod got to her feet and crossed the room to look sternly down into Hannah's angry brown eyes – so like her father's. She said clearly, "This is all done and past. You shall never speak of it again.

"I tried to be a good wife to your father, but it's far easier to fear a man who beats you and treats you with contempt than to love him. I love George Gardner for his kindness and respect. Could you love Will if he struck you, and you feared that he would turn on your son next? Would you still love your father if he beat you?"

"But he didn't," muttered Hannah.

"Well, he beat me," said Herod. "I am with George now; not because he beckoned, but because your father drove me away."

Hannah broke away, saying, "I am going to see what those children are up to in the barn." But as she donned her cloak, Herod heard her daughter growl emphatically, "Papa was never like that to me!"

CHAPTER 22
Early March 1658

ON ONE OF the first sunny days in March, George told Herod, "I cracked my plow blade and must take it to the blacksmith." Herod stared at him dully. In the weeks following Rebecca's birth, she'd felt increasingly lethargic, and nothing seemed to interest her. Then George added, "I'm driving the sledge to carry the plow. It's a fine day, so would you like to ride along? I can leave you with Mary while the smith welds the blade."

The woman's head came up, and the first grin that George had seen for a while crossed her face. "I'd like that. The girls keep me on too short a tether." Despite her depression, Herod was stronger. She'd been walking every day, a little further each time. Yesterday she had gone to see the Stantons for the first time since November.

Herod nestled Rebecca in a sling knit from soft lambswool. The baby rode snug and warm under her loosely tied bodice. Then off they went on the sledge. The oxen skidded their load easily over hard packed snow still covering the road. Soon it would melt, leaving the roads a muddy mess for weeks.

Increasingly excited by her new surroundings, Herod twisted from side to side on the sledge's seat, exclaiming to George about changes along the path. "When did the Coggeshalls put up that shed?"

"Before winter, as I remember."

"It's been that long since I've been to Newport," Herod replied. Rebecca protested when the sledge bounced over rough spots. Herod cradled the infant in her arm to dampen the jolts, and soon her daughter slept. Herod began humming *Lilli Burlero*, a tune she remembered from London, and thought, 'I wish I'd worn a hat. My face will be sunburned, for certain.'

George left her at Mary's gate, but waited until someone opened the door before setting off for the smithy. It was Buzzy Dyer who grinned out at Herod, and then shouted, "Guess who's here?" He said to her, "Hello, GG," his personal shorthand for Goody Gardner.

Buzzy was a year older than Benoni. Herod's eldest son was grumpy about his name, Hebrew for 'son of my sorrow,' but Maher, or Buzzy as people called him, bore his unusual name, Mahershallalhashbaz, with resigned humor.

Mary came out from the back bedroom in answer to her son's call. Her linen sleeves were wet and pale hair strayed from under her cap. She said breathlessly, "Herod, such a surprise! I didn't think to see thee for another month."

"I came with George, and I'm free while he's doing errands."

"Come in, but I warn thee: there's a crowd here."

Herod heard a chorus of tense voices from the bedchamber as she followed Mary across the main room. She asked, "What's afoot?"

Mary stopped in the doorway to reply, "Humphrey Norton is back from New Haven. The Puritans near-killed him." Then she spoke into the room as she entered, "It's Herod Gardner."

There was indeed a crowd. Jane Hawkins had come down from Portsmouth, and Herod recognized Sister Mary Clark. There were two other women she had never seen before; one young, and one older than Mary Dyer.

Humphrey lay in bed, stretched out on his left side. Grimy hair trailed over his pillow and he was gaunt and pale, but there was feverish energy in his eyes that belied Mary's description of 'near death.'

When those glowing eyes found Herod, he smiled sweetly and lifted his bony left hand in greeting. The right hand lay on a bolster in front of him, wrapped from wrist to fingertips. "My dear sister," he said as Sister Clark vacated a seat by his side for Herod. "I heard thou had a trying winter."

"You too, by the look," Herod replied.

"I heard about thy daughter. Is she well?"

"I have her here." Herod pulled the sling out of her loosened bodice, and they all craned their necks. The girl's face was nearly hidden in her sling, and she barely stirred when Herod tweaked off her knit cap to show her fine red curls.

Mary Dyer said, "The Scotts brought Brother Humphrey here two days ago. He was freed from prison in New Haven last week, and all but crawled to their home in Providence. He shouldn't be out of bed yet, but came here with an urgent message."

Mary indicated the two strangers. "Herod, these are my sisters Anne Gibbons and Dorothy Waugh. They came from England last year, and have been teaching in Providence."

"I heard that you two are going to Boston to test their laws," Norton said to them in a husky voice.

"To bring God's warning to those who need it most," said the elder of the two women.

"But first Sister Gibbons and I will visit Salem, where many wish to hear God's word," added Dorothy Waugh.

"I seek not to stop you," said Norton. "This is your mission, just as it is mine. But I have brought my message in the flesh, to ready you for what you face if you go to Massachusetts."

"I have already warned them," said Sister Clark. "They have seen the scars I bear simply for setting foot to Puritan soil."

Norton fixed his intense gaze on the two strangers. "You *will* be whipped, and you will lie in jail until they see fit to free you."

"We know what we face," replied Dorothy. We've both lain in jail in England, and Sister Gibbons was mauled in New Amsterdam."

"The Dutch will do worse if you go thither now," Norton warned. "They have new laws against Quakers, and New Haven is concocting her own as we speak. They had no law to go by when they made an example of me, so they improvised. This is what they did."

He began to lift the cloth draped over his right hand. Jane stirred, but then said, "Go ahead – 'tis time to salve it again."

When Humphrey bared his injured hand, horrified gasps filled the room. Swollen near twice its size, it looked to Herod like a bloated spider, all lurid crimson, sickly purple, and charred black. His fingers protruded like stubby pegs. An ***H*** was seared into the back of his hand so deeply that bone appeared deep in the sodden flesh, blood-smeared and yellowish, or chalky where the bones themselves were burned.

Herod clapped a hand over her mouth, and one of the women behind her began to murmur the Lord's Prayer.

"Heresy was their charge, thus the ***H***," Norton explained. "Massachusetts' law doesn't call for such punishment for women, but you will be flogged."

"Amen," said Sister Clark.

"This is what you shall get." Norton pulled away the sheet which covered him, baring himself to the waist. He was shirtless and skeletally thin. Several welts crossed his ribs, and disappeared from Herod's view as they curved over his side. Humphrey nodded toward his back. "My sisters in Christ: you need to see what they will do to you."

The two Friends walked to the far side of the bed. There, young Dorothy dropped to her knees and closed her eyes, her pale lips moving in silent prayer. Sarah laid a gentle hand on Humphrey's shoulder. "You share the wounds of Christ, Brother Norton. You must feel blessed."

"When they flogged me, I barely knew it," Humphrey told her. "All I felt was God's hand bearing me up."

Jane fetched a small pot from the hearth and cautiously smeared ointment over Norton's burned hand. He sucked in an agonized breath, and the midwife commented, "Young man, I wager you could use God's healing balm now." To Herod she said, "Melted tallow – 'twill keep the scars supple as they heal."

"G-gg-ah," groaned Humphrey. He swallowed, and then rasped, "Praise God for thy skill, Goody Hawkins. I hope to be able to write soon." To Herod he said, "They burnt my right hand to hinder my writing their acts down for our English brethren and Parliament to read.

"Sisters," he called over his shoulder, and the two women came back around the bed so he could see them. "I do not flaunt this to deter you from your mission."

Herod's head rocked back in recognition. Mary told her that God had given every woman and man a mission. Since then, while she nurtured Rebecca and regained her own strength, she had idly wondered, 'What could my mission be?' But she'd felt too melancholy to figure it out.

Before she could think, Herod hurried to the far side of Humphrey's bed. He was drawing up the sheet, so she said unsteadily, "Please wait. I need to see this." The skin on Humphrey's back was taut over puffed flesh, and was the same garish violet-crimson as his hand. Welts, some of them cracked and oozing, criss-crossed his ribs and spine in a horrifying tapestry. "There are too many to count," she murmured.

"Thirty-six," said Norton almost proudly. "I thought they would never stop 'til the hangman's strength wore out. At last someone called from the crowd, 'Do they mean to kill the man?' Even so, God gave me strength to endure."

Mary gently took Herod's hand and led her back to her chair – she was grateful, for she was feeling faint. Humphrey closed his eyes while Jane Hawkins ministered to him. When she was done, his gaze found Herod. His eyes were normally a clear blue, but now his dilated pupils looked like dark wells. "They jailed me in Southold for debating their priest, then took me across the sound to New Haven. I waited two months to be charged, chained to a log in the jail courtyard all winter. No fire; not even a candle." Herod shivered in sympathy.

"At last they tried me, not for trespass, but for heresy, disturbing the peace, and reviling their priests and magistrates. I do admit to the last, for I lost my temper and shouted at their priest when he called us children of the Devil. When I defended myself in court, they jammed the courthouse key into my mouth so," he laid his finger lengthwise between his teeth, "like one gags a horse. They tied it there so I could not speak. Their priest didn't even come to the trial. The court found me guilty, and then they flogged and branded me."

Sister Clark said darkly, "They will strip you to the waist, naked on the pillory for all of Boston's folk to jeer. Bind your hands to a post over your head, then have at you with a three-corded whip. They tie knots in the ends to tear at your flesh. Afterward, with your backs lashed to bits, to the jail you go. Only if you bribe him will the jailer sell you firewood, straw to lie upon, and scraps to eat. When your sentence is done, you must pay the costs of keeping you in prison before they will release you."

Norton added, "I refused to pay the New Haven jailer, but I hadn't money to do so anyway. A kind Dutchman paid my fees, or I would still be there."

Just as she couldn't take her eyes from Humphrey's slashed back, now Herod couldn't break away from his dark gaze. At last she felt Rebecca squirm. Perhaps the thudding of her mother's heart, racing just under the infant's ear, had awakened her. Now her daughter wanted feeding, changing, or both.

With an effort, Herod tore her eyes away from Humphrey's. She cleared her throat and said, "Please excuse me. I must tend Rebecca before she really wakes. She can caterwaul with the best of them."

"Of course," Humphrey said. Herod clasped his left hand before she went out to the hall.

Sister Mary Clark followed her. "Do thou mind if I follow?" she asked tentatively.

"Not at all. Rebecca is damp – would you like to change her?"

The Quaker beamed in response, and then with big, capable hands helped to slide the tiny infant from her sling. She unwound Rebecca's wrapping, and Herod handed her a clean cloth she had brought.

Rebecca wailed steadily while Mary Clark changed her, but the Quaker seemed delighted to have a baby in her hands. She kissed the child's fiery curls, chuckling, "She's a loud little mite."

"Born six weeks early, but she has never looked back," Herod marveled.

"God must have an idea for her." Mary deftly swaddled the child and handed her back to Herod. "We both know what she wants now."

Herod slid Rebecca inside her shift, and then put the infant to her breast. She jerked her head toward the sickroom door and asked Mary, "What think you – is it truly God's plan for them to go to Boston? It seems folly after what the Puritans did to you and Humphrey."

"God is calling my sisters to deliver this message: there will be a reckoning. He will judge them all as harshly as they judge us Friends. It matters not whether they are in Massachusetts, Connecticut, or England. The Dutch, even though they aren't Puritan, savaged one of our brothers in Manhattan. They, too, will stand before God on Judgment Day."

"Those women will be beaten!" Herod cried.

"We can't save them from God's wrath by throwing letters at them," Mary said. "I will happily go whither he calls me next."

"On a mission," Herod mused. "How will you know what God wants?"

"How does anyone know?" Mary countered. "When I first heard Sister Dyer speak in London I was struck dumb. I never heard a woman teach before, but I had to hear more, just as I must breathe. When Sister Dyer called for volunteers to bring God's Light to New England, it was as though a blindfold was removed from my eyes." Then the Quaker noticed that Herod had stopped responding. "Good heaven, enough of my ranting," she said. "What about thee, Herod? Have thou felt that God has a mission for thee?"

Herod didn't answer right away. With her mind in wordless turmoil, she interrupted Rebecca's nursing to gently jostle the infant – perhaps she needed to burp. She put her daughter to her other breast to see if Rebecca would suckle more, then gazed at Mary woefully. "All I have done these last twenty years is bear babies. Now I can't even do that without dying.

"As for God, I've never felt anything from him, not like you and Mary say that you do. Besides, so many terrible things have happened to me. I can't see why a kind God would allow them." Herod's vision blurred.

Mary leaned forward. "What sort of things?"

"My first husband beat me, for one, and my father and brother died horribly when I was but twelve. They had done nothing wrong and we needed them. My mother was left so poor that she shipped me to London rather than feed me. Why would God allow that?"

"A baby bird sometimes needs to be shaken from the nest before it will fly on its own. Perhaps there were lessons in London that thou could not learn at home," Mary Clark suggested.

"How to be a slave to my aunt," Herod scoffed. "Do her every wish or be thrown into the street."

"Thou learned patience and discipline, and thy aunt taught thee to cook, clean, and sew, did she not?" Mary was smiling again.

Herod still didn't feel like joking. "Then why did God give me to John Hicks to maul?"

"Thy first husband?" Herod nodded. "Thy mission lies here, not in England. Would thou have crossed the ocean without him?"

Herod began to catch the Quaker's lighter mood. She admitted, "I would have gone with John Ayshford. He was my friend's brother, and I begged him to take me to Barbados for a maidservant, hoping to escape my fate in London. I haven't thought of him in a long time." Now that Herod pictured him, she realized that with his blue eyes and brown curls, Ayshford had looked a bit like Humphrey Norton.

"So, thy fate lay not with that lad."

"But he left me five pounds when he died, enough to pay our way to Newport from Weymouth."

Mary chuckled again. "Then thy purpose must lie in Rhode Island. Perhaps thou, too, were meant to learn from Sister Dyer, and thy husband was but God's device."

"Perhaps," Herod agreed, but her good humor ebbed. "John is long gone, and my children with him. Our eldest daughter has come back to Newport, but John poisoned her against me. She even looks like him. After Rebecca was born Hannah came to help, but I sent her home. We fought all the time; she, and me, and George. I began to dream of her father shouting and his fists flying at me.

"My Tom was just a babe, and I shall never know him. As for Betty, my second girl – do you know what a dry socket is?"

Mary nodded, "My mum had one. When she lost a tooth, it wouldn't heal and ached for the longest time."

"Betty is my dry socket," Herod told the Quaker. "There is a hole in my heart where she dwelt. Why did God take her from me?"

"Thou are just mopish after birthing that babe," Mary said. "Thou will feel better soon."

"After I learn what my mission is, apart from raising babies and keeping house."

"Ask God and wait for his answer," Mary said earnestly.

"If He answers in my house, one of the kids will interrupt," Herod retorted.

Mary shook her head, but she was smiling. "Thou gained much from thy first husband – the strength and endurance that thou needed to survive."

"Where do those two women get the strength to go to Boston, knowing what they face?" Herod asked.

"Sarah and Dorothy? "They know, just as I knew, that if my trials redeemed but one of the people who witnessed my suffering, it would be worth my pain. Know you of Anne Austin and Mary Fisher?"

"The Quakers who came to Boston last year and were searched for witches' marks?"

Mary nodded. "Like Christ, they suffered to save the Puritans from false priests and cruel acts. I could do no less, and neither can my sisters Sarah and Dorothy."

Herod agreed with many of the Quakers' complaints – John Hicks, like all men in Massachusetts, had been taxed to support Weymouth's Puritan church, though he was not judged fit to join it. The Puritans would allow no other religious practice in their land, and Herod thought that was unfair.

She had heard of the Friends' more controversial acts – prophesying in public and debating other ministers during their sermons. They weren't afraid to shriek out that God would loose the seven plagues upon Massachusetts, and they smudged their faces black with soot in mourning for Boston's coming demise in a rain of fire. While such disruption might be fun to witness, it seemed disrespectful to Herod. But disrespect didn't merit being whipped.

Sister Clark was still talking about the need for the Puritans to change their ways, but Herod's attention was wavering. Just like the Antinomian-Puritan conflict twenty years before, she found the controversy more interesting than the opponents' arguments. But instead of arguing with Mary Clark about the Friends' tactics, Herod let her speak. Rhode Island earned relative peace by letting the Quakers speak freely, and so would Herod.

CHAPTER 23
March - late April 1658

HEROD'S COWS WERE munching the first grass of spring. With her mouth watering at the thought of spring butter with its green, herby flavor, Herod took her churn into the kitchen, saying, "I'm going to bring this myself." The task was one of Herod's favorites because it reminded her of working in her family's springhouse in England's Burlescombe hills.

She poured thick cream into the churn and slid the lid over the dasher handle. Then she cast a quick eye to the bed where Rebecca slept. Nearby, Dorcas was amusing herself with a pair of cornshuck dolls dressed in wool and linen scraps.

George had carved the churn's handle into a comfortable grip, and it fit Herod's palm perfectly. 'My George *is* clever with his hands,' she thought. 'He can make a stool or a bit of harness, and bring down a deer with one shot. He's not the quickest wit, but he's content.

'I wish I could make him happy,' Herod sighed to herself. Wrapping her fingers around the churn's dasher reminded her too much of holding the most male part of George, and of the last time she had lain with him. 'Must have been nine months ago,' she thought, and a surge of erotic longing made the saddle between her legs ache. But was the bliss of lying with George worth risking death?

In the past, they'd toyed with each other when sex wasn't possible; furtive fondlings in the night or a rare moment snatched when the children wouldn't notice. Now George was different, even about that. Several times Herod tried to stroke him intimately, but he pulled away. Once he growled, "Don't start what you can't finish."

He didn't sleep beside her any more. He was always on the far side of a fence of bodies and limbs. Dorcas invariably slept by George, and Rebecca was never far from Herod and her comforting breasts.

Herod switched hands on the dasher. Her mind went to Hannah and the girl's angry words after Rebecca was born. "Papa said you left because you liked *him* better," Hannah cried, aiming a scalding glare at George.

"Who wouldn't?" Herod had cried in exasperation. She hadn't failed John – it was the other way around. Still, it seemed like she had lost Hannah for good. George was upset too, and his sulks never eased until Herod apologized. This predicament was hardly her fault.

'I am weary of apologies to men,' Herod grumbled to herself. 'In Weymouth I showed Reverend Jenner my black eye. He told me to appease John, but never said a word to him. John wanted to be shut of me as much as I wanted to slam the door behind him, but the Puritans would never have parted us. Coddington's no Puritan, but even he kept us together too long. He said it was the law.

'Mary is right – the laws *do* need changing. Laws which took my children, and let them chain Humphrey in the snow and lash him to shreds.' Herod still gagged when she pictured his bloody wounds.

'Laws which order families from their homes or be cast in jail. Now that's happening again,' Herod thought. Just a few weeks ago William Shattuck and his family had stumbled into Newport. After Sister Clark's whipping, Shattuck had refused to attend church and was charged with heresy. Lashing and forced labor couldn't make him submit, so he was banished and given a mere three days to sell their home. The Shattucks had walked sixty miles from Boston with what goods they could carry.

'Walked here from Boston with young children,' Herod thought. 'Sarah and Dorothy are walking there. It must not be so hard to do.' She felt a hint of warmth, as if the sun had broken through the fog. Herod's dasher was moving faster now, up and down in rhythm with her quickening heart.

'What have I done with my life? Nothing important like Mary and her friends. They risk their lives to save Puritans from Hell. I wouldn't do *that*. Besides, all that Seed talk makes little sense. If God planted a Seed in me, I should have felt it by now.

'But what if Mary is right?' Herod laughed aloud as she thought, 'Shall I walk to Boston to shout 'Woe!' and quake in the meeting house?' Her mirth faded, for next she saw the sheriff dragging her before Governor Endecott. Even the name sounded like a lash – Ende … COTT!

Herod could not see herself calling for God to pour his wrath over Massachusetts like blood. However, she could speak of what she had seen

– mutilations and scars, and laws which cast families into the wilderness because they worshipped God a little differently.

As for Hell – and Heaven – Herod didn't know what to believe. It did seem that God was indifferent to human suffering. Maybe he had turned to other matters, letting men bumble through life on their own. If he would not intervene to save the Friends, who would?

Mary said that none of the Quakers had been to Weymouth, so maybe they hadn't heard about the cruelties. The sun shone through Herod's mental fog again. 'Now, *there's* a mission for me. I could tell Weymouth.'

Herod could feel the butter collecting in fat globs on the dasher. She told herself, 'I wouldn't preach a word; just tell them what I have seen. They might elect a kinder man for May court.' Besides, it had been a long time since Herod had an adventure, and she would enjoy seeing old friends again.

Then Herod shrugged, because she knew that Weymouth's citizens weren't going to rise up with torches and pitchforks, any more than she was going to walk fifty miles to plead Mary's cause. But it was a splendid mission, should she ever need one. Plus the butter was ready to turn out of the churn. Things were looking up.

The final days of April were fair, and except for the ongoing tension with George, Herod couldn't have enjoyed them more. Her depression was gone and illness a fading memory. Rebecca was thriving, and filling out as she became more active.

Herod marveled at both her daughters' elfin beauty. Dorcas looked like a delicate golden angel in her simple white gown. Rebecca was ruddy – a newly minted penny with bright curls and skin that flushed crimson when she wailed. 'She'll freckle for sure, just like Henry,' Herod thought.

Both girls were under Nick's watch while Herod worked in the garden. The trio sat in dappled shade under the orchard's unfurling leaves. Rebecca was gazing upward, apparently fascinated by the lime-green leaves or the flickering shadows they cast. Nick had played tag with Dorcas until the little girl tired. Now they sat looking at the ground. Herod couldn't tell what they were doing, but they were content. That was fine with her. If Willy and Georgie were that quiet, Herod would wonder what mischief they were up to.

Herod's musings broke when she saw a couple crest the road to Newport and then walk slowly toward the Gardners' home. One was Mary Dyer. The other person, a man by his clothing and size, moved with care. John Porter would be on horseback. William Dyer, though he was nearly fifty, moved like a younger man. Could it be her old friend, William Jefferay? No matter who was coming, Herod wasn't going to meet him with muddy hands.

She waved a greeting and then dug quick little divots in the row of pea seedlings she was thinning. Where seeds had sprouted too closely, Herod dug out a few to fill gaps in the row. She hastily planted the half-dozen seedlings she'd already uprooted, calling to Nick, "Mistress Dyer's coming with company. Keep Dorcas with you."

Herod hurried to clean her hands. She kept a wash bucket by the door, though it was a struggle to get George and the boys to use it. A quick slosh, and then she dried her hands on her apron.

The visitors were greeting Nick and Dorcas when Herod trotted to the gate. Mary's companion was Humphrey. "How are you?" Herod asked.

"Improving daily. Sister Dyer is a fine nurse." He lifted his hand, still swathed in a bandage, and cautiously wiggled his fingers. "It hurts like the devil when I stretch it."

"Don't stretch it," Herod suggested.

"Have to keep it limber. I practice my writing daily, and Sister Mary is pleased with how the burn is healing."

Herod picked up Rebecca, but when Dorcas and Nick wanted to follow them inside, Herod told them to stay in the yard where she could see them from the window. "If you can walk this far, you must be feeling better," she said to Humphrey.

He gingerly sat at the table. "I measured the distance from northern England to London one foot at a time. I can't stay still long."

"And how was your visit to Providence?" Herod asked Mary. "When I didn't see you at Sabbath last week, Humphrey told me you had gone there."

"Aye," Mary said. The single word was spoken so heavily that the hair on Herod's arms prickled in alarm.

"What's wrong, Mary?" She sat across the table from her friend and held the older woman's cold hands. "What's wrong?"

Just then George entered. "Hello, there. Don't get up," he said to Humphrey. "Henry told me we had company."

Herod had told George about Humphrey a year ago, when she wondered if Mary felt tender toward the handsome man. Now that Humphrey had become Herod's friend too, she wondered how George would react. John Hicks would have been jealous, but George greeted Humphrey with an amiable smile. With another glance at Mary's pale face, Herod told George, "I think Mary has news."

"Do you recall our sister in Christ, Mary Clark?" she asked them.

"Did she come here with you just before Herod birthed Rebecca?" George asked.

Mary nodded. "I have just returned from Providence with heavy news. A ship from there was wrecked, and three of our Friends were drowned." She squeezed Herod's hands.

"Mary Clark?" Herod asked. Her friend nodded again. "That poor girl; she missed her children so. She held Rebecca when I saw you last."

"She spoke of thy girls to me," Mary said. "Sister Clark is in a kinder place now."

Herod asked, "The others who drowned – did I know them?"

Humphrey replied, "No, but one of them recently went to New Haven with our sister," Humphrey bowed his head toward Mary. Mary's hand loosened in Herod's and her eyes slid sideways toward Norton.

"You went *there*?" Herod asked suspiciously.

"Yes," Mary said.

"New Haven branded Humphrey, and you went there."

A shadow of a smile appeared on Mary's face. "I knew thou would not approve. Yes, I went to New Haven, for they are in peril. God will judge them harshly for abusing our brother."

"Are you mad? Just think on what they might have done!"

"Even they couldn't flog two women and an old man," Mary said. "Herod, this is my mission – to save these people who turn away from God's Light and deny it to others. Those ministers, those priests; they stand between God and innocent folk."

Norton added, "Their rulers use fear to keep them in the dark, and their harsh laws to keep us away."

"Why walk into the lions' den and shout, 'Wake up!'" scoffed George. "It seems pure folly to me."

"And me," added Herod. "What did you do; preach at Sabbath?"

"We merely warned them," Mary replied. "Nothing that they could take for heresy."

"How did you get to New Haven – a boat?" George asked.

"We borrowed horses in Providence."

"Two women and an old man riding through Indian country for three days. You've lost your minds."

"It must seem so," Mary said. "We met with the governor and his assistants. They scolded us, then sat us back on our horses and led us half the way to Narragansett Bay."

"Crying, 'Woe be unto you,' while the guard trotted them out of town," added Humphrey proudly.

"You are lucky," Herod told Mary. "You could be in jail now, awaiting your trial."

"Like Sarah Gibbons and Dorothy Waugh in Boston," Humphrey added.

This time, Mary's wordless glance at Humphrey was angry. Then she addressed Herod, "They went to Salem after thou met them, and their message was gladly received there. After two weeks they went to Boston."

"On God's mission," Herod said slowly.

"Yes, they followed God's call," Mary replied. "They were questioned by Governor Endecott and his priests, and will soon stand trial."

"What happens when they are found guilty?" George asked.

"Flogging and more jail. Only God can save them if the Puritans show no mercy," replied Norton.

George said something about the women being crazed, but Herod didn't hear him clearly. 'Perhaps *this* is my mission. I can get my friends to help spare these women,' she thought. Then she felt like she had jerked open the door of a very hot oven. Her musings over the last month snapped into place – the puzzle solved.

"I will go."

Silence followed those quiet words. Herod could only see Mary across the table from her. She smiled tenderly and squeezed Herod's hands once more. Then George demanded, "Have you lost your mind?"

Herod had never told anyone about having seen Anne Hutchinson before Rebecca's birth. She'd passed off the vision as a fever dream, but still felt that she and her daughter had been spared from death by God. Now she had the chance to pay him back.

She stood to look eye-to-eye at George. "I will go, but not to tell the Puritans how to worship. I will speak of what I have seen – good folk abused and cast from their homes. If I testify to such horrors, people may vote for kinder laws. Maybe Mary's friends can be saved."

"Herod, this is not thy fight," Mary said. Humphrey nodded in agreement.

"This is my mission," Herod said to Mary. "You said that I would know it, and I am sure. I will go –"

"You are mad!" George shouted.

"– but not to Boston," Herod finished, breathing hard. "I will go to Weymouth where my friends opposed the Puritans. I will remind them how we hated –"

George sneered, "And you expect them to rise?"

"No," Herod admitted. "But, I will stand up and say, *'This is wrong.'* Ever since my father died, I've been pushed from here to there and back again by – by fate. I've had no say over what I do or where I go. My mother packed me off to London. John Hicks pulled me across the ocean. I wanted to come to Newport, but we didn't leave Weymouth until John was ready. Governor Coddington pushed me to wed."

"But you wouldn't," George reminded her.

"I wasn't saying no to you, George. I said 'No' to him."

"For fourteen years?" George's voice was even more aggrieved.

"It seems that is the sole part of my life that I *can* control," Herod told him. "As dear as they are to me, I've birthed one baby after another with no say in when they come until now, and only because it has become life-or-death. Is my only mission to raise children and grandchildren, waiting for death to catch me?"

"Many women are content so," replied Mary.

"Were you? You were restless as a bird fluttering in a cage before you met George Fox. Now you are a teacher. You led these people," Herod nodded at Humphrey, "across the ocean."

"She merely called," Humphrey said. "I chose to come, just like our other Friends."

"And I choose to ask my Weymouth friends for help," Herod replied. "*I* saved Rebecca when everyone said, 'cast her out.' God spared us both, and I want to spare these hapless women." Herod looked at George in appeal.

"You don't even know their names." George was near tears.

"Herod, God will watch over them," Mary said. "Stay home with thy children."

"Yes, what of Rebecca?" pleaded George. "I can't tend her!"

"I will take her," was Herod's quick answer, but she began to feel less certain. "Perhaps she will soften Endecott's heart even if I cannot."

George pounded on the table. "You near killed yourself to bear her! Now you want to haul her fifty miles through wilderness on a foolish whim. You will never get there."

"You could come with me," Herod said, but George scowled in reply. "Sarah Gibbons walked to Salem and she's twenty years older than me. I'll take Henry for help."

"We are planting corn and I can't spare him."

"Then I'll ask Bob Stanton if I may take his daughter."

Mary motioned to Humphrey as she said, "Herod, I repeat, this is not thy battle. We should leave you twain to talk."

"Not yet," Herod insisted. "Just tell me what you think. If I tell the Puritans that I am not a Friend, do not speak in church –"

"No matters of God at all," added Humphrey. "They can't convict thee of heresy if thou agree with their doctrines and say naught of thy own. They may merely jail and banish thee."

"Would they really jail a mother and her baby?" Herod asked.

"Yes," answered Humphrey emphatically.

"If thou merely plead for mercy," Mary mused. "Their laws punish Friends rising from their own people, but thou art not of them."

George cried bitterly, "You two are as crazed as she is!" Hearing the anger in his voice, Herod nearly renounced her decision. It was a huge risk to not only Rebecca, but to her bond with George as well. She sat at the table and closed her eyes to think.

Mary said, "George, if this is truly God's call, thou cannot stop her. Think thou that William willingly let me go to England so long ago? God sent dreams of my mother until William agreed that I must go. Just imagine his wrath when I said that I could not return home with him. He was grief-stricken, and in the last, cold. We have not bridged that gap."

"I know just how he feels" George growled.

Herod opened her eyes. "I may not save those women, but I must try. If I don't go, I will feel like I've failed them – and myself – for the rest of my life."

"That is how long you will bear the scars after you are whipped," was George's bitter reply.

CHAPTER 24
Late April 1658

QUAKERS WHO HAD walked the region's trails helped Herod plan her trip. Most travelers followed the Pequot Path between Providence and Boston. It had been in use by the Indians long before the exiled Roger Williams traveled it in 1636. Now the path's rivers were bridged or crossed by ferry, and it was so trampled that nobody could get lost. Young men could walk the distance in three days.

However, the path's beeline to Boston was a considerable detour for Herod. Her destination lay twelve miles to the southeast. There was a more direct trail to follow, but it was less traveled. It followed the Taunton River northwest through Wampanoag land toward Plymouth. Humphrey figured that it would take Herod and Mary Stanton five days to reach their goal. Mary said, "Thou will be deep in Indian land all along the Taunton, even if they are friendly. Maybe Humphrey should go with thee."

"His scar marks him as a Quaker, so they would arrest us all," Herod told her.

"Thou and thy children's crusade would do best to travel alone," Humphrey said.

"God will guide them," Mary added.

Two pairs of moccasins, thickly greased to repel water. Extra woolen stockings; scratchy, but still warm when damp. Woolen cloaks, greased for waterproofing. Two thick blankets which Herod had bought yesterday. Their undyed wool didn't catch the eye, but the dense weave promised warmth in the night. A pair of tanned deer hides. The travelers would lie on one, and spread the second over their blankets to fend off rain. Enough cornmeal-rye cakes to last a week, and the same amount of smoked venison pounded into powder, and then mixed with dried apples and bacon grease.

For Rebecca, Herod packed two extra whittles to be supplemented with dried grass, moss, or shredded cedar bark. She took no cooking pots or utensils; just a pair of small knives and a leather bag to carry water. Though George protested, Herod refused to carry a gun. "What could look more harmless than an unarmed woman, a girl, and a baby?" she asked.

"Or more defenseless? You are just inviting brigands with blood on their minds." George squeezed his eyes shut and muttered to himself for a moment. Then he said, "This is madness, but I'll come to keep you safe. I don't want you to be harmed."

Herod was sorely tempted, but she said, "Thank you George, for I know how set you are against this. But Dorcas and the boys need you here."

More wordless grumbling, and then George nodded. "At least two weeks to see you to Weymouth and back, and the crops won't wait. Go ahead with your madness, Herod," he declared. "I pray that you aren't taking those youngsters to their deaths."

Mary Stanton watched solemnly as Herod finished their packs. One held clothing and blankets rolled into a deer hide. Their food was wrapped in the second hide.

Herod slipped two pair of stockings over her callused feet. Over them went moose hide moccasins. They were slippery to the touch from grease which Herod had massaged into the leather. She tied a second pair to her pack, ready to replace the ones she wore when they became soaked. George suggested, "Stuff dry grass in them if your feet get cold or wet."

"Thank you, George, I'll remember that," Herod said quietly. The pack of food was heavier than the blanket roll, so she strapped the clumsy package to her back. Rebecca rode in her lambswool sling, which fit over Herod's left shoulder and crossed her torso. Herod's cloak protected them both.

Mary toted the blanket roll on her own back. George met them at the door with a pair of sturdy walking staves in one hand. He'd sanded the wood and cut grooves into the handles for a better grip. Herod blinked back tears at this small, considerate gift.

"Last chance to give this up," George told her. "It will bring you nothing but trouble."

"You will not be rid of me so easily," said Herod. "I'll be back in two weeks, three at the most. I only hope that I'm not too late to help those poor women."

"You should hope that I'm still here when you return," George said, but without heat. He could have been asking her to pass maple syrup at the table.

"I hope so too," she replied and gently kissed him on the lips. George held her tight for a long moment, with his forehead pressed into her neck. Then he raised his head and his hands slipped away from Herod's shoulders.

She bade her other children goodbye, though she doubted that Nick and Dorcas understood much more than "Mama's leaving." The older boys wished her safe travels and Henry added a tweak to Mary's cap.

Herod looked out at the wet yard and said, "We're off, then." She planted her moccasin into the mud in front of her door. The greased leather skidded, and Herod stopped her slide with George's walking stick. Rebecca banged against her ribs and squawked in protest.

"Watch out for that first step," she said. "It's slick walking." Mary stepped out into light drizzle, pulling her hood tightly around her linen cap. The three of them started northward.

Ocean fogs in late April were drearily common, and mist wrapped Herod and the Stanton girl all the way to Mary Dyer's doorstep. Mary and Humphrey met them at the gate and walked half the way to Portsmouth with them. "Remember, Herod; thou needn't go."

"I'm not going to preach, Mary," Herod reminded her. "I will speak privately with Dick Silvester and my other friends, and ask them to vote those laws down."

"Even so," Humphrey said, "thou risk a whipping if they accuse thee of sedition."

"If anyone asks, I will tell them I came to visit my sister."

"I pray that tale will keep thee safe," Mary said, and kissed Herod farewell.

Ragged patches of blue sky expanded as Herod and Mary Stanton continued northward. "I hope it's sunny soon," the girl said, tossing back her hood. "Dry our cloaks and warm us up."

Herod eyed her servant with approval. Mary was just starting her third year with the Gardners. She was a sweet-smiling, hard worker who did what she was asked, and more. The sturdy child who had come to live with them was growing into a broad-shouldered teen who was good with babies. Rebecca napped contentedly in her arms while they walked.

Herod told Mary, "We'll take the left fork ahead."

"Right one's the way to Taunton ferry," Mary commented.

"Aye, but we'll stop at Mr. Porter's home to ask if he knows anything of the Weymouth path."

Mary laughed. "The likes of him travel by boat. What would he know of a walk like this?"

"No harm in asking," Herod said. She thought it prudent to tell John what she was about to do. Half of Newport knew that she was off to tweak Puritan noses, but he should know too. One of John's partners in his Narragansett land was a goldsmith in Boston, so he might have influence with the governor. It was just a precaution.

Portsmouth was more widely scattered than the larger Newport, where most of the settlers had clustered near the harbor. The Porters lived on the eastern fringe, in a snug home sheltered by a ridge. John had opined that the Gardners needed a better view of the bay, and Herod saw why. All he had to do was open his shutters.

The low-roofed building had been enlarged since Herod last saw it. A clapboarded house with massive stone chimneys on either end was now the main entry point. The half-timbered home that Herod knew clung to the rear.

She tapped on a brass door knocker. After a moment a blond girl opened the door. Around ten years old, she had a pointed chin and alert blue eyes which darted to Herod's face.

"Good morning. Is Mr. Porter in?"

"No'm; no he's not," the girl answered.

"Priscilla, who is that?" a woman's voice demanded.

The child glanced over her shoulder. "'Tain't Percilla, missus, she's gone to the shithouse!"

Herod smiled at the girl's earthy response. From within the house came an exasperated gasp, and then footsteps approached. "Lydia Ballou, I have told you that word is not proper," the same quavering voice said.

Herod had only seen John's wife at a few court days, and those were years ago. Now the mistress of the Porter house was coming to the door.

"Sorry missus; Percilla's in the privy," Lydia amended. Her eyes dropped to her stiff-looking new shoes, but Herod thought that the girl sounded less than contrite.

"That is more appropriate, Lydia." Then fingers gripped the door over Lydia's head. The maid ducked under Margaret's arm and darted out of sight.

The door swung a few inches wider, and into view stepped an elderly woman. Her fine-woven skirt and bodice were tinted a deeper gold than Herod's onion skin dye produced. Around her shoulders Mistress Porter clutched a shawl dyed with expensive indigo and trimmed with lace. She blocked the doorway so Herod couldn't see into the darkened parlor.

"My apologies for that girl's language," she said. "Mr. Porter has just hired her, but I don't understand what he saw in the girl. Her father is a small farmer and charcoal-burner, so she's not from a good background and should not be answering the door. I am Mrs. Porter. What do you want?" The quaver was gone from Margaret's voice.

Herod blinked at the brusque words, but said sweetly, "Good day to you, Mrs. Porter. I am Goodman Gardner's wife, Herod. Is Mr. Porter at home?" she asked, though Lydia had already supplied the answer.

At almost seventy, Margaret Porter was a decade older than her husband, but Herod thought she looked old enough to be his mother. She was not wearing a cap, and her loosened hair may once have been light brown or even red. Now it was a faded pink as white hairs overwhelmed the brown.

Margaret's head barely reached Herod's shoulder. Though her body was plump, her cheeks were caved in and wattles drooped below her chin. Margaret's mouth was set in a grim line like a puckered scar.

"Gardner, Gardner …." Those thin lips barely parted as Margaret mused aloud.

"Goodman George Gardner, of Newport," Herod supplied helpfully.

Margaret's pale eyes flickered to Mary Stanton, and then back to Herod. "My husband has no dealings with any Gardner," she snapped. Again she barely opened her mouth when she spoke, and Herod had to puzzle out some of the mumbled words.

"He hasn't," Herod agreed. "I but sought information."

"Information?" Then Rebecca whimpered and Margaret's gaze shot back to Mary and the baby in her arms. She demanded. "What is that baby doing here?"

Herod replied, "Rebecca is my youngest."

"Not the girl's? Margaret's mouth opened wider, showing decayed teeth. She quickly covered them with her hand and faked a cough. "I thought … why bring it to my doorstep, and what do you want?"

"I am going to Weymouth to visit my sister," Herod explained. "The babe is nursing so I must take her. Mary is coming to help."

Margaret scoffed, "If you seek a boat to hire, you came to the wrong place. Mr. Porter can't help you anyway. He is in Boston; something about that infernal Indian land he is buying."

"In Narragansett?" Herod asked. "We've heard about that in Newport. Will you and Mr. Porter move there soon?"

Margaret's corroded teeth showed again when she snorted, "Me – live among the savages? This village is primitive enough.

"I would rather have stayed in England, but came to Boston to please Mr. Porter. When he and my son-in-law got mixed up with Mrs. Hutchinson, we were forced here." Mrs. Porter swept an age-spotted hand through the air. Herod couldn't tell whether she was indicating her home, Portsmouth, or Rhode Island.

"It is nicer here than in London, or even Boston," Herod said.

"Is that what you think?" Margaret sneered. "I've no time to prattle, Goodwife, so I bid you good day."

Herod said, "Thank you, Mistress," but Margaret closed the door with a decisive thump before she was done speaking.

CHAPTER 25
Early May 1658

"THAT LADY DIDN'T ask us in, Goody. Left us standing on the step," Mary Stanton observed as they walked eastward. The Pocasset crossing was in sight now, a narrow stretch of salt water separating Aquidneck Island from the mainland.

Smiling wryly, Herod said, "I am but Goodwife Gardner. She is *Mrs.* Porter." Even Mary knew the implications of that title. The Porters owned three times the land that George Gardner did, and hired men to work it. George and his sons provided their own labor.

Margaret Porter, when she felt well enough to attend Sabbath, sat in the front pew. As the wife of Goodman Gardner, Herod found a seat in the middle of the meeting house. Before John Hicks was given the right to vote he had no title, and was known to his betters as Hicks or John. At church he and Herod sat in the rear, ignored by the likes of Mistress Porter.

Herod told Mary. "She may have felt ill, but …."

Mary said, "My mum would say she was rude."

When they reached the shore the deeply tanned ferryman told them, "Yer in luck – slack tide just now. We c'n cross without waiting, like we would if the tide was high."

"What happens then?" asked Mary.

"Could get swept down there." The boatman waved his hand at the broad stretch of water south of Pocasset Neck. "Wind and waves'll sink you or drive yer boat on the rocks."

Herod paid the ferryman from the stock of coins Mary Dyer had given her – halfpence each for herself and Mary, but three-month old Rebecca got a free crossing. Released from her wrappings, the baby stretched in her mother's lap while Mary fidgeted in the bow of the ferryman's rowboat. "I've never been off the island before," Mary exclaimed. She shifted to the other side to gawk at the bay. "It's so pretty!" When she turned back to look at Portsmouth the oarsman warned, "Settle down, Missy. You'll tip us."

Glad to have a few minutes off her tired feet, Herod nursed Rebecca. The ferryman asked, "You sure you want to land on the south side?" Most people walked the north bank of the river and lodged in the villages. However, Humphrey had warned Herod to avoid other travelers. "Remember, anyone who questions thee could be Puritan. Let thy plans slip out to him and thou will be marked."

So Herod assured the ferryman that she wanted the southern path. If he wondered why she was leading her little party along the uninhabited bank, he didn't ask why. Rhode Islanders were good at holding their tongues.

After a couple of miles, the walkers passed Common Fence Point, the northmost tip of Aquidneck Island. Now they saw the three-mile width of Mount Hope Bay. Two hundred feet high, Mount Hope stood across the bay to their left. Herod told Mary, "Humphrey says that's where the Wampanoags have their powwows."

Mary shivered. "I'm glad they are on that side. Do you think we'll see any?"

"I hope not," Herod replied. "If we do, remember that Mrs. Dyer says they are friendly. Just smile and say, 'Hello Netop.'"

"Friend," Mary translated. Most Rhode Islanders knew a few Indian words. Some, such as wampum and papoose, were in common usage.

"And if anyone, English or Indian, asks where we are going or if we need help?"

"No, thank you. The Goody is off to help her poor sick sister in Weymouth, and I'm a-helping with the baby," Mary said, fluttering her eyelids innocently.

The sun set behind Mt. Hope, but there was an hour's light left. They were crossing a hayfield and Herod pointed to the forested edge. "See that, Mary? Humphrey said it's about thirteen miles from Newport to where the woods begin. We are in Plymouth territory now. If we keep up this pace, we'll be at Weymouth in four days. For tonight, we sleep in the woods, but I know a little trick. Look for a chestnut branch leaning against a pine tree."

Five minutes later the girl pointed. "Look, Goody, there it is."

"Thirty paces due inland, Humphrey said, and look for felled trees the size of your arm. He made a little shelter there." Sure enough, Herod found a fallen chestnut tree behind a sumac thicket. Several poles lay over a snug little hole between the downed giant's branches. Herod spread one of their deer hides over them while Mary gathered dry leaves for a bed.

"Thou mustn't light a fire," Mary Dyer had warned. "It will attract anyone who smells the smoke. Most travelers are harmless, but the Puritans are not thy only foe." Herod had warned the Stanton girl that they dare not build a fire, but she sighed dramatically when Herod handed her a dry corn cake and cold pemmican for supper.

Both the ferryman and Humphrey had warned Herod that few people had traveled the path since last year. Humphrey said, "Wampanoags use it, but their moccasins leave little trace. Keep a sharp eye for markers – blazed trees and cut branches."

The Taunton ran from southwest to northeast, slowly narrowing from salty estuary to freshwater river. The walkers crossed many cleared fields along the flood plain. Fallow plots were covered with dry weeds and saplings. In others, a few tattered cornstalks were left from last year's harvest, intertwined with decaying vines. Broken squash hulls peered out from the undergrowth, pale brown and domed like human skulls. "These are Indian fields," Herod told Mary. The girl was already unnerved by the macabre squashes, and now she looked around wide-eyed, wondering if the planters might be watching.

The fields were surrounded by blackened forest, and the walkers kicked aside charcoaled branches and scuffed up ash with their moccasins. Wisps of smoke rose from fallen logs in one recently-fired patch. Both of them leapt when a standing chestnut snag spat charcoal and sparks from thirty feet above their heads.

"Goody, I sure thought that was an Indian shooting at us," Mary quavered.

So did Herod, but she dared not show her fear to the girl. "Mrs. Dyer said the Indians are friendly."

"Mum said that I'd better pray that God is watching out for us."

"He is," Herod said, with more confidence than she felt. She thought that God would show his approval of her mission somehow, but so far there was no sign from him. Perhaps he was waiting until she had persuaded her friends to help.

Mary said, "Look, there's a mark ahead." Both of them were watching for hatchet-blazed trees near and far. A prominent hack might mark where a log was felled across a stream, and an alert traveler could cross dry-footed.

"There are many types of markers," Humphrey told Herod. "Piles of rocks, sometimes two or three in a row. If it has a stick or rock on one side, it's pointing the direction you should take. Find them and you can save yourself some trouble."

The travelers bypassed ferries to Swansea and Dighton, circling deep into the woods. When they heard a ferryman's dog bark, they froze. "Do they hear us?" Mary whispered.

"I know not," Herod replied, but nobody paid heed to the dog. When they found the river again it was still over one hundred feet wide, running high with snowmelt. A pine trunk bobbed downstream, turning from side to side as its bare branches caught eddies.

"Look there, someone lost a boat," Mary marveled as a dugout canoe drifted by, so soggy that it was barely afloat. "Do we have to cross?"

"Yes, but there's a bridge," Herod assured her. Mary shivered thankfully.

Their second night was spent in a crude shelter that Herod made. Cold drizzle woke them before dawn. "Damn," muttered Herod. Mary's giggle told her that she hadn't been quiet enough. Light rain lasted through the day, soaking their feet and running down their necks.

The women slogged deep into the woods to sidle around Taunton. Herod told Mary, "Last chance to turn back. Rebecca's traveling well, so I can make it alone."

"Rain and all, I'm having a good time," Mary assured her. "I like the woods and this is better than mucking out the chicken shed."

"I'm glad to have you along," Herod chuckled. "Rebecca's not so much fun to talk to." She had been thinking that the girl would make a good wife for Benoni. 'He's two years older than her, and Bob says that we can keep her until she weds. Maybe Henry – they are friends and the same age. Henry could be the one for her.'

Herod thought that Henry was the most likely son of her bunch. Last fall John Porter had hired him and Benoni to shear sheep. He complimented the Gardners on how hard the boys had worked. "Let me take

Benoni for an apprentice," he suggested. "I need a hand, and the boy will learn his letters and numbers."

Herod had drawn a happy breath, but George frowned. "I need him for my own flocks and wood cutting. He works as well as a man and I can't spare him."

"How about Henry?" Herod had suggested. "He's smarter than Ben, so your numbers will do him more good." Porter agreed, though he wouldn't take Henry until he was fourteen. Herod was glad she could keep her son at home for a couple more years.

Late in the day Herod and Mary made their last evasive maneuver through the forest, hiding from Bridgewater's residents. They waited until dusk to creep over the bridge crossing the Taunton River. This was their most perilous moment. If there was a sentry he was nodding, for their passage went unnoticed. "Say goodbye to the river, Mary," Herod said. "This is the last we'll see of it until we come home."

"Bye bye, Taunton," Mary chanted quietly, waving one damp hand. "And now to bed."

They found another of Humphrey's shelters a little north of the bridge, near the chestnut bough and pine tree combination which marked a dry place to sleep. The branch had fallen during the winter, and Herod helpfully set its top back into the pine tree's limbs. At the fallen log Mary eased off her moccasins. "They are soaked through, Goody. Can't we light a fire to dry them?"

Herod sucked air through her teeth as she thought it over. "I can smell smoke from Bridgewater, so who would notice? Let's do it, but keep it small." Humphrey had tucked shredded bark and twigs under the log for just this purpose. Herod lit them with fat sparks from her flint and iron firestarter, and they gratefully warmed their hands at the little blaze.

Mary dried their moccasins and blankets while Herod toasted clumps of moss and cattail fuzz to stuff into Rebecca's whittle. Warmed pemmican and three-day old corn cakes made a monotonous supper, and Herod cooked more cakes with the rest of the meal. She could barely keep her eyes open to regrease their moccasins with tallow.

The travelers awoke to a frost-needled world. They both groaned as they pulled stiff moccasins onto aching feet, but at least the footwear was dry. So were the leaves they stuffed between doubled stockings for extra warmth. Rebecca was warm in her sling under Herod's cloak, but Mary grumbled about the chill. Herod assured her, "The sun will soon warm us."

Now that they had left the gurgle and rush of the Taunton River behind, their ears were filled with birdsong. Robins sang a long series of 'cheery-up, cheerio' notes from all sides, woodpeckers drummed on hollow snags, and Mary imitated the upslurred whistle of a redbird.

The path didn't look like it had ever been used by Englishmen. Fallen branches blocked the track and sodden leaves lay untrampled. The underbrush was very thick, and Herod's nape prickled like she was being watched. The pair had entered the Ragged Lands.

These woods were once occupied by Massachusetts Indians, which had populated the Atlantic shore from Boston to Rhode Island. However, the Massachusetts had been wiped out by smallpox. The Pilgrims had counted themselves lucky to find the Indians' villages empty in 1620 and believed that God had cleared their new home of hostile rivals.

However, the Englishmen did not burn the woods as the Indians had done, and undergrowth flourished in the Ragged Lands. Bay, laurel, and highbush cranberry stood taller than Herod's head, woven through by grapevine tangles. Greenbrier hid sharp claws under innocent heart-shaped leaves. "They call these the Ragged Lands because we'll be torn to bits by the time we get out of them," Herod grumbled to Mary as the girl untangled a briar snagged around Herod's legs. "Let's tie our skirts up so they aren't shredded."

Humphrey had warned Herod about the rough going, and to watch for trail markers. "Keep thy eyes open and thou will win through. If thou lose the trail, steer toward the rising sun and thou will hit the coast road." It was about fourteen miles from Bridgewater to their destination. Herod figured that each day they had traveled that far, so surely they would make it to Weymouth today! But between freeing themselves from vines and treading carefully through alder bogs, by the day's end they had crossed only half the distance.

"What's one more night in the woods?" Herod said, hoping to cheer the downcast Mary.

"Another night sleeping cold and damp," the girl grumbled.

"We've plenty of pemmican."

"I've had enough of that to last my life."

"Then it's corn cakes for you."

Mary silently picked charcoal from the corn cakes Herod had cooked last night. She moistened it with water from their leather bag, and grimaced when she tasted the cake. "I'm glad we will get to Weymouth tomorrow. I've seen enough of this."

"Me too," Herod said. The girl was anticipating the end of their journey, but Herod was nervous about what tomorrow would bring. Five days on the trail might be simple in comparison to seeking out her old friends and convincing them to help the jailed Quakers. The more quickly Herod could do it, the better chance they had of getting out of Weymouth before the Puritans caught her.

CHAPTER 26
May 10, 1658

A TRAMPLED ROAD, wide enough for two loaded hay wagons to pass, made the footsore travelers beam. The coast road at last! Turn left and you were on your way to Boston. Going right led you to Plymouth. That road would take you all the way to the Cape Cod's curving arm if you wished for a walk on the beach.

A third option was the one that Herod took with her two girls, large and small. A well-used path led straight ahead – the way to Weymouth. Mary was more than ready to be done with her fifty-mile "mud march," as they had begun calling their journey. She was crying when they got up that morning, saying that she didn't know what she was getting into, and soon she would have to follow that same blasted path home.

Herod was impatient with the girl's tears, but equally glad to leave the Ragged Lands behind. Her head eagerly turned from side to side on the Weymouth path. How soon would she see someone she knew? The pinewoods were certainly familiar. She and John Hicks had carved their homestead out of the same young trees. However, Weymouth's woods had been thinned over the last twenty years. The trees were thicker and straighter, for wood cutters had axed the runty and misshapen, leaving straight-trunked timber prospects to mature.

There were many more homes and cultivated fields than Herod remembered. She told Mary, "Look at that – proper clapboard houses. Some even have glass! The village homes must be grand."

Herod didn't know where she was until they reached Whitmarsh's Pond. The mill was still there, but enlarged. And she didn't recognize the teen-aged miller, for he hadn't been born when she lived there.

The brawny lad was tying a sack of corn flour when she came in, and he clapped a cloud of dust from his hands. Herod said, "I've been away for near twenty years. Can you tell me where to find Bess Fry?" That woman had delivered Herod Hicks' daughters, and Herod hoped that she and Mary would be able to stay with her old friend for a few days.

"Bess Fry? No, I – was she married to Bill Fry?" Herod nodded eagerly. "He died some fifteen years ago. His wife got married again, but she's dead five years gone."

Herod sagged, and the miller asked, "Was she kin to you?"

"A friend I hoped to see again."

At least Herod knew where they were now. She told Mary, "We walked right past my old home a few minutes ago. I didn't recognize it."

They backtracked to the dugout that John Hicks had carved into a sandy hill. It wasn't gone after all – now it was part of a barn. Nearby stood a neat little home, with white-washed clapboard walls and a shingle roof.

A family with two little boys had bought the Hickses' home and land. The man was called Nash, but Herod couldn't recall his first name. It was a girl who answered the door, seven or eight years old, with skinny shanks and bare feet sticking out under her knee-length skirt.

"Hello, I'm Herod Gardner. Is your mama or papa at home?"

The girl's nod sent her brown braids swinging. "I'll get 'em," she said. She darted inside, but in a moment she was back. "Ma and Pa are coming."

Herod pictured the sole time she had met Mr. Nash. She was only sixteen then, and since he was twice her age, he had seemed old to her. When she saw Nash she remembered his long nose, but now it was surrounded by fleshy cheeks. The angular, fast-talking man must have gained a pound or two every year since Herod had last seen him. James was his name, and Alice was his wife.

They confirmed that both Bess and Bill Fry were dead. Susanna Reed was another of Herod's old friends, but the Reeds had moved to Boston years ago. Herod said, "I'm sad to hear that they are gone, for they were good friends. I hoped that we could stay a night with Bess so she could see my little one." Alice looked curiously at Mary, but Herod said, "Not her."

Mary was holding Rebecca, but the baby was swathed in a blanket and did not make a large bundle. The girl opened a flap to reveal Rebecca.

The child who had let them in was loitering to listen. She said, "Oh, a baby. Can I see?" Mary tilted the infant toward the girl. "What's its name?" she asked.

"Rebecca," Herod said. Before she could ask, "What's yours?" the brown-haired girl started bouncing on her toes. "I'm Rebecca too! Mama, she's got the same name as me!" The girl's mother smiled as she came to look at the whimpering infant.

"She's tired of travel, as we all are," Herod explained. "We need a place to stay for tonight, since my friends are gone. Is there anyone who takes in lodgers?"

Rebecca peered over Mary's arm at her namesake. "Mama, Papa, can't they stay with us?" She started bouncing again. "They can share our bed and I'll sleep by Rebecca."

The couple shot a worried glance at each other. James replied, "Becky, don't you remember that your sister Sarah is staying the night? 'Twill be too crowded." He said to Herod, "Her sister is bonded to the Whitmarshes, but she's visiting us tonight."

Alice turned hazel eyes just like her daughter's to her husband and said, "Can't –" just as Herod said, "We need nothing fancy. After our nights in the woods, a haypile in the barn will seem like heaven."

Nash said, "We'll see," to his daughter, and then sent her out to look for eggs. The girl left reluctantly. Then he told Herod, "We have to watch who we take in. All that fuss over Quakers, you know. You aren't one of 'em, are you?"

"No, I'm not a Friend," Herod assured him. "I just came to see a friend." Alice looked puzzled as she pondered Herod's play on words, but James smiled thinly.

"A couple of 'em showed up in Boston last week, and Reverend Thatcher says there's a proper nest hiding in Rhode Island. Magistrates say they will be here soon, and we don't want no trouble."

The next morning Herod breakfasted with the Nashes, and then nursed her daughter until the sated infant turned her head away from the breast. Herod left Rebecca with Mary and the delighted Becky Nash, and set out to walk the final couple of miles to Weymouth village. Last night, she had asked James Nash, "What day is it?"

"Third day after Sabbath."

"That means we spent five days on the path here," Herod commented. That also meant that this was Wednesday. Good. She had been warned by Mary Dyer not to interrupt the Puritans' Lecture Day on

Thursday, as the Quakers were wont to do. Herod wouldn't do that anyway. Stand up in front of the congregation to warn them of God's growing wrath? Daub her face with mourning ashes for the governor's damnation? No, Herod didn't want any part of that.

She hoped to meet privately with her old friends; Dick Silvester, Thomas Makepeace, Ambrose Martin, and John Smith. These men had opposed the ouster of Anne Hutchinson's supporters back in 1638. Surely they would agree with Herod, and send a man to the general court who would help repeal these evil laws.

Her inquiries along the path to town were disappointing. Herod learned that Ambrose Martin was gone to Concord. Tom Makepeace? He's in Dorchester now. Nobody could tell her of John Smith.

By the time Herod reached Weymouth's square, her last hope for support was dashed. Richard Silvester was gone too. "You should have took the Plymouth road," said a woman in a russet bodice when Herod asked about him. "He's gone to Marshfield, oh …." She shouted over her shoulder, "Bill, how long has Dick Silvester been gone?"

"Seven, eight years," replied a burly man. He was examining fresh fish heaped on a nearby table. It was market day in Weymouth. There was no garden produce this early in the year, but there were kegs of live lobster, morel mushrooms, buckets of cowslips, fiddleheads, and other spring greens for sale. One table held a dozen species of fish wrapped in seaweed. There were a score of people bargaining over these fresh treats.

Herod's heart raced and her palms grew damp as she told herself, 'You'll never have a better chance than now.' She turned glowing gray eyes on the woman in russet, who was asking if Herod wouldn't like some just-picked greens? "Mistress, who will Weymouth send to General Court?"

"I know not. Bill, who is standing for us at court?" she shouted. Heads swiveled on all sides. Now they were all looking at Herod.

Bill left the fishmonger's table and strode to his wife and Herod. "What d'you need that for?" he demanded.

The woman jerked her head at Herod. She cleared her throat nervously. "Maybe you haven't heard, but there are two kind and gentle women in Boston's jail now. They've done no harm, but under the law they will be whipped."

"They already were a few days ago," said a man pushing his way between shoppers. His graying hair was worn a little longer than the ear-length Roundhead style that Herod remembered from London, but she was wary. He wore no lace or fancy boots, so his clothing was plain enough for a Puritan. Just the sort of man she'd hoped to avoid.

"They were whipped?" Herod asked. "What had they done?"

"Broke our law," Bill said. "They were Quakers, so the law tells them to stay away or get a whipping."

"Thieves and wife beaters should get whipped," Herod countered. "Not women saying a few harmless words."

The gray-haired man bent to speak to a green grocer's lad, and the boy dashed off toward a large building. It stood on the same site where Herod had worshipped with John Hicks. Judging from the fresh appearance of the sawn planks, the new meeting house was only a few years old.

Herod pulled her gaze from the running boy to hear Bill say, "– not just words. Them Quakers interrupt our godly services, arguing with the preachers. I hear that in England them women walk into church stark naked. If that ain't the Devil's work, what do you call it?"

"I'm not a Quaker, so –" Herod began.

The gray-haired man said, "You sound like one."

"I'll never say '*thee*' to you, sir," Herod replied. "And I'll not interrupt a sermon, but those laws are cruel. Does God not turn his face from the unjust?"

"Them Quakers are the lawbreakers," cried Bill. "Lock 'em up!"

Herod replied, "Yes, they break the law, but it's not just jail that they face. With these eyes I saw a man who was flogged until the skin was stripped from his bones. They branded his hand," Herod displayed her own, drawing a big *X* on the back with her finger. "Burned it to the bone. He may never use it again."

"I heard of that," said the gray-haired man. "That was in New Haven, not here."

"Puritan colony, Puritan laws," countered Herod. "How long before they do the same in Boston? I dwelt here twenty years past, when so many were cast from their homes. They caused no riots and killed no one. They merely worshipped in a different way. I live with them in Rhode Island, and we are all at peace."

"Peace, in Rogues' Island?" an unseen man jeered. "You can't even keep a proper government and the towns are at each other's throats. Is that what you call peace?"

Herod shouted, "You know who else lives in Rhode Island? William Shattuck!" A hush fell over the small crowd. "Last month his family was banished, and he could barely walk when they came to Newport. He was one of your own, but flogged for not going to church. We all miss a Sabbath now and then. What will you do when the governor calls *you* a law-breaker, whips you, and gives you three days to be gone before you are hanged?"

Out of the corner of her eye, Herod saw several men approaching. One bore a musket, another wore the black robe and white neck band of a minister. The band was askew, as if donned hastily. They came straight toward Herod. She added quickly, "I but ask you to consider whether these laws are too cruel."

"Governor Endecott will never repeal them," sneered a man in the crowd.

"Maybe you need a new governor!" she cried.

"I'll not be taught sedition by a woman," said Bill, but his wife nudged him. "Let her finish," she said.

"Laws which let the Puritans seize your home. Let them flog you, cut off your ears, brand —"

"We've the right to protect ourselves!" cried the gray-haired man.

"They would have sold William Shattuck's children as slaves. Is that right, to tear children from their mothers' arms?" The group of men was close enough that Herod could see their grim-set mouths and sharp eyes darting over the crowd. She concluded hastily, "What might Endecott do to you if such laws aren't softened? Now, excuse me for taking up your time. I've said too much already."

"By God, you have," growled Bill. He reached for Herod's arm but she backed away. The gray-haired man cried, "Hold her!" but Herod slipped away from Bill's clutching fingers. All he caught was her cap, pulling it from her head. His wife stepped between him and Herod. "You clumsy woman!" he cried, trying to push her aside.

But Bill's wife, whose name Herod never learned, caught the Rhode Islander's eye for just a moment as she obstructed her husband and the gray-haired man, allowing Herod to escape.

CHAPTER 27
May 11, 1658

THE FIRST RAYS of sunlight filtering through cracks in James Nash's barn found Herod wide awake, nursing Rebecca while she mused. Learning that Dorothy Waugh and Sarah Gibbons had been flogged disheartened her, and most of the people in Weymouth's market said the women earned their punishment. Maybe she could find sympathetic ears in Plymouth and Marshfield, but that would do nothing to free the Quakers in Boston.

Last night Mary Stanton had cried herself to sleep after pleading with Herod to go home. Herod's own glowing sense of mission had slipped away, replaced by resignation and a strengthening urge to see her children again – if George hadn't taken them away.

Suddenly James Nash threw open the barn door. He was red-faced and his jerkin was buttoned awry. "The Whitmarsh boy was just here," he said angrily. "He says you started a riot in market yesterday, and the constable is searching for you!"

Taken aback by the hostility in Nash's voice, Herod said, "An argument, perhaps, but no riot. We but spoke of changing the laws –"

"What do you think sedition is?" fretted Nash. "I would never have taken you in if I'd known that you were a Quaker. Now I'm in trouble too!"

"For sheltering a woman and her baby? Maybe *that* law should be repealed too," Herod replied, but her heart was pounding.

"Bah!" Nash spat into the straw. "Get yourselves out of here and be quick about it. If the constable is still at Whitmarsh's you have a few minutes. Cut through my woodlot to the coast road and take yourselves back to Rhode Island!" He looked out the door, and then glared while Mary frantically rolled up their bedding. The girl's chin was trembling and tears dripped from her nose.

Rebecca was still in the soiled whittle that she'd worn overnight, but Herod slid the baby into her lambswool sling. She hugged Rebecca close and threw her cloak over the bundle.

They heard a horse approaching the barn. Nash went pale and said "Damme! I'll take them to the house. Wait a minute, then you go around that way," he pointed away from the rising sun. "If God loves you, they won't see you. Go!" Then Nash strolled outside, whistling. Herod heard him call to the horseman, "A good morning to you, sir!"

"Goodman Nash, have you heard of a Quaker woman in town?"

Watching through a crack in the door, Herod couldn't hear Nash's reply, but he kept the horseman moving away from the barn. It was the gray-haired man from the market place. He was dressed formally and had a pistol under his belt. Beyond him, Herod saw several men armed with muskets coming quickly along the lane from town.

"Mary, they've sent the militia," Herod gasped. The girl swayed, and Herod told her, "Strap on that pack. They will be out of sight in a moment and we'll have to move fast!"

The girl obeyed, and then put her own eye to an opening near Herod's. The horseman and Nash rounded the corner. A few moments later, the militia also passed out of sight behind Nash's home. "Run!" hissed Herod.

Around the barn they slipped, crawling between the rails of Nash's cow pasture. Herod suddenly remembered doing this when she was Mary's age to avoid milking. She bit back a hysterical giggle as they fled across the pasture. Deep into a thicket of pines they ran, and then paused to catch their breath. They could hear nothing but morning birdsong and a crowing rooster. "I think we got away," Mary whispered.

"But stay quiet," Herod replied. "We won't be safe until we get to Rhode Island, and that's five days through the woods." Mary's face crumpled and she began to cry again.

Herod thought furiously, and then she smiled. "We're for Plymouth. Quakers aren't welcome there either, but we'll be safe so long as we keep our mouths shut."

"How far?" asked Mary.

"An hour or two to Marshfield, where I have a friend."

The pair slipped unseen through the pines until they saw the coast road. Herod grabbed Mary's arm. "Listen carefully. The Puritans may have guards on the road, so if we meet anyone tell them that you and I were in

Boston yesterday. We are going to Marshfield to see my uncle, Mr. Silvester. Say nothing else! Got it?"

"Mr. Silvester in Marshfield," Mary repeated, but her reddened eyes worried Herod. She wiped the girl's face, and then pinched her cheeks and chin to make them red too. Perhaps they would think Mary was naturally ruddy.

Herod felt damp seeping through her shift. The baby's whittle was drenched and soon she would be squalling. Best attend to her now so she wouldn't attract attention. Herod quickly removed her whittle, and shook a wad of wet hay from the soiled wrap. Grimacing at the stink, Herod shoved the cloth into her pack. "We'll wash it after we are safe," she told Mary.

Once more she gave Rebecca her breast to stop her fussing, then back into the sling the baby went. Herod settled her clothing and tried to hearten Mary with a confident grin. "Are you ready?" The girl nodded weakly. "Fear not, they won't catch us."

They could see a small stretch of the Plymouth road from their hiding place. It appeared to be safe, so they slipped out to the hard-beaten dirt road and turned south. After ten uneventful minutes, Herod began to relax. Then they heard a whistle behind them. "Hey there, you two! Hold a moment!" A half-dozen armed men were coming toward them at a trot. "Militia," Mary whispered, her breath already hitching in quick gasps.

Herod gripped the girl's hand. "Remember – Boston yesterday, on our way to Marshfield." Mary's face was so white that Herod feared she might faint.

"Good morning, gentlemen," Herod hailed the men. "Can I help you?"

The nearest man ignored Herod's greeting. He crowed, "Tall woman, butternut top, black skirt."

"They didn't say nothing about a girl with her," panted a stout musket-bearer.

"Let's see," the leader said. He jerked the hood of Herod's cloak back, yanking her braided hair. "Look at that! Red, just like Mr. Norton said." Addressing himself to Herod, he said, "Woman, you are coming with us."

"We are going to Marshfield. Why do you stop us?" Herod willed herself to be calm.

"Mr. Norton will tell you," were the only words the armed man said, and back northward they went. They turned onto the Weymouth path and were nearly to the town square when they met the gray-haired magistrate and the rest of the militia. "We got 'em," their captor crowed, "Trying to escape to Plymouth."

Norton eyed Mary closely from head to toe, and then turned his eyes to Herod. "This is the one who preached yesterday. Woman, what is your name?"

"Herod Gardner, sir, and I wasn't preaching," she replied mildly.

"I've not heard your name before. Where do you come from?"

"Newport, in Rhode Island."

"Oh no, she's one of *those*," laughed a round-eyed fellow.

"Those what?" Herod asked.

"Rebels," he jeered.

Mr. Norton spurred his horse closer. "Do you own yourself a Quaker?"

"I am no more a Quaker than you, sir," Herod replied.

"No matter, no matter," Norton declared. "For your incendiary speech, you are off to Boston. Quaker or no, Governor Endecott wants to speak with the likes of you."

It was ten miles to Boston, but they covered the distance before noon. Norton urged his horse along at a brisk pace, perhaps for the pleasure of watching his captives hurry. The militia surrounded them, and silenced the prisoners if they tried to speak.

Mary sniffled steadily. One of the men bumped her with the butt of his musket. "Hurry along, girl. Don't want to make the governor wait."

"Be kind, sir," Herod said. "She's just a servant, come to help carry my baby."

"What baby?" the man scoffed.

Herod threw her cloak aside to reveal the sling where Rebecca rode. "She is in here. Shall I show you my daughter?"

Norton rode back to them and leaned down for a look inside the sling, "So it is," he commented. "Be gentle, men. Let's not harm the babe. The woman may be guilty, but it is blameless." To Herod he said, "I will carry the child so it won't slow you."

She clutched Rebecca so tightly that the baby squawked. "No, Mr. Norton, lead on and I will keep up."

Herod and Mary were stumbling by the time the procession reached Boston. She noted with grim satisfaction that the militia was panting as well. Despite her weariness, Herod proudly kept her head high as they crossed the narrow Roxbury neck. On the far end lay Boston.

The city had grown since Herod arrived from England in 1637, and it prospered as New England's principal port. Painted homes with carved trim and a few shops made of brick lined the streets. Many of the onlookers who gawped at Herod and her escorts looked equally affluent. Lace, silver buckles, and fine fabrics decorated Boston's Puritans, though a person who dressed above his or her station faced a reprimand or even a flogging.

Boston had replaced its church with a larger edifice. Herod's escort passed it by and delivered her to a modest half-timbered building. There, Norton dismounted and led Herod and Mary to the door. A matron in her fifties answered his knock. "Governor Endecott will want to talk to these two," Norton told her.

"The governor is at his dinner," the woman said. She was dressed in clothing so plain that Herod thought she must be Endecott's cook. The woman went off to the next room, leaving them waiting in the parlor.

Herod smelled fresh bread and a savory stew. Her mouth watered, for they had eaten nothing that day. Mary whispered, "I wish we could get some of that." Herod nodded approval of the first spirit the girl had shown all morning.

Now that they had stopped, Rebecca was stirring again. Herod took her out of the sling and cradled her in one arm. When she heard footsteps approaching, Herod squeezed Mary's hand reassuringly.

Last summer Herod's sons had caught a snapping turtle. If she held her arms in the widest circle she could make, that creature's shell would have overlapped it by inches. The boys played with it before George beheaded it with an axe so Herod could clean it for dinner. They waved branches in front of the desperate animal's hooked beak. With one snap it broke a stick thicker than Herod's thumb.

When John Endecott entered the parlor, Herod remembered that turtle. His brown eyes were nestled deep in dark-ringed sockets, and they fixed on Herod with the reptile's burning wrath. He glanced at her, and then appraised Mary. When Endecott's gaze returned to Herod, she thought once more of that turtle, gauging the distance to its target before making a lightning strike.

"So, the King of the Quakers is no longer content hiding behind women's skirts," Endecott sneered. "Now he's sending children to do his work."

Herod replied, "Nobody sent me, sir. I'm here of my own will."

Endecott shrugged. "So they all say. What is it this time? Free the Quakers or God will drown me in blood?"

"I ask you to –"

"*You?*" Endecott's voice rose with that startled word. "Not *thee?* Are you not one of those Quaking fools?"

"No, sir," Herod replied. "But I do ask you to consider what God thinks of your laws." As she spoke, Rebecca began to wail.

The baby had been patient during her peculiar morning, but now Rebecca had had enough. She was hungry, wet, and had been held for too long. Endecott grimaced as the baby's wails grew more piercing. The woman who had answered the door now appeared in the kitchen doorway. "John, what is it?"

"Just a moment, Elizabeth," he said. To Herod he growled, "Can't you silence the brat?"

Herod's eyes narrowed but she answered calmly, "Governor, if your wife has borne children you know that there are times when you can't. If I could feed and change her, we can speak more easily."

"Deliver me," Endecott said in exasperation. "I've sent for the magistrates and Reverend Wilson, but they haven't come yet. You may have your moment. Mrs. Endecott, take them to the kitchen." To Herod he said, "Don't dawdle. When my assistants arrive we won't wait for you to rock it to sleep."

Endecott addressed the magistrate, "Now, Mr. Norton, tell me why this woman and her babies are so dangerous that you needed the militia to bring them." Though Herod wanted to listen, the woman that she had taken for Endecott's cook pulled her into the kitchen.

Elizabeth Endecott was a petite, gray-haired woman with a worry-lined face. Herod told her that she would like to change Rebecca's whittle, so Elizabeth motioned her to a bench by the food-laden table. "Have you a cloth?" she asked.

"Two, but they are both dirty," said Herod. "I've had no chance to wash them."

"I can help you with that, but first," Elizabeth ladled out two generous bowls of stew and gave them to Herod and Mary. "Eat fast," she said as she broke chunks from a loaf of wheat bread. "You have little time."

The two dug into the tasty pottage while Elizabeth rummaged in the pantry. Then the older woman emerged, triumphantly holding up a bundle of cloth. "Three; from my own sons," she crowed. "You may as well have the use of them. Eat, and I'll change that little one." Elizabeth loosened Rebecca's swaddling, and then saw Herod watching her suspiciously. "Eat, and fast! Might be the last meal you will see for a while."

With a whimper, Mary started shoveling her food down as fast as she could chew. Herod picked up her spoon and dug in.

Elizabeth changed Rebecca's whittle, cocking an ear toward the silent hall. "Why are you here? Are you a Quaker?"

Flinching, Herod deflected the question. "I came to visit friends in Weymouth."

"From where?"

"Newport, in Rhode Island."

Elizabeth frowned. "I didn't hear that a boat came in."

"No, we walked," Herod said with a smile.

"Walked? Sixty miles, and with a newborn?" Elizabeth stared down at the tiny Rebecca, who was jerking her fists in the air, howling to be fed. "You must be mad! What is so important that you risk your lives?"

Herod swallowed her bread with difficulty because her mouth was suddenly dry. "Mistress Endecott, I was in Weymouth when Mrs. Hutchinson and hers fled to Rhode Island. Now I live among them. They did nothing against the law, yet they were turned from their homes. William Shattuck was your neighbor but —"

"I know all about that," Elizabeth hissed, looking once more toward the door. "I know what is happening to the Quakers too. Are you one of them?" she asked again.

"No, but the torture must stop!" Herod said, her voice growing louder.

"Young woman, you are on very dangerous ground," said Elizabeth firmly. "Eat up, and heed me. When my husband returns you will apologize, and you had best sound sincere. With luck you will walk out of here with your skin intact."

"But – "

"But nothing! Even if you aren't Quaker, Mr. Endecott will see you flogged as an example."

"To prove that he is not afraid to whip a woman?" Herod said angrily. "He has proven that several times over."

"To show Massachusetts and Rhode Island what happens to people who house Quakers, heed their rants, vote for them …. Why, I would be in trouble for feeding you if I weren't the governor's wife." Elizabeth handed the swaddled Rebecca to her mother. "Nurse her fast – you have little time.

"When Boston sees you get your stripes at the whipping post, word will spread fast about what befell the woman who loves Quakers. And when you show your scars back in Rhode Island, maybe they'll stop disturbing our peace. Stay to home and keep your Quakers with you!"

CHAPTER 28
May 11, 1658

HEROD FINISHED SUCKLING Rebecca and was putting her clothes in order when she heard the house's outer door open. Out in the hall, Endecott greeted the newcomers: two men by their answering voices. "Gentlemen, the Quaker bitches are giving us a hot time this year. Last month it was that pair from Salem. Wait 'til you see this children's crusade!"

Footsteps approached the kitchen. Herod smoothed her skirt, and with Rebecca in her arms stood to meet her inquisitors. Endecott entered, followed by Norton and two newcomers. Before they could speak, Herod nodded at Mary. "Governor, please leave the girl out of this. She's no more Quaker than you. I only brought her to help with my baby."

Endecott eyed Mary, trembling on her bench with stew dripping unheeded from her spoon into her lap. "Leave her with my wife," he finally said. "Leave that baby too."

"I'll keep Rebecca with me," Herod replied.

"I said, leave her!" Endecott's gaze darted to his wife. "Mrs. Endecott, take the child."

"No!" shouted Herod. Elizabeth stepped back uncertainly, so Endecott tried to take the infant. A brief struggle ended with Rebecca wrapped in Herod's arms. She retreated from the Endecotts, bumped into Mary, and gripped the girl's shoulder to keep from falling.

Perhaps mistaking Herod's gesture as including Mary in her refusal, Endecott said coolly, "Then come along and cease wasting our time."

Elizabeth touched the governor's arm. "John, can't you see that the woman is distraught? She's no Quaker, so perhaps this is but a new mother's folly. Be merciful."

"Folly or no, let us see what the woman is made of," was Endecott's offhand reply.

"Where is Reverend Wilson? He should be here by now," Endecott grumbled. He was now seated at a table in the parlor, with papers, quill pen, and ink at hand. Herod stood before him. Mary was almost hidden behind her.

Flanking Endecott was the pair of magistrates, and near the doorway stood Mr. Norton. Endecott nodded to his left, "Mr. Bellingham, my deputy." With a similar gesture to his right he said, "Mr. Atherton, Sergeant-Major of our militia. Gentlemen, constable Norton has escorted this woman from Weymouth. What has she done to merit such attention?"

"She calls herself Hor-rod Gardner, from Newport, in Rhode Island," said Norton.

"Horrid?" asked Bellingham.

"Whore-wood?" Endecott snickered. He couldn't have startled Herod more if he had slapped her. Her head cocked disbelievingly when the governor added, "What sort of pagan name is that?"

Herod reminded herself to remain polite. "The name my parents gave me, Governor."

Norton quickly established that Herod had disturbed the peace at Weymouth yesterday. "Incited sedition, really, by calling on our freemen to overturn their government and undo their laws. She ran off before she could be apprehended, but was tracked down this morning." He concluded, "She *claims* that she's no Quaker."

"I already told you that," Herod said. Endecott glared irritably.

"But she talks like one, except that she doesn't say thee or thou," added Norton.

"Those Quaker women who came hence from Salem were sheltered in Rhode Island," Endecott said. "Now this little parade, also from Rhode Island."

"There's a proper nest of snakes there," mused Major Atherton.

"It didn't take long for the Quaker heresy to catch fire, even if this one says she's not," said Endecott. To Herod he commented, "So, you are no Quaker. What are you?"

"I'm a friend to Friends, even if I'm not one of them," Herod admitted. "But I have witnessed scars given to them in Boston and in other Puritan lands, and it is wrong. You torture them for saying 'thee' or not taking off their hats, but they do you no harm."

"They break our laws and disrupt our godly services," said Bellingham. "You punish law-breakers in Rhode Island, do you not?"

"They would come to no harm if they kept their filthy carcasses in Rhode Island – even better, in England – and left us in peace," Endecott observed. "Do you not have a lock or bar on your door to keep thieves from your home? Our laws are our locks, meant to keep us safe from evil-doers."

"Quakers are not thieves and they do no evil in Rhode Island," said Herod.

"I care not, you ignorant cow," Endecott snapped. "If they break our laws by coming here, they earn the lash. Their blood is on their own hands."

"If they defy our banishments, they'll get worse," Bellingham added.

"Just let them pass peacefully and have their say, and they will leave," Herod told them. "That is what they do in Newport. If you hadn't jailed Mistress Dyer, she –"

"Dyer! Do you know her?" Endecott demanded.

Herod's heart skipped a beat. "I know that she was jailed for months, but she broke no law."

Endecott began, "She broke –"

"A law she knew nothing of!" Herod finished. "How could she? Mistress Dyer was in England for these several years past."

"Did the Dyer bitch send you here?" Endecott asked.

Again the governor's language startled Herod. A pulse began to throb at her temples and she heard a faint, high whine. "No one sent me," she replied cautiously. "I came of my own will."

"Then you are a weak-minded idiot!" laughed the governor.

Bellingham said uneasily to him, "Let the woman take her get and send her home. Clearly, she's not in her right mind."

"Truer word never spoken, sir," said Endecott. "The woman is under Satan's spell." Herod almost smiled, but Endecott's next words sobered her. "Remember Anne Hutchinson's deluded rabble in 1637? They voted in one of their own as governor to repeal our laws and set their own mockery in place. No mere woman was behind that affair – it was Satan! We escaped by turning out Vane, but Hutchinson and the rest of that rabble didn't flee far enough. Now they hold sway in Rhode Island, ruled by Satan!"

"Sir, our president is really Benedict Arnold," said Herod. She kept her tone mild, hoping a jest would lighten Endecott's mood.

It didn't work. He shouted, "Enough of your insolence! This smacks of witchcraft. The Hutchinson bitch cast her spell on Governor Vane. Then she cursed the Dyer woman's womb so that she brought forth a monstrous birth!"

"She blighted her own womb," observed Major Atherton. "Hutchinson birthed her own monster."

"Dyer is the Devil's whore now, sending heretics to torment the godly. This deluded bitch is a fine example." Endecott pointed straight at Herod.

"Where is Wilson?" he cried to Bellingham. "We need him after all. Even better, where is Reverend Mather? He's expert on witchery, is he not?" Herod saw an eerie pinkish fog penetrate the room. Endecott didn't seem to notice it as he shouted coarsely, drawing laughs from his henchmen. He called, "Fetch both Mathers, father and son!"

At first Endecott had frightened Herod with his talk of witchcraft, for witches could be hanged. But the woman who had once fended off her drunken husband with a butcher's knife would not back down now. Herod took a step forward, put her hands on the edge of Endecott's table, and bent to look him in the eye.

"Governor, can't you decide what to do? There are plenty of men here, yet you hesitate like curs snarling at a wolf as they wait for their numbers to grow."

Endecott gaped at Herod disbelievingly. She rushed on. "My uncle in London complained bitterly of Puritans jailed for months and having their ears cut off. Now you have learned to do it too." The governor was trying to speak, but Herod shouted at him, "Just who is under Satan's spell? You call the Quakers fools. Is torture how you cure folly? If you can't be just, at the least you should show mercy!"

"Mercy – to witches?" Endecott rasped. "Give them the lash and then hang them, I say, starting with that whore of Satan, Mary Dyer."

Herod took a deep breath. "Governor, I would tell Satan to claim you, but he already has. You do his work with your whippings and brandings. Your cruel laws damn you and those who vote for you. Who is the wizard who really deserves hanging, Governor Endecott?"

"How dare you!" he cried. "Let's see if ten lashes will drive Satan out of you."

Atherton leaned toward him. "Already there are murmurs in Boston. Those women we whipped last week –"

"Earned it as lawbreakers! We must stand firm, gentlemen. By flogging this stupid bitch," Endecott pointed a shaky finger at Herod, "we show Rhode Island what happens to heretics. Besides, we must nip this invasion before there are enough Quakers here to sway elections. What if they elect one of their own? How soon would they banish us?

"Sedition and peace-breaking is the charge," Endecott declared. "Ten lashes for this arrogant bitch, and for her whelp too."

"Mary is innocent!" Herod shouted. "She just came to help me."

"Help you to spread the Devil's word, so she will share your fate," Endecott added. "To the whipping post with them, at once!"

Bellingham commented, "If we announce the whipping and do it a week hence, we will draw a hearty crowd to learn their lesson."

Endecott frowned. "As Major Atherton said, there are mutterings already. Let us do it fast, for there will be enough witnesses. Then these two can try our jail until they are panting to creep home and warn all to leave us in peace."

"Not the girl!" Herod cried desperately.

"Another word, you stupid bitch, and it will be twenty each to drive the evil out of you!"

Endecott tried once more to force Herod to leave Rebecca with his wife. Convinced that she would never see her daughter again, Herod clung to her, slapping Atherton when he tried to wrest the infant away. Endecott finally snapped, "Leave the brat to her. Let's get this done before real trouble begins."

Atherton took Herod by the arm and pushed her outside, with the weeping Mary stumbling along behind. A crowd had already gathered in the street, attracted by the Weymouth militia and the larger Boston force waiting by the door.

Herod thought that Endecott might address the crowd, but he merely leaned close to her to grate, "Keep your mouth shut, woman. Say one word and it's thirty lashes for each of you, and you won't leave jail until your brat is grown."

The armed men surrounded Herod and Mary, and a pair of lads began to beat drums. The crowd followed, with gleeful children running ahead to shout, "A whipping! There's going to be a whipping!"

Mary wailed to Herod, "Goody, they aren't really going to whip us, are they?"

Herod heard laughs from the people lining Queen Street, but she also saw concerned faces. A woman said audibly, "Are *they* going to be flogged?"

"I'm sorry, Mary," Herod told the sobbing girl. Then she raised her voice. "Neither of us are Quakers. I merely asked –"

"Drummers, beat more loudly," shouted the sergeant. The lads pounded on their instruments in an uneven roll, drowning the rest of Herod's words. She gripped Mary's slippery hand to comfort the girl, but her own fingers were trembling.

Herod's anger was forgotten, and fear took over. Despite the Quakers' confidence that they would not be flogged, they really were on their way to the whipping post! Foremost in Herod's mind was Humphrey's slashed back. Was that how she and Mary would look when Endecott was done with them? Herod almost threw herself at the governor's feet to recant everything and beg him for mercy.

But then Endecott would sneer triumphantly. He might have Herod whipped just for spite, or set her in the stocks so the crowd could taunt and throw filth at the cowardly Quaker. Word would surely reach Rhode Island. Then Herod would face Mary with her once-noble mission as tattered as Humphrey's back. Would admitting failure to her friend – and to herself – be harder to bear than pain from the executioner's lash?

Resolve built once more in Herod's heart, reinforced as her anger returned. She felt a passing gust of resentment at Mary Dyer, who had encouraged her to come here and had said that the Stanton girl would be safe. Then Herod focused on Endecott and his outrageous laws.

She resigned herself to the coming pain. 'You've withstood worse,' Herod told herself. She had borne ten children, and while she hadn't come to welcome birthing pains, at least they meant the end of pregnancy. 'John Hicks broke my bones, but that won me my freedom. If seeing us whipped moves enough people, maybe the laws will get changed after all. So, what can I do to that end?'

Herod pulled Rebecca out of her sling so the people could see her. She cried out, "See what your governor is doing!" Then Major Atherton, now wearing a polished iron helmet, caught her eye. Endecott had said he would worsen Mary's punishment if Herod spoke. Silently, she hoisted her three month-old infant even higher and onlookers pointed at the baby.

Looking up at her whimpering daughter, Herod wondered just what those innocent blue eyes were seeing.

Just beyond the screen of soldiers, a man clad in a long leather apron was shaking his fist at Herod. Was the militia there to protect Boston from Quaker heresy, or were they protecting Herod's vulnerable little trio from an angry mob? Herod tucked Rebecca lower in her arms and shielded her baby's eyes from the furious cobbler and the rest of the shouting rabble.

The procession slowed as the crowd thickened. It was a short walk from Endecott's home to the new town house at the meeting of King and Queen Streets and Cornhill Road. Only a year old, the building dominated the square. Built on squared timbers tall enough so people could take shelter beneath during rain, the huge clapboarded building was crowned by a pair of spires. When they reached the square, Herod saw men coming out of shops and women bringing their children to see this object lesson in crime and punishment.

Individual faces came into brief focus – a stubble-bearded man with mouth agape and eyes glinting. Herod couldn't decide whether he was elated or appalled. A woman's distorted face, all twisted lips and horse-like teeth. She shook a fist at Herod, but her words were lost in the shouts and drum roll. A glance at Mary. Teardrops blotched the girl's faded black bodice, and she dragged at Herod with both hands, crying, "No, no, I won't go there!"

Atherton took Mary's elbow. "Girl, don't make me drag you."

"Yes, Mary," Herod said. "Let's both be strong. Don't let them see you beg."

"But I didn't do anything!" Mary told Atherton. Then the procession halted. The four soldiers in front of them parted, wheeling right and left. The town house now towered over them. Directly in front of Herod stood a rough-sawn plank platform, about two feet high and five feet square. As their escort pushed the women up to the platform, Herod saw that the planks were dotted with dark spots and smears. Irregular lines of black spatter converged at a squared maple shaft, ten feet tall and as broad as Herod's forearm. It, too, was splotched with dried blood. Iron chains hung from the top, their shackles invitingly agape.

With a final drumroll, the militia delivered their prisoners to the executioner. The man wore a knee-length, long-sleeved leather jacket, smeared with the same dark stains that marked the whipping post. This professional – masked to hide his identity – was paid by the town to deal out punishments. He might do a few hangings in a year for murder or witchcraft, or the equally rare branding. A ***T*** would mark a thief's arm or forehead for life, just as Humphrey Norton would forever wear his ***H*** for heresy. Whippings were a common way to teach an unforgettable lesson to both the unhappy soul receiving the lashing, and those who witnessed it.

Herod's eyes met those of the masked executioner, clad in that butcher's coat to keep blood off his clothes. He looked the three prisoners over: a defiant-eyed woman of about thirty-five and her wailing infant, and the trembling twelve-year old.

With one last flourish, the drummers' hands dropped to their sides. An expectant hush fell over the hundred or so people who had gathered to watch the flogging. "These females are guilty of spreading sedition and Quaker heresy in Weymouth!" The strident call to her right made Herod flinch. She turned to see Mr. Bellingham fifteen feet away. The stony-faced Endecott stood beside him. The governor had donned a long black cloak and equally somber hat, and carried a silver-capped walking stick.

"For sedition and disturbing the civil peace, the sentence is ten stripes on their naked backs for each of them!" the assistant concluded. A cheer went up from the watchers.

"Which of 'em first?" the hangman asked. His right hand twitched and Herod's eyes followed the motion. From that hand dangled the whip which he would soon use on them. Not a broad leather strap, which would sting plenty but do little real damage. Not a rope, which would bruise, but not tear the skin. The hangman held a wooden pole, long enough for him to grip with both hands for a more punishing blow. From the end of the rod swung three tightly braided linen cords the thickness of Mary's little finger. A knot tipped each two-foot long cord, the better to tear at flesh and release bright blood.

A spasm went through Herod's body. She shouted at Endecott, "Governor, this girl is innocent. Have mercy and set the child free!"

Endecott replied just as loudly, "For helping you to spread seditious lies, she shall go first. Let us all pray that it saves her from Hell!" Another cheer, mostly male, went up from the crowd and they pressed closer.

"I hate you!" Mary screamed at the governor. A scowl momentarily replaced his imperious expression.

"Mayhap the girl's no Quaker after all," Major Atherton joked nervously. "You've never heard one of them say *that* before."

"Never mind. She is infected with their heresy. Let her return to Rhode Island bloodied, so they see what awaits them for harboring Quakers." Endecott nodded at the executioner. "We are about God's work, and we shall not flinch!"

Herod cried once more, "Let her go!"

"Yes, let both of them go. Can't you see that she has a baby?" called a woman carrying an infant of her own. She struggled through the crowd toward Endecott, but was stopped by a chain mail-clad soldier armed with a halberd.

Ten feet away on Herod's other side, a man shook his fist at her. "Whip the Quakers, I say! Whip the Devil out of them!"

"And from our midst," shouted his neighbor. Both men turned expectantly toward Mary as the executioner set down his lash and took her arm. He pulled her onto the platform and then turned her to face the avid crowd.

"Is this what godly people do?" Herod shouted, holding Rebecca high. "Do they mutilate innocent children?"

Once more the executioner paused. Endecott crossed the distance between himself and Herod in four strides. He hissed, "Speak again, and I'll give the girl ten strokes for every word you utter. Now give me that baby." All eyes were on the pair now.

"You flog old women and children," Herod spat. "By your own laws you'll be cutting off ears next. I'll not surrender my Rebecca into bloodstained hands!"

Endecott leaned close to Herod. His reptilian eyes, their pupils constricted in the sunlight, glared straight into hers. "The babe's blood is on your hands. Pro-ceed!" he said emphatically, his breath puffing on Herod's cheek like a curse.

"Well, miss, will you undress, or must I do it for you?" The executioner's voice was not loud, and it held no real malice. Still, every person in the square shivered, though many from anticipation rather than dread. Mary clutched the top of her jacket and shrank away from him. The executioner sighed in irritation, wishing that they'd jailed the pair for a few days, prepared them for this, and made a difficult job easier. He reached for the trembling girl's laces.

Mary pulled away, fumbling at the ties until she undid the bow. Red-faced, she loosened the laces from top to bottom, very slowly.

The governor jerked his head irritably, and the hooded executioner reached for Mary's laces. Though he gripped her arm with one hand, she slewed away. Major Atherton stepped onto the platform to steady her.

Mary wailed wordlessly as the executioner rapidly unlaced her jacket and dragged it off. She pulled one hand away from Atherton, grabbed for the collar of her long-sleeved shift and clutched the garment to her chest. Atherton caught her hand again, and the executioner jerked at the bow, breaking the tie in his haste. There were cheers and whistles from the crowd as the garment parted.

Endecott cried out, "Order here, or I shall have you all dispersed." The whistles stopped, because few wanted to miss what would come next.

The executioner stripped Mary's shift back over her shoulders, leaving it to dangle at the twelve-year old's waist. Though she still wore her skirt, Mary was left bare from the waist up. For a moment she was displayed thus to the crowd, spread-eagled between the two officials. She turned scarlet from her hairline to her budding breasts as the hot-eyed crowd let forth an expectant sigh.

Herod opened her mouth to beg once more, but the governor tapped his lips meaningfully before turning back to the tableau. The two officials pivoted the bare-breasted girl to face the post and raised her arms over her head. The executioner fastened the dangling manacles around her wrists. Then he picked up his three-tailed lash.

Mary was already sobbing when the first stroke cracked across her back. Three crimson streaks appeared upon her skin and she screamed. Red droplets trickled where the knotted tips had torn her flesh. Then the second blow landed. The girl shrieked, and from the crowd came cheers, jeers, and more than a few cries of, "Mercy!"

The woman who had protested before came pushing back toward Endecott, but the militia barred her way. When she shouted to him the governor merely shook his head before turning back to the flogging.

An eerie calm came over Herod as she watched Mary's torment. The girl was certainly being stung, but it wasn't the slashing that Humphrey had received. That was good. Now, could Herod turn the crowd against Endecott somehow? Not only would that complete her mission, it would be the best, and perhaps the only way Herod could avenge herself. What should she do when it was her turn to face the executioner?

"Four, five, six," children chanted as each blow landed. The wailing Mary writhed, unable to writhe away from the punishing lashes. Blood dribbled down her back and by the time the crowd called, "Ten!" it stained her shift in growing crimson patches.

Atherton and the executioner released Mary as quickly as they had manacled her, and she grabbed for the shift dangling from her waist to cover her breasts. Hoots came from the watchers as the aching, embarrassed girl turned her back to them. She pulled the garment on, crying out in pain as the material dragged over her wounds.

All eyes turned to Herod.

CHAPTER 29
May 11, 1658

"YOUR TURN, GOODWIFE." The executioner held out his hand. Mary's blood smeared his blunt fingers. Her mind was working furiously, but Herod took that bloody hand as daintily as a princess might and stepped past him onto the platform.

Everyone remarked at how serenely Quakers accepted punishment, and it was said to win converts, so that was what Herod must do. But was that enough to turn the crowd and win the vengeance which Herod craved? What would Mary Dyer do? The Stanton girl had been released, so she was safe. Now Herod was free to speak. She turned to face the crowd with the restive Rebecca cradled in her arms. "Are these *your* laws, good people, or do they come from Satan? Whipping children –"

"Executioner, do your work!" called Endecott.

"No, let me –"

The man in the butcher's coat dragged Herod toward the whipping post, saying, "You must surrender your child." Herod tried to struggle free, and then he reached for Rebecca.

When Herod had the fit just before Rebecca was born, the world had turned dark. This time Herod could see and hear, but only as an incoherent blur. Atherton, the executioner, Endecott, distorted mouths, glaring eyes far too close to hers, a crying baby, a woman's raw-throated shriek, "No, you can't take her!"

The last voice was Herod's own. She saw Mary at the back of the platform, head down and weeping. Yes, she could give Rebecca to her. Only that girl could be trusted not to snatch her daughter away and give her into Puritan hands. "Mary, come take Rebecca," Herod called.

"No! I hate you too, and I'm not working for you anymore!" A ripple of laughter ran through the crowd. Mary glared hotly at Herod, and then turned her bloodied back.

Endecott came to the platform, an anxious frown puckering his forehead. This was taking too long and things might soon get out of hand. He said to Herod, "Do you think to stop justice by this refusal?"

"Governor, I walked five days to bear witness to your cruel acts," Herod replied. "Shall I turn back now?"

Endecott motioned to the executioner, who tried to peel Rebecca from Herod's arms. She shouted, "Not this child too!" and clung to the wailing infant. Major Atherton joined the struggle, grasping her other wrist to wrench Rebecca away. His hand brushed Herod's face and without thinking she bit his forefinger, sawing at it with her teeth until she tasted blood.

With a shout, Atherton released her. Herod could see clearly again and focused on Endecott. The crowd had stopped cheering and she could hear angry mutters. A well-dressed man in the rear, his face hidden by a broad-brimmed hat with a gleaming silver buckle, tried to push his way through the onlookers on Queen Street. He was one of a dozen struggling toward Endecott, pleading with him to reconsider.

"We are proceeding, goodwife," the governor warned. "Give me the child now or its blood will be on your hands."

"Innocent blood stains yours, and you will never wash it away," Herod said shakily.

Endecott angrily waved an arm and his walking staff nearly struck a bystander. "Proceed, hangman, and lay it on well!"

The executioner hesitated. "Goodwife, will you cling to your child while I tear your clothes off, or …?"

Herod stepped out of easy reach. She transferred Rebecca to one arm and unlaced her jacket with the other hand. "I will give my back to your lash," she told him loudly, her voice now firm with resolve. "All of you are now witness to what unjust laws do!" She shrugged off the garment. Then, staring straight into Endecott's eyes, she unlaced her shift. His face was stony with resolve equal to hers.

Herod gulped. Part of her had hoped that Endecott would relent, but there would be no mercy. Her fingers were trembling, but not so badly that she couldn't undo her shift.

The mob pressed closer and Herod felt contempt for them, especially the sticky-eyed men who crowded the front rows, aroused and gape-jawed. 'So, I'll give them what they came for,' she thought. With her free hand, she pulled her shift down the arm holding Rebecca. The executioner approached, reaching out helpfully – or was it to hasten her?

Herod stopped him with a glare and shook her arm and hand free. With the deftness of experience, she slid Rebecca into her bared arm and shrugged the shift from her other shoulder. The white cotton dropped to her waist.

'Stare, you vultures,' Herod thought as the throng's eager eyes fixed on her heavy-nippled breasts. With them she had nursed ten children and loved two men. Now they were but amusements for a crowd lusting after blood and helpless flesh. Herod's gaze floated off into the distance.

When she left Rhode Island, Herod intended to address cruel laws, though it meant a difficult journey and perhaps alienating George forever. She had told herself, 'I will not simply wring my hands over my bloodied friends.' That resolve had carried her onward through swamps and the thorny Ragged Lands, all the way to the Puritans' whipping post.

Whether Herod was doing God's work or simply what was right, that flaming sense of *mission* made the blood sing in her ears. Herod was indeed fighting injustice and she would share her bloody tale with all. She dared not speak now lest Endecott worsen her torture, but she thought, 'I protest these cruelties with my blood, and my flogging atones for the evil done to Mary. God, please let these watchers raise their own protest.'

The executioner moved close and said in a near-plaintive voice, "Will you surrender the baby now or make it face the lash?" His black mask was dappled with moisture and sweat ran down his unshaven neck. Herod felt almost sorry for him. He was obeying Endecott's wicked command, but his voice sounded like he would rather be anywhere else.

"I will not give my daughter into bloody hands," Herod told him.

"Then turn about so the people can see, and if you love that child, don't move. I will try not to strike her." He touched her shoulder with surprisingly gentle fingers, steering Herod in a half-turn so her back faced the crowd. Then he picked up his three-lashed whip, glowing wetly with Mary's blood, and stepped out of her sight.

The blood-spattered whipping post loomed over Herod's head. Beyond it, the mob lined Queen Street and massed between the pillars under the town house. Their avid stares revolted Herod, so she raised her eyes to the sky. Her heart was pounding so hard that her body swayed with each beat, but she would not flinch or beg or scream or –

Herod heard the hiss of the three lashes before they landed. A path of fire the breadth of her hand seared across her back. She could not tell where the individual cords had scored her skin, or where the knotted tips had bitten deep. With her eyes focused on the post, Herod willed herself to be just like that foot-square block of bloodstained maple, unable to feel or to move or to cry out – the lashes hissed through the air –

The second blow, higher than the first, sliced across Herod's shoulders, curving around her arm, Rebecca shrieking, oh God, did it hit her and I didn't keep her safe and oh God I should have given her – the lashes sang again –

After the third blow crossed the first, Herod glanced over her shoulder at the executioner. His hands were laced on the whip's handle, and he struck her with far greater vigor than he had used on Mary, muscles bulging beneath the leather jacket as he drew back the lashes again and Herod looked away –

The lashes curved around her waist, just above her skirt and dangling shift. This time Herod could no longer stop her scream, but her body was a marble statue like the ones she saw in St. Paul's cathedral in London. If she stayed still, Rebecca would be safe. Endecott and his magistrates, cloaked like a flock of gore-crows, stood about thirty feet in front of her. Something bright caught her eye – sunlight glinting off a silver-buckled hat. She had noticed the man wearing it before, and now he had shoved through the crowd nearly to Endecott's side –

The fifth blow landed, criss-crossing earlier weals. Herod saw her blood fly in scarlet gobbets, some splattering on the post before her. A woman shrieked in agony, but Herod couldn't tell who made the sound. Her eyes floated away from fresh crimson on the post, back to that man in the expensive hat. Something about him –

Though she managed not to move her feet or let her body sway, Herod's muscles were spasming with the effort. She must have been clutching Rebecca fiercely, but the child had nearly stopped crying, and was breathing in panting little gasps. The man reached Endecott and an argument began –

"Seven!" Part of the crowd was chanting the count, but many had fallen silent. After Herod's scream died away, she heard cries of "Mercy!" His face distorted, the governor gesticulated angrily, Herod blinking tears from her eyes –

"Eight!" More blood painted the whipping post. 'Only two more,' Herod told herself as her throat tore with a shriek when the lash landed, Endecott's squared mouth shouting, walking away, the stranger grabbing the governor's arm –

"Nine!" Herod's back was aflame from her neck to her waist, no, she was being flayed alive, she could give her agony no other name. She must stand still, though, everything in the world depended on it, she looked down at Rebecca, hoping the baby's stillness didn't mean –

"Ten!" Herod's answering croak was barely audible. She held her breath – where was the lashes' hiss as the man in the leather coat readied his next blow?

Nothing. Then a clatter as the executioner dropped his glistening whip on the red-splattered platform. Across the crowd, Endecott was still there, still watching. Their eyes met.

Herod released her grip on Rebecca enough so she could see her daughter. The infant looked up from the cradle of her mother's arms. With a gasp of relief Herod held the infant high so the now-silent crowd could see her too. Rebecca was speckled with the same blood that ran over Herod's arms and bare breasts, but she was unscathed.

Dropping to her knees, Herod called, "Governor!" She saw him scowl. "May the Lord forgive you, for you know not what you do." Her voice cracked as she fired her words at Endecott. A roar came from the crowd – some curses, but most of the people approved Herod's words.

The governor shouted, but Herod couldn't hear him. Was he signaling the executioner to begin again? She held her breath, expecting to feel the lash. Then her eyes filled with relieved tears when Endecott turned and strode toward his home.

The man in the silver-buckled hat looked straight at Herod for a long, anguished moment. It was the first time she had seen his face, but her vision was blurred. When she blinked away her tears, he had turned and was following Endecott.

The executioner was at Herod's side now, bending to take her elbow and help her rise. A murmur came from the crowd, and if any man still stared at Herod's blood-smeared breasts, it was no longer with lust.

Some still cheered the flogging of the Quaker. "Take that, you devil's imp, and tell your Friends that they will get the same," shouted a man standing only one yard from Herod's toes.

"Hush, you!" a matron on the other side of the platform called. "Surely this woman has the spirit of the Lord in her. How else could she do this thing?" She addressed Herod, "Mistress, is the baby unharmed?" Herod nodded silently. "Praise the Lord," the woman called.

Atherton was pressing Herod's elbow now, hastening her toward the town building. Herod stopped to fumble with her long-sleeved shift, which still dangled from her waist. 'I'll never get the bloodstains out,' she thought dumbly. She couldn't drag the garment over her lacerated back so she pulled it up to cover her breasts.

The major tugged her down from the platform and into a rough square formed by the militia. Mary was already there, eyeing Herod with a mix of anger and regret. The drum began to beat, and the little squad moved past the town house and the watchers crowded among its pillars, gaping at the scourged women on their way to Boston's prison.

CHAPTER 30
May 11-12, 1658

"GOODY, I DON'T hate you. I'm sorry I said that. *Him* I hate, but not you," said Mary. A little daylight filtered through cracks in the thick plank shutters covering their prison window. By that dim light, Mary was doing her best to clean Herod's lacerated back with a strip torn from the hem of her knee-length shift.

Rebecca's whittle was changed and the soaked cloth was spread out to dry. The foul rag was only one stride from Herod's feet, but there was no way to rinse it. Herod hissed in pain as Mary dabbed at her tattered skin. The girl pulled back, and Herod rasped, "Don't stop. It must be done.

"Mary, I am so very sorry that you were whipped too. I never thought it would come to this, or I would not have brought you."

"It's not your fault." When Mary hit a particularly painful spot, Herod flinched, dislodging Rebecca from her breast. The baby was too worn out to protest. "Your back is horrible," said Mary anxiously. "Those cuts go every which way and some of your skin is hanging loose."

The executioner was skilled with his lash. He had plowed bloody furrows from Herod's waist to the top of her shoulders, and then cross-hatched them. Herod remembered how Humphrey ravaged back looked, and she winced.

"Just tuck them in, Mary. We'll tear off my sleeves for bandages when you are done."

"Your sleeves aren't big enough, Goody." Mary began sniffling. "I don't know what to do. I wish Mrs. Dyer was here to fix this. 'Twas she who got this done to you."

"No Mary, it was that governor. I wanted to stop this –" Herod coughed violently. Her throat was raw from screaming and she wished desperately for a sip of water to soothe it. There was none in their cell. No stool, no pallet; just foul, damp straw scattered over a dirt floor.

When Herod's throat spasm passed, she whispered, "When Parliament hears what they did to us, surely they will force Endecott to change those laws." But Parliament would not hear of the whippings for a year, and it would take much more violence to make that body act against their fellow Puritans in New England.

Three or four hours passed, judging by how far the splinters of light from the shutter-cracks had crept across the cell's wall. At last they heard footsteps, and then someone fumbled with the lock on their door.

It was their jailer, a man with a sharp-angled nose and cheekbones. He was dressed warmly against the late afternoon chill in a thick jacket, baggy breeches, and tall leather boots. Tossing the jumbled contents of their packs onto the floor, he announced, "My missus is coming with some water." Mary eagerly scrambled toward their belongings as he went out and locked the door behind him.

The girl made a rapid inventory. "Goody, I think everything is here except our knives. Clean whittles for Rebecca!"

"Blankets!" Herod added.

With a bump and a clatter, the jailer's wife entered with not one, but two buckets. One was filled with water, the other was empty. The woman said, "Clean water, and the other's for piss. Don't mix 'em up." She was gone so quickly that Herod barely saw her. Moments later the woman returned, and her husband was with her this time. He dropped an armload of firewood by the tiny hearth and left. His wife bore a steaming kettle and a bundle of rags. She told Herod, "I'll wash your wounds if you like, or the girl can do it."

With a look at Mary's pleading eyes, Herod croaked, "Please, will you?"

The big woman was surprisingly gentle as she bathed Herod's wounds with warm water. "He did a proper job on you," she commented. "I heard that you was holding your baby. Must have made Endecott mad for him to do you like this." Herod nodded, and the woman said heartily, "Well, law-breakers get what's coming to them." With Herod's torn skin clean, she salved the wounds and then told Mary, "Let's have a look."

After assessing Mary's welts, the jailer's wife said, "He went light on you, miss." She rinsed the rag she'd used to wash Herod's back, and then set to bathing Mary's wounds. Herod whispered, "What is your name?"

"Ain't got time for prattling," she told Herod. "They searched your stuff for Quaker books." Herod shook her head, and the big woman added, "Nothing there, so you won't get another whipping. God must love you both."

Lastly, the jailer's wife brought bowls of cold oat porridge, a half-loaf of coarse rye bread, and a pitcher of new milk. "Make this last through morning," she told them. "You won't get no more until dinner."

"How much will this cost?" asked Herod anxiously. She had been warned about exorbitant jailer's fees for food and fuel, which must be paid before they would be released. There was a sack of pennies strapped around Herod's waist beneath her shift, given to her by Humphrey for that purpose. She hoped that she had enough.

To her surprise, the jailer's wife said, "Don't fret about that. I've orders to see you treated well."

Herod and Mary agreed to save their firewood for the morning chill. They had been sleeping outdoors for a week and would be warm enough inside. They had no candle, so when the pair could no longer see by the feeble light creeping through the shutters, Mary laid their deerskins on the foul straw and they huddled together under their wool blankets.

The salve smeared on Herod's wounds eased the pain scalding her back and she slept for a while. Mary woke her, whispering, "I hear voices."

Staring into the darkness, Herod wondered if Mary had been dreaming. Then she heard a furtive murmur, "Who is there? Can thou hear me?"

The jailer had warned them not to talk to anyone, or risk another whipping. Herod hesitated for several anxious heartbeats, and then croaked, "We can hear. Who are you?"

"Dorothy Waugh. I am here with Sarah Gibbons. We have a few minutes to talk because the jailer just went out. His wife cares not if we speak a little. What is thy name?"

"I know you – I met you with Mary Dyer! I am Herod Gardner, and Mary Stanton is with me."

"Praise the Lord," said an older-sounding voice. "But why are you twain here? You aren't Friends."

Herod explained, "I asked people in Weymouth to stop this. Endecott whipped us too, though Mary is innocent of it all."

"We have been jailed a month," said Dorothy, "whipped like thou, and once kept without food for three days. What food the jailer did bring was horrible slop, unfit for hogs. We offered pay for better, but he said we could starve if we wouldn't eat what we were given, and leave our carcasses behind us."

"The jailer already brought food and firewood," said Herod.

There were whispers before Dorothy replied, "Then you two are fortunate."

Sarah added in her quavering voice, "We spoke to some who saw thee whipped. Many were disturbed because thou were holding thy child. Maybe Endecott is worried, so he will treat thee well.

"Quickly now, I must warn thee. You both are in grave danger, so beware who thou talk to. They put spies in jail to whisper as we are now, then turn thee in. The governor locks the shutters so we can't spread 'heresy,' but take care who thee hear through the windows. Lastly, beware Reverend Wilson. Don't match wits with any of them."

Dorothy said, "Wilson called Sister Sarah a witch, and that is a deadly charge. Two years ago they hanged Bellingham's sister as a witch. He was deputy governor then as he is now, but still she hanged. Endecott signed the death warrant. If someone accuses thee …."

"Beware Wilson," Sarah echoed. "He may come to thy cell to pray with thee."

"What should I tell him?" Herod asked.

Dorothy said, "Nothing."

"Perhaps 'I don't know' would be best," Sarah replied. "Thou performed God's work today and he will forgive whatever thou say. Let Wilson pray over thee, play the ignorant fool, and they will free us all in time."

"How long will we be here?" Herod asked.

"There is unrest, so they dare not keep thee and thy baby for long," Dorothy told her. "But Endecott saith not how long he will keep us." Then she said urgently, "Jailer is coming back!"

Sarah said quickly, "God knows what thou did today, Herod, thee and thy maid. He will keep watch over you both, and we will talk anon." The outer door of the jail slammed, and silence fell over the dank prison.

When grey light began filtering between the shutters' boards, Herod noted it with fatigue-dulled eyes. Two shutters, four planks each, as broad as her hand. Brightening slits marked minor cracks, and a few shrunken knotholes let in rich half-circles of light.

If Herod concentrated on those bright slivers and lay perfectly still, the pain in her lacerated back quieted. However, she'd been lying on one side for too long with only matted straw and a deer hide between her shoulder, hip, and the cold dirt floor. Eventually she must turn, and the throbbing pain would flare again so that every gash, bruise, and three-cornered tear pulsated with fire. Then it slowly subsided and Herod got scraps of sleep before Mary brushed against her or Rebecca whimpered to be fed.

The light brightened, conversations and cart traffic increased in the street outside, but no pedestrian spoke to them through the shutters. After the Quakers' warning, Herod wouldn't have answered.

Footsteps came to their door a couple of hours after sunrise. When the unseen person inserted a key into the lock, Herod sat up. She muffled a cry as scabs on her back split and began to bleed afresh. The jailer stuck his head into their cell. "Everyone still alive?"

Mary blinked in the sudden light and said a hasty, "Yes."

Herod asked, "Can we have water to clean the baby's wraps?"

"My missus will see to it," he replied, and then ducked out and relocked the door. He walked heavy-footed to the Quakers' cell; their lock clicked and the door creaked. "Come on you two, get your duds and don't dawdle. Governor's waiting for you."

They walked quickly past Herod's door with the jailer's boots pounding behind them. "Herod …," Dorothy said, but nothing more. The jail's outer door slammed.

Herod listened for their return, but the morning stole silently by. It was nearly midday when the next person arrived at their door. This time it was the jailer's wife, toting bread, cheese, another pitcher of milk, and a pail of water. She bathed Herod's wounds again. "It ain't too bad, Goody. Looks clean, and not much bleeding."

Though she wouldn't tell Herod her first name, Goody Salter was satisfied with how Mary's back was progressing. "Scabbing over nicely, but you'll bear scars to explain to your husband."

Herod begged, "Where have the Quakers gone?"

"Never you mind. You shouldn't be taking any interest in them, if you get my drift. You get out of here sooner if Endecott thinks that you aren't one of them."

"Can I send a message to Newport?"

"That's up to the governor, so ask my husband when he comes. He's had a busy morning or he'd have got to you sooner. I'll bring supper before dark. Mind that you save some to break your fast in the morning."

After Goody Salter left, Herod and Mary settled down to wait. An hour later, they heard two people stepping toward their door. Herod's panicky thought was that Endecott was coming with the jailer. It was Salter, but he was followed by a wizened man at least seventy years old, with a gray beard that reached his collarbones. He was a minister by his clothing – black skull cap, white neck band, and a severe black suit.

The jailer announced, "This is Reverend Wilson, with a few questions to ask of you." He spoke directly to Herod, as if Mary did not exist. To Wilson he said, "Sir, I will wait for you in my office." He closed the door behind him but did not lock it.

So this was the fanatic from Sarah and Dorothy's warning. The man studied Herod as intently as she eyed him. His faded brown eyes flicked over Mary before he said genially to Herod, "You are the woman and infant I heard about. Is the babe well?"

"Yes," Herod replied, but she was startled by Wilson's gentle tone.

"I'm not forgetting you, young miss. I hear that your name is Mary."

"Mary Stanton." The girl's face brightened. "Thank you, sir."

"And are you recovering after yesterday's ordeal?"

"Yes, Reverend." Mary broke out in the first smile that Herod had seen on the girl's face since the night they spent in Nash's barn. "Reverend, can I ...."

Wilson turned his back on Mary, leaving the girl's words to fade in midair. Those pale brown eyes fixed on Herod. "I understand that your name is Gardner," he said, still with that gentle, fatherly tone.

"Yes, sir," Herod said. She reminded herself of the need for courtesy in hopes of receiving the same.

"Goodwife?" Herod nodded. "Well, Goodwife Gardner, I also hear that you come from Rhode Island."

"From Newport. I once lived in Weymouth and went to show an old friend my new daughter." Wilson nodded. "Mary is my maidservant, helping with Rebecca."

"Pray continue."

Herod found herself wanting to please the elderly minister. Why, he didn't seem like the ogre that the Quakers had described. She told him, "My friend died and I hadn't heard."

"Such a long walk you had for nothing," Wilson said sadly.

"Yes, Reverend."

"So, you went to the Weymouth market," he prompted.

"Looking for others I once knew."

"And talked with some people there."

"Asking about my friends."

"Goodwife, you were whipped for supporting Quaker heresy! I know all that you said. Those fools have disrupted Sabbath all over Massachusetts, sowing discord and seeking converts wherever they go. You claim that you are not one of them?" Wilson's fatherly tone soured and his faded eyes were suddenly piercing.

"Mr. Wilson, I am no Quaker, but they have been treated far too harshly and so have I," Herod said. She was wary and more than a little angry now.

"Goodwife Gardner, that is not true. We make laws to protect our people from evil. When Quakers break those laws they are punished."

"What evil? Taking a ship to Boston as Mary Dyer did on her way home from England?"

"Mistress Dyer. Hmm. As for you and your servant, you were scourged to drive Satan out of you, as well as for law-breaking. Make no mistake – it is Satan who sent you here."

"Mr. Wilson, I came of my own will."

"Do you find this amusing?" he snapped.

"No sir," Herod replied warily.

"Were you not sent by one of that Quaker horde infesting Rhode Island?" There was no hint of kindness in Reverend Wilson's voice now. Mary was shrinking away as if she feared he might slap her, but Wilson's attention was fixed on Herod.

"They told me not to come. I but wanted to see my friend –"

"Yet you were inciting insurrection in the common. Even at the whipping post you defended those heretics. If it wasn't Mary Dyer who put such words in your mouth, then 'twas surely Satan himself!"

Herod might have laughed if her situation weren't so perilous. "Mr. Wilson, I see Satan's handiwork in the scars borne by those Quakers. Is this truly what God wishes?"

"If this is what it takes to keep the Devil from Massachusetts, then yes!" Wilson cried. "I would burn every Quaker in the world to save innocent souls! Governor Endecott and I are charged by God to keep murderers, witches, and heretics away from his people. We will do whatever we must, even if it seems cruel to simpletons like you.

"Some here see witchery in the Quakers' pernicious ways. Have you seen marvelous happenings in Rhode Island? Do they call down God's curse on godly Puritans?"

"I've not been to their meetings," Herod said, feeling a bit of giddy humor return. "I hear that they sit together to pray or sing. That doesn't sound like witchery to me."

"Goodwife, bewitchment takes all forms. Blasphemy and fits are easy to see, but evil can wear a friendly face and speak soothing words." Wilson's voice was now an angry rasp. "Pride and rebellion are sins, so who can say that Satan is not behind the Quakers' words and deeds?"

"I know not," Herod replied calmly. "But are you and Governor Endecott not proud to be doing God's work here?"

Wilson's eyes narrowed in fury. "We are *humbled* that God chose us for this glorious task! He set us here to demonstrate that a people guided by his word will prosper, and that those deluded by Satan will surely fall!"

Herod could have told Wilson that Rhode Island was prospering too, but he gave her no chance. "Just as God sent Indians to remove the Hutchinson woman and her heretical soul from this world, so does the Devil use human agents to strike at the godly! Proud and haughty women: Hutchinson, Dyer, and now you flaunting yourself at the post yesterday. 'Tis a wonder that God didn't strike you dead for mouthing our Savior's words!"

"Will you ...." The minister's voice faltered. He coughed and then said more strongly, "Will you and your maid pray with me, Goodwife? Pray for God to drive Satan from your hearts and steer you back to salvations' path?" His cheeks had turned pale, and he rubbed his eyes.

Herod said, "Mr. Wilson, we've a pastor of our own in Newport. I will pray with him."

Wilson turned to the door and rapped feebly on it. "Mr. Wilson, are you well?" Herod asked. Without looking at her, he straightened and knocked harder. They heard the jailer's footsteps approaching.

The minister's voice was stronger when he turned back to Herod. "Goodwife Gardner, you and your maid are in grave peril." Herod felt like laughing once more, for that is how Sarah Gibbons had warned her about Wilson. "Satan has gathered in Mistress Dyer and those Quakers, and he is plucking at you. You must pray with me whilst you are still jailed or with your pastor when you are released."

The door swung open, and the jailer stuck his sharp-nosed face in to see what was amiss. Wilson turned once more to Herod. "Make no mistake about this: your soul rests in Satan's hands. Naiveté will not protect you on Judgment Day." With a whispery swirl of his cloak, Wilson was gone, leaving Herod and Mary in their dark cell.

CHAPTER 31
May 25, 1658

AT FIRST, EVERY footstep their cell meant near-panic for Herod and Mary. Neither the jailer nor his wife would tell them what became of the Quaker women. Had they been punished again, put on a boat to England, or driven into the wilderness? And when would Endecott or Wilson come to torment their prisoners again?

Despite their fears, nothing happened. Goody Salter brought food and tended their healing wounds, but wouldn't give them information. Her husband supplied clean straw and a daily armload of firewood. Wilson never returned, nor did Endecott disturb the silence.

Terror became tedium. Other prisoners came and went, but none were housed near the Rhode Islanders' cell. The world beyond that small, dark room was nonexistent as far as Herod and Mary could tell.

They talked of their lives, learned each other's songs, and made cats-cradles with a cord braided from torn strips of their shifts. Rebecca was pampered and allowed to sprawl unswaddled. Her fists could find her mouth now, and she began to hold up her head. Mary's scabs were flaking away. Herod's itchy back protested when she moved, but she could finally wear her bodice and jacket.

On their first morning, Herod used a fork to gouge one of the rough-sawn boards of their cell. She added a new mark every day. This morning she had added the fourteenth scratch and counted them yet again. Yes, fourteen. Two weeks in this dank hole reeking of moldy straw and the slop bucket. That morning the jailer's wife came early with their food. She dressed Herod's wounds, but then secured the bandages with a cloth strip wound around her torso.

Herod was sharing a hard chunk of bread with Mary when the jailer poked his head into their cell. "Get your stuff together and hurry up about it. Governor's waiting for you."

Herod's heart leapt, not with fear, but with hope. "Are we being freed?"

Salter didn't answer this question any more than the others that they'd asked in the past fourteen days. He merely said, "Let's go."

Rolling their blankets into packs was familiar work, and Mary did it quickly while Herod prepared Rebecca to move. She told the girl quietly, "Sarah and Dorothy must have gotten word to Mary Dyer." Salter cast an irritable glance at her. Herod's hope lightened her feet as she followed the jailer to his tiny office. There stood John Endecott.

The governor was red-cheeked, and the folds circling his eyes were as dark as bruises. He glared sourly at his three prisoners, large and small. "Have you enjoyed your stay in our fair city?" he sneered.

If being humble meant release, then Herod would gladly grovel. "Yes, governor. Your jailer has been very kind to us."

"Kinder than you deserve. Do you still think our laws unjust?"

Herod paused for a breath. "They are your laws, governor. I am taking my daughter and Mary home, so I am no longer concerned with them."

"That is the only wise thing you have said this month," Endecott replied. "Do you understand what will happen if you ever spout your deviltry in Massachusetts again?" Herod nodded, but Endecott told her, "A whipping far worse than the one you just got, and you will work for your keep. It will be a long, long time before you crawl home to Newport again. Understand?"

The last word was spoken directly into Herod's face. She swallowed hard and said, "Yes, governor."

"Do you?" Endecott demanded of Mary. The cowed girl merely nodded. "Then leave me. There is a man outside who will escort you from Massachusetts. Speak to no one as you go, and if I ever see you again …."

"Thank you, sir," Herod said meekly, and Mary echoed, "Thank you."

Endecott tossed an irritable wave in their direction, saying, "Away with you." Herod turned so quickly that scabs on her back cracked. She bit her lip to keep from crying out, for she wouldn't let Endecott see her pain.

Reaching for the latch, she thought, 'He said there is a guard to take us out of town.' She pictured a pike-toting lout trailing them down the Pequot Path to Rhode Island, driving them when they needed to rest and jeering at their weariness. She opened the door and blinked in the first sunlight she had seen in two weeks.

A man waited outside, but he wasn't carrying a pikestaff. He was a few inches taller than Herod, with long, dark hair braided into a neat queue. His stylish black felt hat bore a woven silk band with a glittering silver buckle. This was the man who had tried to halt her flogging. Herod stopped cold when she recognized John Porter.

"By God, it *is* you," he said, reaching out to help her down a pair of steps. Herod's hands were chilled by fear, so when she clasped his hand, it was the warmest, most comforting sensation she had felt in years. The last time she had felt this safe was the night that George Gardner had taken her into his home after she fled John Hicks' attack. "Have they treated you well?" Porter's dark eyes were red-rimmed, as though he had slept poorly last night. "Do you want to rest?"

"No, just get us away from here," Herod replied. She glanced back at the jail door, where Endecott stood watching them dourly.

"Give me one of those packs, Mary. I'm sorry this happened to you," Porter said.

"Thank you, Mr. Porter," Mary replied. She was pale and grimy after two weeks in their foul cell, but wore a cheerful grin that broadened with every step away from their prison.

Herod blinked in surprise when she saw Goody Salter waiting in the town house square. John asked Herod once again, "You say that you were treated well? Decent food and firewood?" She nodded.

"Then, goodwife, you have earned this," John said. He hand the jailer's wife a coin.

"Thank you, sir," she said. "'Twasn't right keeping that baby in jail. I don't know what the governor was thinking."

"Nothing good. Thank you, Goodwife," John said to her. Then he took Herod's arm to help her along the street toward the docks.

"Goody Salter wrapped my wounds this morning," she told John.

"She should have. I promised to be generous if you were treated well."

"But I didn't pay Endecott," Herod said worriedly. "The Quakers said I must pay before they'd release us."

"I paid your fees this morning."

"Oh." Herod turned to look John in the eye, though the scabs on her back pulled. "I can repay you, for the Quakers gave me coins."

246

"If you wish, but I slept better these last two weeks knowing that you were well-fed," John told her.

A hard knot of tension was unwinding in Herod's chest and she chuckled. "Then I thank you, John. Where are we going now?"

"I hired a boat, so we're off to Newport," he said casually.

Herod burst into a delighted giggle. "Mary, we don't have to go back through the Ragged Lands!"

"Huzzah!" the girl cheered.

"Even by water, it's going to be hard on you," John said. "We can stay at my inn for a few days."

"No," Mary and Herod said simultaneously. They eyed each other and laughed. Then Herod took in Mary's greasy, soot-streaked face and a louse crawling in the girl's hair. She felt just as filthy all over.

"We need to stop there for my things," John was saying. "Let's have a meal, and I'll have the innkeeper heat bathwater for you."

Herod exclaimed, "And then get me on that boat!"

Porter's hired boat was a good-sized coaster. It had a tiny cabin, but Herod said, "I don't want to be stuck in there. Mary and I have seen enough close quarters to last us for years." The captain and his teenage son rigged up a sail over the foredeck for shade. Then they hauled a thick mattress out of the cabin and placed it beneath the canopy.

"Here you go," said John.

"Not yet. I want to watch us leave this accursed place."

Then the captain told Porter, "The tide's about turned against us. We don't sail now, we'll be here 'til tomorrow."

"Don't fret – your cargo won't rot," John said. He explained to Herod, "Near three weeks ago I hired the captain to haul a load of cloth to Portsmouth, but then I waited for them to set you free."

"I'm sorry I kept you," Herod said.

John chuckled, "Don't worry about Captain Brown. In Portsmouth I have a load of pelts I got from the Narragansetts. He'll carry it back to Boston and pull in a fine profit. That will stop his complaining."

The captain's son untied the ship and shoved it away from the dock with an oar. Then the captain manned the tiller as his son hauled up the sail. The canvas bellied out over Herod's head with a pop, the ship heeled and began to glide eastward. Herod stood at the rail to watch Boston's wharves dwindle. The nervous knot in her chest vanished.

"Goodbye, Boston," Mary said.

"Amen," Herod said. Then she asked John, "When did you come here?"

"Near a month past," John replied. "John Hull is one of my partners and I came to talk to him about our land. As long as I was here, I bought that cargo. Hull and I had finished so I was ready to sail, but after what happened to you, I waited." John smiled ruefully. "I was supposed to represent Portsmouth at General Court last week. They may fine me for not appearing."

"That's terrible," Herod said.

"Don't fret. I asked Robert Westcott to tell them that I took ill."

"Who is Westcott?" Herod asked. The coaster had cleared Boston's harbor and was threading southeast through the outer islands. Herod looked back at Castle Island, just as glad to leave it behind as she was delighted to see it after crossing the Atlantic in 1637. "Goodbye Massachusetts, and goodbye Endecott," she murmured.

"Goodbye, indeed," added John. Mary blew kisses to the vanishing town.

Herod turned back to John. "Westcott?" she asked again. She felt sleepy but wanted to savor her escape. It was a wondrous ending to the worst two weeks she had seen since her father had died of plague.

"Robert Westcott is President Arnold's brother-in-law, and a friend of mine. He was with me in Boston when you were whipped."

Herod blushed. She wondered if they – if John – had seen her stripped. 'No matter: a hundred people saw you bare that day,' she told herself. To Porter she said aloud, "I saw that fancy hat but didn't know it was you."

"Like it?" John doffed the hat and placed it on Mary's freshly washed hair. "There are more in that cargo of mine. As for Endecott, he shouted me down, but I was too late to stop that whipping. I tried these last two weeks to get him to release you, or simply let me see you, but he refused. Either his heart is dead set against Quakers, or just you. What did you say to him?"

Herod waved a weary hand. "I'll tell you later. Finish with Westcott, then let me sleep."

"Robert Westcott bore my humbles regrets to President Arnold, and he also took those two Quaker women back to Rhode Island. I gave him money to pay their jail fees, since I didn't want Endecott to think me tender-hearted toward all Quakers."

"Thank you," Herod told John. "We didn't know when we'd be freed until today, and I never heard that you tried to see us."

"Endecott wanted you to be afraid." Herod murmured her agreement, and then yawned and rubbed her eyes. John added, "Herod? Tell me you won't go back."

"No, John, I've had my say."

Herod dozed the day away, waking only to nurse Rebecca. The sea air was cold, but she was kept warm by that wonderful downy bed. The captain steered his ship around Cape Cod's point, and into the shallow waters off Provincetown. John pointed to a couple of large whitewashed buildings set among several lesser homes. "There are inns onshore," he told Herod. "Would you like a room?"

"It's calm, so let's stay here," Herod said. They dined on cold roast mutton, bread, and hard cheese, watching as the captain's son tossed out fishing lines. After they supped, Mary went to watch and chat shyly with the lad. Then his line went taut, and the boy began hauling it in hand over hand.

Herod walked unsteadily to watch the boy's catch emerge. The silver fish wore black stripes from nose to tail, and was longer than her forearm. It fought vigorously, splashing the laughing young people.

"Striped bass," John said from behind her. "Some of them are longer than me."

"I caught a fish once," she told him. "When we came over I caught one like that," she held a hand at shoulder level.

"With tentacles?" John wiggled two fingers at his chin. Herod nodded, and he said, "Cod. Some of them are longer than me too."

"How do you know their names?" Herod asked.

"I'm often on the water," John told her. "Fishing is fun, and the crew tells me what we've caught."

Herod said, "My boys have a canoe and bring home plenty of fish and such, but George doesn't like to go."

"How about you?" John asked.

"You're addled!" Herod laughed.

"I wasn't sure. You weren't afraid to walk the Ragged Lands, so I thought you might like canoeing too."

Later, wrapped in her thick wool blanket, Herod watched John and Captain Brown drag her bed into the tiny cabin. It was a new tick, and was the softest – and quietest – bed she had ever slept on. Straw or cornshucks were noisy, and Herod's own bed contained too many feathers with sharp quills. After sharing a damp deer hide with Mary and Rebecca for the last three weeks, Herod looked forward to a fine night's sleep. She said happily, "John, I've never slept on such a bed before."

"Don't you have geese to pluck?"

"I hate plucking them live – it hurts them so," Herod said. "I save feathers when we eat birds, but my tick is only that thick," she held her fingers a few inches apart. "I've been saving them since I got sick, and have a full sack to add. I'll do it when I get back, and take the quills out now that I've tried this bed."

"You will have to lie quiet for some time."

"Sewing is light work," Herod told him.

"You can lie on this bed to do it," John said with a grin. "It's yours."

The sun was touching the horizon, and sky and water blazed with a hundred shades of orange and red. The reflections tinted Herod's face, but her cheeks turned even pinker at John's words. She asked incredulously, "Mine?"

"I bought the thing on a whim. You will be hurting for some time, so you may as well keep it." Herod didn't believe him at all. She would bet with the Devil that after John rented the boat he ran out and bought it just for her.

"I can't – you've already spent so much. This boat –"

"Is carrying my cargo and will sail back to Boston loaded with my furs." John laughed, "I am making money on this trip."

"Well, thank you, then." Herod said, flustered by John's generosity. "You paid my jail fees too."

John had been watching gulls dive into the ocean for baitfish. When he turned to face Herod she caught her breath. He was hatless now, showing a high, pale forehead, and his tanned cheeks were washed with ruddy light. Where many men his age were losing their teeth, John still had all of his. His mouth could look severe in repose, but tonight John Porter was grinning like a boy at the birds' antics.

'John looks happy enough to kiss the whole world,' Herod thought, 'He's old enough to be my father, but there stands the most handsome and generous man I know.' She forced herself to listen as John said, "A couple of pounds to settle my sins with God." He snapped his fingers. "If it makes you feel better, I will sell my splendid new hat and recoup more in the sale than I spent on you."

John looked straight into Herod's gray eyes. "You matter more than any hat. I ...." He cleared his throat. "You three are healthy and healing, and that pleases me. Now, let's get you to your cabin before the light fades. You shouldn't get chilled."

"I don't take chills easily," Herod told him.

"That's what I like about you," John said. "Margaret takes chills, and faints, and balks worse than a mule. There once was a little adventure in her. Margaret had a daughter from her first marriage, and she and Sarah would ride with me."

"Why did they stop?"

John's smile faded and he looked out over Cape Cod Bay. "We had our daughter Hannah, and came over from England not long after. That ended our rides." Then the corners of his eyes crinkled again. "As for you: you aren't afraid to try things. You just jump in there and do it! This trip of yours is a fine example. I'd wager that everyone told you not to. I would have."

"George was furious," Herod replied. "He said it was folly and that I couldn't change anything. He was right."

"I'm afraid so," John said. "Even if you did persuade your Weymouth friends to send a friendly representative, Endecott's Puritans would outvote him. That is what I would have told you, but it matters naught.

"Walking sixty miles through wilderness seems folly, but people will remember that a woman with a babe in her arms stood up against the rankest Puritans in New England! I am so very proud of you." Herod's face grew hot, but she couldn't keep from smiling. John added, "I just wish that you'd told me your plans first."

Herod said, "I stopped to ask you about the path, but your wife said you were gone."

"Margaret talked to you?" Herod nodded. "Was she courteous?"

"Well ...."

John laughed heartily. "When she saw you and Mary toting that baby, I'm sure that she thought the worst."

"How so?"

"Margaret probably thought the girl was your daughter, and that I got either you or Mary in trouble. She just couldn't tell which one. Poor old girl; she must have been relieved to learn what you really wanted. So, what did you think of her?"

"She's not very happy, is she?" Herod commented.

"Margaret hasn't felt well for a long time. She's a good ten years older than me – almost seventy now. Says she has heart trouble and those fainting spells, but …."

"Do you doubt her?"

John shrugged. "When we first came to New England, she hated walking muddy roads instead of riding in a carriage, so she wouldn't go out. Next she was embarrassed by her bad teeth. Now I don't know how far she could go. Even on this calm sea and with your down bed to lie on, I don't think that Margaret could travel as far as Providence."

"Poor woman."

"I feel sorry for her too," John said. "But I refused to stay home all these years just because she wouldn't go out, and I won't stay shut in now." With a twinkle in his eye, he added, "If Margaret was to take this trip, she would have three maids to attend her, and I would need a keg of brandy. If it didn't ease her pains, it might help mine."

During the night the breeze shifted from north to east, which sped John's chartered ship along. They tacked southward along the flat beaches of Cape Cod, and then sped past the southern elbow with its broad shoals and sand bars. Soon Narragansett Bay was in sight.

Herod's bed had been hauled back outside, but when the ship entered the bay she stood to watch. John pointed to a long bluff on the eastern shore. "See there? That's Point Judith. No white man lives on this side of the bay for another twenty miles; not 'til you get to Richard Smith's trading post."

"What smoke is that?" Mary asked, pointing to small gray plumes rising from woods near the shore.

"Narragansett camps. Their main villages are inland, but they come to the shore to raise crops and fish." John turned to Herod. "We could be back in Newport before nightfall, but ...." He was smiling with his lips pressed together, like a man with a secret to tell.

"But what?" she asked mischievously.

"The weather is fair, so we could go west and I'll show you my Pettaquamscutt land. We'll anchor in the river for the night, and it's an easy trip to Newport in the morning."

The captain added, "Should be a westerly breeze tomorrow. Cross the bay in an hour."

A slow smile came to Herod. She was feeling much stronger after the last two days. John's dark eyes were dancing, and though her back still ached, she had caught his adventurous mood. After three weeks, what was one more night away? There would be outcry from the Stantons, but Herod had earned whatever she heard from them, and from George. He would surely keep her close to home from now on, so this might be her last chance to go roaming.

"John, I would love to see your land."

CHAPTER 32
Late May 1658

PUSHED ALONG BY a southwest breeze, the little ship skimmed along the Narragansett shore. Mary sat by Herod with her chin on the rail, watching as fields and forest, clean rocky shores, and reedy salt marsh slid by to their left. Every time the girl saw a wigwam surrounded by cornfields, she cried out, "Look, there are Indians!"

In late afternoon, John pointed to a low ridge about a half-mile inland. "See that rock?" A gray knob thrust like a bald man's head from the forest, rising about one hundred feet above the bay. "That's Pettaquamscutt Rock. The tribes meet there at treaty time, and that's where Kachanaquant and I signed the deeds when I bought their land."

"You bought Indian land?" Mary asked.

"My four partners and me. Ever since we passed Point Judith you've been sailing by our land." John's tone was offhand, but Herod could see that he was very pleased with himself and his purchase.

Mary's mouth fell open. "You own all of this?"

"Our land goes inland further than you walk from Goody Gardner's home to Newport town and back again."

"And how much did you pay?" Herod asked.

"Less than two hundred pounds." Now it was Herod's turn to gape, and John's smug grin broadened. "Other sachems are willing to sell, so we'll own more soon.

"There is the Pettaquamscutt River mouth," Porter gestured at an inlet just off their bow. "The tongue of land between the river and sea is still Indian. But the far side of the river, up to the Rock and far beyond, is ours." John shouted to the captain, "Turn in here!"

The ship slipped into the lower Pettaquamscutt River. When they turned northward and lost the sea breeze, the sail went slack. "This little river valley – isn't it pretty?" John asked.

Mary breathed, "It sure is," and Herod nodded her agreement. All of this land was John's! George had over two hundred acres of pasture, woodlot, and cornfield, but John and his partners owned more land than all of Newport and Portsmouth combined. All for no more money than it took to buy a few cows and some English clothing.

The valley was indeed pretty. Beyond the tide line lay one field after another, planted with the Indians' favored crops – corn, beans, and squash. Some wooded patches remained, but most of the land along the river was cleared. Above the fields lay a low, tree-covered ridge. It was crowned by Pettaquamscutt Rock, just as John's silver buckle decorated his fancy new hat.

" – is mine," John was saying.

Herod hadn't been listening, and asked, "What?"

"The western shore up the river as far as we can see, and to the ridge and beyond, is my own," John told her. Herod shook her head in disbelief.

Mary said, "Are you going to move here?"

"Someday soon, I hope," John replied.

"What about the Indians?" Herod asked, nodding at a cluster of bark-covered huts. Their Narragansett occupants were visible; women and children working around a small fire or tending the corn. A few men stood on the riverbank watching the ship.

"They have agreed to move as long as we let them fish in the river. There are plenty of cornfields inland, and their main villages are there. These are just summer camps."

"Your wife told me that she won't live with the savages," Herod told John.

He laughed. "Margaret would rather muck out pigsties than move here. But I want to, and badly."

They were now about a mile inland. John told the captain, "We'll stop here." The captain's son hauled down the slack sail and they dropped anchor. Though the Pettaquamscutt Rock blocked their view of the sunset, Herod stood at the rail with John until nearly dark. Glowing clouds overhead painted his face with gold while he told her of his plans.

"Just imagine – a few hearty families can put up homes in a few weeks. We would have a fine village in a year. Those fields are cleared for us and the soil is the best I've seen in New England. Crops will all but plant themselves. The Bulls, the Dyers, my son-in-law and his family; we are making our plans already. Half of the boys, and the girls' husbands, want land here or just over that ridge.

"Herod, you and your sons, and your daughters' husbands will all have your own farms in this valley. Fifty acres apiece, and hundreds inland. I hold the deeds and my partners agree that this valley is mine, so I can charge whatever I like. What say you to twenty-five pounds for two hundred acres? Or a free grant for helping me build?"

Herod's eyes went dreamy. They could sell their rocky farm, with its ocean gales and thin, overgrazed soil. Land enough to make her sons rich and dower her daughters properly. She could see their homes already, nestled side-by-side in this lovely river paradise. "John, I want this more than anything in my life!"

"Now let's see if we can convince your husband."

Her physical pain, and George's anger, and the Quakers' anguish had all melted away. The sun dipped behind Pettaquamscutt Rock while John described the land which Herod hoped would be hers. Her future and that of her children, all with prosperous farms of their own, glowed even more brightly than the sun.

They couldn't linger in the morning. Clouds shaped like mares' tails were forking across the sky from the southwest; gauzy veils which foretold change in the weather. They were accompanied by a freshening wind out of that quarter. The captain couldn't see the sky west of Pettaquamscutt Rock, but said to John, "We'd best go before it gets choppy. Might be a hard crossing for your lady friend."

Reluctantly, Herod watched her new-found Eden disappear as the river bent east toward the bay. "John, I must get George to see this. He will be so excited!"

"I'll hire young Will Dyer to bring all of us over in his ketch. Margaret can come too, but she'll only come if Christ himself carries her over in his arms. She would never assent to a boat ride like this."

Herod lay on her mattress as the coaster sped along, scudding on wave crests or yawing in the troughs. Increasing swells slapped the little craft in the main channel, but after the ship passed the northern tip of Conanicut Island, they were more sheltered from the wind. The much gentler ride let Herod sit up to watch Newport draw near. "I should tell Mary Dyer that I've returned," Herod said reluctantly.

John said, "We can hire one of her boys to cart you home."

Home! Telling Mary about her ordeal no longer interested Herod. George and her children were all that she could think about. Fierce longing for them had gnawed at her in prison, but the excitement of her release and that sublime opportunity in Pettaquamscutt had dampened it. Now, more than anything, she wanted to be home.

As it turned out, there would be no delay with Mary Dyer. Her son Maher resignedly told them that she was off to Providence, "to hobnob with that whole Quaker flock. Those two ladies came back from Boston jail a couple of weeks ago, and they told Ma what happened to you. Now they are going in all directions to preach."

The teen hitched up the Dyers' carthorse to haul Herod and Mary home. He laughed when John Porter directed them to the dock to pick up Herod's featherbed. "I sure was sorry to hear that you two got flogged, but you came home in comfort," Maher said. He helped the captain's son haul the mattress out of the boat and they laid it in the wagon bed.

"Ride here if you'll be more comfortable," John told Herod.

She gave him a mock-scornful stare. "You must mistake me for …." Herod nearly said, "your wife," but altered it to, "Someone who is sick. I don't need to wallow in there like a hog in mud."

"Not wallow – recline," John told her. "Like a Roman empress out to take the air."

"A row-man what?" Herod asked.

"A queen in ancient Italy. Maher and I are your loyal guards, ready to protect you."

Maher flourished his whip at an imaginary brigand. "Stand aside, you villain – make way for our queen!"

Herod laughed, but when the cart hit a rut she couldn't hide a wince. John said, "If I sit back here with you and Rebecca, and young Mary sits up there with Maher, will you ride?" She nodded.

Before long they pulled up at the Stantons' home to let Mary out. Herod apologized once more to Mary for getting her into such difficulties. The girl said, "It wasn't your doing, Goody."

"But I'm the one who took you there. I will never forget how you helped me, and you are the bravest girl that I know."

Mary blushed, and then gasped with delight when John Porter produced a polished pewter mirror and presented it to her. "For taking such good care of Goody Gardner and Rebecca."

Then the Stantons' door flew open. Avis, followed by Bob, ran into the yard. Before she got to the gate, Avis was shouting, "Herod Gardner, you said nothing could go wrong, but you got my poor girl whipped! How do you explain that?"

Herod said, "I am so sorry. The Quakers said that the Puritans wouldn't touch Mary, but it's my fault."

"I'm not bad hurt, Ma," Mary said, jumping down from the wagon seat to demonstrate.

John told Avis, "Mary saved Goody Gardner and her little girl by taking such good care of them. Your daughter is very brave and you should be proud of her." Then he drew Bob aside.

Avis glared at the men, and then turned her narrowed eyes back on Herod. "Come inside, Mary, and show me those wounds," she said loudly. She snatched Mary's bundle of clothing, and then pushed the girl toward the house. "No doubt they are festering from neglect," she said, glancing over her shoulder to make sure that Herod had heard.

Mary also looked back, but when she waved goodbye to Herod there was a smile on her face. In her hand was the mirror that Porter had given her.

On the far side of the cart, John spoke quietly with Bob for a few minutes. Herod thought she saw John pass something to Mary's father. Bob thumped the older man's shoulder, saying, "Think nothing of it, John. Thank you for bringing our wandering girls home."

John climbed up to the wagon seat beside Maher, but sat backwards on it, with his feet in the cart's bed. "Almost home, Herod," he told her.

She rode quietly, saddened by Avis' wrath. Finally she said to John, "How did the Stantons know? We just got back."

"Maybe Robert Westcott spread the word," John said. "He brought those Quakers back to Providence two weeks ago."

"Oh." If the Stantons knew that they had been whipped, then surely George knew too. "He's going to be so angry," Herod said in a small voice.

"George?" Herod nodded. John said, "Probably so."

Herod suddenly felt exhausted. No, exhaustion was too tiny a word for what she felt. Elation at her release from prison, two weeks of fear and not enough sleep, that whipping, and worrying whether George and their children would still be at home. Herod felt like she had plunged into a well and was fathoms deep under water.

Tears welled into her eyes and Herod blinked them away. If John saw them, he would think her in pain or try to comfort her. She could hold those emotions back unless he spoke – then she would dissolve. Her chin quivered once, and then her face was still.

The cart rolled past the fence separating Robert Stanton's hayfield from Mark Lucar's corn. John eyed the seedlings. "Corn's not far along this year. It's been a cold one."

Herod swallowed hard. "Yes. George was still planting when …." She gulped again and her shoulders slumped. Rebecca had suckled earlier, and now she was asleep in one of her mother's arms. The other hand lay desolately in Herod's lap, palm facing upward as though she were pleading.

John said casually, "The corn looks hearty enough." He switched the reins to one hand. With the other, he rummaged in a pocket tied around his waist under his unlaced jacket. Then he nudged Herod's elbow and dropped something into her upturned palm. "For Rebecca."

Her hand closed automatically around the unseen object. Her fingers told her it was several hard, rounded pieces, still warm from John's pocket. Herod opened her hand and then sucked in her breath.

There lay a circlet of teething beads, large enough to slip around her wrist. The round coral spheres were the size of a strawberry, and their glowing red-orange was nearly the same color. John said, "The child won't need them for a while, but you can hold them for her."

Herod almost refused the gift. Why had John had given her so many things? Was it improper for her to keep them? Then she saw how his jet-dark eyes were sparkling, not from guile, but from pleasure. She said, "Thank you, John. I'll tell her about how you rescued us from Boston."

John's grin broadened. Then he stretched his closed hand over hers again. Herod gasped as a strand of the sky dropped into her palm.

Herod's fingers brought the necklace up before her unbelieving eyes. The only time Herod had seen that color on a woman was at St. Paul's cathedral. A woman wearing a black velvet cloak and satin dress had swept by Herod. Around her throat she wore a silver necklace wrought like glittering flowers. Their centers sparkled with five stones in that same sky blue.

The beads in Herod's hand were translucent glass, like the red necklace her father gave her the year she turned twelve. John's strand was the size of blueberries, but tinted the exquisite blue of robins' eggs. "John, I can't —"

"Sure, you can. John Hull sent to Holland for a sack of these; presents for Kachanaquant and the other sachems. I have plenty, so I'd like you to have these."

"They are beautiful," Herod breathed. She held the necklace up to the sun, and the heavenly blue glow doubled. She thought the strand would graze her collarbones when she tied it around her neck. "Like the ones my father gave me," she said.

"You haven't worn them in many years. Did Hicks take them?"

"No. When he burned our house, they burned too."

John said gently, "Now you have a strand to replace them."

CHAPTER 33
Late May 1658

WILLY SAW THEM coming when they crested the hill. He dashed to the house, shouting, "Pa, Pa, they're back!" For all of Herod's fears, her home wasn't empty. Her children, from Benoni to Dorcas, spilled out through the open door. And there behind the rowdy mob came Herod's lanky, smiling husband, glad to see her after all! George and John helped her to the ground, and Herod tried not to grimace as her wounds pulled and flexed.

When George reached to hug her, Herod flinched, and said, "Very gently. I suppose that you heard what happened in Boston."

"I did," George replied briefly, and altered his embrace to gently grasp her forearms with warm hands. Herod leaned against his chest to kiss him, and then burrowed her face into his dusky blond hair. When she straightened, George said, "We are just sitting down to dinner. Mr. Porter, would you stay? How about you, Maher?"

Maher nodded and John said, "I'd like that. Mrs. Porter doesn't know I'm back yet, so she won't miss me." Before they went inside, John asked, "George, will you lend a hand with this?" He reached into the wagon and lifted a corner of the feather bed.

George peered over the wagon's side. "What on earth is that?"

"A feather bed, and it is yours," John told him. "I'll help you take it inside."

"No, let the boys get it," George said. He turned to Herod. "Did you get that in Boston?"

"I got it when I heard how badly Herod was hurt," John explained. "It eased her trip, so she didn't have to stay in Boston to heal." George couldn't argue with that, but he was frowning as he followed Benoni and Henry inside. The two boys were nearly engulfed by the luxurious sack of fluff.

With the bed stowed away, George refused Herod's help in serving a simple meal of fried venison and cornmeal mush. He told the noisy boys,

"Take your food and go out so we can talk." The girls stayed with them, and Dorcas sat close to her father, gazing warily at the stranger.

At the foot of the table, John leaned back in his tall chair to dig into his pocket. He produced a small white bundle and tossed it to George. "Embroidery from France. Herod can sew it on Dorcas' gown."

George removed the cloth wrapper and held up a long, white band decorated with a diamond pattern. "Pretty stuff, Mr. Porter. Thank you." His voice was more bemused than gruff. Then George gave it to Herod.

The band's length was nearly the full span of her arms. "So pretty," Herod cried. "Enough for a yoke, sleeves, and a border at the bottom. Thank you, John." She said to George, "He gave teething beads to Rebecca for when she's older." But she did not tell George about the blue necklace, not until she knew more about his humor, and she had asked Porter not to tell him. John Hicks' jealous rages still haunted Herod's dreams and she did not want to awaken such a mood in George. Instead, she asked him, "So, what did you hear from Boston?"

"We heard that you and the Stanton girl were whipped and jailed at the governor's whim," George replied. "Nobody could say when you might be freed. We heard no more until you came down the lane." He gazed somberly at her. "How bad was it?"

"Bad enough, but getting better," Herod assured him.

"I told you that would happen. I said –"

"You were right," Herod told him. "You said that I wouldn't make any difference, and you were right about that too," she said bitterly. "I talked with Governor Endecott himself, but all I did was put that poor child and me at the whipping post. Nothing changed."

"Their court met while Herod was jailed," John said. "The Puritans made their laws against Quakers even stronger."

"You missed our court," George mused. "They said you were sick."

"I was in Boston these last four weeks," John replied. "I meant to return for court, but when I heard that your wife had been whipped, I stayed."

"John helped us get out of jail, George, and brought us home, too."

"I'm glad you were there," George told Porter.

"George, I'll never say that I'm glad I went. That whipping …." Herod shuddered. "But now that it's over, I'm not sorry that I tried."

George's eyes narrowed but before he could speak, John said smoothly, "You'd have been proud to see her, George. She faced the lash braver than any man, and they didn't even chain her. Afterward she prayed on her knees for God to forgive them. That should have shamed them, but you know how Puritans are. They think they are God's handmaidens, doing his work in New England. How can they do any wrong?"

"Did you see it?" George asked John.

The older man's eyes slid sideways to Herod. "See her whipped?"

"He tried to stop it," Herod said. "John talked to Endecott, but he wouldn't listen."

George took that in silently. After a moment he said, "They didn't chain you. Why not?"

Herod sighed. "Because I was holding Rebecca."

"You held our daughter while they whipped you?" George asked incredulously.

"I thought if I let go of Rebecca, I'd never see her again," Herod explained. "I held her close and the lashes never touched her."

Herod's eyes pleaded with George to leave the subject for later. He began, "You …." Then instead of continuing, he took a bite of cornbread and chewed it slowly.

"The governor could have merely scolded your wife," John said. "He admitted that she's no Quaker, but says that his actions are just. The next Quakers who turn up in Boston will be sorry, because there is no mercy in that man."

"They know what they face," Herod said.

"And are you going back too?" George asked caustically.

"I tried my best," Herod replied. "I'll warn them, but I won't go."

"That's good." George mopped his forehead theatrically.

"Besides, John has other things to tell you about. Tell George about your beautiful land." So Porter described his paradise with its deep, fertile soil for planting with corn or hay. House lots by the river and cornfields already cleared. Timber close at hand. A spring spewing water which tasted better than wine. "George, you can't buy that sort of land in Newport. A thousand Pettaquamscutt acres each will let your sons prosper and dower your daughters."

George ran a hand through his hair but said nothing.

"Come and look at it," John urged. "Let Herod heal, then we'll all go. Bring your sons and we'll make an adventure of it."

Herod looked to George in appeal. "Indian land," he muttered. "Starting over. It's hard work, Herod. Build a house, split the rails, plant the fence posts. I've done it twice already and helped others. I'm over forty, and that sort of work is meant for younger men."

"You have five sons for help," Herod said. "John says that others are coming; Henry Bull's son, Sam Dyer."

"Some of the Sherman boys," John added. "It's just talk now, but I am choosing hearty men with young families, ready to plant our own 'city upon a hill.' That's what the Puritans called Boston when we arrived in Massachusetts, and they have prospered. Just think what we can do."

"Come and see it, George," Herod urged.

Slowly, George began to smile. "Why not?" he said to Herod. "I haven't had a sail since last year. When you are ready, let's go have a look."

George's good mood vanished when he got a look at Herod's back. Her wounds were well-scabbed but he still swallowed hard. "They did this to Mary too?" he asked.

"Not half so bad. I begged Endecott to spare her, but he flogged her anyway."

"Why?"

"To set an example, or so he said," Herod replied. "Who will dare stand up to him after that?"

George growled, "So you got Mary whipped. Then, after all you went through to bear Rebecca, you took her under the lash."

"I feared they would steal her." George looked skeptical, and Herod added, "I tried to give her to Mary, but she was crying and wouldn't listen. I wanted so to keep Rebecca safe, but I couldn't let go of her."

"Keep her safe?" George shouted. "You risked her life with that stupid trip! What kind of mother are you?"

"I didn't think ...." Herod's voice cracked as she began to weep.

George squinted at her and asked, "Didn't think what?" He bit at his words like a dog cracking dry bones.

"I didn't think they would do it!" Herod cried out.

Dorcas sat up behind Herod, whimpering, "Papa?"

"Hush, now, little girl," George told her. "Mama and Papa will be quiet." Dorcas lay down and he turned back to Herod to whisper, "So ... you held our daughter for a shield?"

"No – I don't –" Herod sat doubled over on the edge of the bed. She took a deep breath and said, "That man with blood on his hands, trying to take her. I couldn't."

George let out a long breath and then finished wrapping Herod's wounds. He gently helped slide her shift over her head, and then brushed her waist-length bronze hair. At last he said, "I'm glad you are both home and safe. I love you, and it frightens me to think of losing either of you."

"You were right about everything, George," Herod said in reply. "But I had to try." Dorcas had gone back to sleep on her parents' new feather bed, and George lay down beside her. He grunted in surprise.

"What?" Herod asked.

"This really is a fine bed," George said. He punched the tick, and by the last firelight watched his fist sink into the down stuffing. "I must thank John Porter for this." Herod smiled at her husband when he added, "And go to see his land."

CHAPTER 34
Late May 1658

THE NEXT DAY Hannah Haviland and her family came to call. George dragged a bench to Herod's bedside for Hannah and Will. Herod opened her arms to hug her grandson Joseph, now four years old. The boy had dark curls to his shoulders and thick lashes surrounding wide brown eyes. "Joe Haviland, you are going to break girls' hearts," Herod told him.

The puzzled boy turned toward his mother, who said, "Joey, Grandmama's teasing. Now, go play with Nicholas." Hannah sat on the edge of Herod's bed, saying, "What did …." When she sank into the new feather bed, she exclaimed, "What's this?"

So Herod described Governor Endecott's wrath and the floggings. She explained about Mr. Porter's kindness, getting this soft bed so she could sail home without waiting to heal. She ended with, "And Mr. Porter gave this bed to us, since he has one of his own."

"How is your little girl?" asked Will.

Herod smiled at the infant, recently fed and drowsing at her side. "Rebecca scarcely knows that she had a journey."

Hannah eyed the yawning baby, with her head crowned by fuzzy red curls. "Mama, she looks just like you."

"She's got George's cute little nose," Herod said, and Hannah rolled her eyes. "She is well, I'm better, and poor, innocent Mary Stanton's almost healed."

"But Bob told us that Avis won't let her work for us anymore," George said quietly. "I don't blame her."

Herod said, "I thought –" just as Hannah began, "I'm sorry –"

They stopped simultaneously, and then broke into laughter. Herod motioned to Hannah to continue. "Mama, I'm sorry that you were hurt and about everything I said. Papa shouldn't have hit you, and you were brave to help those Quaker ladies."

Herod's face grew hot. "Thank you, Hannah, but you were right. Endecott is still governor. Those who watched it may have flinched, but they voted for him again."

George got up to stir a kettle hanging over the flames, and then shoved it to one side so the contents would cool enough to eat. Watching him, Hannah said, "Mama, you don't have a servant now. Would it help if I stay 'til you are on your feet again?"

A happy grin lit George's face and Herod said, "Why, Hannah, that would be good of you. I hope that all of you can stay."

Will shook his head. "Thank you, Mother Gardner, but we've two big flocks of chicks and they need a lot of tending. Joe and I will go home this afternoon."

"Sooner, if you don't have enough dinner for all of us," Hannah added.

As it turned out, there was plenty in the pot. "I'm sorry that we have no beer," Herod told Will. "But we have five fresh cows, so there's plenty of milk."

"I have a bit of applejack left from last year's cider," George told Will. "Like a taste?" George handed an ounce or two of weak apple brandy to the young farmer. Will took a sip and breathed an appreciative "Ahhh."

A memory of John Hicks with his nose in a mug of liquor came to Herod and she suppressed a shudder. She willed that image away and said to her daughter, "Hannah, I never told you that we saw your father a few years after he took you to Flushing. I begged for news of you, Betty, and Tom. He wouldn't say much, but at least told me that you were well. We gave some applejack to him." Herod winked at Will. "That brought it to my mind." Will smiled in response and took another sip.

"Papa wouldn't touch it now," Hannah said. "The morning he took us, he threw that jug off the ship when we got to sea. He sometimes takes a drink with the Dutch magistrates, but only one."

"Good news," Herod said. "If John hadn't drunk so much, maybe he wouldn't have driven me away."

"He said …." Hannah's face reddened. She bit her lip and took a big bite of stew.

"I have a funny tale," said Will. "When Hannah and I found out that we had to marry, I was nervous because I thought Father Hicks would be furious. Instead, he takes me aside and says, 'Well, I've got a joke for you.' That's just what he said. 'When I married Hannah's mother, she was only thirteen. I thought she was older, and she let me think so.'"

Will said to Herod, "He first saw you on a street in London. You had a basket of vegetables on your arm and were clomping around in big wooden clogs like you were mucking out a cow barn. He told me, 'I never saw anyone more beautiful than that red-haired girl. She simply glowed while she nattered with the greengrocer.' He followed you home to a woolen shop, and for a couple of weeks he watched you whenever he could get away."

George laughed and asked Herod, "Did you see him?"

Herod shook her head, telling Will, "Don't stop there!"

"Mr. Hicks said he was a salter, packing meat for sea voyages –"

"John told me that he was a scholar at Oxford," Herod said indignantly. "What a fraud!"

Everyone laughed this time. Encouraged, Will took another sip of applejack and continued, "A minister Mr. Hicks knew was leading a party to Massachusetts, so he bought passage too. He got that salter job to pay for it. He watched you but never saw suitors, just your parents, or so he thought. So he went to meet you, but said he wanted to buy clothes."

"I cannot believe it! John told me that it was by chance that he came to my uncle's shop," Herod told her family. "He must have been a mighty slick watcher because I never saw him. Go on," she added, utterly fascinated.

"Mr. Hicks couldn't believe his luck," Will said. "You were all alone in the world, with your father dead and your mother didn't care what came of you. You were …." Will blushed and said hastily, "beg your pardon, but he said you were bold as brass, asking him to meet you at the well and talking like you wanted to go to New England with him.

"So, Mr. Hicks says that he went straight to his church at St. Olave's, across the Thames in Southwark, where he figured that they didn't know you at all. He tells them that he intends to marry you."

"What cheek!" Herod said, but it was her turn to blush. Had she truly led John to believe she would wed him so easily, or was he spinning a yarn for his son-in-law? Will looked worried, perhaps thinking that he'd offended Herod. She said, "Not you, Will. Please, don't stop."

Will took another sip. "Mr. Hicks thought you were sixteen at the most, but told them at St. Olave's that you were twenty-one and your father gave his permission. He made up a name for your father – William –

but when they asked him for your name, he wasn't sure how to spell it. You say it different than him – you say Horrud, and he says Harwood."

"John always called me Harwood," Herod said. She had never told her family that her full name was Herodias, and wondered, 'Should I tell them now? No, let that wait.' Instead, she told Will, "Go on."

"Mr. Hicks went back to see you on Saturday, just like you told him, with that marriage intention in his pocket. Then you said that you wanted to get clean out of your uncle's home and asked him to marry you."

"Mother!" For the last several minutes Hannah had been looking back and forth between her husband and mother. Judging by her shocked expression, she had never heard any of this.

"I did not!" Herod exclaimed. "What a liar."

"That's what he said," was Will's defensive reply.

"I didn't mean you, Will. I asked John if someone in his party needed a maidservant, but he did the proposing. All I did was say 'yes' and tell him of a preacher at St. Faith's who would marry us without banns."

"That was the funniest part of all, so Mr. Hicks said." Will grinned nervously. "By chance he put the right date on that marriage license, and told them St. Faith's because it was near your home. He said it was all he could do to keep himself from laying in the street to laugh."

Herod scoffed, "The joke was on him with that lying license."

"Might get him in trouble with God," George commented. He was also listening intently, but seemed amused by the entire tale.

Will drained his mug. "I got one more surprise. Mr. Hicks said after you got married you told the minister your name was Herodias. He couldn't believe you had such a name."

Hannah giggled, "Herodias? Mother, is that true?"

"It really is Herodias! Never heard that before, did you?" Herod jeered. Hannah shook her head. Then the girl broke into red-faced, tears-rolling-down-her-cheeks laughter. Herod joined in, along with the rest of the family. She dried her eyes and called to Will, "You can't stop now! What else did John say?"

"Not much, Mother Gardner. But Mr. Hicks did tell why he filled out that paper and followed you around, looking into the shop window like a thief. He said the first time he saw you, you were laughing with the other girls. When he was battling with you, you never laughed anymore and he missed it. Anyhow, Mr. Hicks said you were so beautiful, that he wanted to marry you at the first glance."

Will turned to Hannah. "I know just how he felt. The first time I met you, we were both young but I never stopped thinking about you. I'm sorry that we had to marry so young, but I never regretted it."

"Nor I," Hannah said to her husband, squeezing his hand.

"That *is* a funny tale, Will," Herod told him. "John fooled me good and proper. He seemed so helpful, but he was planning it all week! Of course, I fooled John right back, since I was only thirteen. I just had to get out of my aunt's house.

"I am sorry, even now, that John and I were such a horrible match. I was young, he was hot-tempered, and we struck sparks worse than horseshoes on a flint road. If we met ten years later perhaps we would still be together. Hannah, your father was a good man in many ways. He and I went sour on each other, and there was no fixing it. What sorrows me most is that I missed you, Betty, and Tom so; hearing your voices, telling you stories, and watching you grow up."

"We missed you too," Hannah admitted.

Herod looked at her Gardner children, silently listening to a tale that most of them didn't really understand, and at George, that patient and tender man. She said to them, "I don't regret my life since then for one minute. I love all of you, and believe me, Hannah; George is much, much better for me. No jealousy, no wrath, and no battles. If John has changed as you say, then I am proud of him."

"And I am proud of what Herod did, going to Boston like that," said George from his hearthside seat. "I wouldn't put myself in harm's way for a pack of strangers, but it took guts. I have never been prouder of you, Herodias."

CHAPTER 35
Late May 1658

A FEW DAYS later, Hannah and the youngest Gardner boys were weeding Herod's kitchen garden when a woman and man on foot crested the hill from town. Hannah said, "Who could that be?" She came to where Herod sat under a tree with her two daughters.

Herod shaded her eyes, but she knew the slim woman's gait and the proud carriage of her head and shoulders. "That's Mistress Dyer, but I don't know him – wait – that's Humphrey Norton!" Herod smiled in anticipation of a visit with her dearest friend and her Quaker companion, but Hannah rolled her eyes and commented, "Here comes trouble."

Herod's grin broadened. Who could see trouble in gentle, forty-five year old Mary? However, her daughter said, "I'll tell them that you are sick and can't visit."

"I went to Boston of my own will," Herod reminded Hannah.

"You wouldn't have thought of it on your own," Hannah replied skeptically. She opened the gate for Mary and Humphrey, and Herod heard her tell the Quakers, "Excuse me, I've laundry to tend." Heavy-footed with anger, Hannah walked quickly around the corner of the Gardners' home, leaving the pair at the open gate. Herod waved a welcome at them.

The Quakers came to where she and her daughters sat under apple trees already loaded with tiny green fruit. Herod painfully struggled to rise, and Humphrey said, "Let me help thee."

With Herod on her feet, Mary gently embraced her. "We were in Providence with the other Friends when we heard that thou were returned home. We came as fast as we could."

"I am glad to see you," Herod told them.

"And I praise God thou were released from prison so quickly," Humphrey said. "We heard how thou fared at Endecott's hands. How are thy wounds?"

"I am healing well. Hannah is a fine nurse, and so is George."

"Is he angry with thee?" Mary asked.

"George feels better since I promised I will never return to Puritan soil," Herod said warily. Would they now urge her to return to Massachusetts to test the depths of Governor Endecott's cruelty?

Instead, Mary and Humphrey both nodded in approval. Humphrey told Herod, "Thou did God's work, and thy part in our battle is over."

Herod sighed in relief. "Now, please tell me that you two won't go there either."

Humphrey said, "When God calls me, I shall go where he wishes."

"Herod, for now, my task is here on Rhode Island," Mary said. "My Friends need a place to rebuild their strength, much as thou are doing now. They have a haven at the home of Sister Scott. Here in Newport, my home is also theirs."

"How does William feel about that?" Herod asked.

For a moment, the corners of Mary's mouth turned downward. She said, "Surely thou must suspect. Ever since I went to England he and I have grown apart."

"You can't be surprised." Herod said bluntly.

Mary shook her head. "We live separate lives. I have my Friends and our godly struggles. William has his own affairs; shipping horses and salt mutton to the Indies, brawling in court with Mr. Coddington, and defending his actions in the Dutch war."

Herod knew about the suits and countersuits: Dyer vs. Coddington and Coddington vs. Dyer. The two men had lived parallel lives for many years, with their fortunes rising and falling in near-concert. Like Coddington, William Dyer now concentrated on increasing his wealth, but they were still turning their frustrations on each other.

Mary told Herod, "I have no illusions that William will become a Friend, but I hope that the rift between us will close some day."

Herod shook her head, certain that event would never happen. She said, "I have heard nothing of Sarah Gibbons and Dorothy Waugh since I spoke with them at Boston jail. Are they in Providence?"

Humphrey said, "Yes, and they have recovered well. Others are there too, but not for long."

"Not Boston again," Herod groaned.

"Massachusetts, Connecticut, and Plymouth all have their bloody laws, and are in great peril," Humphrey said. "What can we do but try to save their townsmen from Hell?"

"Leave the Puritans to save themselves."

Mary replied, "What if they cannot, because their governors and ministers lead them astray?"

"It's their affair, and not yours! See here," Herod tugged at the neck of her shift, pulling it down to reveal livid scars snaking over her collarbone. Thick scabs still marked where the whip's knotted ends had bitten deep. "This is Puritan work, and a hundred people watched. Did my suffering soften their hearts? No! Endecott still governs.

"He will flog you until his whips are worn out, but he will just get new whips. When he cuts your ears off and burns holes through your tongue the crowd will cringe, but nothing will change. Nobody cares."

"God cares," Humphrey said. "He bore thee up, and brought thee home –"

"It was John Porter who brought me home," Herod cried. "What did God do for me at the whipping post? Nothing!"

"He gave thee strength to endure," Mary said. Herod didn't trust her tongue enough to reply. "Thou are angry, but in time thou will see God's hand in this." Again Herod stayed silent.

Mary sighed. "Sisters Sarah and Dorothy are coming to Newport, and they would like to thank thee –"

"No!" Herod said flatly. "I met your Sister Clark and we became friends. Now she is drowned at sea on one of your errands. I no longer want to befriend you Quakers, only to hear that you have been lashed to bits." Herod was in tears now. "I can't do it, Mary, I simply can't! Maybe it is God who calls you, but Endecott is the very Devil. If you test his resolve you will lose your ears, and then your life."

"Plymouth, Herod. God has called me to Plymouth, where Endecott has no power," Humphrey said quietly.

"They have whips in Plymouth too," Herod said. "Let me warn you of this peril, Mary: Endecott and Wilson both say that you were bewitched by Anne so you gave birth to that monster, and you are now a witch yourself; casting spells on me and on your Friends. Know you what happens to witches?" Herod asked. "They are hanged! Endecott said that he whipped Mary Stanton and me to drive out the Devil. Just think on what he will do to you."

"But we must try," Mary told Herod. "Even Endecott's black soul can be saved."

Humphrey held up his scarred hand. The **H** seared into his flesh was still crimson. "A few who saw this done had their hearts touched. Now they raise their own voices in protest. Even now Parliament is hearing of these cruelties, and they will surely command mercy from their brethren here."

Mary added, "Those wretched souls under Puritan rule are doomed unless someone helps them. If God calls us, we must go."

"But not to Boston," Herod begged.

"Not yet," was Mary's serene answer.

The Quakers' visit left Herod feeling gloomy. The English Friends turned their determined eyes to Boston, Plymouth, and Salem, but there was nothing more Herod could do. Singly or in pairs, the Quaker men walked northward and were tossed into jail to await their fate. Herod could only take dim satisfaction that she had tried to stop them.

Her next visitors pleased her far more. Just a couple of days after she saw Mary and Humphrey, a cart full of people came to her home, accompanied by three men on horseback. One was John Porter on his blaze-faced Thor. Herod vaguely recognized the other riders and the family in the cart. She had seen them at elections, but never at her gate. They were the Shermans. Like John, they lived in Portsmouth. Also like Porter, the Shermans had followed Anne Hutchinson twenty years ago, and were expelled from Boston.

John introduced them in a volley of names. Philip Sherman, a sober-faced man near fifty, was the cart's neatly dressed driver. He held the horse's reins as John helped Sherman's wife step down from the wagon seat. John told Herod, "This is my step-daughter, Sarah, who is wed to this fine man." Sarah held his hand for a long, affectionate moment.

Herod eyed the woman, whose chestnut hair tumbled over her shoulders and knitted shawl. So this was Margaret Porter's daughter by her first marriage. Herod hadn't been aware that Sarah was only about ten years younger than John.

The two other riders were Eber and Peleg, the Shermans' oldest sons, both in their early twenties. From the cart's bed tumbled more of the Sherman brood – Edmund, Samson, Mary. Benjamin, the youngest, was about eight. "We've five more, but couldn't fit them all in the cart,"

Sarah explained. Even so, the Sherman family filled the Gardners' home to overflowing.

"You look fit," John commented to Herod. "I told Sarah and Philip about what the Puritans did to you."

"'Twas brave of you to speak out so," Philip said.

"Even braver to take that little one for a five-day journey on foot," Sarah added, peering at Rebecca.

"There rests the best-known baby in Rhode Island," Porter said. Herod was pleased, but George looked annoyed. She could hear him thinking that his daughter was famed for her mother's folly.

"We won't keep you," John was saying. "We are going to visit Mr. Brenton." William Brenton's Hammersmith Farm occupied the southwest tip of Rhode Island. "Before we leave, I've a pair of proposals for you.

"Tomorrow I'm taking Philip and his boys over to Pettaquamscutt. George, we've plenty of room on the boat – why don't you and your older lads come? I'd like for you to see that land."

Herod stiffened. Was this to be an all-male excursion? But if George agreed to buy some of that beautiful riverside acreage, she could swallow the snub. As if he felt Herod's indignation, John turned to her. "Here's my other idea. Herod, Mr. Jefferay told me that you are without a girl to help you."

"Avis Stanton wouldn't let Mary come back to us," Herod admitted. "How did William Jefferay know, and how did you learn so quickly?"

John chuckled, "You can't hide a thing from that man. He has a nose for gossip like nobody else, and passes it along to the right party."

"Our daughter Mary has just turned thirteen," said Philip. "A good age to leave home and work for you."

Herod's gaze flew to the brown-haired girl standing by her mother. The girl's wide eyes met Herod's and she smiled hesitantly. 'I wasn't much older when I wed John,' Herod thought. 'This child must be terrified.'

Sarah Sherman put a comforting hand on her daughter's shoulder. "Mary's a fine cook and a great help with my little ones. She can stay with you until you are well again. Longer, if it suits you both."

Mary's eyes darted from Herod to her mother and back. They looked damp, but the girl met Herod's gaze. "Would you like to stay with us, Mary?" Herod asked.

The slender girl's chin trembled, but she bobbed a curtsey to Herod. "Yes, Goody. Grandpapa Porter says that you are very kind, and I would like to help you." Herod was pleased to see that girl's resolve, and in response, Mary flashed a winning smile of her own.

"It's settled, then," said John to Herod. "Tomorrow, you ladies can get acquainted." He turned to George. "And you and your boys can have a look at Pettaquamscutt with us."

"Good!" said George with genuine enthusiasm.

Herod couldn't hide a delighted grin. Philip and Sarah's coltish daughter might be the perfect replacement for Mary Stanton, and George couldn't possibly resist that riverside paradise. When George turned away, John caught her eye and winked.

Herod enjoyed her day with Sarah and Mary, while the Pettaquamscutt expedition sailed to the west side of Narragansett Bay. Mary was not prone to asking questions, but her dark-lashed eyes took in everything with interest. 'The girl is just shy,' Herod decided. She had shown grit, and Herod liked the easy relationship between daughter and mother. After she finished showing the Shermans around their home and outbuildings Herod said, "I have to rest."

"I heard about what happened to you," Sarah said. "You must be hurting."

"It's not so bad now," Herod said as they sat at the kitchen table. "Mr. Porter was a great help to me in getting back from Boston. I'm very grateful to him."

"He's a kind man – very kind."

Impulsively Herod said, "He was only ten years older than you when he wed your mother. It must have felt odd having your step-father so near your age."

Dimples appeared in Sarah's cheeks. "Not so odd. He seemed much older when he married Mama, and it wasn't for a few years that I noticed that we were close in age. He got a pony for me and we rode together until we crossed the ocean, and I had to leave my pony behind. I wed Philip soon after we came to Boston, so no more riding," the older woman said ruefully. "So sad. I loved my morning rides with Father Porter."

Late in the afternoon, George and the boys returned, tired and sunburned. Sarah and Mary went off with the rest of the Shermans, promising to bring Mary and her belongings the next day.

"What did you think?" Herod asked her husband eagerly.

"It is beautiful land, just as you said," replied George. "But the boundaries aren't clear. Massachusetts claims it and so does Connecticut. Parliament has yet to decide who owns that land. If I buy now and it is granted to Massachusetts, will they honor my deed?"

"Surely that won't happen," Herod scoffed.

George shrugged. "Porter says that they aren't selling land yet, so we can wait and see what happens. It will still be there in a year or two."

"Very well, George," Herod said. It always took George a while to make up his mind. Surely he would leap at that land when as he convinced himself that it was his idea, and not Herod's.

CHAPTER 36
June 1658 - June 1659

HEROD HAD DONE her best to shame the Puritans and to warn the Quakers that the torture would continue. Though she tried to numb herself to the Friends' suffering, Endecott's triumphant smirk and the leering crowd haunted her dreams.

Her whipping was mere overture for a grueling six months for Quakers who had come on the *Woodhouse*. Herod was nauseated when she heard that shortly after her ordeal, Humphrey stood at Boston's whipping post. She also learned that three other Quakers had defied their order of banishment. Each was sentenced to have an ear sliced off by Boston's busy executioner.

Friends and converts converged on Boston to pray for the prisoners. However, Mary Dyer assured Herod that she was not going to join the protest. "Last year my husband gave his word to Endecott that I would trouble them no more," Mary said. "For now I will not cause him to break that vow."

On the same September day that the three men's ears were slashed from their heads, the grandmotherly Katherine Scott was given ten lashes. New laws were applied to the unwanted Quakers. They were banished. If they returned, they would hang. Sister Scott's response? "If God calls us, woe be unto us if we come not."

"We are as ready to take your lives as you are to lay them down," was Endecott's reply.

"That man will do as he says," Herod told Mary when they heard that executions were now the law. "If he hangs you, your deaths will change nothing."

"Parliament will hear of them," Mary assured her. "While Humphrey was jailed over the summer, he wrote down all that has befallen us. His book will be printed in England, and thou art in it, Herod; thou and thy poor servant. Henry Vane will use those pages to bring our pleas to Parliament."

"I will be in a book," Herod marveled.

"Thou and thy babe," Mary said with a smile. "Thou hast said all these months that thy suffering was in vain, but soon Parliament will hear of thee." Herod enjoyed telling a handful of friends, including John Porter, about her literary future.

Though Herod expected the blood bath to continue, most of the Quakers went south at the end of 1658. Humphrey Norton said goodbye to her in March of the next year, and sailed to England to seek Parliament's sympathy and to publish his book. Was it worth her agony to be in a book? Herod was amused by the notion, but what difference would it make? Endecott was still governor and his laws were even more brutal. Nothing had changed.

And George Gardner still wouldn't commit to buying John Porter's land. No, nothing had changed at all.

With no storms on her personal horizon, Herod immersed herself in her family. Rebecca passed her first birthday and was beginning to walk. Dorcas had attached herself to her father when Herod was ill. Now, irked by the time her mother spent with Rebecca, Dorcas gravitated to Benoni and to Mary Sherman.

Mary, with six older brothers to acquaint her with good-natured teasing, had settled into place with the Gardners as easily as a new-grown tooth. The fourteen-year old handled Herod's sons with a combination of guts and guile.

The older boys began to compete for the girl's attention. After young George brought Mary a bunch of flowers, Henry shooed an aggressive rooster out of the way to collect the eggs for her. When Ben brought a load of kindling far heavier than his brothers could tote, Mary sped to unload his arms.

Herod thought that her placid Benoni would make a perfect match for the soft-spoken Sherman girl. Apparently Mary thought so too, because she was far more likely to spend free hours with Ben than to flirt with other Newport boys – or his brothers. Dorcas reluctantly accepted her brother's presence at Mary's side, and was soon begging the pair to take her with them. Herod chuckled as she watched Ben hoist Dorcas to his broad shoulders for a Sabbath stroll with Mary.

Governor Endecott must have been pleased when few Quakers appeared in 1659. Surely it was his death penalty which had brought peace. His administration celebrated by passing laws against observing holidays. A family who said 'Merry Christmas' or held a feast would be fined five shillings. Playing at cards or dice would earn the same fine, for Massachusetts sought to turn colonists' minds from fun to more solemn affairs. However, despite Puritan prayers to deliver them from Quakers, home-grown converts took on their troublesome ways.

Rhode Island was nearly empty of Friends. Herod heard of only two new arrivals, William Robinson and Marmaduke Stevenson. Herod saw the pair with Mary in late May but kept her distance. Why make new friends only to see them suffer?

A couple of weeks later her fears were justified. It was Avis Stanton who carried the news. Though Bob and George had remained close friends, Herod and Avis barely spoke. Now Newport's biggest gossip sneered to Herod, "Did you hear those Quaker-men are jailed in Boston? Will you chase after them?"

"Avis, it concerns me not," Herod said coolly.

"There's a little girl in that jail too. She's eleven years old, so they say. You could take that Sherman girl and get her whipped like my poor daughter," Avis jeered.

"Have you not heard the Puritans are hanging Quakers?" Herod replied. "I'll not go there to stretch by a noose, and neither will anyone on my account. Good day to you." She strolled south along Thames St. to leave Avis and her stinging tongue behind. However, what Herod heard about the jailed Quakers stuck. Was this to be another bloody summer?

As far as Herod knew, the only Quaker left in Newport was Mary Dyer. When Mary's thin, tanned face came into Herod's mind her nape prickled. The last time they had spoken, Mary sounded almost triumphant when she said, "Endecott has exchanged his whip for a noose. If my brothers must lay down their lives to repeal those wicked laws, they will do it. So will I!"

With Mary's words echoing in her mind, Herod's unwilling feet described a U on Thames Street. She followed Newport's waterfront northward, away from her home. She absently watched the docks pass by on her left. Rhode Island was trading livestock and dairy goods to the southern colonies and West Indies. Herod sold a few kegs to those merchants every year. She marveled at the big ships which would soon carry her butter over the seas.

A long line of warehouses and shops lay on Herod's right, crafted from neatly sawn timber. Most were painted or whitewashed. Twenty years ago, Newport was a handful of huts and there wasn't a pane of glass to be found in town. Now nearly every shop had glass windows, and there were some three-story buildings.

Herod followed Town Creek uphill to the spring, admiring new taverns and Coddington's big, solid home. 'What a prosperous town we have become,' Herod thought. 'Boston may be larger, but our Newport is prettier.'

Out to the Dyers' new house Herod went, though she wasn't sure who would be home. Everyone knew that William and Mary were estranged, though they still lived in the same dwelling when Mary was in town.

Like his sons who had been fined for refusing to train with the militia, William was also in trouble with Rhode Island's court. Nicholas Easton had delivered enough information about their privateering to be exonerated, but William refused. His case was still not resolved.

The last time Herod had seen Mary, her friend cried, "An innocent man will speak to clear his name, so why does William remain silent? Was our house built with tainted money and furnished with stolen goods?" Herod told her that people claimed he kept much for their new home. "That is not my home," Mary had said, leaving Herod to wonder just where Mary thought her home was now.

Now Herod pounded on Mary's door, channeling frustration and anxiety into her fist. When the door swung open Herod looked into beloved blue eyes. Mary was thin, honed by trips on foot from Newport to Providence. Her face brightened when she saw Herod.

"You are here – thank God!" Herod gasped.

"Where did thou think to find me?" Mary asked. Her voice was too cheerful, making Herod even more suspicious.

"Boston," she said bluntly.

Mary ushered her friend inside. Nobody else seemed to be home, not even the maidservant. Were Mary's children too uncomfortable to stay with their controversial mother? Then Herod forgot about Mary's family.

William had replaced the scarred table that stood in the Dyers' kitchen for twenty years. The new table was longer, its sanded planks waxed until they gleamed. A pack lay on that table; a bundle of clothing tied with a strap to sling over a walker's shoulder.

Herod looked pointedly at the pack, and then at Mary. Her friend said a bit uneasily, "Fear not. I am on my way to Providence where I will wait with my sister Katherine. Her daughter Patience lies in jail."

"In Boston," Herod added. "Swear that you will not go there to protest."

"God has not called me." Mary swept a few crumbs from the table and tossed them into the fireplace, glanced out the window, and then at her pack. Finally she met Herod's eyes and reached for her friend's hands saying, "Thou –"

When Herod pulled away, Mary's eyes widened. "You horrify me," Herod said. "You send banished people there, knowing that they could hang. How dare you push another child into that lions' den? That girl will be jailed until Endecott sees fit to turn her loose. I pray that he doesn't beat her bloody first!"

"I sent them nowhere, any more than I sent thee," Mary replied indignantly. "Remember that Humphrey and I both begged thee not to go?"

"You put the notion in my head with your talk of missions." Mary opened her mouth, but Herod rushed on, "I know: 'God put it there.' Perhaps we did God's work, Mary Stanton and I, but blood has flowed like a river in Boston. Endecott is bloodthirsty yet."

Mary's disbelieving face hardened. When Herod paused for breath, she said, "Just why *did* thou go to Weymouth? Were thou doing God's work or just seeking excitement?"

"Do you think me a mere thrill-seeker?" Herod shouted. "Your sad Friends bleed for no sensible cause, and so did Mary Stanton and I!"

Mary said sternly, "Thou know the cause. And though I have not been scourged, the damned cry to me in my dreams. I have salved my friends' wounds – *thy* wounds. It may be that God requires blood, just as our dear Jesus shed his to save us."

"You are not Christ, Mary."

"Neither is Endecott, though he and Wilson prate that they do God's work. Perhaps we cannot move them, but their deluded –"

Herod laughed bitterly. "Endecott says that it's *you* who are deluded by Satan, who sends you hurling yourself at the Puritans' feet. Who is of God, Mary, and who is bewitched?"

"Thou shall know us by our works, and it is not Friends who wield the lash," Mary said patiently. "Can souls in Massachusetts be turned from Endecott's bloody course by prayers uttered in Rhode Island?" Herod did not answer, and Mary asked again, "Can they?"

"It seems not," Herod admitted.

"Thou went there to speak to them, and placed your life in God's hands as my friends do now," Mary said. "If their ordeals open Puritan eyes, then they are content."

"Content to die."

"If that serves God best."

"What of your family's needs?" Herod asked.

Mary quivered as though her friend's words had struck deep. She patted Herod's hand. "If I would reach Providence before dark, I must go now."

"To Providence, but then to where?" Herod asked, sickened by this talk of God, and blood, and sacrifices.

"If God calls me to Boston, Herod, I shall go. For now he merely calls me to Providence." Mary opened the door and shouldered her pack, standing to one side so her friend could go out first. Feeling dismissed, Herod went home, wondering when – and if – she would ever see Mary Dyer again.

CHAPTER 37
June - October 1659

WILLIAM DYER SAID that Mary had reached Providence, but rumors persisted that she had kept going northward. Nearly every Sabbath Herod asked William about his absent wife. The first time he told her politely, "Mrs. Scott said she has heard nothing." Later, he merely said, "I know not."

At the end of July, William told Herod, "I didn't want to worry you, but Mary was arrested in Boston for visiting jailed Quakers. The Court of Assistants will not try her until September."

Herod's first coherent thought was that William had lost his mind. He had spoken so serenely that he might have been asking for a piece of bread. She cleared her throat and asked cautiously, "Will you go to court and plead for her?"

William gave a humorless laugh. "Do you truly think Mary needs me to speak for her? She has words enough to make Endecott wish he'd left her alone." Herod smiled uneasily, and he added, "I have no influence with Endecott, but I would like to speak with him about mercy." There was frustration in William's voice now. "Mary will lie in jail all summer without trial, and for no real wrong-doing. If speaking to Quakers is all it takes to make a 'Friend,' then Endecott and Wilson are staunch Quakers."

"But won't you –"

"Herod, I pleaded with Mary to stay at home, but it did no good. She knows full well what might happen. Let her lie in a cell until they banish her in September, and maybe she will give up this mad crusade. However, I will write to Endecott." Herod nodded reluctantly and forced herself to remain calm.

With the confidence of a former attorney general who dealt with governors and the eloquence of a husband fearing for his absent wife, William Dyer picked up his quill pen and wrote to Massachusetts' Court of Assistants:

> *Having received some letters from my wife, I am given to understand of her commitment to close prison. Had you no commiseration of a tender soul that being wett to the skin, you cause her to be thrust into a room whereon there was nothing to sitt or lye down upon but dust? Had your dogg been wett you would have offered it the liberty of a chimney corner to dry itself, or had your hoggs been penned in a sty, you would have offered them some dry straw. Alas, Christians now with you are used worse than hoggs or doggs.*
>
> *You have done more in persecution in one year than the worst bishops did in seven, and now you add more towards a tender woman. She only came to visit her friends in prison and intended to return to her family, as she declared the next day to the Governor. What house entered she to molest, that like a malefactor she must be hauled to prison, or what law did she transgress? She was about a business justifiable before God and all good men. Hath not people in America the same liberty as beasts and birds to pass the land or air without examination?*
>
> *Ye have no rule of God's word in the Bible to make a law against Quakers nor have you any order from the Supreme State of England to make such laws. Remember what Jesus Christ said, 'if the light that be in you is darkness, how great is that darkness.'*
>
> *My wife writes that she has been jailed above a fortnight and had not trod on the ground, but saw it out your window. What inhumanity is this, had you never wives of your own, or ever any tender affection to a woman, that you deal so with a woman?*
>
> *Mine and my family's want of my dear yokefellow will crye loud in your eares. I question not God's mercy, but at present my self and family are by you deprived of the comfort and refreshment we might have enjoyed by her presence.*
> *her husband*
> *W. Dyre*
> *Newport this 30 August 1659*

However, William would not carry this plea to Boston himself. When George asked him why not, William said, "When your wife disappeared in Massachusetts last year, did you go chasing after her?" Herod scowled, but George shook his head by way of agreement.

"I've pleaded with that woman to stay home, but she's off to Providence more often than not," William told them. "Mary is gone from us as surely as she was dead. 'Tis her restless ghost who reminds us of what we have lost. So, I'll not leave my family to fend for themselves while I trot off to Boston. I pray that my words will stand for themselves."

"And if she goes back again?" asked George.

"Your wife came to her senses," said William. "Mine may not."

George said, "I would drag Herod from Boston if –"

Herod abruptly walked away from the men with her face burning. 'With my own body I tried to stop the floggings, which is more than William can say,' she thought indignantly. 'He risks nothing, but still refuses to testify for Mary when she could hang!'

At the same time, Herod couldn't help agreeing with William, and even with George. Mary had put herself in peril, just as Herod had done. Herod was satisfied that she had done her part in shaming the Puritans. She hoped that banishment would satisfy Mary.

Governor Endecott's assistants met in early September. The Puritans' most pressing issue was the Quakers filling their jail. A few days later William Dyer, with his face set like rough-hewn granite, drove his cart to Herod's gate. "Please come speak with Mary," he said.

"She's back?"

"Two days ago," William told Herod. "I argued myself hoarse yesterday, pleading with her to give up this fatal cause. Mary replies, 'If God calls me, I must go.' I doubt she will listen, but please talk to her one more time."

With Rebecca on her lap, bundled against the late September breeze, Herod rode through Newport town on the seat beside William, watching the carthorse's rump. Its muscles worked right, left, right, tensing and thrusting, each step drawing Herod closer to Mary, to say ... what? 'Last time we argued so. Will she even speak to me?' Herod thought. 'What can I say to stop her? She'll go back, I know she will, when one of those accursed Friends is sentenced to hang.

'Quakers put those ideas in Mary's head, and she helped them do it to me. *Go shame the Puritans*, they said. But when I shamed Endecott – *if* I shamed him at all – his laws just got worse.' Just picturing Endecott made Herod ill. Those dark-circled eyes sparkling with sadistic glee as he watched Herod's whipping, murmuring to his assistants as she screamed and bled, their aroused, twisted smiles ….

Herod tore her mind back from that image and tried to think clearly. 'What can I tell Mary to make her stay with us?' When William halted the carthorse at his own gate, she still didn't know. He helped Herod and Rebecca to the ground, and then took the horse's bridle to lead it away. "Aren't you coming in?" she asked.

"No," William said dully. "Please talk to her."

When Mary opened the door, she was thinner than ever after a diet of jailhouse slop for eight weeks. "What a surprise to see thee!" The skies were gray that day, and her wary eyes reflected that bleak color.

"Why?" Herod asked. "Did William not tell you that he was fetching me?"

Instead of answering Herod's question, Mary said, "Thou brought Rebecca." She took the blanketed baby from her friend. "Little one, it is good to see thee. How old is she?"

"Two years next February. You should remember. You helped me birth her when I nearly died," Herod said tonelessly.

"Seventeen, eighteen months now," said Mary. Stroking Rebecca's curls, she turned to the great chair at the head of the table and settled into the seat. The child plugged a thumb into her mouth, ready to let the women talk in peace.

Herod asked, "What happened?"

"We had a long wait in prison, my brethren and I, but God strengthened us for our trials." A smile grew on Mary's face. "The court barely let me speak before passing their sentence of banishment."

"You sound vexed," Herod commented.

Mary shrugged. "Thou would have been proud to watch Patience set the magistrates on their ears. She is only eleven, but the child has the wisdom of a woman grown. Recall thou when Christ met with the priests in Jerusalem? He was but one year older than Patience, yet he was their equal. I heard mutterings that Satan lay behind Patience's logic, but the court said that she was too young to grasp her own words. They admonished her, and pray that they will never see her again."

Herod let out a relieved sigh. Though she had never met Patience, Herod had been haunted by visions of the girl being whipped at the post. Despite her fears, the child was safe.

"My brothers Robinson and Stevenson were on dangerous ground when they testified that God had called them to Boston. Thou know what Puritans preach – God has spoken to no man since Moses. They have hanged many a heretic, and I feared that Reverend Wilson would accuse my brothers."

Mary told Herod that the men were banished, but that William Robinson did not go quietly. When informed that he would be put to death if he returned, he told the court, "Upon that day, you will shed innocent blood." The bailiff shoved a handkerchief into his mouth, but that did not silence the irrepressible Quaker. The sergeant-at-arms dragged him from the courthouse, Robinson's shirt was torn away, and he was lashed.

After the treatment dealt to Robinson, Marmaduke Stevenson held his tongue, nodding mutely as his order of banishment was read. Then they all were given their liberty, and also a stern warning that they must be gone from Massachusetts in two days, or die.

Herod listened silently, watching Mary's face. Color came to her cheeks as she spoke, and her words quickened. But now Rebecca had heard enough. The toddler squirmed, saying, "Down, down, down," with increasing intensity. Mary set her on the floor and watched her walk straight to an open chest to examine the linens within. "How well thy child is doing, Herod. Thou must feel fortunate."

"Yes, Mary. I thank God every day that she is alive. I came so close to losing her."

"And we feared that we would lose thee," Mary added.

"And now I am afraid again."

"Of what?" Mary leaned toward Herod, even as she stuck out a toe to turn Rebecca away from the fireplace.

Herod watched the maneuver. "You see how easy it is to turn Rebecca from peril?" Mary's smile vanished. "How can I turn you from peril, Mary? I wake every night in fear that I will soon lose you." Mary sighed heavily and Herod rushed on. "You know what William called you? A ghost haunting your family. Your children no longer have a mother and he no longer has a wife. If you don't turn from this – this spell that you are under, I will no longer have my dearest friend."

She reached for Mary's hands, clenching them firmly. "These," Herod shook their entwined fists in front of Mary's face, "these brought life to my children. My hands brought your babies into this world. Why can't I hold you here, safe and sound? Why can't William?"

"Because God calls," Mary replied. "He speaks to my soul with his own voice. You lie awake fearing to lose me, but every night I hear him, and those poor, damned souls in Massachusetts calling for help because their bloody rulers are leading them to Hell."

"Let them save themselves, Mary."

"What if they don't know how?"

"Perhaps they deserve it. Those people laughed and lusted when I was whipped. They *should* burn!"

"Nobody deserves that, not even Endecott," Mary said severely. "Puritans think they made those accursed laws, but it is Satan's doing. God himself revealed this to me. My life is torture so long as I hear those damned souls crying out. My Friends sacrifice themselves for our Lord, and so will I."

"Is it sacrifice or is it suicide? Two sins, Mary – suicide and pride."

Mary goggled at Herod. "You think me proud?"

"You believe you are so …." Herod searched for the proper word. "Righteous! You are so righteous that you can bend Endecott and Wilson to your will. Is that not pride?"

"Not at all, Herod," Mary replied. "It is not me, but God who will humble Endecott for his evil works and Wilson for his evil counsel."

Herod cried out, "You will hang, and nothing will change!"

"Nothing?" Mary smiled tenderly. "I will go to eternal joy with God upon that day."

Herod stood and kissed her friend on the forehead. "Farewell, then, Mary. It's a shame that you won't live to see your grandchildren. I have two now, and they are such a joy. But I see that you are set on this, and I will miss you."

She scooped up Rebecca. The child giggled as she soared into the air, safe in her mother's arms. "Mary, I would rather be with my family on earth. Goodbye." Herod left her friend quickly and told William that she would walk home. She wanted to weep in private.

CHAPTER 38
October - November 1659

THE INK ON Mary's order of banishment was barely dried when she, Marmaduke Stevenson, and William Robinson were again arrested in Boston for speaking to jailed Friends. News of them came to Rhode Island in pulses, like spurts of blood from a severed artery. "She is jailed." That word arrived after Mary's October 9 imprisonment as quickly as a horse could trot. It was followed by, "They will be tried." On October 22 Newport heard, "Mary Dyer and the two Quaker men are sentenced to hang a week hence."

In the meeting house at Sabbath, enough people eyed Herod and muttered asides to their companions that she finally asked Betty Bull, "What ails them?"

"You and Mistress Dyer," Betty replied. "Mr. Dyer will not go to plead with Endecott for her life. I've heard talk that you might."

"Why should anybody think that?"

"The scars you got last year," was Betty's blunt answer.

"You can tell the gossips that I'll not go either," Herod said angrily. She spotted a cluster of women – Avis Stanton among them – staring at her from the aisle. "I will not go!" she snapped at them. Avis hustled away with the flustered group.

Betty eyed Herod warily, and she thought, 'Am I going mad? Why else would I shout at women who have done me no harm, and make a scene in the meeting house like a Quaker. Will they soon lock me up?'

A deep male voice just behind Herod made her and Betty leap. "Should those nosy hens bother you again, tell them that my son has sailed to Boston to plead for his mother." Those words rang out in the suddenly-hushed meeting house.

William Dyer stepped into view beside Herod, meeting the crowd's eyes in challenge. Heads swiveled away and coughs and whispers filled the room. Then William sat beside Herod. People glanced covertly, but nobody dared to snicker.

Herod joked nervously, "Do you need spectacles? You are in the women's seats."

"Let 'em talk," William replied. "One more bit of my life for them to chew over. Tell me, Herod, has this been hard for you too? Hearing whispers whether you will go preach against Puritans again?"

William's words were bitter, but Herod knew immediately that his anger was not directed at her. She felt a surge of affection, for she hadn't felt so close to Mary's husband for a long time. "At least no one ever hinted that I drove Mary off," she replied.

"To Boston – or to England, for that matter," William agreed. "I heard talk that she ran away from me."

"I'm sorry, William."

"Why? Did you say that too?" A genuine smile proved that he was joking.

"Never!" Herod said with a grin of her own. "Believe me; I know what you endure."

William laughed. "Yes, you would, Herod. You have seen some hard times in Newport. John Hicks was nothing but trouble for you."

"The best thing he ever did was leave," Herod commented. "Still, the gossips fattened on us for years. Him, me, George, Tom Painter. Now it's your turn – you and Mary."

"Not me," William said. "It was Mary who abandoned me."

Herod thought of the chatter about William's naval campaign, but held her tongue. Instead she told him, "I'll not be the next fodder for tattle-tales. No more scandal for me."

In the early morning on October 27, Herod climbed to a low hilltop above her home. She looked out, but not northward to Boston, fifty miles away. Instead she took in the blue line of the Atlantic Ocean painting the horizon to her south. Herod said a brief prayer for Mary. She had seen no mercy in John Endecott's heart, so she asked God to make Mary's death painless and to take her straight to heaven.

A few days passed, and then up to the Gardners' gate rode William Dyer, slumped wearily on his horse. Herod's first thought was that he had fetched Mary's body home. To save him the pain of saying the words, she asked, "When will you bury her?"

To Herod's amazement, William smiled. "Not for years, I hope. Endecott hanged the two men, but Mary has come home."

Herod dropped to the ground like a rag doll, and tears she had suppressed for days came flooding out. "I didn't mean to shock you," William said, extending a hand to help her rise.

"It's just that I am so happy."

William nodded. "We will have a thanksgiving dinner tomorrow. George, would you and your family come? Please, no talk of Quakers or Puritans. I wish to remind Mary what it feels like to break bread with friends."

"Good luck with that," was George's skeptical reply.

After William rode away, Herod started a huge batch of bread dough. When it had risen, she built a fire in her hearthside oven to heat it for baking. She pounded and tore at the yielding dough; kneading it until her shoulders ached. Herod molded and shaped it to her will, as she could not do with Mary Dyer's turbulent life.

With the loaves set in a warm corner to rise again, Herod and Mary Sherman peeled and sliced apples for a cobbler. They seasoned the fruit with honey and cinnamon, and then baked it in an iron coffin. Embers piled on its lid turned a topping of oats, flour, and molasses into a chewy, delicious crust.

With the bread nearly done, Herod looked around to see what else she could bake while her oven was still hot. "Perhaps a pudding," she mused, but the Sherman girl told her, "Goody, we are near out of flour and sugar."

"You have made enough bread for us and the Dyers both," George said. "Mary won't have to bake for a week."

Herod said, "I've been thinking all this time, but still don't know what to say to her."

George suggested, "How about, 'Welcome back.' Mary may speak of Boston if she will, but let's simply remind her of what she is missing at home."

When the Gardners drove up to Newport the next day, the cobbler was kept secure by Herod's feet so the younger boys who filled the wagon bed couldn't sneak bits with sticky fingers. William and Hannah Haviland, with Joseph and year-old Benjamin, joined them near the Dyers' home. William Dyer had assented when Herod asked if she could bring her daughter's family, and Hannah was happy to have been included.

The Dyers' big home was fragrant with the scent of fowl roasting in a metal oven. Young Mary Dyer was stirring a kettle hanging over the flames and the bondservant Catherine worked by her side. 'She must be near eighteen now,' Herod thought. 'I wonder if she will stay when her bond is ended?'

The hearth had recently been rearranged. Pans and tongs now stood at the left side of the fireplace, and kindling and log wood were stacked to the right. The arrangement would have been awkward for Herod, and she watched Catherine to see if she was left-handed.

Then Mary came into the room and Herod forgot about the servant. She went to hug her friend, saying, "Look, Mary, I brought bread and cobbler." The words seemed inane, but at least Herod had found something to say.

"I am grateful, Herod. God must have whispered to thee that I had no time to bake."

"I thought so," Herod replied. But then silence fell between the long-time friends and Mary busied herself at the hearth, nudging Catherine out of the way.

The room filled with people; William and five of their six children. Samuel was over twenty, and Herod heard that he was courting Anne Hutchinson, granddaughter of the revered Anne. Young Mary, Maher, and Henry, all in their teens now, were mingling with Herod's brood. Mary's youngest son, Charles, was following Catherine like an orphaned puppy.

A knock on the door announced a couple who raised Herod's eyebrows – William and Ann Coddington. He and Dyer had battled each other in court for years, but now here he was, ready to break bread and talk genially with his old adversary – and friend.

After a blessing said by William, the children were encouraged to slap roasted goose on slabs of Herod's wheat bread, and most of them trooped out to the barn to see William's new stallion. He'd bought it in Massachusetts, but the boys assured the party that it was a purebred from Spain. John Porter was not the only man in Rhode Island who wanted to improve the colonists' horse kind.

With the children's noise abated the group fell to their meal, excepting for Mary. She sat at the end of the table, a slender woman clad in dark gray with a white cotton cape over her shoulders. Herod's friend looked even more exhausted than her husband. Though Mary's eyes went from one person to another, Herod didn't know if she was actually seeing them. Saying hardly a word, she picked at her goose and corn pudding. The food seemed to do Mary good, for a little color came into her cheeks and she even had a second helping of Herod's apple cobbler.

At last William raised a glass of cider laced with rum. "Thank you for coming, my friends. We go back a long way. Most of us were in Boston for those first years and the wild times with Sir Henry Vane. Remember how we thought we'd voted him in to govern us all? It lasted only a few months, then the Puritans cast us out and we tumbled south.

"Now we are lords of our own Newport, but we've lost some friends along the way. The Hutchinsons and John Coggeshall – gone to their graves. John Clarke, away these eight years to England, and probably no closer to getting a charter for us than when he left.

"I have much to be thankful for, but not the least is that I have worked with such fine men to make our Newport prosper. I am grateful for such fine friends and for my family – *all* of them," William finished with an eye cocked at Mary. He raised his cider cup. "To all of you!"

Mary flushed, but sipped at her cider in a toast. The others also saluted William, some with cider and rum, and others with plain apple juice. Herod savored her freshly-pressed drink, a fine mix of tart and sweet apples pressed at the Dyers' orchard. There was froth on the top of her glass and tiny bubbles stung her nose – the cider had begun to work.

Then Ann Coddington asked, "Where is your son William?" Mary's eyes flashed in the first real emotion she had shown. Was it anger, or the concern of a mother for her absent son?

Coddington nudged his wife's arm, but William Dyer said, "Off to the Azores with a boatload of cheese and such to trade."

"Trade," said his wife, with strength growing in her voice. "What did our son trade with the Puritans for my life, husband?"

"Nothing but words, Mary," William said gently. He explained to the party, "Two years past when Mary was jailed, I went to bargain with Endecott for her release. I gave my word that Mary would trouble them no more. Since my vow has now been broken, last week it was our son's turn to plead for his mother's life."

"A life which is not Endecott's to spare or to take," Mary added. "I placed that life into God's hands, as did my brethren who are in Paradise now."

A stir went around the table. William stabbed his knife into a scrap of goose on his plate, and then flicked it to the family's dog who sat hopefully by the door. The bit of skin vanished in a single bite. The Coddingtons murmured to each other.

Did everyone know what had transpired in Boston but Herod? "Mary, what happened?" she asked. William Dyer shot an irritated glance at her, but Mary smiled serenely.

"My brothers and I were judged guilty of sedition and I watched them hang. They were brave and true to the end, and are now with our Lord. I climbed the gallows happily, for 'twas like climbing the stairs to Heaven. When they snugged the noose around my neck I, too, offered my life in service to the Lord."

When Herod pictured Mary; bound, hooded, and teetering between life and death, she could barely keep from vomiting. However Mary met her anguished gaze with another of those placid, surreal smiles.

"Thou art dearer to me than any sister, Herod. I was loath to leave all of you, but it was obedience to God's will which placed me there. When I heard them cry, 'Stop, she is reprieved!' I could not move. They had to pull me down and carry me back to prison."

"At least Governor Endecott showed mercy to you," Ann Coddington said.

Anger flickered across Mary's face. "Mistress Coddington, I wrote two letters to that servant of Satan; one after my brothers and I were condemned, and another after they were put to death. Now I tell you all what I wrote: 'the mercies of the wicked are naught but cruelty.' Endecott may claim that he gave me my life, but I would rather have gone to our Lord than suffer life among the damned."

Ann looked affronted and William Dyer slapped his palm on the table. Herod cried, "How can you –"

"Thou are not damned, Herod," Mary said quickly. "The wicked reveal themselves by their works. But it was torture to watch my brothers give their lives so willingly, and yet my own sacrifice refused. I can only believe that it was God's plan.

"We are so close to breaking those accursed laws. While we waited for the hangman they had to build fences around the jail, for people thronged to the windows to speak to us. Endecott needed his full militia to lead us to the gallows for fear that Boston would rise. Surely he cannot uphold those evil laws much longer."

"Surely he can," Dyer sneered. "Those people may be curious or even pity you, but they will follow where Endecott orders. If you go back there, he will hang you. No remorse, no more reprieves. You will hang."

Ann Coddington spoke up again, "I can scarce believe they would hang a woman."

"How many Indian women and children died at Puritan hands during the Pequot war?" Mary asked. "How many were sold into slavery? Anne Hutchinson was the most saintly woman I've ever known and they cast her soul to Satan. But they could not defeat her. I have seen her at God's feet in Heaven."

"The Puritans earned their fate," Herod said to Mary. "Let Endecott burn. Why trouble yourself further?"

"Dear Herod, I admire thee. When thou decide on a course nothing can stand in thy way. Would that I had such freedom, but this life is God's now, and mine no longer. *Greater love hath no man than this; that he lay down his life for his friends.* Though I am a woman, it is love which drives me; love for even such as Puritans."

"Bah!" barked William Dyer. "What of your family?"

"Do you truly need of me?" Mary asked him. "Samuel will soon marry. One by one the others will go. Even Charlie no longer needs me."

Mary looked from one of her uneasy friends to the next. "Think of your own children. Do you not wish to protect the weakest? To make them whole and strong? Herod, think of Rebecca. Thou risked thy life for her. Thou art blessed in God's eyes and with that sweet child you now have." Herod looked down at her daughter, sitting in her lap and sucking on bread dipped in cobbler juice. Mary told her, "Rebecca needs thee more than George does, for she is weak and he is a man grown."

William Dyer began to speak, but Mary overrode him, "My husband and children are strong, even to the youngest, but deluded Puritans will follow Endecott and Wilson to eternal doom. If my life redeems their souls, I shall rest happy in the bosom of our Lord."

Her husband scowled, but Mary's sweet smile never wavered. "I am tired and my soul aches after seeing how my friends have suffered. If God requires my blood to end the torture, so be it. I am content, so long as the Lord's will be done."

CHAPTER 39
May 27 - 30, 1660

RHODE ISLAND'S GENERAL Court was nearing its end when electrifying news arrived for William Dyer. He had managed to delay – yet again – delivering a full account of the Dutch goods he had seized so many years ago. With another extension granted, he could snooze through the rest of the assembly.

But then word came that William's wife had been arrested in Boston again. That colony showed no inclination to elect a softer-hearted leader, so John Endecott would still hold the governor's chair, wielding the same harsh laws. Mary would be tried on the thirty-first and she was apparently doomed.

William wrote once more to Endecott, saying that he hadn't seen his wife in six months and did not know that she had gone to Massachusetts. He concluded:

> *Let not your Compassion bee conquered by her inconsiderate maddnesse. I know you are all sensible of my condition ... yourselves may be husbands to wife or wives, so am I ... pray give her to me once again and I shall be so much obliged for ever, that I shall endeavor continually to utter my thanks and render you Love and Honor most renowned: pity me, I begg itt with teares.*

George Gardner had gone to vote for Rhode Island's president, but had then returned home. Therefore, he and Herod had not heard of Mary's arrest or trial.

Herod was dicing shriveled turnips from last year's crop while keeping an eye on Rebecca. She tossed them into a kettle of stew and stirred it well. The dried green beans, known as leather-breeches for their toughness, had finally softened but were the unappetizing color of old cow dung. With luck they would disintegrate before it was time to eat.

"Rebecca, get away from there," Herod called. The toddler was trying to pry the lid from the salt pork keg again. Why she was so attracted to the slimy mess, Herod didn't know. At that age, Dorcas was content to sit with a kitten in her lap, sucking her thumb and twiddling her hair. Rebecca wanted to know about everything – the fire, the kettle, the pigpen. Herod, Mary Sherman, or one of the boys had to watch her every waking minute.

Willy darted into the house. "Mr. Porter's at the gate!" he called.

The disappointing stew vanished from Herod's mind. She swished her hands in water fetched to wash the breakfast trenchers. After swipe on her apron to dry her fingers, Herod gave her head a quick feel – were her cap and hair neat? Then Herod picked up Rebecca and strode to the door. "No!" the toddler protested, squirming in her mother's arms. She set the girl down outside.

John was standing at the garden gate. He held a black horse which Herod hadn't seen before, a big-bodied animal with a thick tail which brushed the ground. The horse's eyes were nearly lost in its dense forelock but they showed white rings as the creature watched Herod's mob of children.

Rebecca darted to join Willy. He, Nicholas, and Dorcas were already clustered by the gate, clamoring, "Mr. Porter, can I have a ride?" John had overcome Dorcas' shyness with bits of rock sugar candy, and now the girl was reaching up to pat his jacket hopefully.

"Another time," Porter told them. "I've come to see your parents." He gently pushed Dorcas clear of the horse's hooves. Then his eyes found Herod. John looked tense, but he grinned as she ran to catch Rebecca.

Young George offered to take the horse. Usually when John came to call, his mount rested in the Gardners' barn or lazed in their pasture with the milk cows. This time he told George, "Thank you, but this mare is skittish. I'll put her in the barn myself."

When John returned to the yard, Herod was surprised to see how haggard he looked. Usually clean-shaven, John now wore a stubbly beard and his sleeves were dusty. He asked urgently, "Have you heard about Mrs. Dyer?" Mary had vanished shortly after William's dinner party and it was rumored that she'd spent the winter in Providence or on Long Island.

Herod blanched. "Not in a half-year."

"She is jailed in Boston and their court begins tomorrow. Endecott will be quick to act because he's worried about a riot. They will try her then or on the day after."

"Maybe they will reprieve her again," Herod said hopefully.

John shook his head. "Think you that she would accept it?"

Herod scowled. "No, but perhaps if I talked to her .... If I left now, could I get there in time?"

"We. I am going to Boston anyway, so I will take you," John said.

"No!" The cry made them both jump. George, red-faced and damp-shirted from hoeing weeds in the sun, had just come around the corner of the house. "Herod, are you mad? Do you want to hang, too?"

"Herod will be safe," John assured him.

George sneered, "So you say. I thought you were sweet on my wife." Herod gasped, but he ignored her. "Why would you drag her into such peril?"

"There is no peril," John explained. "Herod hasn't been banished – I saw to that two years ago. Her name isn't even in their records."

"George, no one is dragging me!" Herod snapped, but both men ignored her.

George told Porter, "There's no reason for Herod to go at all. Let William chase his wife."

John said, "Both he and their son pledged Endecott that she would not return. She broke their word, so William will not chase after her."

For a moment Herod stood motionless, and then she pounded her fist against the door. "If William won't go, why should I risk *my* life?" she exclaimed. "Mary cares so little for us that we've heard nothing from her. I even wondered if she went back to England to see that George Fox. Why should I rush off to Boston, when she will surely refuse my plea?"

George's face lit triumphantly, but John merely watched Herod with dark, impassive eyes. With her mind in turmoil, she couldn't look away from him. At last she said, "If I do nothing, Mary will hang."

"Let her!" George cried. "That is her wish. All she has done these last three years is disturb her family's peace, and ours as well!"

Herod's anger rose at George's callous statement, but she said to John, "I dare not go. Even if my name is not in their books, Endecott will remember me."

"I will speak to him first," John assured her. "If you can convince her to come away with us and never return, Endecott will be grateful. He doesn't want to hang a woman."

"Hah!" George cried. "He will hang Mary, jail Herod, and perhaps you too. Come here, children, and kiss your mother farewell. You will never see her again!"

Herod looked at a semi-circle of confused, embarrassed faces. Even Rebecca knew that something was amiss. Herod told them, "Off to your chores now, and let us talk." The older children moved away reluctantly but Dorcas and Rebecca stayed close by.

George scoffed, "Though Connecticut's governor is Puritan, he begged Endecott not to hang those Quaker men last fall. Said he'd crawl on his knees from New Haven to Boston to take them away. His plea changed nothing."

"Endecott can't afford to hang Mary," John told him. "With Cromwell dead, there's talk of putting a king on the throne again. Charles' son is most likely, and he might be out for revenge because the Puritans chopped off his father's head."

"Then go beg for Mistress Dyer yourself," said George. "Leave my wife out of this."

"Let her decide," John suggested.

Herod stared at John, and then at George. Yes, a decision must be made, but it felt almost like she was choosing between the two men. She could stay home to please George, but her failure to act would set Herod up for a lifetime of regrets.

Dashing off with John might not be safe or wise, and Herod knew that much hung in the balance, including her life with George. Still, it appealed irresistibly to her. She might save Mary's life, and Herod sensed that other gains were possible.

Then John said, "Herod, you told me in March that you feared for Mrs. Dyer. You begged me to ask my friends in Boston if she was there. What do you want to do?"

"Save her! I will hate myself if she dies when I could have stopped it." George glared at her and Herod told him, "Let me speak. Remember our last dinner with Mary, when she said that she loved the weakest the most. I haven't been able to put that out of my head.

"George, remember our little Dorcas, when she was so small that she could fit in your hat. You did anything you could to keep her alive. So it is for me, George. Remember how I was with Rebecca?" George rolled his eyes, and Herod felt a touch of hope. At least he was responding to her. "Whose grip on life is weakest now, and most likely to die?"

"What of me? What of our children, Herod?"

"Rebecca is nearly weaned, and you have Mary Sherman to help you. I'll only be gone a few days."

"Hah!" said George again, but Herod saw defeat in his eyes. He swallowed hard and then turned away. With his back turned to hide his action, Herod saw him brush at his eyes. Then he walked quickly away. Dorcas trotted behind him, saying anxiously, "Papa, Papa."

Herod's heart fell as she watched them disappear around the house's corner. Would this open a rift which could never be healed? John also seemed uneasy. He said, "Herod, maybe you shouldn't do this. It could tear you two apart, just as their parting did to the Dyers."

Herod laughed nervously. "I was just thinking of them, but this is different. Mary was gone to England for six years, but I will be back in a week. George will forgive me."

A long silence followed. Then Rebecca squatted to watch a green looper caterpillar inching along the path. The girl turned it this way and that with gentle fingers, sending the translucent little creature scurrying for safety. Then she made a grab for it, but Herod called to her, "Let it be, Rebecca. You might hurt it."

Then she told John, "I will go to Boston with you. It's my last chance to turn Mary from the gallows."

A brief smile brightened John's face. "Mine too," he replied. "So, Herod, if I take you to Boston we must ride fast. The wind and tide are good, so we can sail to Providence today. We'll hire a horse there. Do you think that you can ride?"

"I don't know. How long will it take?" Herod asked.

"It's fifty miles from Providence to Boston. I used to ride it in a day, but I'm not a young man anymore. I hope we can do it in two. We'll rest at an inn and get a fresh horse there."

Then John told her, "It will wear out your legs." He rubbed his inner thigh in warning. "Whether you ride pillion or sidesaddle, it will rub you in places that I shouldn't speak of to a woman. Which of the boys' breeches would fit you the best?"

John's question flustered Herod out of her melancholy, and she giggled, "I don't know. Henry, maybe? Ben is nearer my height, but he's big around the waist. I think his would fall off me."

A little grin quirked one side of John's mouth. "Get Henry's, then. While you are at it, fetch the longest stockings you have, and stout leather shoes. Put the stockings on and wear the breeches under your skirt."

"Wear a man's clothes?" Herod gasped.

"Believe me, you'll be more comfortable. The breeches will protect your legs. One last thing: take a little pot of grease. It will ease your skin if it gets rubbed. Nothing with salt in it, mind you, because it would sting like the blazes. Take salt pork and you will be sorry."

Herod scurried about, selecting her cloak from its peg by the door, and opening a storage chest for a clean skirt. She was trying not to think about what she might lose in this mad dash to Boston, but Rebecca sensed her mother's distress. The toddler followed Herod, whimpering and tugging at her skirt. Herod dug deeper into the chest for a pair of winter stockings, and her fingers touched something hard.

It was the blue necklace John had given her after she was whipped, tied into a linen scrap. Herod untied the knot and poured the strand into her hand. When Rebecca reached for it, Herod looked for another of John's gifts. The red teething beads were the girl's favorite toy, but somehow they had been put out of her reach on the fireplace's mantle.

"Here you go, baby girl," Herod said, slipping the circlet around Rebecca's wrist and tying it to the child's sleeve. Come to think of it, Rebecca was wearing a third gift from John. Herod had sewn the band of French embroidery on Dorcas' gown, but she had outgrown it. Now Rebecca was wearing the white, lace-trimmed dress. Herod smoothed the gown's yoke, admiring the eyelets she had added to the garment.

Her eyes went back to the blue necklace, and she tied it around her own throat. The cold weight settled over Herod's collarbones, and she wished for a mirror so she would know how they looked.

"Mama, Mama!" Rebecca tugged on her skirt again and Herod picked her up. The girl closed her fingers over her mother's necklace, and Herod feared she might break the delicate linen cord. She loosened the baby's grasp and Rebecca's face puckered.

"Here, 'Becca. These are your beads," she said, curving Rebecca's fingers around her own circlet. The girl clutched them, but her face remained a somber reflection of her mother's anxious mood.

Herod held her close, staring into space for several long moments as she thought about George's pain and John's gifts, and her own future with both men. John's generosity sprang from friendship, and Herod's impulsive action would not harm her bond with George. Besides, Mary's life hung in the balance, and perhaps only she could persuade the Quaker to return home. Herod had no choice but to try.

She set Rebecca down and returned to her packing. The blue necklace shifted, reminding Herod that it still circled her throat. 'I never have told George about this,' she thought. 'I must do it when I get back.'

Herod removed the necklace, but instead of stowing it among her stockings again, she hid it among the embroidered bed curtains that she had stored for the summer. She hoped that George wouldn't find it before she returned home.

CHAPTER 40
May 30, 1660

GEORGE HAD NOT reappeared by the time Herod was ready to go. She called for him, but the boys didn't know where he had gone. She was relieved that there wouldn't be a last-minute argument, but also saddened. There would be a reckoning for her impulsive act.

Wearing Henry's breeches felt strange – Herod was almost waddling like a duck as the leather rode up between her thighs. "How can you men bear these things?" she asked John. A broad smile was his only response.

Herod gave instructions to Benoni, Henry, and Mary Sherman – stir the stew, feed the livestock, churn the butter. She especially told Mary to watch Rebecca and feed her soft foods, not salt pork and rye bread. Then she bid goodbye to her children.

Ben nudged Henry, and he spoke up for his siblings, "Ma, why are you doing this? Shouldn't you wait for Pa before you go?"

"Henry, your father could be gone for hours. They will probably try Mrs. Dyer tomorrow, so we must leave now if we are to save her from the hangman. You and Ben are old enough to mind the others."

John told them, "First let's see if your mother can ride to Portsmouth. If she can't, I'll bring her back today." He fetched his mare from the barn. A few wisps of hay still trailed from the animal's lips.

Herod asked, "Where is Thor?"

"Resting a sore leg. Besides, I wanted to try this new mare. Now, the first thing we do is get you up there." Herod eyed the tall beast dubiously.

John folded his light woolen cloak into thirds, and then laid it over the horse's back behind the saddle. "What's that for?" Herod asked.

"You are going to sit on it." Giggles came from Herod's children, who were circled around to watch their breeches-clad mother climb onto that horse.

"That? Astride?"

"If you sit sideways, you'll slide off in a second. Yes, you have to ride astride. Now, watch how I do this, because you will follow." John gathered the mare's reins in his left hand, snug enough to keep the animal from walking away. He stuck his left foot in the stirrup and stepped easily up, swinging his right leg over the horse's back. He looked down at Herod's upturned face. "See how I did it?" She nodded, pink-cheeked with excitement.

John tied her bundle to a saddle ring. Then he lifted his left toes out of the stirrup and swung his leg forward. The horse shifted its weight. "Steady, girl," Porter said. "Ben, keep a good grip on her. I have no idea whether she's packed double before."

When the mare stood quietly, John told Henry, "Give your mother a boost if she needs it." He nodded at the stirrup dangling before Herod's eyes. "Left foot in there, take my hand, pull yourself up, and swing your right leg over her back. Ready?"

Herod gulped. She hiked up her skirt and took John's hand. With her left foot in the stirrup and a couple of hops, she pulled herself up. When she settled behind John's saddle the horse tossed her head. Herod reached back tentatively and patted the broad rump behind her. "Good girl," she told the mare.

With an approving nod, John said, "Both of you."

John's cloak padded the mare's spine reasonably well, and Herod soon became used to the animal's walk. "Relax and let your back swing with hers," he advised. Herod felt him doing exactly that – moving as one with the horse, and she tried to match her balance to his.

It worked better if she snuggled close to John and wrapped her arms around his waist. 'It's almost like lying with George,' Herod thought, blushing so deeply that she was glad Porter couldn't see her. She must have tensed, because he said, "Just relax. Isn't this fun?" Herod took a deep breath and blew it out, willing her pulse to return to normal.

John told her, "We won't be able to walk the whole way. It's the easiest gait to ride, but we'd need a week to get there. You know what a trot is?"

"I rode my sister's horse when it trotted," Herod replied apprehensively, thinking of the carthorse's jarring gait.

"We'll do a lot of it," John said. "A horse can go miles at a trot. Hold tight to me, don't look down and don't pull your knees up. If you don't bounce, it will be easier on you and Salome both."

"Salome?"

"That's the mare's name, and a good one for a big girl like her." John let out a hearty chuckle. "Now that I think of it, Salome was Herodias' daughter in the Bible. Fancy that! So, be gentle with your little girl."

When the animal broke into a slow trot, Herod bounced helplessly on the mare's back. "Let your legs hang down and just sit there like a bag of meal," John advised.

Herod tightened her grip on John's ribs and her chin banged into his shoulder. "Sorry," she muttered, thinking irritably, 'He sits like there's pitch on his saddle so he's glued tight.' But with her thighs pressed close and her body nestled against him, Herod felt how John absorbed the mare's strides in his lower back. Soon she was doing the same.

The mare relaxed when Herod did and the roughness in her stride eased. Herod chuckled, feeling as though she had finally conquered riding. John loosened the reins and the mare's speed increased. She was moving differently now, swaying gently from side to side.

"Feel the difference? She's pacing now. Nice and easy, isn't it?" John commented over his shoulder. "I don't know if she does it naturally, but that's why I bought her. If she passes this lovely gait to her foals, I'll have the best riding stock in Rhode Island." Then John pulled the mare back to a walk. "Not so bad, was it?"

"No!"

"Think you could do that all day?"

Herod sobered. "It's not bad now, but …."

"Your legs will ache tomorrow." John's voice was serious now. "By nightfall you'll be raw, but you will have another day to ride. Any doubts, and I'll take you home now."

"John, I want to try," Herod told him.

"Well, so do I. Let's give you a try at the canter. Remember, it will be easier with a proper pillion. You know what a canter is, right?"

"Gallop along, yes." Herod's heart was pounding. She'd never cantered before, but it looked thrilling – and scary.

"It's gentler to sit than a trot, and Salome's gait is easier than many. Hold on tight, now." Herod leaned against John and flexed her arms. "Ready?" She nodded. John gripped her wrist and clucked to Salome. The animal bounded forward, covering the ground in twelve-foot leaps.

The ground flew below Herod in a dusty haze, and for a moment she was terrified. John called back, "Don't look down!" Her head snapped up to look resolutely past his right ear. Soon Herod caught the new rhythm, moving as a single being with John and the horse, their bodies rising and falling as Salome propelled them forward. Herod sensed overwhelming power between her thighs; the animal's great curving ribs and thickly-muscled back, John's muscular thighs pressing against her own, and his waist and curving ribs moving as he breathed in rhythm with Salome's strides.

The world was going by impossibly fast, pastures and fences unrolling in a multicolored blur. Now Herod knew how it felt to race like a deer. No – to soar over the earth like a bird. When they passed a woman on the road, Herod looked down at the top of her cap. A glimpse of the woman's astounded gape at Herod, clad in her son's breeches, and then they sped by.

Herod tipped her head back to giggle in delight at the thrilling, perilous power of man and horse barely contained between her own legs and arms. And, Herod admitted, she also rejoiced at her unasked-for freedom from family and chores. John Porter was taking her to save Mary Dyer! She laughed once more, a hopeful peal as Salome cantered northward.

John chuckled; a deep, upwelling sound. Perhaps he, too, had been nervous about this improbable jaunt, but now he shouted, "On to Boston!" and jabbed a triumphant fist into the air.

"To Boston!" Herod echoed, brandishing her own fist for a quick, exultant moment. Then Salome's weight slewed sideways when her hoof landed in a rut. A nervous thrill prickled the hairs on Herod's neck, but she felt safe clutching John with her encircling arms.

CHAPTER 41
May 30, 1660

WHEN JOHN AND Herod neared his Portsmouth home, he told her, "Margaret knows that I planned to see John Hull after court was over. It will go easier if she doesn't know that I'm taking you. If you don't mind waiting in the barn while I get my stuff...."

"And keep quiet," Herod added.

"Smart girl!"

John turned the mare westward and they dropped downhill toward the bay. When the road leveled out they passed a long fence line. A small herd of horses galloped toward the road and Salome nickered to them. There were about a dozen mares with foals born a few months ago, and several older animals in shades of brown and gray. "Like them?" John asked.

"So pretty," Herod commented. "Look at those babies!"

The foals raced along the fence, and then circled off to buck and nip at each other. Salome broke into a trot. John pulled her back as he told Herod, "They are mine. I breed and raise horses, then sell them here or ship them off to the Indies."

"You bring goods from Boston to sell," Herod commented.

"And from England. I dabble in many things." Then a loud whinny rang out. Salome's ears pricked and she called in response. John nudged her, and she moved forward reluctantly.

He pointed to a small barn on the other side of the lane. It stood within a sturdy fence six feet tall. The top half of the door was open, and a dark bay horse thrust its head and neck out over the bottom half. It bugled eagerly at Salome, and the mare pranced and shook her head.

"Love at first sight," John explained. "I got that stone-horse last year. There's a lot of Arab in him so he's not as big as Salome, but she has size enough for both. He sired those foals, and I couldn't be happier with them. Soon I'll be breeding the finest horses in New England."

By the time they reached John's house, Herod was more than ready to dismount. John stopped Salome at the far side of the barn where they couldn't be seen from the house. He told Herod, "Get a grip on my belt, swing your right leg over her rump and slide down." Herod thought it looked like a ten-foot drop from Salome's back, and her feet protested when they hit the ground.

John dismounted with practiced ease and patted Salome's neck approvingly. "I do like this mare! Now, how do you feel?"

"Weak at the knees," Herod replied.

"How's your hide?"

Herod rubbed the inside of one knee but felt no real discomfort. Henry's breeches felt strange, and people who had seen her in men's clothes were sure to talk, but the leather had protected her. She nodded to John. "Good."

"You just rode ten miles. There's another fifty to ride before we get to Boston. Two days, maybe three, and we could be too late," he warned. "Do you still want to do this?"

"Yes."

"I think that Endecott will let us talk to her, but what will you do if Mary refuses to come back with us? She's stubborn – almost as bad as you." Herod eyed John scornfully, but he did not respond with the mischievous grin which she expected. Instead he said earnestly, "How will you feel if Mary looks you in the eye and says, 'No'?"

"She has already done it," Herod told him. "I was against her journey to England years ago, and I've begged her a hundred times to not go into the Puritan colonies. I am doing my best, so let Mary say what she will. Let's go."

John looked at the ground for a moment, kicking at a rock embedded in the dirt. "I'm a fool for long odds," he said. "At races, I bet on a horse that others spurn. Something in its eye tells me to take that chance …." He toed the pebble again, and then looked straight at Herod and patted her shoulder. "Let's go. No man can say that we didn't try."

John led Salome into the barn and Herod closed the door behind them. He loosened the saddle's girth as he said, "I'll turn the mare out and get my stuff. Then we'll be off."

Thor was standing in a stall at the end of the barn. He stuck his white-blazed nose over the rail and nickered. Herod went to pet him, and he sniffed her hands hopefully. "I'll turn him out too," John said.

Thor's legs looked fine to Herod, so she said, "I thought you said he had a sore leg."

"It's not bad. Mostly I wanted to try Salome." With the mare at his heels, John hung his saddle on a stand and put the bridle on a peg. When he reached into a lidded keg, both horses nickered eagerly.

John poured several kernels of corn into Herod's palm and showed her how he fed the grain to Salome. "Fingers together, hand flat. Give that to Thor." The gelding's whiskers tickled Herod's hand, and she stroked his nose as he crunched his treat.

Suddenly the barn door opened. A girl came inside, saying to herself, "Now, who closed that door?"

Salome started toward the girl, and she gasped. Then John called, "Lydia, I'm back from Newport." The blond girl's eyes flew to John, and then to Herod. She remembered seeing the servant two years ago; a skinny child with country speech that Mrs. Porter had disdained. Lydia must be about twelve now. The girl's body was filling out and she would soon be drawing attention from Rhode Island's boys.

John was saying, "Lydia, do you know Goodwife Gardner?"

"Ummm …." The girl examined Herod again, taking in those unconventional breeches with an unconscious "tsk." Lydia answered triumphantly, "I saw her a while back. She came here for you, but you was off to Boston."

"And I'm off again," Porter told her. "Goody Gardner's sister in Providence is having a baby, and she's going to help. I promised her husband that I would see her safely there, and then ride up to Boston to see Mr. Hull."

Herod nodded her agreement to John's tall tale. Lydia's pale eyes took her in again, and then swung back to her employer. "Does Mrs. Porter know she's here? She didn't tell me about no dinner for you and her."

"We won't stay for dinner, Lydia. We must leave quickly to make Providence by dark. Mrs. Porter doesn't know, and let's not bother her with it. You know how things upset her." The servant groaned in agreement. Herod remembered trying to please her own critical aunt back in London. It looked like the girl also hated catering to her mistress' moods.

Then John dug into his pocket. "See here, Lydia." Those quick eyes brightened when he held up a coin. "Margaret might need extra help while I'm gone. This is for your trouble, and there's another just like it if she is content when I return. No upsets, and get her what she needs, you see?"

Lydia nodded happily, clenching the silver in her fist. She even called gaily, "I wish your sister well, Goody," as John gently pushed her to the barn door.

"I'll be along in a moment, Lydia – need to see to the horses first," he told the servant. To Herod he said, "I'll be back quick as I can. I apologize for abandoning you in my barn, but really, it will be quicker."

"Don't worry," Herod told him. "Your barn is a palace."

John unbarred the rear door so Salome could go out to pasture. Then he opened Thor's stall to let him follow the big mare. Thor went out eagerly and John called after him, "Watch out for that mare – she's twice your size. Thor's in love," he told Herod.

She giggled, but then asked, "Don't you fear that Lydia will tell Mrs. Porter about me?"

"Lydia doesn't enjoy Margaret in a snit any more than I do. She's a clever little girl and will do as she's told." Years later, Herod would remember what John said about Lydia's obedience. She would also wonder what else Lydia had done for Mr. Porter, but by then, it no longer mattered.

It took John a little longer to get ready than Herod expected. When he returned, he had shaved his black and silver stubble. Herod fingered her own chin in query and John smiled. "I daren't face Endecott looking like a bearded old reprobate."

While they rode up from Newport, Herod's nose was inches away from John's head. She couldn't help but notice that white hairs were scattered there, too. Now John's hair was freshly washed and braided into a tidy queue. As they walked the path toward Portsmouth's docks Herod asked impulsively, "How old are you, John?"

He laughed, "Too old to ride to Boston in two days!"

"How old?" Herod insisted. "Mama said I was born the year before the bad plague in 1625."

"You are thirty five? What am I doing with such an old woman?" Herod playfully slapped his arm. "I'm near sixty. Old enough to be your father."

"I only have one sister; right, Papa?"

John chuckled. "That's right. Her name is Hannah and she was married ten years ago."

"So your wife will be all alone. Will she be lonely?"

"Margaret enjoys having me out of the house," John replied. "She's got Lydia, and Priscilla and her husband to do for her while I'm gone. He minds the stock and keeps firewood in the house, Priscilla tends the garden, and Margaret complains to all of them."

"Won't she miss you?"

John glanced away, as though judging the wind on the bay. He said wistfully, "I wish that it were so, but the answer is no. In truth, I won't miss her either. She doesn't like my horses." John's voice went up an octave when he whined, 'Just look at those boots! You are tracking filth through the house.'

"I like living at the farm where I can see the sea. Margaret would rather stay in Portsmouth town, but she preferred Boston. She was cross-eyed with rage when we were forced out with Mrs. Hutchinson. She would have been happiest if we had stayed in England. Most of all, Margaret hates my land in Pettaquamscutt because she knows that I want to live there."

"And she won't go," Herod said. "She told me so two years ago." She thought that Porter was keeping a good pace – not too fast, like George when he was in a hurry. But then, John was only an inch or two taller than Herod, where George topped her by a handspan. At least Porter wasn't doddering along like an elder with one foot in the grave.

John explained, "Margaret is terrified that I will leave her behind. I'm not going anywhere for a few years, but she believes it's better to upset herself now than to wait for later. So Margaret is curt, and I don't mind spending two weeks in Boston with Hull, or sailing to Narragansett to meet with the sachems. It keeps us out of each other's path. And now, here we are at the dock."

John paid a neighbor's son to sail them up the Providence River. He told Herod, "We're as lucky as we can be with a flood tide. We could be there in a couple of hours." They sat together on a bench in front of the sail. The boat was skipping along briskly enough for water to splash over the bow. Herod had taken off her breeches while she waited for John, and now wished that she hadn't. They would have kept her dry. John said, "The wind is with us. I'd have paid double if the lad had to row."

"Row? I thought you said it was twelve miles there."

"Ten years ago, I could have done it. Roger Williams still does, and he's my age."

"Then why don't you?" Herod teased.

"Shoulder," John said easily. "Took a tumble off Thor when he was young and foolish. I could cross to Bristol, but to Providence? Ow!" John gripped his left shoulder and grimaced.

A little while later, as they passed the whale-shaped hump of Prudence Island, Herod asked, "Why are you doing this, John?"

"Going to Boston?"

"I am mad to do this again, so what are you?"

"It's not the first crazy thing I've done, but it will be hard on you," John commented. "First the ride, and then you face Endecott again."

Her smile faded. "And Mary may refuse to see me. She has always done as she pleases." Herod looked away to scratch at something crusted on the gunwale. Then she admitted, "I think that we will fail. And poor George …. This hurt him so much, but I had to try anyway. But why are you going?"

John rubbed a hand over his jaw. "Several reasons," he finally said. "The easiest? I was already going for Hull's signature on that deed. Another is that I don't think much of Puritans and their ways. The Church of England was overly rich and needed reform, but the Puritans overreached as they grew in power. When they chopped off King Charles' head, they went too far for me. I was glad that I was already in New England."

The sun was reflecting off the river, and Herod shaded her eyes with one hand. "When did you come over?"

"In 1635, but I was no part of the grand Puritan experiment. I'm a trader – buy here, sell there. I wanted to get in early on this new world with all the opportunity it offers. After two years in Boston with Winthrop's narrow-minded ilk, I was ready to get away. Harry Vane was a fine governor, and I thought that Mrs. Hutchinson's folk had the right to say what they liked. But next thing I knew, the Puritans were demanding that I surrender my gun. I could have recanted and stayed in Roxbury, but why live under bullies?

"Now those same greedy men are reaching out from Massachusetts and Connecticut to steal our lands. Even Plymouth lays claim to Rhode Island. Our charter makes our boundaries plain, but that doesn't stop them from trying, and they are getting worse every year. Now they are after the Narragansett lands. Humphrey Atherton bought a chunk I had my eye on."

"I know that name," Herod told him, shaking her head irritably. "Can't put my finger on it. Go on."

"Remember my land by the Pettaquamscutt River? Atherton bought the east bank, everything between the river and the sea. Damme, I wanted that land."

Not even John's mild curse offended Herod. Her father had said that sort of thing when he was upset. She felt strangely honored that Porter trusted her enough to say such things. If John Hicks had uttered that word, Herod would have been nervous, wondering if violence would follow.

Porter was saying, "Just last year, Connecticut complained that our Narragansetts were harassing their Mohegan tribe, and the Puritans fined them a huge amount. Atherton paid those debts and forced the Narragansetts to mortgage their lands to him. Now he calls for those debts to be paid or they must surrender their lands. What if the whole tribe goes to war over this? I will lose my land, but people in Providence and Warwick may lose their lives."

"Will you speak to Endecott about your land?" Herod asked.

"Not this time. We have more urgent matters to discuss," John reminded her. The Providence River was narrowing, and he commented, "Not long 'til we reach town. Now, what was I saying?"

"Why are you going to Boston?"

"I was horrified enough when they whipped you, but hanging? Gah! What Endecott is doing to those Quakers is dead wrong. If I can help you save Mistress Dyer, then I'm happy. It would please me to stick a thumb in their eyes too, but for now I will beg Endecott for mercy, just as sweet as preserves on pancakes."

"If he will offer mercy."

"And if Mistress Dyer will take it."

"What of her?" Herod asked. "I didn't know you regarded Mary so."

"Mistress Dyer has the finest mind of any woman in Rhode Island."

Herod chuckled. "Even me?"

"If you had Mary's education, you would be her equal. I don't know where she learned her letters, but she's as eloquent as Mrs. Hutchinson. Your friend stands for all of us in Rhode Island. She *is* Rhode Island."

"We are outcasts – some fled England, and many were expelled from Massachusetts with Mrs. Hutchinson. It galled me, but I now believe that we Rhode Islanders are better for it. We are the hard-headed ones who would not recant.

"Miss a few Puritan Sabbaths and the deacon comes a-knocking on your door. They force you to tithe for their minister. You will go to jail if you refuse. They don't tolerate other church ways at all. Just look at us – we have Baptists, Church of England, Quakers, Jews, and even a few Catholics. Nobody tells us how – or whether – to worship."

"We're crusty folks," Herod said, and John grinned at her.

"That's right. We won't be told what to do, but in times of trouble we cling together. We won't take no for an answer. That is exactly what Endecott and his Puritans have learned about Mary."

Herod chuckled in response, but John didn't smile. "You know, Herod, there is one more reason that I am doing this. They will probably hang Mistress Dyer. I hope that taking you on this mad dash will make it easier to bear than if you sat at home and did nothing. As for me, it's no hardship to have your company on this trip, if I'm not too bold."

"Not at all. I enjoy your company too." Herod said demurely, but her cheeks were burning.

CHAPTER 42
May 30-31, 1660

LATE IN THE afternoon their boat sailed up to the Providence docks. Herod looked around curiously. So this was Providence! Rhode Island's first settlement was a few years older than Newport. Herod was used to the notion that Newport had outstripped the older Portsmouth in size, but she was surprised to see that her home town was larger than Providence as well. Houses and shops were clustered near the docks, but most of Providence's homes lay on long, narrow strips of fenced land.

Before they docked, John said to Herod, "I hope nobody recognizes us. I don't want talk to start. If anyone asks, tell them your name but say that your sister is in Medfield. Say nothing at all about Mary or Quakers."

"What if they ask my sister's name?"

"Make one up. Oh ...."

"Anne Ball." John eyed her quizzically and Herod said, "She really is my sister. Just happens that she never came over from England."

"No lie, no sin," John chuckled. Nobody challenged them as they walked up Providence's main street and he pointed out the sights. "There's the Scotts' home. They are –"

"Strong-brewed Quakers," Herod finished for him.

"Shall we ask what they've heard from Boston?"

If the Scotts knew for certain whether Mary had been hanged, it would save them a long, hard ride to Boston. But Herod blamed them in no small part for Mary's unswerving course to martyrdom. Had they ever once asked her not to go? Herod doubted it. "John, I don't want to see them," she said.

"Understandable. Let's see what we can learn at the inn." Across from the town's spring, John pointed out a large house with a bleaching wood-shingled roof. "Roger Williams lives there."

"Really?" The famed founder of Providence lived in an unpainted clapboard house surrounded by a garden and orchard, much like Herod's own home. "Your house is grander," she told John, and he shrugged.

Then a male voice called in a London accent, "John Porter, is that you?"

"Blast," Porter muttered. "I dare not ignore him."

John and Herod stopped by the fence to meet Roger Williams. Herod had seen the man when he presided over George's adultery trial, but had barely taken notice. Now she gave him a closer look.

So, this was the man who had been cast out of Massachusetts by the Puritans in 1636. Williams and several like-minded friends had gone south, bought Indian land, and built their Providence upon it.

Though he was near sixty, Roger was powerfully built, with broad shoulders and big, weathered hands. The fashionable Mr. Coddington wouldn't be seen in Roger's plain clothing. He was clad in linsey-woolsey breeches, a smudged linen shirt, and heavy leather shoes that had clearly been worn in a cow pasture. Herod was amused to see that the great man was spreading chicken manure under the trees in his orchard. Why didn't he have a servant do such a menial task?

"Grand day for a bit of gardening," Williams told them.

"Your apples look good, Roger," said John.

"Should be a prime crop, God willing," Williams replied. "Off to Boston so soon after court? I just got home yesterday." Then Williams' eyes went to Herod and he nodded courteously.

"Roger, this is Goodman Gardner's wife from Newport. You know George, that tall, blond fellow. Goody Gardner's sister in Medfield is having a baby and I offered to see her there."

"Your servant, Mr. Williams," Herod said nervously.

"My pleasure, Goodwife." Roger Williams had kind, sparkling eyes, but Herod hoped fervently that she wouldn't be asked for more information.

"Yes, I'm off to Boston again," John said, diverting Williams' attention. "The court gave their permission to buy that new Pettaquamscutt tract, so I'm going to get John Hull's signature."

"How much?"

"Land? Ten miles by twelve, for one hundred thirty-five pounds."

"Some well-needed money for the Narragansetts, but not enough to pay their mortgage to Atherton," Williams said. "That could be trouble."

"They may have to sell more land," John agreed. "We'll buy whatever we can."

Then Williams asked, "Are you sure you want to go to Boston? Mr. Dyer's wife will stand before Endecott soon. If he hangs her, might be you will see a riot."

Herod's stomach lurched, but John said calmly, "It shouldn't amount to much. Who would defy such a well-armed militia for long? So, they haven't condemned the poor woman yet?"

"Their court opened today with elections," said Williams. "Mistress Dyer has gambled her life that she can shame Massachusetts into rewriting their laws. She should have waited. England's Puritans are losing their grip and Charles will be restored to the throne any day. Until then, all Mistress Dyer can hope for is mercy."

"From Puritans?" John scoffed. "You, of all people, know the sort of mercy they show. They drove you from your home in wintertime."

Williams smiled. "It *was* a mercy. I no longer had their preaching in my ears, or paid tax for their ministers. As for Mistress Dyer, I fear it will go badly for her. They are too proud to back down."

"And so is Mistress Dyer," Herod said impulsively.

Williams' hazel eyes swiveled back to her. "Very true, Goodwife. The Quakers are a proud breed for people who claim to be humble. I pray that God will bring Mistress Dyer to her senses. Governor Endecott too, for hanging a woman may not set well with Parliament."

"Or with King Charles," John said.

"God's will be done," Williams replied.

They made their farewells and Roger Williams returned to his orchard. John and Herod headed for an inn on the north edge of Providence. When they were out of hearing, John asked, "What did you think?"

"Of Mr. Williams? He speaks fair, but thinks little of the Quakers."

"That is so," John said. "They are brave, but who can blame Puritans for taking offense when Quakers disrupt their services? It's rude, but no hanging offense in Roger's mind. He doesn't like Puritans either. He got chased out of Boston, Salem, and Plymouth as a radical." Then John chuckled. "Roger has a few things in common with your friend Endecott."

"No friend of mine," Herod scoffed.

"Fancy that! Williams agrees that Satan might be leading the Quakers to Hell by spurring them to rebel. Also, for a time he and Endecott both thought that women should be modestly veiled whenever they leave their homes."

"The day I wear a veil is the day they put a Pope on the English throne," Herod said tartly.

Roger Williams was the first – and last – Providence resident which Herod spoke to. At the town's northern border, John paid for lodging. The easiest way to keep from spilling information was to say nothing, so Herod acted like she was hard of hearing. The innkeeper's middle-aged wife openly pitied the "poor deaf thing. I hope she's not simple too," the woman said to John.

"She's slow, but takes orders well so long as I shout them loud enough," Porter replied, earning a surreptitious, but indignant nudge from Herod's elbow.

Herod shared a sagging rope bed with a woman and her teenage daughter bound for Hartford. Her husband and John Porter slept in the next room with a couple of other male travelers. Herod thought that she would not be able to sleep for worrying about Mary. Instead, she fell asleep within minutes of crawling under her threadbare blanket.

When John tapped on the door before daylight, Herod was already awake. She quietly slipped into her outer clothing and breeches, trying not to wake her bedmates. They shared a quick breakfast of bread and cheese and John bought more to carry in a saddlebag.

The hostler brought out a short-legged beast with hooves as large as nail kegs and a shaggy red coat. "It don't look like much," he told John, but 'twill carry two." A pillion was strapped behind the animal's saddle. It was a thick leather blanket with a stuffed seat. Herod would sit sideways on the horse's rump, with her right shoulder almost nestled against John's back. A handle for her left hand and a platform for her feet promised more comfort than Herod had enjoyed yesterday.

John mounted the horse, and then the hostler helped Herod clamber from mounting block to pillion. She suppressed a whimper as her tired muscles flamed. However, sitting sideways instead of straddling the horse would spare those chafed spots inside of her thighs. The hostler told John, "Now, you can trade for another hack a couple hours north if this one's jaded."

"And at Wrentham beyond that," John replied. "I've traveled this road before."

Then they were off, walking northward on the Pequot Path. The sky was gray, and only the brightest stars twinkled like snow dust overhead. The waning moon had set long ago, and the eastern horizon showed light enough to follow the well-beaten path.

Herod fidgeted, arranging her skirt so it draped behind her over the horse's rump. "This cursed thing – I wish I dared go without," she told John.

"Go ahead," he chuckled. "Those breeches will keep you decent."

Herod laughed, "What a sight! Even in Newport they would put me in the stocks."

"I've seen odder wear on travelers, including a trapper wearing a bear hide for a cape. He used the head for a hood, looking out through the mouth." When they could see the road clearly, John kicked their mount into a trot, and that put an end to conversation.

The hired horse had a rougher gait than John's big mare, and Herod said through gritted teeth, "Endecott had better not deny me after all this."

"Do you want to rest?"

"Let's go," Herod told him. "If I get down, I'll never get back up." Her muscles were quivering, but they had to keep moving if they hoped to reach Boston that day. Herod leaned her head against John's shoulder, seeing Governor Endecott's dark-ringed eyes, harder than a pair of icy pebbles. If she blocked that image then she pictured Mary, fragile, but resolute, standing defiantly before the Puritan court.

The Pequot Path was barely wide enough for two carts to pass, but at times the travelers blinked in full sunlight in marshes or cornfields. Most of the undergrowth was cleared by fire, and the woods were bright and full of birdsong. Occasionally they found a stretch of virgin forest untouched by axes: a lofty green tunnel which reminded Herod of the Ragged Lands.

Though they seemed to make no progress, the sun sped westward. As the light waned, John reluctantly told Herod, "We can't reach Boston tonight. We'll have to stop at Dedham, but we'll be lucky to get there by nightfall. Not enough moon to press on after dark."

"If they condemned Mary today, they could hang her tomorrow," Herod fretted.

"We'll get back on the path early," John replied. "Should reach Boston around nine."

"But what if they hang her at nine?"

"Endecott likes to do his hanging after a hearty sermon from Wilson to convince one and all that this is God's will. We'll get there on time."

John finally got Herod laughing by inventing tales about the Dedham inn. "It's called The Kettle of Beans because that is all you can expect for your supper. There's a big brass kettle in three colors on their signboard. The proprietor is named …."

"Old Musket Blast," suggested Herod.

"Because that is how he sounds an hour after dinner," added John.

Herod collapsed against his back and giggled. She said in hitches, "He keeps – us awake – all night."

"Because we share one bed – you, me, Old Musket Blast, Mistress Musket Blast, and her granny." Unseen by Herod, John was grinning.

"Five children," said Herod.

"The sow and her litter, and the old hound dog."

"At least we will sleep warm," Herod concluded. But her leg muscles were screaming, and she bit back a sob when John kicked their mount back into a jolting trot.

CHAPTER 43
May 31 - June 1, 1660

WHEN THEY ARRIVED at the inn, the woman working the ale-tap had ominous news from Boston. "They tried a Quaker woman and she's going to hang. It ain't right to hang a woman, if you ask me."

"Did you hear when?" Herod asked.

"Tomorrow, but I heard talk of a reprieve."

The woman went back to the kitchen to fetch their supper, and Herod hissed to John, "We should go now!"

"We can't see the road, our horse is tired, and the hostler has no fresh mounts," John told her. "Tomorrow we will leave as soon as that nag can see where to put his feet. It's only ten miles to Boston so we'll be there in two, three hours. Now, off to bed as soon as you finish eating. Get some sleep."

But Herod lay awake, seeing Mary surrounded by militia with pikes and muskets, just as they had escorted Herod and the Stanton girl to the whipping post. The jeering, pleading mob pressing close, smelling of sweat and liquor. Mary, facing a ladder propped against a sturdy gallows, a noose dangling before her pale face.

When John and Herod mounted their weary horse in the morning, the approaching sunrise turned the eastern horizon to gold. However, streamers of fog hid the ground and their mount stumbled over shadowed ruts in the road. A particularly hard lurch threw Herod against John's back, and she heard a clank as the animal scrambled to keep its footing. John urged it forward, and it took a couple of uneven steps before halting.

"Hellfire! He cast a shoe." John dismounted awkwardly, throwing a leg over the horse's neck and sliding down the animal's shoulder. He picked up the muddy hoof, and Herod craned her neck to see the horse's twisted shoe dangling awry. Nails on the other side still held the shoe tight to the horse's hoof.

John mumbled beneath his breath. Holding the hoof between his knees, he wrenched at the bent shoe, but the nails wouldn't give way. He let go of the hoof and the horse stamped a couple of times. The misshapen shoe clanked loudly. "Well, now we are in a pickle," John commented.

With her stomach roiling, Herod asked, "Can we go on?"

"We must. There's a tavern about two miles from here. With luck, they have a horse for us – and this one won't go lame before we get there." John led the beast forward, its head bobbing with each step.

Herod dared say nothing. Her first husband would have seethed silently until she made a mistake and diverted his wrath to her. George would also brood, answering questions with grunts until he worked out what to do. How would Porter react?

After a few minutes, John patted the horse's neck, whistling a musical fragment. "Tell me, Herod; is this trip to Boston worse than your last?"

She was clinging with both fists to her pillion handle as the horse limped along, rocking her hard with each stride. Her reply was, "John, let me down!"

John looked over his shoulder and smiled. "That won't do." He helped Herod slide to the ground, and then tugged the resistant animal along the path.

Herod walked gingerly on sore legs at first, but then her stride lengthened. The sun was over the horizon, and she thought, 'Now Endecott is dressing in his finest blacks, just like a crow. Sit down to eat, then off to church.'

"You didn't answer me."

John's question startled Herod out of her gloom. "What?"

"Is this visit to Boston easier than your last?"

"I can't say. Which is harder, carrying a baby through swamps for five days, or straddling a red-hot barrel for two?" John winced in sympathy. "God is getting his sacrifice from my hide," Herod said grimly. "Maybe that will satisfy him and he'll let Mary live."

A half-hour passed before they found a farmer feeding his sheep and goats. The husky young man removed the offending shoe, hammered it as flat as he could, and nailed it back onto the horse's hoof. The animal seemed sound, so the farmer boosted Herod back onto her pillion and the travelers returned to the path. After a quarter-mile the horse's gait altered.

John slid to the ground and checked the shoe. "Can't see anything amiss," he mused. "Could be a nail into the quick, or the hoof cracked. I dare not ride," John told Herod. "If that sorry beast carries us both it will be dead lame before we reach Boston."

He marched forward, towing Herod on her reluctant steed. This time there was no banter or whistling. Herod's mood blackened steadily, for the sun was well clear of the treetops. "We'll never get to Boston in time," she told John.

"It's not yet eight. With luck, we can stop this nonsense," he told her. "Endecott must break his fast – can't hang a defenseless woman when your guts are as empty as your heart."

John was wrong, for the Puritan leaders were in a hurry on the first day of June, 1660. Six months ago there were objections when William Robinson and Marmaduke Stephenson hanged. Many of Boston's citizens still remembered Mary as a friend and neighbor, and they might protest.

Hang a woman who smothered an unwanted infant or killed her husband, and an approving crowd would cheer and bring their children to watch. Mary had done nothing but visit her jailed Friends. She hadn't preached heresy or disturbed the peace, as other Quakers had done. There was talk that Endecott should relent and put Mary on a ship to Barbados or England. Soon a rumor was spreading that a mob might rescue her.

In response, Endecott acted with ruthless speed. At 9:00 in the morning, the marshal came to escort Mary to the gallows. She calmly asked him for a few more minutes, for she would be ready presently. But the marshal told her, "I cannot wait for you."

At that moment, John and Herod were entering Roxbury, a half-mile from Boston's gate. They could not see armored men with muskets and razor-keen pikes in their hands, spreading through Boston's crooked streets. Soldiers would quell any rescue before it began.

Herod and John did not witness Captain James Oliver and his men gathered at the prison when the thick-planked door swung open to reveal Mary Dyer's serene face. Marshall Michelson gave the slender Quaker to the militia. The well-armed men formed a phalanx to escort her to the gallows at Roxbury Neck.

Drums beat loudly so that any heresy uttered by Mary would be drowned out, sparing Boston's folk from words put into her mouth by Satan. As John and Herod pressed forward through Roxbury's lanes, they could hear those distant drums rustling as innocently as dried leaves. Herod swallowed hard and John bit his lip anxiously.

On the day that Mary walked to the gallows, Boston was nearly an island. The peninsula was connected to the mainland by a thread; a strand of gravel and mud so low that the highest tides washed across it. The tide was low, leaving reedy mudflats exposed on both sides of Roxbury Neck. Herod could smell the rich marsh, and the thick, salty odor was also strong for Mary that morning.

Years before, Boston's early settlers had built a wooden palisade across the narrowest part of the neck. They closed the gate at night to keep out hostile Indians and wild animals. Attacks were unlikely now, but that gate was still barred overnight.

Mary heard the gate creak open on wooden hinges, sending her forth from Boston Town for the final time. She had been surrounded by a crowd which accompanied the procession from the jail. Many jeered, but a large number pleaded with Mary to repent and save herself. The militia shoved the crowd back behind the town wall, and then the gate was closed. Mary's execution would not be prevented by a mob.

She had been in jail for two weeks and welcomed the sun on her back. It glinted off musket barrels and halberds held by the militia, and lit the men's stony faces. More people tried to crowd onto Roxbury Neck from the mainland — families who brought their children to see the heretic hang, mourners, and the curious. They were held well away from the gallows by a line of soldiers. Mary looked away to spring-green hills protruding above the sea fog and did not hear their cries.

As John led Herod through Roxbury's lanes on her limping mount, they were surrounded by people headed toward Boston. "They are like shad swimming up a creek to spawn," John muttered. Then the crowd came to a halt where roads converged at Roxbury Neck. Herod clung to her mount's coarse blonde mane with trembling hands. From her saddle she could see over the crowd. "John, everyone is stopped."

"They may have closed the gate. Can you see it?"

"No, but the road is full of people. We can't get through."

A moment of thought, and then John shouted, "Way, make way! This woman is giving birth! Make way!"

Heads swiveled, and Herod turned crimson. She hadn't worn her breeches so she wouldn't attract attention, but now John was drawing all eyes to her. What should she do now? Then he cried out again, "This woman is birthing!"

Herod clutched her belly, and a few people stepped aside. John flashed a triumphant look over his shoulder. She doubled over to hide her flat abdomen and uttered a theatrical groan. More people gave way and they lurched onto the southern end of Roxbury Neck. There they came to a halt. Over the horse's head Herod could see that the path was blocked by people held in place by militia.

However, Herod could also see the northern end of the neck only five hundred feet away. There, near Boston's gate, a ladder leaned up against the gallows – a thick crossbar raised twelve feet into the air on sturdy pillars. Clustered around the gallows' foot, with their backs to Herod, were the magistrates dressed in their somber cloaks and white neckbands.

A thicket of musket-bearing militia approached the gallows, accompanied by a battery of drummers. Their instruments rattled noisily until the group reached the black-cloaked men. Then silence fell. Herod strained to hear, but the crowd was too noisy. She called, "Quiet!" but the only response was irritable glares.

At the foot of the gallows-ladder the executioner, masked to hide his identity, took Mary Dyer's arm and led her to her fate. She climbed the rungs willingly, and then turned to face the crowd. Her gaze found the implacable Governor Endecott, there to witness his court's sentence carried out, and to watch Satan's handmaiden return to her master.

Endecott coldly pitied those who had followed Mary from the jail, pleading with her to repent and accept mercy, for those weak-minded souls were on the verge of damnation. Even worse in his mind were those perverse, critical souls who had, after the Quakers hanged last fall, labeled Endecott and his court as bloody persecutors. No doubt some of them were watching now. No matter – General Atherton's men were well-prepared to maintain order.

Nevertheless, to appease those tender hearts, Endecott would give Mistress Dyer one last chance to slink off to Rhode Island. He nodded, and one of his assistants called to Mary, "Goodwife, if you promise to go home and never return, you can come down and save your life." The crowd fell silent.

Mary's voice was clear and unwavering when she replied, "Nay, I cannot. I came hence in obedience to the will of the Lord. In His will I abide, faithful unto death."

"Mistress Dyer, you were banished, and know well that your death is the penalty," the assistant told her. "You broke our law in coming again. Therefore, you are guilty of your own blood."

"Nay, I came to keep the blood guilt from all of you," she told him. "Your magistrates must repeal this unrighteous law against the innocent servants of the Lord." Mary climbed two or three rungs higher to call out, "For you who take my life, I ask the Lord to forgive you." A roar came from the crowd.

Massed at the foot of the gallows were Boston's ministers: John Norton, Richard Mather, and John Wilson, the old warrior of God who had questioned Herod in prison. Wilson cried out, "Repent, oh, repent! Be not deluded and carried away by the deceit of the devil."

Mary looked the elderly Wilson in the eye – he who was once her pastor. "Nay, man, I am not now to repent."

Herod could hear none of this, for she and John were too far away. But she saw the slender woman clad in gray climb the gallows, and then turn to face the crowd. Herod called down to John, "I see Mary. They are going to hang her!"

John shoved Herod's left foot out of the stirrup, stuck his own boot in, and hauled himself up to look over the crowd. He gasped out a muffled oath and then his shoulders sagged in defeat. With a deep sigh, John lowered himself to the ground.

"Mary, Mary!" Herod screamed, though she could not be heard at this distance. Her words were drowned out by hundreds calling out their protests – or encouragement – to the hangman. Mary still stood on the ladder, apparently speaking to people at her feet.

Once more John tried to clear a path for Herod and her steed. He shoved people aside, then slapped the horse's flanks and tugged the nervous animal's reins. It reared, and then dug all four hooves into the ground. "Kick it, Herod, make it move!" John cried to her.

"John, we're too late!"

The crowd's eyes were on the pair now. "What, are you some of those Quakers?" a beefy man asked. More angry comments rose.

"Not me," John replied. "My wife is ill – I must get her to a doctor." Though Herod moaned again, barely needing to fake it this time, there was no moving forward. Herod's wet eyes went back to the gallows.

Two men were working around Mary now. Even at that distance, Herod saw that one had climbed high enough to place a noose around

Mary's neck, and tie her unresisting hands behind her back. The other tied her friend's feet, securing the skirt around her ankles so modesty would be preserved during Mary's death struggle.

John said, "If your friend is right, in a moment she will stand before God," he said.

"Mary told me that is her sweetest wish," Herod replied. However, Mary's choice baffled her. Herod loved waking next to George, with their children at her side. Could the joys of Heaven possibly outdo a sunset over Narragansett Bay or the taste of a sun-warmed apple? No angel's song could please her ear more than the liquid trills of thrushes and warblers. Life was sweet for Herod and she wanted it to go on forever.

The last time she saw Mary, her friend had said in response to Herod's pleas, "Of course I am tempted to give it up! I might make peace with William, befriend my children again, and dandle my grandchildren. But, Herod, it is so hard! How can I live safe at home so long as my Friends suffer and so many souls are in peril?

"Christ gave his life to redeem us all, and I can do no less." Herod had started to protest, but Mary stopped her. "Should my death cause men and women to turn away from those evil counselors, then I am content. On that day I shall enter eternal happiness."

Herod watched as a man reached a white cloth up to the trio on the gallows ladder. She later learned that it was Reverend Wilson who had volunteered his neckcloth to cover Mary's face.

Herod felt John grip her foot. "I am well," she told him. His upturned cheeks were dusty and streaked with sweat and tears. "Mary told me that she is on the path to paradise." John dried his face on his sleeve and squeezed Herod's ankle again.

Then, with Mary securely bound and blindfolded, the men climbed down from the gallows ladder. She was poised on the rung, almost tiptoe. Her concealed face tilted up, as though she was rising toward the sun.

Herod murmured, "No ...."

The burly man standing to John's left frowned at them again. "Say no more," John muttered. "No tears. Bring no attention to us." Herod could not speak without choking, so she reached down to John. He gripped her hand tightly and urged, "Don't watch."

The drums rolled in a brisk, rattling tattoo. Abruptly, Mary spun out into the air, twirling free from the ladder. A gasp and cry rose from the watchers, as "Mary ...." issued from Herod's ashen lips.

Spooked by the drums, a flock of pale birds rose from the marsh; wailing gulls turning on narrow wings, and crook-necked egrets wheeling over Roxbury Neck. Their shadows rippled over Mary's body dangling peacefully from the gallows as the birds turned toward the ocean and disappeared into the luminous sea-fog.

The crowd began to stir. It thinned as watchers, both satisfied and mourning, headed back to their homes. Others pressed toward Boston when the militia opened the city gate. John, Herod, and their jaded horse stood quietly, letting the people eddy around them. Herod gazed out to sea, hoping to see the white egrets return. It had been a long time since she last saw the graceful birds, and they were her favorite.

A man and woman wearing commoners' clothing walked out from Boston, and paused to take in the magistrates and ministers lingering at Mary's bound feet. Then they crossed the neck. As they passed by Herod and John, the woman exclaimed to her companion, "I say that's the wickedest thing they've done yet."

The man replied, "They aren't hanging Quakers in England, so I wonder what Parliament will make of this?"

"I hope they put a stop to it," said the woman emphatically. The couple passed on without speaking to Herod and John.

The fog had lifted and a southern breeze blew gently against Herod's face. She could see the Dorchester shore now. Beyond it, unseen, was Weymouth, but Herod's mental compass was now pointing southwest. "Can we go home now?" Her gray eyes, dry now, turned back to John as she spoke.

"We need a fresh horse, or I'll hire a boat in Boston." John nodded toward the city gate and the gallows nearby. "Can you go there?" Herod felt a brief thrill of fear. She dared not place herself in the hands of men who had just hanged her friend. What if they recognized her? Then John added, "We'll stay away from Endecott and you'll be safe with me."

At the gallows, Mary's skirt had come loose from its bindings and was billowing in the breeze like a flag. There was still a fair-sized crowd at her feet, but the Puritans must be sated by blood, for they were paying little attention to passers-by.

Herod told John, "I can go, for *that's* not really Mary. Her labors are over. Even now she is entering heaven." The knot in Herod's stomach had unraveled and shock was bearing her up. For now she took shelter in the peace enfolding her. There would be time enough for grief later.

Then Herod remembered the couple who had just walked by. She told John, "Those people we saw were moved. Maybe others are too."

"They may force Endecott to soften, or vote him out. What that man said about Parliament is partly right," John said. "I heard talk of restoring Charles to the throne on his birthday, and that was a few days ago."

"We could have a king again." Herod mused.

"A king who rules over Massachusetts. The Puritans may soon regret today's work."

Herod smiled vengefully when she said, "The Quakers will tell him about this, just as Humphrey Norton wrote about my whipping in a book."

"You and Rebecca, and all the others," John agreed. "Your suffering will not be in vain, and neither will Mistress Dyer's death."

"For now, are you ready to go into Boston?"

"Yes, if that means going home," Herod told John. "I want to go back to Newport. I wounded George gravely, and I would mend that. I want to hold my children and tend my garden. I'm glad we tried to stop … that … but no more adventures for me."

"That sounds good," John replied. "Margaret will fuss, but it will be good to see the old girl again." They were nearly alone on Roxbury Neck now, and John tugged the horse's reins. It took a halting step toward Boston, and then another.

"Let's go home," Herod said.

THE END

Author's Notes

Which is it – fact or fiction? Read on to find out:

RESEARCH SINCE I completed *Rebel Puritan*'s manuscript has turned up information about Herodias Long and her family, some of which is at odds with my tales. The first item is the London marriage allegation for John Hickes and Harwood Long:

14to Martij 1636 / W[hi]ch daie appeared p[er]sonally John Hicke [sic] of the parish of St Olaves in Southwark Salter and a batchelour aged about 23 yeares and alledged that he intendeth to marrie with Harwood Long Spinster aged about 21 yeares the daughter of William Long Husbandman who giveth his Consent . . . [signed] John Hickes

This allegation contradicts Herodias' 1665 petition for divorce. There, she asserts that her father had died before Herodias' mother sent her to London, and that she was only thirteen when she married John Hicks. It is possible that both John and Herodias bent the truth in their favor. However, I believe that John was strongly motivated to lie about his impending marriage to a girl who was far under age. I also think that since by 1665 Herodias had little reason to lie about her marriage, and her testimony was closer to the truth.

Elizabeth Hicks is a controversial addition to the family of John and Herodias Hicks. Her existence was hinted at when John Hicks called Josiah Starr "son-in-law" in his 1672 will, and genealogists of yesteryear said that Josiah's wife was named Elizabeth. However, "son-in-law" could be used interchangeably with "stepson," which was also the relationship between John Hicks and Josiah Starr. Nevertheless, I chose to add Elizabeth to *Rebel Puritan*, and also to keep her in The Reputed Wife. Elizabeth Hicks is almost certainly fictional, but so are my novels.

Few of my characters are fictional, and they are noted below. All other persons are real, though at times they are handled fictitiously. In particular (genealogists take note!) *Herodias Long, George Gardner, and John Porter's backgrounds in Rebel Puritan and The Reputed Wife are completely fictional.* Furthermore, Herod's dash to Boston with John Porter in 1660 is entirely my invention. I encourage readers to check my website at www.rebelpuritan.com/more for information about Herodias Long and her family.

Rhode Island:

In *Rebel Puritan* I used Gardner and Dyer for the names of my characters, instead of Gardiner and Dyre. Gardiner is used by many Rhode Islanders, but George was also called Gardner and even Gardener in Rhode Island records. Also, Gardner is the most familiar variant for me, since my grandmother's name was Gardner.

Though Dyer is the most familiar variant, William Dyer used Dyre, and Mary titled herself Dyar in her letters. All description of Mary's background in England is my invention. The Dyers' bondservants are fictional, but Catherine is based on a real person whose surname is unknown.

Ages of many colonial Rhode Islanders are estimates. Newport's vital records, along with deeds and probates were destroyed during the American Revolution. In addition, Newport's acts from 1647-1653 are missing from the colony's records. Entries about William Coddington were undoubtedly damaging to men on both sides of that controversy, so in 1656 they were cut out of the book and given to Coddington as a goodwill gesture.

Rhode Island and Providence Plantations is the colony's and the state's official name. The island where Newport and Portsmouth stand is also called Rhode Island, but was first named Aquidneck Island. To avoid confusing island with colony, I continue to refer to it as Aquidneck.

The hanging of Captain Partridge is – in part – my invention. Governor Stephen Hopkins penned a history of Rhode Island in 1765, with access to Newport's records which were destroyed by the British in 1778. He wrote, *About the year 1653 an inhabitant of Newport, of very considerable note, was charged with a capital crime, and was brought before the town meeting, there tried and condemned to death, and the sentence immediately executed in their presence.* I am not the first to speculate that Partridge was executed.

Thomas Painter lived in several Massachusetts towns in the 1640s, and settled in Newport about 1652. However, it is my invention that Painter was ever connected with John Hicks, or ever lived at Flushing or elsewhere in New Netherland. I based my account solely on Painter's accusing George Gardner of adultery in the same month that John Hicks received a divorce in New Netherland.

There is speculation that Mary Dyer studied Quakerism with George Fox and Thomas and Margaret Fell, but no proof. As for my calling Mary Dyer a Quaker minister or preacher, that is not a term the Friends would have used. Any Quaker could speak in meeting, which was not led by an individual. A person who adopted Quaker beliefs was 'convinced.' An influential, highly-regarded Friend would be called 'weighty.'

Sarah Grand is fictional. Jane Hawkins of Portsmouth was widely known as a midwife, but was quite elderly and probably could not attend Herod Gardner's birthing in winter.

William Jefferay performing Church of England rites is fictional.

It is conjecture that Mary Stanton is Robert Stanton's daughter, but it is likely. The Stantons owned land adjacent to George Gardner, and George and Robert bought land together in 1662. To my knowledge, there were no other Stanton families in Newport at the time.

I have abridged Mary William Dyer's letters, modernized some spelling, and added punctuation to increase ease of reading. When Mary and the other Quakers refer to 'priests' they are talking about Puritan ministers, not Catholic priests.

Massachusetts:

The residents and officials of Boston and Weymouth are real. Herodias Long's whipping is not found in any Massachusetts record, but was well-described by Humphrey Norton in 1659.

DOCUMENTS

I have added paragraph breaks, some capital letters and punctuation, and filled in abbreviations to make the intent clear in the colonial records below. They are abridged, and so I have placed the full records on my website at www.rebelpuritan.com/.

December 3, 1643
Harrwood Hicks complained to Rhode Island's governor that her husband was beating her and requested a divorce. John Hicks was bound to keep the peace, and later in 1644 the couple was granted a separation:

This witnesseth that in the yeare 1643, decemb. the 3d Harrwood Hicks, wife to John Hicks, made her Complaint to us of Many greevances, & Exstreeme violence, that her Husband used towards her, uppon which she desired ye peace of him.

Uppon ye Examination whereof we found such due grounds of her Complaints by his Inhumane & barbarous Carriages; such Crewell blows on Divers parts of her body, with many other like Cruelties, that we, fearing the ordenarie & desperate afects of such barbarous Cruelties, murthering, poysioning, drowning, hanging, wounds & Losse of Limbes, Could not but bind him to ye peace.

Moreover we found him soe bitterly to be Inraged, & soe desparate in his Expreshions, uppon which the poore woman fraught with feares, Chose Rather to subject herselfe to any Miserie than to Live with him; He also as desirous thereof as She, Solicited us to part them, with much Impretunyty.

We therefore diligently observing & waighing, ye premeses Conceived & Concluded, that it were better, yea farr better for them to be separated, or devorced than to Live in such bondage being in such parfect hatred of one another ... being perswaded that god had separated them soe Inmeewtablie, that they were free from that marriage bond before god ...
William Coddington

Rhode Island General Court records

December 12, 1644 or 1645

An extract of a letter from John Hicks was entered into the Rhode Island court records between June & July 1647 as proof that Herod Gardner had been permanently abandoned by her first husband. The letter was dated December 12th but the year was not given. However, Hicks was probably in Flushing before December 1644.

Taken out of a letter from John Hicks to Mr Coggeshall dated at Flushin the 12 of decemb:

Now for parting what way ther is seeing she have carried ye matter so subtilly as she have I know not, but if ther be anyway to bee used to untie that Knott, which was at the first by man tyed that so the world may be satisfied I am willing there unto, for the Knot of affection on her part have been untied long since, and her whoredome have freed my conscience on the other part, so I Leave my self to yor advise, beeing free to condissend to yor advice if ther may be such a way used for the finall parting of us.

Rhode Island General Court records

May 19-21, 1647

After John Coggeshall became Rhode Island's governor in 1647, the colony updated their laws. When a married man or woman has sexual relations with a person other than their spouse, that act is adultery. If both man and woman are unmarried, they commit fornication. Both acts were illegal, but where adultery was once punishable by death, now it earned a fine of 13 shillings:

… the Most High shall judge them. Adultery is declared to be a vile affection, Whereby men do turn aside from ye natural use of their own wives, and do burn in their lusts towards strange flesh. And we do agree, that what penalty the Wisdom of the State of England have or shall appoint touching this transgression, the accessaries and effects shall stand throughout the colony.

As single persons, Herod and George Gardner were not guilty of adultery, but they were breaking another of the new laws:

It is agreed, and ordered by this present Assemblie, for the preventing of many evills and mischiefs that may follow thereon, that no contract or agreement between a Man and a Woman to owne each other as Man and Wife, shall be owned from henceforth threwout the

Whole Colonie as a lawfull marriage, nor their Children or Issue so coming together to be legitimate or lawfullie begotten ... that man that goes contrarie to this present Ordinance established, shall forfeit five pounds to the parents of the Maid, and be bound to his good behaviour; and all the accessories shall forfeit five pounds a man, halfe whereof shall go to the grieved parents and the other halfe to the Towne.

Rhode Island Colonial Records

Another of the 1647 laws applied indirectly to George and Herod Gardner:

No person, in this Colonie, shall be taken or imprisoned, or be disseized of his Lands or Liberties, or be Exiled, or any other otherwise molested or destroyed, but by the Lawfull judgment of his Peeres, or by some known Law...

In 1644 John Hicks left Rhode Island after he and Herod agreed to separate. It can't be told from the records if John voluntarily abandoned his home, or if it was taken from him. In March 1649 the following deed was entered into Rhode Island's records. However, it is my invention that John claimed that his land was illegally seized, and that he was compensated by this sale:

Memorand that on ye 1 day of March _____ 1648 [Old Style; now 1649] John Ridgman of Newport did enter upon record his purchase of a parcel of Land that the said John purchased of John Hicks contayning fifty acrs more or less which was Layd forth to the said John at Newport Cliffs, Lying on the Northwest side of Road Iland bounded on ye east end vidzt: partly by Robt Stantons Land & partly by the high way ...

Rhode Island Colonial Records

October 15, 1651
Approximately 2/3 of Rhode Island's men signed a petition asking that Coddington be removed as governor-for-life. However, I do not know whether George Gardner signed the petition. In October or November John Clarke and William Dyre sailed to England, accompanied by Roger Williams:

We ... earnestly request Mr. John Clarke to do his utmost endeavours in soliciting our cause in England; and we do hereby engage ourselves to the utmost of our estates to assist them, being resolved in the mean time peaceably to yield all due subjection unto the present power set over us [William Coddington].

Rhode Island Colonial Records

February 19, 1652
Coddington wrote from Newport to John Winthrop Jr.:

My commission hath not hitherto succeeded as was expected by me, for some ... have endeavored an interruption, not to say a rebellion, which have chiefly been occasioned by some proceedings against Mr. Dyre ... [He] made over his estate, & so did Jeremy Gould, & both of them fitted themselves for England. Mr. Dyre sent his wife over in the first ship with Mr. Travice, is now gone himself for England, & so is Jeremy Gould, and hath made over his estate to defeat me of my righte.
Newport Begins Lloyd A. Robinson 1964

William Dyer sailed to England in early November 1651. It seems from Coddington's wording that Mary left Rhode Island before her husband, perhaps on the first ship to leave New England in March or early April 1651. Mr. Travice is Captain Nicholas Trerise.

June 1, 1655
John Hicks was granted a divorce from Hardwood Long at New Amsterdam. Not long afterward, he married Florence Carman.

We the councillors of New Netherland having seen and read the request of John Hicks sheriff on Long Island, in which he remonstrates and presents that his wife Hardwood Longh has ran away from him about 9 years ago with someone else with whom she has been married and had by him 5 or 6 children. His wife having therefore broken the bond of marriage (without him having given any reason thereto) he asks to be qualified and given permission to marry again an honorable young girl or a widow
New Amsterdam Colonial Records

June 28, 1655
At the June Court of Trials held in Portsmouth, Thomas Painter accused George Gardner of adultery. The case would be heard in October after an investigation and solicitation of testimony:

George Gardner presented as followeth:
I present George Gardner for keeping John Hicks his wife as his owne Contrarie to Law
Portsmouth this 26 of June 1655
Thomas Painter his T marke
Records of the Rhode Island Court of Trials

October 12, 1655

Thomas Painter's adultery charge against George Gardner was tried at Newport. The account of Herod's 1643 divorce petition and her 1644 separation from John Hicks were entered into the court record along with the resolution of George Gardner's trial:

This presentment being found by the Grand Inquest, it is traversed. The petitt juries verdict thereon as followeth The pla(intiff) not having made good his charge, we therefore find for the Deff't. Damage 6d & costs of the Court, further it being proclaimed by an Opus Eust that if any could further accuse or had further to say they might be heard, but none apeering he was quitt by proclamation in the court.
     The Deff't not withstanding of his owne free will paid the costs of Court.
                              Records of the Rhode Island Court of Trials

October 14, 1656

Massachusetts' Puritans discussed the Quaker menace at General Court. The first anti-Quaker laws were passed on that date – any captain who knowingly brings in a Quaker is fined £100, any Quaker will be jailed and severely whipped, anyone importing their literature is fined £5 per book, anyone who reviles a magistrate or minister will be severely whipped or fined £5:

Whereas there is a cursed sect of haeritickes lately risen up in the world, which are commonly called Quakers, who take upon them to be immediately sent [by] God, and infallibly assisted by the spirit to speake & write blasphemous opinions, despising government & the order of God in church & commonwealth, speaking evill of dignities, reproaching and reviling magistrates & ministers, seeking to turne the people from the faith, & gaine proselytes to their pernicious wayes.
         Records of the Governor and Company of the Massachusetts Bay

January 20, 1657

The Pettaquamscutt Purchasers made their first Narragansett land purchase from Quassaquanch, Kachanaquant, and Quequaquenuet, chief sachems of Narragansetts. The partnership eventually owned twelve square miles of prime fields and woodlands. The Purchasers were John Hull of Boston, and John Porter, Thomas Mumford, Samuel Wilbore Jr., and Samuel Wilson of Portsmouth. Several years later, Benedict Arnold and William Brenton of Newport also became partners. The partners paid £17 and other gifts for:

All the land and the whole hill called Pettaquamscutt, bounded on the south & SW side of the [Pettaquamscutt] rock with Ninigret's land, on the E with a river, northerly bounded 2 miles beyond a great rock in Providence, W bounded by a running brook beyond the meadow, together with all manner of mines.
Rhode Island Land Evidences Dorothy Worthington 1921

May 11, 1658
In May, 1658 Herod Gardner walked from Newport to Weymouth, MA to protest the abuse being dealt out to Quakers by the Puritan colonies. She and her maidservant Mary Stanton were arrested and taken to Boston where each was whipped ten lashes. Herod refused to surrender her infant daughter, so she was whipped while holding the baby in her arms.

Most researchers believe Herod was a Quaker. If so, it was not for long. She is not found in Rhode Island Quaker records, and neither was her immediate family. Whether her protest arouse from faith or conscience, Herod struck a brave blow for religious liberty and her efforts were noted by the Quakers Humphrey Norton, John Copeland, and George Bishop:

Horred Gardiner, a mother of many children, and an inhabitant in Newport upon Road-Iland, being moved by the measure of God to go on his message unto Weymouth, took with her the youngest babe that fed upon her brest, such a journey that no flesh that had looked upon it with the fleshly eye, could have expected (considering her condition) she could have accomplished, but her faith was made strong through weakness.

And according to the will of God finished her testimony at Weymouth in Boston Collony, where the witness in the people answered unto her words; but the baser sort hurried her away the day following, before John Indicot Governor of Boston, who after abusing her with unsavory language and much threatening committed her and the girle that assisted her to bear her child (Mary Stanton by name, with reviling language) unto the Gaolor where they received ten stripes a piece with the threefold cord of their covenant.

Such a barbarous article of their faith is this, as I have not heard the like, as to whip a woman who bare two babes, sucking the breast at the time, one visible, and the other invisible, who after that execution of this their cruelty, kneeled down saying, The Lord forgive you for you know not what you do; a woman standing by, said, Surely if she had not the spirit of the Lord she could not do this thing.

Thus they continued them in prison about fourteen days, not suffering any of their friends to come at them ... this cruelty was acted on them about the eleventh of the third moneth 1658.
New England's Ensigne Humphrey Norton 1659

August 30, 1659

Mary Dyer went to Boston in summer 1659 to visit jailed Quakers, and was herself imprisoned. William Dyer wrote to Governor Endecott and his assistants begging for the release of his wife. She banished upon pain of death, and then released in September. William Dyer's abridged letter:

Gentlemen:

Having received some letters from my wife, I am given to understand of her commitment to close prison ... had you no commiseration of a tender [soul] that being wett to the skin, you cause her to thrust into a room wheron was nothing to [sit down upon] or lye downe upon but dust (as is said) hadd your dogg been wett you wold have afforded it the [liberty] of a chimny corner to dry it self, or had your hoggs been pend in a sty you would have afforded them some dry straw, or else you wold have wanted mercy to your beast, but alas Christians now with you are used worse than hoggs or dogs, oh merciless crueltie ...

You have done more in persecution in one yeare than the worst bishops did in seven, & now to add more towards a tender woman in that condition, that gave you no just cause against her; for did she come to your meetings to disturb them as you call itt, or did she come to reprehend the magistrates?

[She] only came to visit her fren[ds in] prison, & when dispatching that her intent of returning to her family as she declared in her [statement] the next day to the Governor, therefore it is you that disturbed her, else why was she not let alone ...

My wife writes me word and information, that she had ther been above a fortnight and had not trode on the ground, but saw it out your windowes; what inhumanity is this, had you never wives of your own, what can man that is borne of a woman, or ever any tender affection to a woman, deal so with a woman? ... so s[ai]th her Husband
W. Dyre
Newport this 30 August 1659

Massachusetts Archives

October 8, 1659

Mary Dyer was released, but she immediately returned to Boston and was arrested. She, Marmaduke Stevenson, and William Robinson were sentenced to death for defying the orders of banishment already placed against them. After her trial, Mary wrote this [abridged] letter to the General Court to protest their judgment:

From Marie Dire to the generall court now this present 26th of the 8 month 59 assembled in the towne of boston in new Ingland: Greetings of grace mercy and peace to every soul that doth well : tribulation anguish and wrath to all that doth evell ...

To make such lawes as by him is intended utterly to root out and keep back from among you that holy people and seed wch the lord hath blesed for ever : caled by the children of darknes (cursed quakers) ... therefore in the boweles of love and compasion I becech you to repeall al such lawes as tend to this purpose and let the truth and servants of god have fre pasage among you : for verily the enemie that hath don this cannot in any measure countervail the great damage that wil fal upon you. If you continue to keep such laws, woe is mee for you ...

Its not my owne life I seek for (I chuse rather to suffer with the people of god then to injoy the pleasures of eqypt) but the life of the seed wch I know the lord hath blessed ... To me to live is christ and to die is gaine though I had not had your 48 houers warning for the preparation of the cruel and in your esteme cursed death of mee marie d[ire] ...

In love and in the spirit of meeknes I againe beceche you for I have noe enmity to the persons of any; but you shal know that god is not mocked but what you sow that shal you reap from him ...

Massachusetts Archives

Coming in 2015 from Neverest Press:

A Scandalous Life:
The Golden Shore

THE GOLDEN SHORE continues Herodias Long's saga as the Gardner family, Rhode Island, and the region's Native Americans all struggle to secure their futures. Battles and hard decisions lie ahead, and Herodias may be forced to choose between love and security. Or can she have them both? Here is a sample from *The Golden Shore*:

Fall 1663

THE COASTER – A single-masted boat broad in the beam, but responsive to the tiller – slipped easily into the Pettaquamscutt River's mouth. Benoni Gardner sat at the oars, but the boat barely needed extra power as it rode the rising tide. He lowered the sail then sculled gently along, steering the boat between flooded salt marshes.

    A pair of snow white egrets rose from the eastern bank, trailing long black legs as they flapped heavily by. Herodias Gardner shaded her eyes and cried out, "Look! I haven't seen those in so long!" One of the birds uttered a harsh croak. Herod commented, "I have always thought such a beautiful bird deserved a sweeter song."

    "Stand here in the spring and you are beset by song," John Porter told her. He nodded at the tall ridgeline to their west. "Those trees are so full of warblers that you can't hear yourself think." The ridge was a glorious swath of fall color – golden ash, scarlet maple, and pumpkin-colored sassafras. Giant white pines with wispy green branches, and oaks which hadn't yet turned accented the hillside with green. Above it all rose Pettaquamscutt Rock; an austere tan dome.

Then the sun cleared a fog bank lingering over the bay. Thin wisps of cloud muted the eastern light, but behind Herod a warm glow swelled. She turned to look westward, and then gasped. Over their heads, the Rock had turned to gold, glittering where sunlight reflected off flecks of mica and quartz. "Ah, I'd hoped that the fog would clear," said John.

They had spent the night at Richard Smith's home at Wickford, where Smith had opened a trading post on the Pequot Path nearly three decades ago. John had roused the Gardners early, and they set sail before sunrise to travel the few miles to his land.

John said to Benoni, "We'll anchor here." The young man back-paddled to stop the boat. Then John picked up an iron anchor from the shallop's bottom and dropped it over the side. One might think that a man over sixty would struggle with that anchor, but Porter handled the weight easily. Then he sat on the bow seat and casually hooked one boot-clad leg over the other knee. "George and Herod: behold my empire!"

Herod rose from her seat for a better look. George Gardner levered himself up from the bench behind her, and held her shoulder with one broad, warm palm. "It's just as beautiful as I remembered," Herod told him. The sunlit foliage reminded her of a giant posy of dandelion and hawkweed; scarlet, bronze, and yellow puffs strewn across the ridge.

A sloping plain stretched beyond the narrow band of reeds at the water's edge. To measure its width, a man would have to step along briskly for a good ten minutes before he reached the ridge's base. Clumps of hickory and maple were scattered among the fields, but most of the plain was planted with corn or sown with English hay. The cornstalks and hay stubble were sere and brown, nipped by a hard frost a few days ago.

"Where are the Indians?" Herod asked. She told George, "They had little bark houses among the fields when I was last here."

"That was five years ago," John said.

Herod murmured, "Just after I was whipped." George squeezed Herod's shoulder for a moment, and she felt comforted.

John told them, "The Narragansetts moved to their winter fort beyond the ridge. They did not live here this summer, and won't be coming back. Kachanaquant agreed to leave these lands when he sold them to me.

"Last spring your son George helped to plant these fields. See the smoke?" John pointed at a patch of trees halfway to the ridge. "That's where his wigwam lies. He lived there all summer while he tended the fields, and now he's pulling the ears. In return, that piece of land is his. He and

Will Haviland will build proper homes here next year, and in return they'll get more land on the ridge and beyond." Will had married Herod's eldest daughter, Hannah Hicks, and had also been working for Porter that summer.

Herod shaded her eyes, but couldn't see young George or Will. The last clouds overhead lifted, and the sun dappled the river with sparkles. The dried cornstalks had lost their green, but even their tawny leaves glowed in the morning light. Herod felt dizzy, and realized that she was holding her breath. She let it out and clutched the mast to steady herself.

John was saying, "Jerry Bull is building down past the bend, where we came in from the bay, and your son-in-law is building next to him. But this stretch here, from the bend to that far grove, is mine to grant as I please – or to keep. This is my home now, and the lads are building a house for me." John pointed a hundred yards upstream, to a finger of sand angling out into the river. Uphill, near a thicket of crimson sumac, stood a house's square frame; roofed with thatch and already half-covered with planks.

"Are you moving next spring?" George asked. Herod was unable to speak, consumed with longing for a house on that hillside with a view of the river.

John grinned. "I all but live here now. Part of the summer I was right here with young George and Will. The rest of my time was spent down on Point Judith. My partners and I built a fence across the neck and had a drive to chase off the wolves and bears. Our horses and cattle are grazing there now, fat and safe."

"What of your wife?" Herod asked. "You said that she didn't want to move here."

"Margaret's been home all summer, cared for by servants. She believes that I plan to return to Portsmouth. I will – to settle some affairs and get the rest of my stuff."

George stiffened and his hand dropped from Herod's shoulder. "You are abandoning her? The woman is nigh seventy – what will she do to live?" Herod sank back to her seat, her eyes fixed on John.

The trader's lips compressed. "I've told Margaret many a time that she is welcome to come here with me. When she sees me packing, I hope that she'll change her mind. If she won't, I will keep plenty of servants to see to her comfort. I'll give her the increase from our farm for her support, but I will live here. It's the fairest place I've ever seen, and I want to spend the rest of my years here."

Then John uncrossed his legs and bent forward persuasively. "George, I have a proposal. Come here in the spring and build houses and fencing. In the fall, I will grant you and Herod a home lot on the other side of mine, and farmland beyond the ridge."

"And me!" called an eager voice from behind the mast. Benoni had shipped the oars and was shading his eyes for a better look. "I'm nineteen now, so I can own land. Mr. Porter, I'll work for you next year. I'll even spend this winter in Georgie's wigwam for a piece of that riverbank."

"Done, Benoni!" John told George and Herod's eldest son. "Now, George, what do you think?"

"Please, George, say you will," Herod urged. But the tall farmer remained silent.

With rising exasperation, Herod told him, "We can't afford Newport land since you and Bob Stanton bought that useless swamp from the Indians." George quivered at the bitter reminder, but Herod would not be daunted. "I can tell from here that the soil is deep. Ours is played out and full of stones, but look at that corn! We haven't grown such corn for years. George, we have to come here."

George had sunk back to his seat, and he stared silently out at Porter's land. Herod's beseeching hand on his thigh went unnoticed, so she turned to John.

Porter smiled gently at them. "George, I've been here in the winter. That rise to the east shelters this spot from ocean gales. You could almost grow cabbages year round here. With a summer's work, the land is yours. 'Tis the same deal my partners and I gave to young George. John Tefft, Bill Bundy –"

"And Hannah's husband," Herod reminded George.

"All of them are getting land along the coast and over the ridge," John said. "We'll have a true village here in five years. Each of your sons, as soon as they turn eighteen, get their own grant. I'll even dower your daughters. I want you and your fine family here that badly," Porter concluded.

"Please, George ...."

"Very well," George said. His hand went back to Herod's shoulder again and he patted it gently. "It's a fair deal and fine land, and I can't deny Herod what she wants so dearly. We'll take the deal, Mr. Porter."

Jo Ann Butler has spent most of her life digging up New England's past as a colonial archeologist, genealogist, and in writing Rebel Puritan and The Reputed Wife. An 8th-great granddaughter of Herodias Long, Ms. Butler can be contacted at www.rebelpuritan.com